MIRACLE ON KAIMOTU ISLAND

BY
MARION LENNOX

MILLS & BOON

First published in Great Britain 2013
by Mills & Boon, an imprint of Harlequin (UK) Limited.
Harlequin (UK) Limited, Eton House, 18-24 Paradise Road,
Richmond, Surrey TW9 1SR

© Marion Lennox 2013

ISBN: 978 0 263 89907 8

Harlequin (UK) policy is to use papers that are natural, renewable and recyclable products and made from wood grown in sustainable forests. The logging and manufacturing process conform to the legal environmental regulations of the country of origin.

Printed and bound in Spain
by Blackprint CPI, Barcelona

KAIMOTU ISLAND

BY
MARION LENNOX

ALWAYS THE HERO

BY
ALISON ROBERTS

MILLS & BOON

EARTHQUAKE!

One day, one drama, one chance for love…

A huge earthquake has hit the beautiful island of
Kaimotu, the local doctors are on red alert and rescue
paramedics have been flown in. They will need
all their skill, love and courage to help the survivors,
but amongst the medical personnel are two sets
of star-crossed lovers who have one chance
to heal their love amidst the chaos.

Can happiness really come out of tragedy?
Can love triumph over adversity…?

**MIRACLE ON KAIMOTU ISLAND
by Marion Lennox**

**ALWAYS THE HERO
by Alison Roberts**

Dear Reader

New Zealand is known as 'the shaky isles' for good reason. Last year an earthquake ripped apart the New Zealand city of Christchurch, leaving the city we've all grown to love in ruins.

My friend, fellow author Alison Roberts, was in the centre of it, back working as a paramedic, doing all she could for the city she calls home.

Afterwards we talked about the emotions such an appalling event engenders, how tragedy can so often bring out the best in us. Of course then, as romance writers, our thoughts went to *What if?*

An earthquake such as Christchurch's was simply too big, too dreadful for us to contemplate writing about, but what if we took the same event in a closed community—a tiny island where the islanders need to work together, where past emotions are put aside for present need, where men and women are placed in deadly peril and by that peril discover the things that are most important to them?

In life, love can be hidden, pain can be concealed, but when the earth shakes everything is raw and exposed. Humour, courage, love…they're the cornerstones of our lives, but often it takes tragedy to reveal it. We hope you love reading our *Earthquake!* duet as our heroes and heroines find happiness amid a world that's shaken and is now resettling on a different axis.

Marion Lennox

Marion Lennox is a country girl, born on an Australian dairy farm. She moved on—mostly because the cows just weren't interested in her stories! Married to a 'very special doctor', Marion writes Medical Romances™, as well as Mills & Boon® Romances. (She used a different name for each category for a while—if you're looking for her past Romances search for author Trisha David as well.) She's now had well over 90 novels accepted for publication.

In her non-writing life Marion cares for kids, cats, dogs, chooks and goldfish. She travels, she fights her rampant garden (she's losing) and her house dust (she's lost). Having spun in circles for the first part of her life, she's now stepped back from her 'other' career, which was teaching statistics at her local university. Finally she's reprioritised her life, figured out what's important, and discovered the joys of deep baths, romance and chocolate. Preferably all at the same time!

Recent titles by the same author:

THE SURGEON'S DOORSTEP BABY
SYDNEY HARBOUR HOSPITAL: LILY'S SCANDAL†
DYNAMITE DOC OR CHRISTMAS DAD?
THE DOCTOR AND THE RUNAWAY HEIRESS

†*Sydney Harbour Hospital*

**These books are also available in eBook format
from www.millsandboon.co.uk**

Dedication

To the men and women of Christchurch—
and to one amazing paramedic.
Rosie, you're awesome.

PROLOGUE

No ONE KNEW how old Squid Davies was. The locals of Kaimotu could hardly remember the time he'd given up his fishing licence, much less when he'd been a lad.

Now his constant place was perched on the oil drums behind the wharf, where the wind couldn't douse a man's pipe, where the sun hit his sea-leathered face and where he could see every boat that went in and out of Kaimotu harbour. From here he could tell anyone who listened what he knew—and he did know.

'She'll be a grand day at sea today, boys,' he'd say, and the locals would set their sights on the furthest fishing grounds, or 'She'll be blowing a gale by midnight,' and who needed the official forecasters? Kaimotu's fishermen knew better than to argue. They brought their boats in by dusk.

But now...

'She's going to be bigger'n that one that hit when my dad's dad was a boy,' Squid intoned in a voice of doom. 'I know what my grandpa said, and it's here now. Pohutukawa trees are flowering for the second time. Mutton birds won't leave their chicks. They should be long gone by now, leaving the chicks to follow, but they won't leave 'em. And then there's waves hitting the shore on

Beck's Beach. They don't come in from the north in April—it's not natural. I tell you, the earth moved in 1886 and this'll be bigger.'

It had to be nonsense, the locals told themselves nervously. There'd been one earth tremor two weeks back, enough to crack a bit of plaster, break some crockery, but the seismologists on the mainland, with all the finest technology at their disposal, said a tremor was all there was to it. If ever there was a sizeable earthquake it'd be on the mainland, on the fault line, through New Zealand's South Island, not here, on an island two hundred miles from New Zealand's northern most tip.

But: 'There's rings round the moon, and even the oystercatchers are keeping inland,' Squid intoned, and the locals tried to laugh it off but didn't quite manage it. The few remaining summer tourists made weak excuses to depart, and the island's new doctor, who was into omens in a big way, decided she didn't want to live on Kaimotu after all.

'Will you cut it out?' Ben McMahon, Kaimotu's only remaining doctor, squared off with Squid in exasperation. 'You've lost us a decent doctor. You're spooking the tourists and locals alike. Go back to weather forecasting.'

'I'm only saying what I'm feelin',' Squid said morosely, staring ominously out at the horizon. 'The big 'un's coming. Nothing surer.'

CHAPTER ONE

PREDICTIONS OF EARTHQUAKES. Hysteria. One lone doctor. Dr Ben McMahon was busy at the best of times and now there weren't enough hours in the day to see everyone who wanted to be seen. His clinic was chaos.

There was, though, another doctor on the island, even though she'd declared she was no longer practising medicine. Up until now Ben had let Ginny be, but Squid's doomsday forecasting meant he needed her.

Again?

The last time Ben McMahon had asked anything of Guinevere Koestrel he'd been down on one knee, as serious as a seventeen-year-old boy could be, pouring his teenage heart out to the woman he adored.

And why wouldn't he adore her? She'd been his friend since she was eight, ever since Ginny's parents had bought the beautiful island vineyard as their hobby/holiday farm and Ben's mother had become Ginny's part-time nanny. They'd wandered the island together, fished, swum, surfed, fought, defended each other to the death—been best friends.

But that last summer hormones had suddenly popped up everywhere. On the night of his ill-advised proposal Ginny had been wearing a fabulous gown, bought by her wealthy parents for the island's annual New Year's Eve Ball. He'd been wearing an ill-fitting suit borrowed from a neighbour. Her appearance had stunned him.

But social differences were dumb, he'd told himself. Suddenly it had seemed vital to his seventeen-year-old self that they stay together for ever.

Surely she could change her plans to study medicine in Sydney, he told her. He planned to be a doctor, too. There was a great medical course in Auckland and he'd won a scholarship. If he worked nights he could manage it, and surely Ginny could join him.

But the seventeen-year-old Ginny had smiled—quite kindly—and told him he was nuts. Her life was in Sydney. The tiny New Zealand island of Kaimotu was simply a place where she and her parents came to play. Besides, she had no intention of marrying a man who called her Carrots.

That had been twelve years ago. Ben had long since put the humiliation of adolescent love behind him, but now there was a more important question. Ginny had been back on the island for six months now. She'd signalled in no uncertain terms that she wanted privacy but Ginny Koestrel was a doctor and a doctor was what the island needed. Now. Which was why, even though looking at her brought back all sorts of emotions he'd thought he'd long suppressed, he was asking yet again.

'Ginny, I need you.'

But the answer would be the same—he knew it. Ginny was surrounded by grapevines, armed with a spray gun, and she was looking at him like he was an irritating interruption to her work.

'I'm sorry, Ben, but I have no intention of working as a doctor again. I have no intention of coming near your clinic. Meanwhile, if these vines aren't sprayed I risk black rot. If you don't mind...'

She squirted her spray gun at the nearest vine. She wasn't good. She sprayed too high and lost half the mist to the breeze.

Ben lifted the spray pack from her back, aimed the gun at the base of the vine and watched the spray drift up through the foliage.

'Vaccination is one of my many medical skills,' he told her, settling a little, telling himself weird emotions were simply a reaction to shared history, nothing to do with now. They both watched as the spray settled where it should, as emotions settled where they should. 'There's a good vine, that didn't hurt at all, did it?' he said, adopting his very best professional tone. 'If you grow good grapes next year, the nice doctor will give you some yummy compost.' He grinned at the astounded Ginny. 'That's the way you should treat 'em, Carrots. Didn't they teach you anything in your fancy medical school?'

Ginny flushed. 'Cut it out, Ben, and don't you dare call me Carrots. In case you haven't noticed, it's auburn.' She hauled her flaming curls tighter into the elastic band, and glowered.

'Ginny, then.'

'And not Ginny either. And I'm a farmer, not a doctor.'

'I don't actually care who you are,' Ben said, deciding he needed to be serious if he was to have a chance of persuading her. 'You have a medical degree, and I'm desperate. It's taken me twelve months to find a family doctor to fill old Dr Reg's place. Dr Catherine Bolt seemed eminently sensible, but she's lived up to her name. One minor earth tremor and she's bolted back to the mainland.'

'You're kidding.'

'I'm not kidding.' He raked his hand through his hair, remembering how relieved he'd been when the middle-aged Catherine had arrived and how appalled he'd felt when she'd left. He really was alone.

'Every New Zealander has felt earth tremors,' he told Ginny. 'We're not known as the shaky isles for nothing. But you know Squid's set himself up as Forecaster of Doom. With no scientific evidence at all he's been droning on about double flowers of the pohutukawa tree and strange tides and weird bird behaviour and every portent of catastrophe he can think of. There's something about a shrivelled fisherman with a blackened pipe and a voice of doom that gets the natives twitchy. 'As well as losing us our doctor, I now have half the islanders demanding a year's supply of medication so they can see out the apocalypse.'

She smiled, but faintly. 'So you want me on hand for the end of the world?'

'There's no scientific evidence that we're heading for a major earthquake,' he said with dangerous calm. 'But we do have hysteria. Ginny, help me, please.'

'I'm sorry, Ben, but no.'

'Why on earth did you do medicine if you won't practise?'

'That's my business.'

He stared at her in baffled silence. She was a different woman from the one he'd proposed to twelve years ago, he thought. Well, of course she would be. His mother had outlined a sketchy history she'd winkled out of the returning Ginny, a marriage ending in tragedy, but…but…

For some reason he found himself looking at the elastic band. Elastic band? A Koestrel?

Ginny's parents were the epitome of power and wealth. Her father was a prominent Sydney neurosurgeon and her mother's sole purpose was to play society matron. Twice a year they spent a month on the island, in the vineyard they'd bought—no doubt as a tax deduction—flying in their friends, having fabulous parties.

The last time he'd seen Ginny she'd been slim, beautiful, but also vibrant with life. She'd been bouncy, glowing, aching to start medicine, aching to start life. Ready to thump him if he still called her Carrots.

In the years since that youthful proposal he'd realised how wise she'd been not to hurl herself into marriage at seventeen. He'd forgiven her—nobly, he decided—and he'd moved on, but in the back of his mind she'd stayed bouncy, vibrant and glowing. Her mother had carefully maintained her fabulous exterior and he'd expected Ginny to do the same.

She hadn't. The Ginny he was facing now wore elastic bands. Worse, she looked…grim. Flat.

Old? She couldn't be thirty, and yet… How much had the death of a loved one taken out of her?

Did such a death destroy life?

'Ginny—'

'No,' she snapped. 'I've come back to work the vineyard, and that's all.'

'The harvest is long over.'

'I don't care. I'm spraying for…something, whatever Henry told me I had to spray for. When I finish spraying I need to gear up for pruning. Henry's decided to retire and I need to learn. I'm sorry, Ben, but I'm no longer a doctor. I'm a winemaker. Good luck with finding someone who can help you.'

And then she paused. A car was turning into the driveway. A rental car.

It must be Sydney friends, Ben thought, come over on the ferry, but Ginny wasn't dressed for receiving guests. She was wearing jeans, an ancient windcheater, no make-up and she had mud smeared on her nose. A Koestler welcoming guests looking like a farmhand? No and no and no.

'Now what?' she said tightly, and she took the spray pack from Ben and turned to another vine. 'Have you brought reinforcements? Don't you know I have work to do?'

'This isn't anyone to do with me,' Ben said, and watched who was climbing out of Kaimotu's most prestigious hire car. The guy looked like a businessman, he thought, and a successful one at that. He was sleek, fortyish, wearing an expensive suit and an expression of disdain as he glanced around at the slightly neglected vineyard. The man opened the trunk and tossed out a holdall. Then he opened the back car door—and tugged out a child.

She was a little girl, four or five years old. She almost fell as her feet hit the ground, but the man righted her as if she was a thing, not a person.

'Guinevere Koestrel?' he called, and headed towards them, tugging the child beside him. 'I'm Richard Harris, from Harris, Styne and Wilkes, partners in law from Sydney. You were expecting me? Or you were expecting the child?'

There was a long silence while Ginny simply stared, dumbstruck, at the incongruous couple approaching.

'I…I guess,' she managed at last. 'But not yet.'

The lawyer was tugging the child closer and as he did…

Down's syndrome, Ben thought. The markers were obvious. The little girl was beautifully dressed, her neat black hair was cropped into a smart little cut, there was a cute hair ribbon perched on top—but nothing could distract from the Down's features.

He glanced back at Ginny, and he saw every vestige of colour had drained from her face. Instinctively he put out a hand to steady her and she grabbed it, as desperately as if she'd been drowning.

'I didn't expect…' she said. 'I thought…this wouldn't happen for months. The legal processes…'

'Our client was prepared to pay whatever was needed to free her to go to Europe,' the man said, clipped and formal. 'We sent you emails. We received no response and we had no phone contact. Our client left the country last Friday, giving us no choice but to bring her. We had a nanny accompany us to New Zealand but the girl gets seasick and refused to come on the ferry.'

He gazed down at the child, and at the look on his face Ben wondered how much leverage had been applied to make such a man do a job like this. A lot, he was sure.

'I don't…I don't check emails any more,' Ginny managed, and the lawyer looked at her as if she was a sandwich short of a picnic. A woman who didn't check emails? His expression said she must be as disabled as the child beside him.

But… 'No matter,' he said, making a hasty recovery. 'My only fear was that I wouldn't find you, but now you're here this is the official handover. According to the documents we mailed to you last month, you've accepted responsibility for her. Her mother's left for Europe. Her instructions were to deliver her to you and here she is.'

And he propelled her forward, pushing her away from him, a little girl in a pretty pink dress, with pink sandals and an expression that said she didn't have one idea of what was happening to her.

If she weren't a Down's child, she'd be sobbing, Ben thought, but he knew enough about the syndrome to know sobbing was a last resort. But still…

'Oh, my…' Ginny said faintly, and Ben's hold on her tightened still further. He'd seen patients in shock before, and Ginny was showing every symptom.

'Ginny, what is this? What's going on?'

Ginny gave herself a shake, as if trying to rid herself of a nightmare. She, too, was staring down at the child. 'I… This is…'

She stopped and looked helplessly towards the lawyer and then at the little girl beside him. 'Tell him,' she said weakly. 'Please…tell Ben.'

And the lawyer was happy to comply. He was obviously wanting a businesslike response and it looked like he'd decided Ben was the most likely to give it.

'This is Barbara Carmody,' the man said, clipped and efficient, not even looking at the little girl as he introduced her. 'The child's the result of an extra-marital affair between my client and Dr Koestrel's late husband. Her mother raised her with her other two children but unfortunately her husband has finally discovered that the child isn't his. He's rejected her. The marriage has failed and Mrs Carmody has left for Europe.'

'Her parents have deserted her?' Ben said incredulously.

'There are provisions for her care,' the lawyer said smoothly. 'Dr Koestrel's late husband left funds in his will for this eventuality, and there are institutions that will take her. On Mrs Carmody's instructions we contacted Dr Koestrel for the release of those funds but instead of releasing money she's agreed to take on her care. So here she is. The paperwork's all in her suitcase. If you need to contact her mother, do it through us—the address is with her papers. If you could sign the included documents and forward them to our office I'd appreciate it. If you'll excuse me, I don't wish to miss the return ferry. Good afternoon.'

And he turned back towards the car.

The little girl didn't move. Neither did Ginny.

The man was about to walk away and leave the child behind.

No.

Ben strode to the car, slammed closed the car door the lawyer was attempting to open then set himself between lawyer and car while Ginny stood in stunned, white-faced silence.

The little girl didn't move. She didn't look at the lawyer. She didn't look at anyone.

'Abandoning a child's a criminal offence,' Ben said, quite mildly, looking from the little girl to Ginny and back again. Ginny was staring at the child as if she was seeing a ghost. 'There must be formal proceedings…'

'I'll miss my ferry,' the man said. 'Dr Koestrel has

signed the most important documents. Additional paperwork can be sent later.'

'You can't dump a child because you'll miss your ferry,' Ben said, and folded his arms, settling back, not understanding what was going on but prepared to be belligerent until he did.

'Dr Koestrel's agreed to take her. I'm not dumping anyone.'

'So…what did you say? Barbara's the result of an affair between some woman and…Ginny's late husband? Ginny, can you explain?'

'W-wait,' Ginny managed. She looked helplessly at the little girl and then something seemed to firm. Shock receded a little, just a little. She took a deep breath and reached out and took the little girl's hand.

She led her to the edge of the vines, where a veggie garden was loaded with the remains of a rich autumn harvest. Lying beside the garden was a hose. She turned it on and a stream of water shot out.

'Barbara,' she said, crouching with water squirting out of the hose. 'Can you give my tomatoes a drink while we talk? Can you do that for us?

The little girl looked at the hose, at the enticing stream of water. She gave the merest hint of a smile. Whatever had been happening in this child's life in the last few days, Ben thought, she needed time out and somehow Ginny had a sense of how to give it to her.

'Yes,' the girl said, and Ginny smiled and handed over the hose then faced Ben and the lawyer again.

'James…died six months ago,' she managed. 'Of non-Hodgkin's lymphoma.' Then she stopped again and stared across at the little girl fiercely watering tomatoes. She looked like she could find no words.

'So tell me about this child.' Ben still had his arms folded. The guy in the suit with his professional detachment in the face of such a situation was making him feel ill, but he glanced at Ginny again and knew he needed to keep hold of his temper. He needed facts. 'What's her full name?'

'I told you…Barbara Louise Carmody. Everything's in the case. All her paperwork. Get out of my way, please,' the lawyer snapped. 'I'm leaving.'

'Ginny…' Ben said urgently, but Ginny wasn't looking at him. Or at the lawyer. She was staring at the tiny, dark-eyed girl.

'This…this little girl broke my heart,' she whispered, and Ben suddenly figured it out. Or the bones of it. Her husband had fathered a child with someone else. She'd faced her husband's death, and now she was coping with betrayal as well as loss.

How could anyone expect her to accept this child? he wondered incredulously. How could she even bear to look at her? But she'd reacted to her with instinctive protectiveness. At such an age, with Down's, with a hose in her hand and plants to water, the hurtful words around the little girl would disappear.

But…*she'd said she'd take her. Indefinitely?*

'Do you have her medical records in her luggage?' Ginny asked, in a cold, dead voice.

'Of course,' the lawyer said smoothly. 'I told you. Everything's there.'

'Did you know she's Down's?' Ben demanded, and Ginny nodded.

'Yes, I did. I'm sorry, I should be more prepared. This is fine.' She took a deep breath, visibly hauling herself together. 'You can go,' she told the lawyer. 'You're right, the documentation can happen later. Thank you for bringing her to me. I regret I didn't receive the emails but I'd still rather have her here now than have her spend time in an institution.'

Then she stooped down and took the little girl's hands in hers, hose and all, and she met that long, serious gaze full on as the water sprayed sideways. And Ben saw the re-emergence of the Ginny he knew, the Ginny who faced challenges head on, his brave, funny Ginny who faced down the world.

'I was married to your…to your father,' she said. 'That means I'm your stepmum. If it's okay with you, Barbara, I'll look after you now. You can live with me. I need help watering all my plants. I need help doing all sorts of things. We might even have fun together. I'd like that and I hope you'll like it, too.'

CHAPTER TWO

THERE WAS NOTHING else Ben could think of to say. The lawyer climbed into his rental car and drove away. The car disappeared below the ridge, and the sound faded to nothing.

There was a long, long silence. Somewhere a plover was calling to its mate. The sea was a glistening backdrop, the soft hush-hush of the surf a whisper on the warm sea breeze.

Ginny's world had been fragmented and was now floating in pieces, Ben thought.

He thought of her blank refusal to practise medicine. He thought of the unknown husband's death. He thought of her accepting the responsibility for a child not hers, and he knew that fragmentation hadn't happened today. It was the result of past history he knew little about.

He'd hardly talked to her for years. He knew nothing of what had happened to her in the interim except the bare bones she'd told his mother when she'd returned to the island, but now she was kneeling beside the tomatoes, holding Barbara, looking bereft, and he felt his heart twist as…as Ginny had made his heart twist all those years before.

But now wasn't the time for emotion. He flipped

open the child's suitcase and searched, fast. If the medical and legal stuff wasn't there he could still stop the lawyer from leaving the island.

But it was all there, a neat file detailing medical history, family history, lawyer's contacts, even contacts for the pre-school she'd been going to.

She might not have been loved but she'd been cared for, Ben thought grimly.

How could a family simply desert her?

'She has Mosaic Down's,' he said out loud, skimming through the medical history, and Ginny closed her eyes. She'd know what that meant, though. Mosaic Downs meant the faulty division of chromosomes had happened after fertilisation, meaning every cell wasn't necessarily affected.

But it was still bad. Barbara had the distinct look of Down's. Who knew what organs were affected?

Taking on a child was huge, Ben thought. Taking on a Down's child…

Barbara had gone back to watering. She was totally occupied in directing the hose. They could talk.

They needed to talk.

'Ginny, are you serious?' he said urgently. 'I can still stop him.'

'And then what'll happen?' She shook herself. 'No. I'm sorry. I'm not handling this well. I did know this was coming. I did agree to this, even if it's happened sooner than I thought. I *will* look after her.'

'No one can ask that of you,' Ben said, and Ginny met his gaze head on. There was a long silence and then she gave a decisive nod, a gesture he remembered.

'No,' she said. 'They can't, but I will. Veronica and James did exactly what they wanted. Their selfishness was boundless but there's no way this little one should suffer. James's death set me free, and Barbara should be free as well, not stuck in some institution for the disabled.' She managed to smile at the little girl—but then she felt silent again.

She was overwhelmed, Ben thought, and rightly so. Her world had just been turned on its head.

And Barbara? She was totally silent. She didn't look upset, though. She simply stood patiently watering, waiting for what came next.

Down's syndrome…

A man could mount arguments, Ben thought, for giving the whole human race Down's. Yes, it took Down's kids longer to learn things. Down's kids seldom reached average intellectual milestones, but, on the other hand, the Down's patients he had were friendly, selfless and desired little more than for those around them to be happy.

He walked forward and crouched beside Barbara. Ginny seemed almost incapable of speech. Maybe she'd said what she needed to say, and it was as if she didn't know where to go from here.

'Hi,' Ben said to the little girl. 'I'm Dr Ben.'

If he was right about this little one being well cared for, physically at least, then she'd be accustomed to doctors, he thought. Strange places would be associated with medical tests. Using the term 'doctor' might make this situation less strange.

And he was right. The little girl turned her gaze to him, but not to him personally. To his top pocket.

The arc of water went wild and no one cared.

'Jelly bean?' she said hopefully, and he grinned because some things were universal. Doctors' bribes.

'Jelly baby,' he said, and fished a yellow jelly baby from a packet in his shirt pocket. She took it gravely and then continued gazing at him—assessing him for more?

'Do you like jelly babies, Barbara?' he asked, and she frowned.

'Not…not Barbara,' she whispered.

'You're not Barbara?'

'Not Barbara,' she said, suddenly distressed. She looked down at her pink dress, dropped the hose and grabbed a button and pulled, as if trying to see it, as if trying to reassure herself it was still there. 'Button.'

'Button?' Ben repeated, and the little girl's face reacted as if a light had been turned on.

'Button,' she said in huge satisfaction, and Ben thought someone, somewhere—a nanny perhaps—had decided that Barbara was far too formal for this little girl, and Button it was.

'Your name is Button,' Ginny whispered, and Ben saw a wash of anger pass over her face. Real anger. Anger at her late husband and the unknown Veronica? He watched as she fought it down and tried for calm. 'Button, your mum's sent you to me so I can look after you. Maybe watering these tomatoes can wait. Would you like to come inside and have a glass of lemonade?'

'Yes,' Button said, and Ginny smiled. And then she looked uncertain.

'I have nothing,' she faltered. 'I really wasn't expecting her until next month. I don't know…'

'Tell you what,' Ben said, rising and dusting dirt from his knees. What was happening here was dramatic but he still had imperatives. Those imperatives had seen him take time out to try and persuade Ginny to be a doctor. That was a no go, especially now, but he still had at least twenty patients to see before he called it a day.

'You take Button inside and give her lemonade, then go through her suitcase and see what she has. When you have it sorted, bring her down to the clinic. I can give Button a good once-over—make sure everything's okay…'

'I can do that.'

'So you can,' he said. 'You're a doctor. Okay, forget the once-over. But our clinic nurse, Abby, has a five-year-old and she's a mum. If you don't need a doctor, you might need a mum to tell you all the things you're likely to need, to lend you any equipment you don't have. I have a child seat in the back of my Jeep—I use the Jeep for occasional patient transport. I'll leave it with you so you can bring Button down. I'll have Abby organise you another—the hire car place has seats they loan out.'

'I… Thank you.'

He hesitated, and once again he felt the surge of emotion he thought he'd long forgotten. Which was crazy. One long-ago love affair should make no difference to how he reacted to this woman now. 'Ginny, is this okay?' he demanded, trying to sound professionally caring—instead of personally caring. 'Are you sure you don't want me to ring Bob—he's the local cop—and have him drag the lawyer from the ferry?'

She looked at him then, really looked at him, and it was as if somehow what she saw gave her strength.

'No. I'm okay,' she said. 'I need to be. I don't have a choice and neither does Button. Thank you for your help, but we'll be fine.'

'You will bring her to the clinic?'

She hesitated. 'Yes,' she conceded at last.

'Big of you.'

She gave a faint smile. 'Sorry. I guess I'm not up for awards for good manners right now. But I am grateful. I'll come to the clinic when I need to. Thank you, Ben, and goodbye.'

She watched him go and she felt…desolate.

Desolate was how she'd been feeling for six months now. Or more.

Once upon a time her life had been under control. She was the indulged only daughter of wealthy, influential people. She was clever and she was sure of herself.

There'd been a tiny hiccup in her life when as a teenager she'd thought she'd fallen in love with Ben McMahon, but even then she'd been enough in control to figure it out, to bow to her parents' dictates.

Sure, she'd thought Ben was gorgeous, but he was one of twelve kids, the son of the nanny her parents had hired to take care of her whenever they had been on the island. At seventeen she'd long outgrown the need for a nanny but she and Ben had stayed friends.

He had been her holiday romance, welcoming her with joy whenever her parents had come to the island, being her friend, sharing her first kiss, but he had been an escape from the real world, not a part of it.

His proposal that last year when they'd both finished school had been a shock, questioning whether her worlds could merge, and she'd known they couldn't. Her father had spelled that out in no uncertain terms.

Real life was the ambition her parents had instilled in her. Real life had been the circle she'd moved in in her prestigious girls' school.

Real life had become medicine, study, still the elite
social life she'd shared with her parents' circle, then
James, marriage, moving up the professional scale...

But even before James had been diagnosed with non-
Hodgkin's lymphoma she'd known something had been
dreadfully wrong. Or maybe she'd always known something had been wrong, she conceded. It was just that
it had taken more courage than she'd had to admit it.

Then her father had died, dramatically, of a heart at-
tack. She'd watched her mother, dry eyed at the funeral,
already gathering the trappings of rich widow about her.

The night of the funeral James had had to go out.
'Work,' he'd said, and had kissed her perfunctorily. 'Go
to bed, babe, and have a good cry. Cry and get over it.'

Like her mother, she hadn't cried either.

She'd thought that night... She'd known but she
hadn't wanted to face it. If she worked hard enough,
she didn't have to face it.

'Lemonade or raspberry cordial?' she asked Button.
She sat her at the kitchen table and put lemonade in front
of her and also the red cordial. Button looked at them
both gravely and finally decided on red. Huge decision.
Her relief at having made it almost made Ginny smile.

Almost.

She found herself remembering the day of James's
funeral. It had been the end of a truly appalling time,
when she'd fought with every ounce of her medical
knowledge to keep him and yet nothing could hold
him. He'd been angry for his entire illness, angry at
his body for betraying him, at the medical profession
that couldn't save him, but mostly at Ginny, who was
healthy when he wasn't.

'—you, Florence Nightingale.' The crude swearing

was the last thing he'd said to her, and she'd stood at his graveside and felt sick and cold and empty.

And then she'd grown aware of Veronica. Veronica was the wife of James's boss. She'd walked up to Ginny, ostensibly to hug her, but as she'd hugged, she'd whispered.

'You didn't lose him. You never had him in the first place. You and my husband were just the stage props for our life. What we had was fun, fantasy, everything life should be.'

And then Veronica's assumed face was back on, her wife-of-James's-boss mantle, and Ginny thought maybe she'd imagined it.

But then she'd read James's will.

'To my daughter, Barbara, to be held in trust by my wife, Guinevere, to be used at her discretion if Barbara's true parentage is ever discovered.'

She remembered a late-night conversation the week before James had died. She'd thought he was rambling.

'The kid. He thinks it's his. If he finds out…I'll do the right thing. Bloody kid should be in a home anyway. Do the right thing for me, babe. I know you will—you always do the right thing. Stupid cow.'

Was this just more? she thought, pouring a second glass for the obviously thirsty little girl. Guinevere doing the right thing. Guinevere being a stupid cow?

'I'm not Guinevere, I'm Ginny,' she said aloud, and her voice startled her, but she knew she was right.

Taking Button wasn't doing something for James or for Veronica or for anyone, she told herself. This was purely between *her* and Button.

They'd move on, together.

'Ginny,' Button said now, trying the name out for

size, and Ginny sat at the table beside this tiny girl and tried to figure it out.

Ginny and Button.

Two of a kind? Two people thrown out of their worlds?

Only she hadn't been thrown. She'd walked away from medicine and she'd walked away from Sydney.

Her father had left her the vineyard. It had been a no-brainer to come here.

And Ben…

Was Ben the reason she'd come back here?

So many thoughts…

Ben's huge family. Twelve kids. She remembered the day her mother had dropped her off, aged all of eight. 'This woman's looking after you today, Guinevere,' she'd told her. 'Your father and I are playing golf. Be good.'

She'd got a hug from Ben's mother, a huge welcoming beam. 'Come on in, sweetheart, welcome to our muddle.'

She'd walked into the crowded jumble that had been their home and Ben had been at the stove, lifting the lid on popcorn just as it popped.

Kernels were going everywhere, there were shouts of laughter and derision, the dogs were going nuts, the place was chaos. And eight-year-old Ben was smiling at her.

'Ever made popcorn? Want to give it a go? Reckon the dog's got this lot. And then I'll take you taddying.'

'Taddying?'

'Looking for tadpoles,' he'd said, and his eight-year-old eyes had gleamed with mischief. 'You're a real city slicker, aren't you?'

And despite what happened next—or maybe because of it—they'd been pretty much best friends from that moment.

She hadn't come back for Ben; she knew she hadn't, but maybe that was part of the pull that had brought her back to the island. Uncomplicated acceptance. Here she could lick her wounds in private. Figure out where she'd go from here.

Grow grapes?

With Button.

'We need to make you a bedroom,' she told Button, and the little girl's face grew suddenly grave.

'I want Monkey in my bedroom,' she said.

Monkey? Uh-oh.

She flipped open the little girl's suitcase. It was neatly packed—dresses, pyjamas, knickers, socks, shoes, coats. There was a file containing medical records and a small box labelled 'Medications'. She flipped this open and was relieved to find nothing more sinister than asthma medication.

But no monkey.

She remembered her mother's scorn from years ago as she'd belligerently packed her beloved Barny Bear to bring to the island.

'Leave that grubby thing at home, Guinevere. You have far nicer toys.'

'I want Monkey,' Button whispered again, and Ginny looked at her desolate little face and thought Button couldn't have fought as she had. Despite her mother's disgust, Ginny had brought Barny, and she'd loved him until he'd finally, tragically been chewed to bits by one of Ben's family's puppies.

But fighting for a soft toy wouldn't be in Button's

skill range, she thought, and then she realised that's what she'd taken on from this moment. Fighting on Button's behalf.

She tried to remember now the sensations she'd felt when she'd received the lawyer's initial documents laying out why Button was being deserted by the people who'd cared for her. Rage? Disgust? Empathy?

This was a child no one wanted.

Taking her in had seemed like a good idea, even noble. Veronica and James had acted without morality. She'd make up for it, somehow.

Alone?

She was glad Ben had been here when Button had arrived. She sort of wanted him here now. He'd know how to cope with a missing Monkey.

Or not. Don't be a wimp, she told herself. You can do this. And then she thought, You don't have a choice.

But...he had offered to help.

'I guess you left Monkey at home,' she told Button, because there was no other explanation but the truth. 'I might be able to find someone who'll send him to us, but for now...let's have lunch and then we'll go down to Dr Ben's clinic. I don't have any monkeys here, but Dr Ben might know someone who does.'

Ben had told her the clinic would be busy but she'd had no concept of just how busy. There were people queued up through the waiting room and into the corridor beyond.

Plague? Ginny thought, but none of the people here looked really ill. There were a few people looking wan amongst them but most looked in rude health.

She'd led Button into the reception area, but she took

one look and tugged Button backwards. But as she did, an inner door swung open. Ben appeared, followed by a harassed-looking nurse.

Ben-the-doctor.

She'd seen him a couple of times since she'd returned to the island. She'd met him once in the main street where he'd greeted her with pleasure and she'd been calmly, deliberately pleasant. But dismissive. She'd returned to the island to get some peace, to learn about vineyards, but to treat the place as her parents had treated it—an escape. She'd had no intention of being sucked into island life.

Then this afternoon he'd asked her to help him—and then he'd helped her. She'd been incredibly grateful that he'd been there to face down the lawyer on her behalf.

But now he was facing, what, twenty patients, with one harried-looking nurse helping.

He looked competent, though, she thought, and then she thought, no, he looked more than competent.

At seventeen they'd shared their first kiss after a day's truly excellent surfing, and there had been a reason she'd thought she'd fallen in love with him. He'd been her best friend but he had been an awesome surfer, he'd been kind and…cute?

There was no way she'd describe Ben as cute now. Twelve years had filled out that lanky frame, had turned boy into man, and the man he'd become…

He was tall, lean, ripped. He had sun-bleached brown hair and sea-blue eyes. Did he still surf? He looked a bit weathered, so maybe he did. He was wearing chinos, a shirt and a tie, but the shirtsleeves were rolled up and the tie was a bit askew, as if he'd been working hard and was expecting more work to come.

He'd taken time out today to visit her. That was why the queue had built up, she thought, and then she thought taking time out must have been an act of desperation. He'd made himself later still in an attempt to get the help he desperately needed.

He was surrounded by need. He looked harassed to the point of exhaustion.

'Ginny,' he said flatly as he saw her, and then managed a smile. 'Hi, Button.' He sighed. 'Ginny, I need to spend some time with you and Button—I reckon she does need that check-up—but as you can see, I'm under pressure. Do you think you could come back in an hour or so? I hadn't expected you so soon.'

An hour or so. She looked around the waiting room and thought…an hour or so?

She knew this island. There was a solid fishing community, and there were always tourists, but there was also a fair proportion of retirees, escapees from the rat race of the mainland, so there were thus many elderly residents.

What was the bet that Ben would have half a dozen house calls lined up after clinic? she thought, and glanced at his face, saw the tension and knew she was right.

'Can I help?' she said, almost before she knew she intended to say it.

His face stilled. 'You said…'

'For this afternoon only,' she said flatly. 'But you helped me with Button.' As if that explained everything—which it didn't. 'If there's someone who could care for Button…'

'You're sure?' Ben's face stilled with surprise, but before she could speak he shook his head. 'Stupid, stupid, stupid. The lady's made the offer in front of witnesses.' And before she could speak again he'd knelt by Button. 'Button, do you like making chocolate cake?'

'Yes,' Button said, a response he was starting to expect. She was puzzled but game.

'This is Nurse Abby,' Ben said, motioning to the nurse beside him. 'Abby's little boy is making chocolate cupcakes with my sister, Hannah, right now. We have a kitchen right next door. When they're finished they'll decorate them with chocolate buttons and then walk down to the beach to have fish and chips for tea. Would you like to do that?'

'Yes,' she said again, and Ginny thought, God bless Down's kids, with their friendly, unquestioning outlook on the world. If Button had been a normal four-year-old, she'd no doubt be a ball of tension right now, and who'd blame her? But Down's kids tended to accept the world as they found it.

She would get her Monkey back for her, she thought fiercely, and she picked Button up and gave her a hug.

'You're such a good girl,' she said, and Button gave a pleased smile.

'I'm a good girl,' she said, and beamed, and Abby took her hand and led her out to where chocolate cupcakes were waiting and Ginny was left looking at Ben, while twenty-odd islanders looked on.

'Everyone, this is…' Ben hesitated. 'Dr Ginny Koestrel?'

'Yes,' she said, and turned to the room at large. She had no doubt what the islanders thought of her parents but she'd never changed her name and she had no intention of starting now.

'Many of you know my parents owned Red Fire Win-

ery. You'll know Henry Stubbs—he's been looking after
it for us, but he hasn't been well so I've come home to
run it. But Ben's right, I'm a doctor. I'm an Australian
and for this afternoon I'm here to help.' She took a deep
breath, seeing myriad questions building.

Okay, she thought, if she was going to be a source
of gossip, why not use it to advantage?

'Ben says many of you are just here for prescrip-
tions,' she said. 'If you're happy to have an Aussie doctor, I can see you—we can get you all home earlier that
way. I'll need to get scripts signed by Dr Ben because
I don't have New Zealand accreditation yet, but I can
check your records, make sure there are no problems,
write the scripts and then Dr Ben can sign them in between seeing patients who need to see him for other
reasons. Is that okay with everyone?'

It was. First, Ben's face cleared with relief and she
knew she was right in thinking he had house calls lined
up afterwards. Second, every face in the waiting room
was looking at her with avid interest. Guinevere Koestrel, daughter of the millionaires who'd swanned around
the island, splashing money around, but now not looking like a millionaire at all. She'd been on the island for
months but she'd kept herself to herself. Now suddenly
she was in the clinic with a little girl.

She knew there'd have been gossip circulating about
her since her arrival. Here was a chance for that gossip
to be confirmed in person. She could practically see
patients who'd come with minor ailments swapping to
the prescription-only side of the queue. She glanced at
Ben and saw him grin and knew he was thinking exactly the same.

'Excellent plan, Dr Koestrel,' he said. He motioned to

the door beside the one he'd just come out of. 'That's our second consulting suite. I'm sorry we don't have time for a tour. You want to go in there and make yourself comfortable? There's software on the computer that'll show pharmacy lists. I'll have Abby come in and show you around. She can do your patient histories, guide you through. Thank you very much,' he said. 'And you don't need to explain about Henry. Henry's here.'

He turned to an elderly man in the corner, and she realised with a shock that it was her farm manager.

Henry had been caretaker for her parents' vineyard for ever. It had been Henry's phone call—'Sorry, miss, but my arthritis is getting bad and you need to think about replacing me'—that had fed the impulse to return, but when she'd come he hadn't let her help. He'd simply wanted to be gone.

'I'm right, miss,' he'd said, clearing out the caretaker's residence and ignoring her protests that she'd like him to stay. 'I've got me own place. I'm done with Koestrels.'

Her parents had a lot to answer for, she thought savagely, realising how shabby the caretaker's residence had become, how badly the old man had been treated, and then she thought maybe she had a lot to answer for, too. At seventeen she'd been as sure of her place in the world as her parents—and just as oblivious of Henry's.

'This means I can see you next, Henry,' Ben said gently. 'We have Dr Ginny here now and suddenly life is a lot easier for all of us.'

She'd said that her help was for this afternoon only, but she had to stay.

Ben had no doubt she'd come to the clinic under

pressure, but the fact that she'd seen the workload he was facing and had reacted was a good sign. Wasn't it?

It had to be. He had a qualified doctor working in the room next door and there was no way he was letting her go.

Even if it was Ginny Koestrel.

Especially if it was Ginny Koestrel?

See, there was a direction he didn't want his thoughts to take. She was simply a medical degree on legs, he told himself. She was a way to keep the islanders safe. Except she was Ginny.

He remembered the first time she'd come to the island. Her parents had bought the vineyard when he'd been eight and they'd arrived that first summer with a houseful of guests. They'd been there to have fun, and they hadn't wanted to be bothered with their small daughter.

So they'd employed his mum and he'd been at the kitchen window when her parents had dropped her off. She'd been wearing a white pleated skirt and a pretty pink cardigan, her bright red hair had been arranged into two pretty pigtails tied with matching pink ribbon, and she'd stood on the front lawn—or what the McMahons loosely termed front lawn—looking lost.

She was the daughter of rich summer visitors. He and his siblings had been prepared to scorn her. Their mum had taken in a few odd kids to earn extra money.

Mostly they had been nice to them, but he could remember his sister, Jacinta, saying scornfully, 'Well, we don't have to be nice to *her*. She can't be a millionaire and have friends like us, even if we offered.'

Jacinta had taken one look at the pleated skirt and pink cardigan and tilted her nose and taken off.

But Ben was the closest to her in age. 'Be nice to Guinevere,' his mother had told him. He'd shown her how to make popcorn—and then he'd shown her how to catch tadpoles. White pleated skirt and all.

Yeah, well, he'd got into trouble over that but it had been worth it. They'd caught tadpoles, they'd spent the summer watching them turn into frogs and by the time they'd released them the day before she'd returned to Sydney, they'd been inseparable.

One stupid hormonal summer at the end of it had interfered with the memory, but she was still Ginny at heart, he thought. She'd be able to teach Button to catch tadpoles.

Um…Henry. Henry was sitting beside him, waiting to talk about his indigestion.

'She's better'n her parents,' Henry said dubiously, and they both knew who he was talking about.

'She'd want to be. Her parents were horrors.'

'She wanted me to stay at the homestead,' he went on. 'For life, like. She wanted to fix the manager's house up. That was a nice gesture.'

'So why didn't you?'

'I have me dad's cottage out on the headland,' Henry said. 'It'll do me. And when I'm there I can forget about boss and employee. I can forget about rich and poor. Like you did when she were a kid.'

Until reality had taken over, Ben thought. Until he'd suggested their lives could collide.

Henry was right. Keep the worlds separate. He'd learned that at the age of seventeen and he wasn't going to forget it.

Think of her as rich.

Think of her as a woman who'd just been landed

with a little girl called Button, a little girl who'd present all sorts of challenges and who she hadn't had to take. Think of Ginny's face when the lawyer had talked of dumping Button in an institution…

Think of Henry's indigestion.

'Have you been sticking only to the anti-inflammatories I've been prescribing?' he asked suspiciously. Henry had had hassles before when he'd topped up his prescription meds with over-the-counter pills.

'Course I have,' Henry said virtuously

Ben looked at him and thought, You're lying through your teeth. It was very tempting to pop another pill when you had pain, and he'd had trouble making Henry understand the difference between paracetamol—which was okay to take if you had a stomach ulcer—and ibuprofen—which wasn't.

Ginny…

No. Henry's stomach problems were right here, right now. That was what he had to think of.

He didn't need—or want—to think about Ginny Koestrel as any more than a colleague. A colleague and nothing more.

CHAPTER THREE

GINNY WORKED THROUGH until six. It was easy enough work, sifting through patient histories, checking that their requests for medication made sense, writing scripts, sending them out for Ben to countersign, but she was aware as she did it that this was the first step on a slippery slope into island life.

The islanders were fearful of an earthquake—sort of. Squid was preaching doom so they were taking precautions—buying candles, stocking the pantry, getting a decent supply of any medication they needed—but as Ginny worked she realised they weren't overwhelmingly afraid.

Earth tremors had been part of this country's history for ever. The islanders weren't so worried that they'd put aside the fact that Guinevere Koestler was treating them. This was Ginny, whose parents had swanned around the island for years and whose parents had treated islanders merely as a source of labour.

She hadn't been back since she'd been seventeen. Once she'd gone to medical school she'd found excuses not to accompany her parents on their summer vacations—to be honest, she'd found her parents' attitude increasingly distasteful. And then there had been this thing with Ben—so the islands were seeing her now for the first time as a grown-up Koestler.

The island grapevine was notorious. Every islander would know by now that she'd been landed with a child, and every islander wanted to know more.

She fended off queries as best she could but even so, every consultation took three times longer than it should have and by the time she was done she was tired and worried about Button.

Button?

Where was she headed? She'd spent the last six months building herself a cocoon of isolation. One afternoon and it had been shattered.

She needed to rebuild, fast.

She took the last script out to the desk and Ben was waiting for her.

'All done,' she said. 'Mrs Grayson's cortisone ointment is the last.' She handed over the script she'd just written. 'This'll keep that eczema at bay until Christmas.'

He grinned and greeted Olive Grayson with wry good humour, signed the script and watched the lady depart.

The waiting room was empty. The receptionist was gone. There was no one but Ben.

'Button…' she started, and headed towards the kitchenette, but Ben put a hand on her shoulder and stopped her.

It shouldn't feel like this, she thought, suddenly breathless. Ben touching her?

For heaven's sake, she wasn't seventeen any more. Once upon a time she'd thought she was in love with this man. It had been adolescent nonsense and there was no reason for her hormones to go into overdrive now.

'I hope you don't mind but I sent her home with our nurse, Abby,' he said.

'You...what?'

'Abby's a single mum and the tremors happening when she can't be with her son are doing her head in. So my mum's taking a hand. Abby will be having dinner with us, so I suggested she and Hannah—my sister—take both kids back to our place. They'll have put them to bed, and dinner's waiting for us. Mum says there's plenty. I have a few house calls to make but they can wait until after dinner if you'd like to join us.'

'You...'

'I know, I'm an overbearing, manipulating toad,' he said, smiling. 'I've manipulated you into working for us this afternoon and now I've manipulated you into a dinner date. But it's not actually a dinner date in the romantic sense. It's Mum, Dad, whichever of my siblings are home tonight, Abby, Button and you. It's hardly candlelit seduction.'

She smiled back, but only just. This was exactly what she didn't want, being drawn into island life. She wanted to work on her vineyard. She wanted to forget about being a doctor. She wanted...

Nothing. She wanted nothing, nothing and nothing.

'Why not medicine?' Ben said softly, watching her face, and she thought almost hysterically that he always had been able to read her thoughts.

'What...what do you mean?'

'I mean I did some research when I heard you were back on the island. You've got yourself a fine medical degree. And yet...'

'And yet my husband died of cancer,' she said flatly, almost defiantly

'And there was nothing you could do? You blame yourself or your medicine? Is that it?'

'This is not your business.'

'But you walked away.'

'Leave it, Ben. I changed direction. I can't let the vineyard go to ruin.'

'We need a doctor here more than we need wine.'

'And I need wine more than I need medicine. Now, if you don't mind…I'll collect Button and go home.'

'My mum will be hurt if you don't stop and eat.'

She would be, too.

She'd popped in to see Ailsa when she'd arrived back at the island—of course she had. Ben's mum had always been lovely to her, drawing her into the family, making her time on the island so much better than if she'd been left with the normally sullen adolescent childminders her parents had usually hired on the mainland.

But she'd explained things to Ailsa.

'I need time to myself—to come to terms with my husband's death.' To come to terms with her husband's betrayal? His anger? His totally unjustified blame? 'I'm done with relationships, medicine, pressure. I need to be alone.'

'Of course you do, dear,' Ailsa had said, and had hugged her. 'But don't stay solitary too long. There's no better cure than hugs, and hugs are what you'll get when you come to this house. And if I know our kids and our friends, it won't only be me who'll be doing the hugging.'

Nothing had changed, she thought. This island was a time warp, the escape her parents had always treated it as.

She wanted this island but she didn't want the close-

ness that went with it. For six months she'd held herself
aloof but now...

'Irish stew and parsley dumplings,' Ben said, grinning and putting on a nice, seductive face. His left eyebrow rose and he chuckled at her expression. 'Who
needs candlelight and champagne when there's dumplings?' He held out his hands. 'Mum says it's your favourite.'

She'd remembered. Ailsa had remembered!

'And the kids are already sorting toys for Button,' he
said, and tugged her toward the door. 'Come on home,
Ginny.'

Home.

She didn't want to go. Every sense was screaming
at her to go back to the vineyard.

But Button was asleep at Ailsa's. Ailsa had made
parsley dumplings.

Ben was holding her hands and smiling at her.

What was a woman to do? A woman seemed to have
no choice at all.

'Fine,' she said.

'That doesn't sound gracious,' he said, but still he
smiled.

She caught herself. She was sounding like a brat.

'I'm sorry. It's very generous...'

'It's you who's generous,' he said gently. 'If you
hadn't helped I wouldn't be getting any dinner, and
Mum knows that as well as I do. So thank you, Ginny,
and don't feel as if by coming you're beholden. Or even
that you're somehow putting your feet into quicksand.
You can draw back. You can go back to your vineyard
and your solitude but not before you've eaten some of
Mum's Irish stew.'

* * *

There were eight people around Ailsa's kitchen table, and the kids were asleep on the squishy living-room settee just through the door. The children were still in sight of the table. They were still part of the family.

It had always been thus, Ginny thought. Not only had Ailsa and her long-suffering Doug produced twelve children, but their house expanded to fit all comers. Doug worked on one of the island's fishing trawlers. He spent long times away at sea and when he was home he seemed content to sit by the fire, puffing an empty pipe.

'I know you smoke it at sea, but not in the house, not with the children,' Ailsa had decreed, and Doug didn't mind. He regarded his brood and Ailsa's strays with bemused approval and the house was the warmer for his presence.

Eight was a small tableful for these two, but the kids were mostly grown now, setting up their own places. Ben was the third of twelve but only the three youngest were home tonight. Becky, Sam and Hannah were fourteen, fifteen and seventeen respectively, and they greeted Abby with warmth and shoved up to make room for her.

Abby, the nurse who'd worked with her that afternoon, was already there. The nurse had impressed Ginny today, not only with her people skills but with her warmth. She looked at home at the table, as if Ben often had her here.

Abby and Ben? A question started.

Ben was helping his mother ladle dumplings onto plates. Doug hardly said a word—it was up to the kids to do the entertaining, and they did.

'It's lovely to see you again,' seventeen-year-old Hannah said, a bit pink with teenage self-consciousness as she said it. 'We missed you when you went.'

'Ginny was Ben's girlfriend,' fourteen-year-old Becky told Abby, with no teenage self-consciousness at all. 'I'm too young to remember but everyone says they were all kissy-kissy. And then Ginny went away and Ben broke his heart.'

'Becky!' her family said, almost as one, and she flushed.

'Well, he did. Maureen said he did.'

Ginny remembered Maureen. Maureen was the oldest of the McMahon tribe, self-assertive and bossy. She'd come to see Ginny on the last night Ginny had been on the island, all those years ago.

'You could have been kind. Ben's so upset. You could say you'll write. Something like that.'

How to say that she couldn't bear to write? That even at seventeen all she'd wanted to do had been to fling herself into Ben's arms and stay? That she'd talked to her parents about the possibility of university in Auckland but she hadn't been able to divorce the request from the way she'd felt about Ben, and her parents had laid down an ultimatum.

'You're being ridiculous. The boy has no hope of making it through medicine—twelve kids—they're dirt poor. Cut it off now, Guinevere, if you want to be kind, otherwise you'll simply distract him from trying. You're going to university in Sydney and if there's any more nonsense, we'll send you to your aunt in London.'

The boy has no hope of making it through medicine. You'll simply distract him from trying.

The phrases had stung but even at seventeen she had been able to see the truth in them.

Ben had wanted so much to be a doctor. He'd dreamed of it, ached for it. Since he'd been fifteen he'd worked on the docks after school, unloading fish and cleaning them for sale. It was a filthy, hard job, and every cent of what he'd earned had gone to his doctor training fund.

You'll simply distract him from trying.

And then her father had issued another ultimatum, this one even worse.

Okay. If she couldn't study in Auckland... If she couldn't be with him...

She'd made a decision then and there, a Joan of Arc martyrdom, an adolescent burning for a cause. She'd renounce him and prove her parents wrong. She'd tell him not to write, to forget her, to focus purely on his career. Then, when they were both qualified doctors, she'd come again, appear out of the mist, probably wearing something white and floaty, and the orchestra would play and...and...

She found herself smiling, and everyone at the table was looking at her oddly. Even Ben.

'Sorry,' she said. 'I was just remembering how romantic it was. Our first love. I hope your heart wasn't broken for long, Ben.'

He grinned. 'For months,' he said.

'I thought you started going out with Daphne Harcourt that same summer,' Hannah retorted. 'Now, *they* were kissy kissy. And then there was that painted one you brought home from uni.'

'And Jessica Crosby with the weird leggings and piercings,' Becky volunteered. 'She was hot. And now Mum thinks Abby—'

'Enough,' Doug said, breaking in abruptly. 'Leave the lad alone.'

They subsided as everyone always did when Doug spoke, and why wouldn't you subside when Ailsa's Irish stew was in front of you? But Ginny couldn't help thinking…thinking…

So Ben hadn't carried a flame for her. That was good, wasn't it? Yeah, it was, for of course at seventeen she hadn't carried a torch for him all that long either. She'd immersed herself in university life, she'd had a couple of very nice boyfriends, and then she'd met James.

He'd been older than her, his parents had moved in her parents' circle and he'd already been a qualified surgeon. She'd been thrilled when he'd noticed her, even more thrilled when he'd proposed.

And that same naivety that had had her dreaming of returning to Kaimotu in clouds of white mist with orchestra backing had then propelled her into a marriage that had been a disaster.

'Ginny,' Ben said gently, and she looked up and met his gaze. He looked concerned. Drat, he'd always been able to read her face and it was disconcerting. 'Are you okay? Did we work you too hard?'

'Would you like to stay here the night, with the little one?' Ailsa asked. 'Ben says you've been dropped into parenthood and it's hard. She's sound asleep now. She'll be right here.'

It was so tempting. She could step back into the McMahons' protection, she thought, as she'd stepped into it all those years ago.

Its warmth enfolded her. This family…

And then she glanced at Abby, who was looking

fiercely down at her dinner plate, and she thought, What am I messing with? If there was something between these two, the kids talking of past loves must really hurt.

Joan of Arc syndrome again? Move aside, Ginny?

It wasn't dumb, though, she thought. There were no white mists and orchestras in the background now, just hard reality that had been drummed into her ever since she'd made her wedding vows.

'Thank you but no,' she managed. 'It's a lovely offer but Button and I will be fine.'

'I've put together a wee pack of toys for her,' Ailsa said. 'She likes Ben's old stuffed turtle, Shuffles.'

She flashed a glance at Ben at that, and then looked away fast. Noble doctor donating his Shuffles… It was dumb but why did that tug her heartstrings?

'Thank…thank you.'

'If there's anything else we can do…'

'I can babysit,' Hannah said. 'I'm supposed to be at uni but I copped glandular fever and missed the first two months of the semester. We figured it was best if I took the next two months off as well and start again at mid-year. So if you want to help Ben at the clinic I can keep helping out with Button. I…I do it for money,' she said, a trifle self-consciously. 'I mean…I'm sort of saving to be a doctor, too.'

'We'd love some help,' Ben said. 'Wouldn't we, Abby?'

'And you know, Ginny, it might help Button settle,' Ailsa said softly. 'She'll find it strange just the two of you. Ben seems to think she's been used to babysitters, so maybe stretching the care might help her adjust. Hannah looks after Abby's little boy, Jack, after school. The little ones played really well tonight. It might help

you, too, and as Ben says, we need all the medical help
we can get.'

They were all looking at her. The pressure…the pressure…

'No,' she said, and seven lots of eyebrows went up.

'Whoops, sorry,' she said, realising how petty her
'no' had sounded. 'It's just…'

'It's very fast,' Ailsa said, and came round the table
to give her a hug. 'Ginny, we all know your husband
died and we're very sorry. We should give you space.
It's just…we know how hard Ben's pushed.'

'When I'm qualified, I can help,' Hannah said, and
Ginny glanced at the girl and saw how much she meant
it.

They all wanted to help—and she could.

'I'm sorry,' she managed. 'It's just…I can't.'

'Then you can't,' Ailsa said solidly, and glared at
Ben. 'If she can't then she can't, so don't ask it of her.
Ben, I know Ginny and I know she's been through a
bad time. You're not to nag and you're to leave her alone
until she's ready. Thank her very much for this afternoon and let her be.'

'Thank you very much for this afternoon,' Ben said
gravely, and then he smiled at her.

It was the smile she remembered. It was the smile
that had twisted her seventeen-year-old heart.

It was a white-mists-and-orchestra smile.

Enough.

She focussed on her dumplings and the talk started
up again, cheerful banter as there always was around
this table. As she'd always remembered.

People didn't look at her at this table. They didn't

focus on her manners, they didn't demand she join in politely, they simply…were.

She glanced up and Ben was still watching her. His smile was faintly quizzical.

He wouldn't push. This whole community wouldn't push. They'd settle for what she was prepared to give.

How mean was it of her not to help?

She…couldn't.

'Call yourself a doctor… Stupid cow, you can't even give an injection without shaking…'

It wasn't true. She'd been okay until James…until James…

'Call yourself a doctor…'

'It's okay, Ginny,' Ben said gently. 'No pressure.'

She flushed and tried to look at him and couldn't. She'd been a doctor that afternoon, she told herself fiercely. Why couldn't she keep going?

Because Button needed her, she thought, and there was almost relief in the thought. In one day she'd become a stepmother. It was scary territory, but not as scary as stepping back into…life?

The chatter was starting up again around the table. No pressure.

This family was full of friends, she thought ruefully, and maybe…maybe that was what she needed. She could accept friendship.

Without giving anything in return?

It had to wait, she thought. If she said yes… If she got her New Zealand registration, she'd be expected to be a real doctor again.

'Call yourself a doctor…'

'No pressure at all,' Ailsa said gently beside her. 'The

island can wait. Your friends can wait. We can all wait until you're ready.'

She smiled at Ginny, a warm, maternal smile.

Friends, Ginny thought, and tried to smile back. Friends felt…good.

So much for isolation, she decided as she tried to join in the cheerful banter around the table, but at least she'd left the white mists and orchestras behind her.

Ben walked her out to the car. He helped her buckle the sleeping Button into her newly acquired child seat, and then stood back and looked at her in the moonlight.

'We tried to blackmail you,' he said softly. 'The lawyer and then me. I'm sorry.'

'I… You didn't.'

'I manipulated you into helping this afternoon.'

'I did that all by myself.'

'Sort of,' he said wryly. 'I know how conscience works. Mrs Guttering met me in the supermarket last week and started complaining about her toe. Before I knew it she had her boots off and I was inspecting her ingrown toenail between the ice cream and frozen peas. How do you say no? I haven't learned yet.'

'And yet I have,' she said, trying to smile, trying to keep it light, as he had, and he put a hand out to cup her chin.

She flinched and moved back and he frowned.

'Ginny, it's okay. Saying no is your right.'

'Th-thank you.'

The lights were on inside. The kids were still around the table. Someone had turned the telly on and laughter sounded out through the window.

Kids. Home.

She glanced away from Ben, who was looking at her in concern. She looked into the car at Button and something inside her firmed. Button. Her stepdaughter.

Out of all of this mess—one true thing. She would focus on Button. Nothing else.

'You want her,' Ben said on a note of discovery, and she nodded, mutely.

What had she let herself in for? she thought, but she knew she wanted it. The moment she'd seen that clause in James's will...

When she and James had married, a baby had been high on her list of priorities, but James hadn't been keen. 'Let's put it on hold, babe, until our careers are established. The biological clock doesn't start winding down until thirty-five. We have years.'

But for Ginny, in a marriage that had been increasingly isolating, a baby had seemed a huge thing, something to love, something to hold, a reason to get up in the morning.

As medicine wasn't?

It should be, she thought. There'd never been a time when she hadn't thought she'd be a doctor. Her parents had expected it of her. She'd expected it of herself and she'd enjoyed her training.

She'd loved her first year as an intern, working in Accident and Emergency, helping people in the raw, but it had never been enough.

'Of course you'll specialise.' That had been her father, and James, too, of course, plus the increasingly ambitious circle of friends they'd moved in. 'You'd never just want to be a family doctor. You're far too good for that, Ginny.'

She was clever. She'd passed the exams. She'd been

well on the way to qualifying in anaesthetics when James had got sick.

And after that life had been a blur—James's incredulity and anger that he of all people could be struck down, James searching for more and more interventionist cures, the medical fraternity around them fighting to the end.

'I should have frozen some sperm,' James had told her once, but she'd known he hadn't meant it—he'd never considered it. The idea that he was going to die had been inconceivable.

She'd watched as medical technology had taken her husband over, as he'd fought, fought, fought. She'd watched and experienced his fury. At the end he'd died undergoing yet another procedure, another intervention.

She remembered standing by his bedside at the end, thinking she would have liked to bring him here to this island, to have him die without tubes and interventions, to lie on the veranda and look out to sea…

James would have thought that was crazy.

'Can you tell me why you've decided to give up medicine?' Ben asked, and she shrugged.

'It couldn't save James.'

'Is that what you hoped? That you could save everyone?'

'No.'

'Then…'

'There was too much medicine,' she said flatly. 'Too much medicine and not enough love. I'm over it.'

'I'm sorry,' he said, as the silence stretched out and she stared out at the moonlight to the sea beyond—the sea was never far away on this island—and tried to figure where her life could go from here.

'We will find another doctor,' he said gently. 'This
need is short term.'

'Are you still saying I should help?'

'I don't see why you can't. You were great today.'

'I need to look after Button.'

'That's not why you're refusing. You know it's not.'

'I don't need to give you any other reason.'

She looked into the back seat again, at the little girl
curled into the child seat, sucking one thumb and hugging Ben's disreputable Shuffles with her spare arm.
Ailsa and Abby had presented her with a dozen soft
toys, from glossy teddies to pretty dolls, and Button
had considered with care and gone straight for Ben's
frayed turtle with one eye missing.

She looked like James, a little, and the thought was
strange and unsettling, but even as she thought it Button
wriggled further into her car seat and sighed and she
thought, no, she looked like Button. She looked like herself and she'd go forward with no shadows at all. Please.

Ben was smiling a little, watching her watch Button
hugging Shuffles. 'Mum never throws anything out.'

'You'd never have let her throw Shuffles out?' she
asked incredulously, and amazingly he grinned, tension easing.

'Maybe not. Actually not. Over my dead body not.'

'Yet you let Button have him.'

'Button will love him as Shuffles needs to be loved,'
he said, and then he looked at her—he really looked
at her. 'Will you love her?' he said, and she stared at
Button for a long, long moment and then gave a sharp,
decisive nod.

'Yes.'

'And if her parents reclaim her?'

'They won't.'

'If they do?'

'Then I'll cope,' she said. 'Everyone copes. You know that. Like us thinking we were in love when we were seventeen. You move on.'

'Button needs a greater commitment than we were prepared to give,' he said, and she flushed.

'You think I don't know that?'

He gazed at her gravely, reading her face, seeing... what? How vulnerable she felt? How alone? How terrified to be landed with a little girl she knew nothing about?

Kids with Down's had medical problems to contend with, as well as learning difficulties. Heart problems, breathing problems, infections that turned nasty fast...

She'd cope. Out of all the mess that had been her relationship with James—his betrayal, his fury that she be the one to survive, his death—this little one was what was left.

James's death hadn't left her desolate but it had left her...empty. Medicine was no longer a passion. Nothing was a passion.

If she could love this child...

But nothing else, she told herself fiercely. Nothing and no one else. She'd seen how fickle love was. Her parents' relationship had been a farce. James's professed love had been a lie, leading to bleakness and heartbreak. And even Ben... He'd said he loved her at seventeen but he'd found someone else that same summer.

'You moved on, too,' he said mildly, which brought her up with a jolt.

'Don't do that.'

'I don't know how not to,' he said obtusely, but she

knew what he meant. That was the problem. She'd always guessed what he was going to say before he said it and it worked both ways.

'Then don't look at me,' she snapped, and then caught herself. 'Sorry. I didn't mean…'

'I know what you mean.

'Ben…'

He smiled wryly and held up his hands in surrender. 'Okay, I'm mentally closing my eyes here. Tomorrow afternoon, then? One o'clock?'

'No.'

'Ginny…'

'No!' She hesitated, feeling bad. Feeling trapped. 'In an emergency…'

'Isn't a host of panicked islanders an emergency?'

'Tell the islanders Squid has something obtuse like delusional encephalitis. Lock him in your quarantine ward until he starts prophesying untold riches instead of earthquakes.'

He grinned at that. 'It'd need back-up medical opinion to confine him. You'll sign the certificate?'

She smiled as well, but only faintly.

'I can't sign,' she said gently. 'I don't have New Zealand registration and I don't intend to get it.'

'Not if…?'

'No.'

He gazed at her for a long, long moment, reading her face, and she shifted from foot to foot under his gaze. He knew her too well, this man, and she didn't like it.

'Ginny, if I'd known you were having such an appalling time…' he said at last.

'I wasn't. Don't.'

'I should have written.'

'I told you not to.'

'And I listened,' he said obtusely. 'How dumb was that?' He shrugged. 'Well, you're home now. There's no need for letters, but I won't pressure you. I'll cope. Meanwhile, just see if you can open up a little. Let the island cure you.'

'I'm not broken. I've just…grown up, that's all.'

'Haven't we all,' he said, and his voice was suddenly deathly serious. 'Even Button. Cuddle her lots, Guinevere Koestrel, because growing up is hard to do.'

It was a night to think about but Ginny didn't think. She didn't think because she was so tired that by the time she hit the pillow her eyes closed all by themselves, and when she woke up a little hand was brushing through her hair, gently examining her.

It was morning and she was a mother.

She'd taken Button with her into her parents' big bed, fearful that the little girl would wake up and be afraid, but she didn't seem afraid.

She was playing with Ginny's hair and Ginny lay and let the sensations run through her, a tiny girl, unafraid, sleeping beside her, totally dependent on her, bemused by her mass of red curls.

She hadn't had a haircut since James had died—she hadn't been bothered—but now she thought she wouldn't. James had liked it cropped, but Ben…

She'd had long hair when Ben had known her. Ben had liked it long.

Ben…

It was strange, she thought. She'd been such good friends with Ben, but she'd barely thought of him for years.

She didn't want to think of him now. The sensations he engendered scared her. She'd fought so hard to be self-contained, and in one day…

It wasn't his fault she'd been landed with Button, she told herself, but she knew the sensations that scared her most had nothing to do with Button.

Button…Button was here and now. Button was her one true thing.

She found a brush and they took turns brushing each other's hair, a simple enough task but one Button found entrancing. Ginny enjoyed it, too, but she didn't enjoy it enough to stop thinking about Ben. To stop feeling guilty that she'd refused to help.

If she'd agreed… She wasn't sure about Australian doctors working in New Zealand but she suspected there'd be no problem. She might even be able to do more than write scripts.

She'd thought she wasn't missing medicine but yesterday, watching the diverse group of islanders come through her door, she'd thought…

She'd thought…

Maybe she shouldn't think, she told herself. The thing to do now was just whatever came next. It was her turn to brush Button's hair.

She brushed and it felt good. Making Button smile felt good. Sharing her home with this little girl felt…. right.

She thought of last night, of Ailsa's table, and she thought homes were meant to hold more than one.

Button was winding her curls around her fingers. 'Red,' she said in satisfaction.

'Carrots,' she said, and Button considered—and then giggled.

'Carrots.'

Family, Ginny thought, and then suddenly found herself thinking of Abby, Ben's clinical nurse.

She seemed lovely. She was a single mum and a competent nurse. She worked beside Ben, and his parents obviously cared for her.

Good. Great, she told herself. It was lovely that he had a lady who was so obviously right for him.

Wasn't it?

Of course it was, she told herself harshly, and then it was her turn to brush so she needed to focus on something that wasn't Ben and Abby.

For there was no need to think of anything past Button and the vineyard.

No need at all.

Ben woke early and thought about Ginny. He should think about Abby, he told himself. His family had been matchmaking with every ounce of coercion they could manage. Abby was lovely. She was haunted a bit by her past but she was a gorgeous woman and a true friend.

As Ginny had been a friend?

See, there was the problem. One hot day in his eighteenth year Ben had stopped thinking of Ginny as a friend. They'd been surfing. It had been a sweltering day so there'd been no need for wetsuits. They'd waited, lying at the back of the swell for the perfect wave, and when it had come they'd caught it together.

They'd surfed in side by side, the perfect curve, power, beauty, translucent blue all around them.

The wave had sunk to nothing in the shallows and they'd sunk as well, rolling off their boards to lie in the shallows.

Her long, lithe body had touched his. Skin against skin...

He'd kissed her and he'd known he would never forget that kiss. It had him still wanting to touch her after all these years. Still unable to keep his hands away from her.

What he felt for Abby was friendship, pure and simple. But Ginny... Seeing her today, spending time with her, watching her care for Button...

Yeah, the hormones were still there.

Hormones, however, could be controlled. Must be controlled.

'There should be pills,' he told himself, and then thought there probably were.

Anti-love potions?

Except he didn't need them. It was true he'd got over his adolescent lust. He'd had other girlfriends, moved on.

Out of sight, out of mind? Definitely. He'd had a few very nice girlfriends. Nothing serious, but fun.

The problem was that Ginny wasn't out of sight now and the physical attraction had slammed straight back...

But the class thing still held true. He remembered that final night, in his shabby suit, Ginny dressed as if she'd just come off the Paris catwalks, and he remembered her gentle smile.

Impossible.

Yeah, so class, social standing had been important then, he told himself. Not so much now.

But then there were her ghosts. Big ones, he thought. A guy who'd betrayed her? A past that made her want to give up medicine? He didn't know it all. He could only guess.

If he wanted her...

What was he about, still wanting her?

He didn't, he told himself. This was nostalgia speaking, surely.

'Get over it,' he told himself harshly. 'She's rich, independent and wants nothing to do with you. She doesn't want to be a doctor any more and she can surely afford to do what she likes. It's her call. Leave her alone. One haunted society doctor who doesn't want to be a doctor at all—no and no and no.'

The week wore on.

Down on the docks, Squid's doomsday forebodings were increasing rather than fading.

'She'll be a big one. I'm telling you, she'll be a big one.'

Ben thought longingly of Ginny's suggestion of quarantine and locks and keys and thought he could almost justify it.

But despite Squid's doom-mongering, the islanders were calming down. They were growing accustomed to his prophecy; starting to laugh about it. The urgent medical need faded.

He received a couple of applications for doctors to take Catherine's place, but neither of them was prepared to come to the island for an interview. What sort of commitment was that? he thought, trying to figure out how he could find time to take the ferry to Auckland and interview them.

Maybe Ginny could help.

Maybe he couldn't ask her.

A couple of days after their dinner, she booked Button into the clinic, brought her in and together he and Ginny gave the little girl a complete medical assessment. That was weird, a mixture of personal and medical. It made him feel...

Like he didn't want to feel.

'You haven't changed your mind?' he asked, labelling blood samples to send to the mainland for path. testing. He was...they both were...a bit concerned about Button's heart. Heart conditions were common in Down's kids. He thought he could hear a murmur. There was nothing about a murmur in her medical records but Ginny thought she could hear one, too.

'Button needs me,' she said simply, and it was true, but it worked both ways, he thought. He could see how much she cared for the little girl already.

He looked at them both, Button playing happily with Shuffles, calmly accepting his ministrations, seemingly unperturbed that her life had been turned upside down—and he looked at Ginny's pale, strained face.

'Maybe you need Button more than she needs you,' he said gently.

'No.'

'I won't go there, then,' he said equitably, and lifted Button from the examination couch and popped her on the floor. Ginny took her hand and backed away—almost as if she was afraid of him.

'I'll let you know when the results come through,' he said.

'Thank you.'

'Ginny...'

'Thank you,' she said again, and it was like a shield. Patient thanking doctor.

Nothing personal at all.

* * *

Once in the car she could block out the personal. Once out of sight of Ben.

She kind of liked taking Button home. No, more than liked. She was trying to hold back, aware at any minute that Veronica or Veronica's husband could change their mind and want her again, but Button was a little girl who was easy to love, and she found her heart twisting at the thought of her being discarded.

She might even fight for her, she thought. What rights did a stepmother have?

Maybe none, she thought, but there was a real possibility she'd be taking care of Button for life—and right now Button was filling a void. Button needed her and she intended to do the best job she could.

Which meant she was justified in refusing to help Ben, she decided, and squashed guilt to the back of her mind. One of her girlfriends had once told her, 'Don't have kids, Ginny. The moment you do, every single thing is your fault. No matter what you do, you feel guilty.'

So she was just like other mothers, she decided, and thought she should ring Ben up and tell him.

Or not.

Focus on Button. And the vineyard? She wasn't actually very good at growing grapes. She should find someone to replace Henry. She didn't actually have a clue what she was doing.

But, then, so what if she missed a harvest? she decided. The world had enough wine and she didn't need the money. Henry popped in to see her and worried about it on her behalf, but she calmed him.

'Next year, when I'm more organised, I'll hire staff and do it properly. I should have done it this year but neither of us was organised. And you're not well. Thank you for dropping by, but I'll manage. Did Ben...? Did Dr McMahon give you something that'll help?'

'He wants me to go to the mainland and have a gas-gastroscopy or something. Damned fool idea. You want me to teach you about—?'

'No,' she said gently, thinking of the old man's grey face. 'Let's put this year's harvest behind us and move on next year.'

That was a great idea, she decided. She'd put the whole of the last year aside. She'd refuse to be haunted by shadows of the past.

She and Button could make themselves a life here. She watched Button water her beloved tomatoes—watering was Button's principal pleasure—and thought... she could almost be happy.

But happiness was a long-ago concept. Pre-James.

Happiness went right back to Ben—and there was the biggie.

But why was it unsettling her? Once upon a time she'd thought of him as her best friend. Friends instead of lovers? Why not again?

He wanted her to do more. She could, she conceded. Hannah could look after Button.

Working side by side with Ben?

Why did she keep remembering one hot day in the surf?

Why did the memory scare her stupid?

CHAPTER FOUR

RUNNING A SOLO practice was okay, was even feasible, except in emergencies.

With only ten beds, Kaimotu Hospital was not usually used for acute care. Acute-care cases were sent to the mainland, and now, with only one doctor, it was a case of deeming more cases acute.

With two doctors on the island they could cope with routine things like appendicitis, hernias, minor surgery, but with only one…well, the Hercules transport plane from the mainland got more of a workout.

The islanders hated it. They loathed being shipped to the mainland away from family and friends, but Ben had no choice. Until they found another doctor, this was the only way he could cope.

He did cope—until the night Henry's ulcer decided to perforate.

Why did medical emergencies happen in the small hours more often than not? Someone should write a thesis, Ben thought wearily, picking up the phone. His apartment was right by the hospital. He switched his phone through to the nurses' station while he slept, so

he knew the nurse on call had overridden that switch. This call, therefore, meant he was needed.

'Ben?' It was Margy, the island's most senior nurse, and he knew the moment he heard her voice that he had trouble.

'Mmm?'

'Henry's on the phone. I'm putting you through now.'

'B-Ben?'

The old winemaker wasn't voluble at the best of times, but now his voice was scarcely a whisper.

'Yeah, Henry, it's me. Tell me what's wrong.'

'Me guts,' Henry whispered. 'Pain...been going on all night. Took them pills you gave me and then some more but nothing's stopping it and now...vomiting blood, Doc. Couple times. Lotta blood.'

To say his heart sank would be an understatement. He was already out of bed, reaching for his pants.

'You're at home? Up on the headland?'

'Y-yeah.'

'Okay, I want you to go back to bed and lie very still while I wake Max and Ella up,' he told him. Max and Ella were the nearest farmers to Henry's tiny cottage. 'They'll bring you down to the hospital. I reckon you might have bleeding from your stomach. It'll be quicker if they bring you here rather than me go there.'

Besides, he thought, he needed to set up Theatre. Call in nurses.

He needed to call on Ginny. Now.

'I might make a mess of their car,' Henry whispered, and Ben told Henry what he thought about messing up a car compared to getting him to hospital fast.

Then he rang Max and Ella and thanked God for good, solid farming neighbours who he knew would take no argument from Henry. There'd also be no tearing round corners on two wheels.

Then he rang Ginny.

Ginny was curled up in her parents' big bed, cuddling a sleeping Button—and thinking about Ben.

Why did he keep her awake at night?

He didn't, she conceded. Everything kept her awake at night.

Memories of James. Memories of blame.

'You stupid cow, how the hell can you possibly know how I feel? You're healthy—healthy!—and you stand there acting sorry for me, and you can't do a thing. Why can't you get this damned syringe driver to work? How can you sleep when I'm in pain?'

The syringe driver *had* been working. It wasn't pain, she thought. It was fear, and fury. He'd had twelve months of illness and he'd blamed her every moment of the way.

So what was she doing, lying in bed now and thinking of another man? Thinking of another relationship?

She wasn't, she told herself fiercely. She was never going there again. She was just…thinking about everything, as she always did.

And then the phone rang.

She answered it before Button could wake up.

'Ginny?'

Ben's voice did things to her. It always had.

No.

'Ben?'

'Ginny, I need you. Henry has a ruptured stomach ulcer. He's been bleeding for hours. There's no time to evacuate him to the mainland. Mum and Hannah are on their way to your place now to take care of Button. The minute they get there I need you to come. Please.'

And that was that.

No choice.

She should say no, she thought desperately. She should tell him she'd made the decision not to practise medicine.

Not possible.

Henry.

'I'll come.'

'Ginny?'

'Yes?'

'How are you at anaesthetics?'

'That's what I am,' she said, and then corrected herself. 'That's what I was. An anaesthetist.'

There was a moment's stunned silence. Then… 'Praise be,' Ben said simply. 'I'll have everything ready. Let's see if we can pull off a miracle.'

Henry needed a miracle. He'd been bleeding for hours.

Ginny walked into Theatre, took one look and her heart sank. She'd seen enough patients who'd bled out to know she was looking at someone who was close.

Ben had already set up IV lines, saline, plasma.

'I've cross-matched,' he said as she walked through the door. 'Thank God he's O-positive. We have enough.'

There was no time for personal. That one glance at Henry had told her there was hardly time for anything.

She moved to the sink to scrub, her eyes roving around the small theatre as she washed. He had everything at the ready. A middle-aged nurse was setting up equipment—Margy? Abby was there, slashing away clothing.

Ben had Henry's hand.

'Ginny's here,' he told him, and Ginny wondered if the old man was conscious enough to take it in. 'Your Ginny.'

'My Ginny,' he whispered, and he reached out and touched her arm.

'I'm here for you,' she told him, stooping so she was sure he'd hear. 'I'm here for you, Henry. You know I'm a doctor. I'm an anaesthetist and I'm about to give you a something to send you to sleep. We need to do something about that pain. Ben and I are planning on fixing you, Henry, so is it okay if you go to sleep now?'

'Yes,' Henry whispered. 'You and Ben…I always thought you'd be a pair. Who'd a thought… You and Ben…'

And he drifted into unconsciousness.

She was an anaesthetist. *Who'd a thought?* Henry's words echoed through Ben's head as he worked and it was like a mantra.

Who'd a thought? A trained anaesthetist, right here when he needed her most.

Ben had done his first part of surgery before he'd returned to the island. It had seemed sensible—this place was remote and bad things happened fast. He'd also spent an intense six months delivering babies, but if he'd tried to train in every specialty he'd never have got back to Kaimotu.

Catherine had had basic anaesthetic training, as had the old doctor she'd replaced. For cases needing higher skills they'd depended on phone links with specialists on the mainland. It hadn't been perfect but it had been the best they could do.

Now, as he watched Ginny gently reassure Henry, as he watched her check dosage, slip the anaesthetic into the IV line he'd set up, as he watched her seamlessly turn to the breathing apparatus, checking the drips as she went to make sure there was no blockage in the lines, he thought... He thought Henry might just have a chance.

Henry had deteriorated since Ben had phoned Ginny. By the time Ginny had walked into Theatre he'd thought he'd lose him. Now...

'Go,' Ginny said, with a tight, professional nod, and she went back to monitoring breathing, checking flow, keeping this old man alive, while Ben...

Ben exposed and sutured an ulcer?

It sounded easy. It wasn't.

He was trained in surgery but he didn't do it every day. He operated but he took his time, but now there was no time to take.

He cut, searched, while Margy swabbed. There was so much blood! Trying to locate the source of the bleeding...

'One on each side,' Ginny snapped to the nurses and they rearranged themselves fast. Ben hadn't had time to think about it but the way they had been positioned only Margy had been able to swab, with Abby preparing equipment.

'I can do the handling as well,' Ginny said calmly. 'Get that wound clear for Dr McMahon. Fast and light. Move.'

They moved and all of a sudden Ben could see...

A massive ulcer, oozing blood from the stomach wall.

That Henry wasn't dead already was a miracle.

'Sutures,' he said, and they were in his hand. He glanced up—just a glance—in time to see that it was Ginny who was preparing the sutures. And monitoring breathing, oxygen saturation, plasma flow.

No time to think about that now. Stitch.

Somehow he pulled the thing together, carefully, carefully, always conscious that pulling too tight, too fast could extend the wound rather than seal it.

The blood flow was easing.

How fast was Ginny getting that plasma in?

He glanced up at her again for a fraction of a moment and got a tiny, almost imperceptible nod for his pains.

'Oxygen saturation ninety-three. We're holding,' she said. 'If you want to do a bit of pretty embroidery in there, I think we can hold the canvas steady.'

And she'd taken the tension out of the room, just like that. He and both the nurses there had trained in large city hospitals. They'd worked in theatres where complex, fraught surgery took place and they knew the banter that went on between professionals at the top of their game.

Ginny's one comment had somehow turned this tiny island hospital into the equal of those huge theatres.

They had the skill to do this and they all knew it.

'Henry's dog's name's Banjo,' Margy offered. They were all still working, hard, fast, not letting anything slide, but that fractional lessening of tension had helped them all. 'We could tell him we've embroidered "Banjo" on his innards when he wakes up.'

'He'd need *some* mirror to see it,' Ben retorted, and went back to stitching, but he was smiling and he had it sealed now. That Henry had held on for this long...

'Oxygen level's rising,' Ginny said. 'That's the first

point rise. We're aiming for full within half an hour, people. Margy, can you find me more plasma?'

And Margy could because suddenly there was only the need for one to swab. Ben was stitching the outer walls of the stomach closed then the layers of muscle, carefully, painstakingly. Ginny was still doing her hawk thing—the anaesthetist was the last person in the room to relax—but this was going to be okay.

But then… 'Hold,' Ginny said into the stillness. 'No, hold. No!'

No!

They'd been so close. So close but not close enough. Ben didn't need to see the monitors to interpret Ginny's message—he had it in full.

A drop in blood pressure. Ventricular fibrillation.

He was grabbing patches from Margy, thanking God that at least the bulk of the stitching was done, but not actually thanking God yet. Saying a few words in his direction, more like.

Or one word.

Please… To get so close and then lose him…

Please…

The adrenaline was pumping. If Ginny hadn't been here…

Please…

'Back,' Ginny snapped, as he had the patches in place, as he moved to flick a switch…

A jerk… Henry's body seemed to stiffen—and then the thin blue line started up again, up and down, a nice steady beat, as if it had just stopped for a wee nap and was starting again better than ever.

'Oh, my God,' Margy said, and started to cry.

Margy and Henry's daughter had been friends be-

fore they'd both moved to the mainland, Ben remembered. That was the problem with this island. Everyone
knew everyone.

'Every man's death diminishes me.' How much more
so on an island as small as Kaimotu?

'He... I think he'll be okay,' Ginny said, and Ben
cast her an anxious glance as well. Henry had worked
for her parents for ever. Did she consider him a friend?
The tremor in her voice said that she did.

'We'll settle him and transfer,' Ben said, forcing his
hands to be steady, forcing his own heartbeat to settle.
'I want him in Coronary Care in Auckland.'

'He won't want that,' Margy said.

'Then we transfer him while he doesn't have the
strength to argue,' Ben said. 'I'm fond of this old guy,
too, and he's getting the best, whether he likes it or not.
Thank God for Ginny. Thank God for defibrillators.
And thank God for specialist cardiac physicians and
gastroenterologists on the mainland, because if we can
keep him alive until morning, that's where he's going.'

It was an hour later when he finished up. Henry seemed
to have settled. Margy had hauled in extra nursing staff
so he could have constant obs all night. Ben had done
as much as he could. It was too risky to transfer Henry
to the mainland tonight but he'd organised it for first
thing in the morning. With his apartment so close he
was just through the wall if he was needed.

Enough.

He'd sent Ginny home half an hour ago, but he
walked out into the moonlight, to walk the few hundred yards to the specially built doctors' quarters, and

Ginny was sitting on the rail dividing the car park from the road beyond. Just sitting in the moonlight.

Waiting for him?

'Hey,' she said, and shoved up a little on the rail to make room for him.

'Hey, yourself,' he said, feeling…weird. 'Why aren't you at home?'

'You reckon I could sleep?'

'I reckon you should sleep. What you did was awesome.'

'You were pretty awesome yourself. I didn't know you were surgically trained.'

'And I didn't know you'd done anaesthesia.'

'Once we were friends,' she said softly into the night. 'We should have kept up. I should have written. I should have let you write. One stupid summer and it meant we cut our friendship off at the knees.'

'As I recall,' he said carefully, 'it was a very nice summer.'

'It was,' she said, and smiled. 'We had fun.'

'You were the best tadpole catcher I ever knew.'

'I'm going to teach Button,' she said, and he wanted to say he would help but it wasn't wise. He knew it wasn't wise. She was opening up a little just by being here, and he wouldn't push for the world.

Except…he needed to ask.

'Why did you give up medicine?' he asked into the stillness, and the night grew even more still.

'You know,' she said at last, 'that when the world gets crazy, when there are things around that are battering down in every direction, a tortoise retreats into his shell and stays there. I guess…that's what I've done.'

'Your shell being this island.'

'That's the one.'

'But medicine?'

'While James was dying… We tried everything and I mean everything. Every specialist, every treatment, every last scientific breakthrough. None of it helped.'

'You blame medicine?'

'No,' she said wearily. 'But I thought… My dad pushed and pushed me to do medicine and James pushed me to specialise, and when both of them were in trouble…Dad and then James…they both turned. They were so angry and there was nothing I could do. I used to go to bed at night and lie there and dream of being… I don't know…a filler-up of potholes. A gardener. A wine-maker. Something that made it not my fault.'

'It wasn't your fault your dad and James died.'

'No,' she said bleakly. 'But you try telling them that.'

'They're dead, Ginny.'

'Yes, but they're still on my shoulder. A daughter and a wife who didn't come up to standard.'

'That's nuts,' he said, and put a hand on her shoulder. He felt her stiffen.

'No,' she said.

'So you've rejected medicine because of them. You're rejecting friendship, too?'

There was a long silence while they both sat and stared out over the moonlit sea. He kept his hand where it was, gently on her shoulder, and he felt her make a huge—vast—effort to relax.

What had those guys done to her—her father and her husband? He thought back to the laughing, carefree girl who'd been his friend and he felt…

Yeah, well, there was no use going down that road. He couldn't slug dead people.

He wanted to pull her closer. It took an almost superhuman effort to keep it light, hold the illusion that this was friendship, nothing more.

'I'll come out eventually,' Ginny said at last. 'I can't stay in my shell for ever and Button will haul me out faster.'

'You'll go back to the mainland?'

'No!' It was a fierce exclamation.

'This island's not for hiding, Ginny,' he said softly. 'Life happens here as well.'

'Yes, but I can take Button tadpoling here.'

'She'll love it.' He hesitated but the urge was too great. 'Let me in a little,' he said. 'We used to be friends. I'm the second-best tadpoler on the island. We could… share.'

She stiffened again. 'Ben, I don't… I can't…'

'Share?'

'That's the one.' She rose, brushing away his touch. Her face was pale in the moonlight and he wondered again what those guys had done to her. Unbidden he felt his hands clench into fists. His beautiful Ginny…

'It's okay,' he made himself say, forcing the anger from his voice. 'Treat the island as a shell, then. You have Button in there with you, though, and I have a feeling she'll tug you out. And you came out tonight. Henry's alive because you came out, and you can't imagine how grateful I am.'

'It's me who should be grateful,' she said. 'Henry was my friend.'

'Henry *is* your friend.' And then, as she didn't reply, he pushed a little bit further.

'Ginny, no one on this island judged you because of who your parents were. You stayed here for ten summers and there are lots of islanders who'd call you their friend. My family almost considered you one of us. We're all still here, Ginny, waiting for you to emerge and be our friend again.'

'I can't.'

'No,' he said, and because he couldn't stop himself he touched her cheek, a feather touch, because the need to touch her was irresistible and she was so beautiful and fearful and needful.

So Ginny.

'You can't,' he said. 'But tonight you did.' And then, before he knew what he was going to do, before she could possibly know for he hadn't even realised he was about to do it himself, he stooped and kissed her, lightly, on the lips.

It had been a feather touch. He'd backed away before she'd even realised he'd done it, appalled with himself, putting space between them, moving away before she could react with the fear he knew was in her.

But he had to say it.

'We're all here, waiting,' he said into the darkness. 'We'll wait for as long as it takes. This island is as old as time itself and it has all the patience in the world.'

And as if on cue the world trembled.

It was the faintest of earth tremors, exactly the same as the tremors that had shaken this island since time immemorial.

A tiny grumble of discord from within.

Nothing to worry about? Surely not.

'Or maybe it's saying hurry up,' Ben said, and grinned, and Ginny managed a shaky smile.

'It'll have to wait.'

'Maybe the island's giving you a nudge. Like we gave you a nudge. You saved Henry tonight, Ginny, so there's a start. No pressure, love, but when you come out of your shell, we're all waiting.'

No pressure.

He watched as she put her fingers to the lips he'd just kissed. He watched as she watched him, as something fought within her.

What had her father and husband done to her?

'I...I need to go,' she faltered, and he didn't move towards her and God only knew the effort it cost him not to.

'Yes, you do.'

'Ben...'

'Don't say anything more,' he said softly. 'You've done brilliantly tonight. I love what you're doing with Button—we all do. One step at a time, our Ginny, that's all we ask.'

He tugged open the door of her car and watched as she climbed in.

He didn't touch her and it almost killed him.

'Goodnight, Ginny,' he said softly, and she didn't say a thing in reply.

He stood back as she did up her seat belt, as she started the engine, as she drove away, and he thought...

She looks haunted.

Not by him, he thought. She needed time.

He would give her time. Except for emergencies. Even knowing she was on the island, another doctor...

Who was he kidding? Even knowing she was on the island...his Ginny.

He would give her time. He had to.

She reached the vineyard. The lights were on inside the house. Ailsa and Hannah would be there, keeping watch over Button, waiting for her, anxious about Henry.

This island was like a cocoon, she thought, a warm, safe blanket that enveloped her and kept her safe from the real world.

Did she ever need to go back to the real world?

Kaimotu was time out, a holiday isle, a place of escape.

She could make it real.

But if she did, would the world move in?

She thought back to her marriage. The fairy-tale. A big, gorgeous, clever man her parents had approved of, dating her, making love to her, making her feel like the princess in a fairy-tale. She could have her parents' life. She could have a happy-ever-after.

Yes, she'd had a childhood romance with Ben but that had been years before. She'd felt that what she'd found with James had been real, wonderful, a grown-up happy-ever-after.

And she'd stepped into James's world and realised that grown up wasn't fantasy. Not one little bit. Grown up was trying to meet expectations, climbing the career ladder, accepting scorn when you failed.

Grown up was realising that medicine couldn't save lives—that you could do nothing to help your father or your husband.

Grown up was learning to hate yourself as well as copping hate from those around you.

'I need a shrink,' she said out loud, and then closed her eyes, took a deep breath, stared up at the starlit sky and figured she didn't need a psychiatrist. She needed to move on. Move forward.

But not very much, and certainly not in the direction of Ben.

Ben had kissed her.

Ben was real.

No. He'd be just the same as all the other fantasies, she told herself. She no longer trusted her judgement. She no longer trusted men who told her she was capable, beautiful, wonderful.

She no longer trusted.

'My job is to take care of Button and to make wine,' she told herself, and thought that actually she hadn't managed very well in the picking and processing department and there wouldn't be all that much Chardonnay coming out of the vineyard this season.

'It doesn't matter,' she said stubbornly. 'Button's the important thing.' Like Henry was important. She'd helped save Henry.

Yes, but for how long? He'd have another coronary, he'd arrest, he'd die and she'd feel...she'd feel...

'I'm not going to feel,' she said savagely into the dark. 'If Ben's desperate I'll help but nothing else. I will not be responsible for anything else but Button. It won't be my fault.'

'That's a cop-out and you know it,' she told herself, and she bit her lip and turned resolutely towards the house.

'I know it is,' she told herself. 'But it's all I'm capable of. And if Ben McMahon thinks he can change my mind just by kissing me... Pigs might fly, Ben McMahon, but you are not stuffing with my life.'

Sleep was nowhere. Ben lay in the dark and stared at the ceiling and all he could think about was that kiss.

He'd wanted her when he'd been seventeen, and he wanted her still. Crazy or not, his body was reacting to her as it had at seventeen.

He wanted her.

But while he wanted her as a woman, as the desire he'd felt all those years ago surged back to the surface, he needed her as a doctor. The skill she'd shown had knocked him sideways. He had to persuade her to join him; with her skills the island could have the medical service it deserved.

All sorts of possibilities had opened up as he'd watched her work. Islanders with cancer pain often needed to be transported to the mainland, at a time when they most wanted to stay here. He didn't have the skills to help them.

As an anaesthetist, Ginny had those skills.

So…was he messing with that need by making it personal? By letting his desire hold sway? He'd kissed her and she'd shied away like a frightened colt.

'So don't kiss her,' he said out loud, knowing that was easier said than done.

She'd been injured by the men in her life, he thought. She'd been injured by the arrogant bully he remembered her father being, and a husband who sounded like a bottom feeder. Ben wasn't seeing her as a victim, though. With her determination to keep Button, with the skill and humour she'd shown in Theatre tonight, he knew that underneath the battered armour there was still the lovely, feisty, carrot-haired girl he'd fallen in love with all those years ago.

'It was an adolescent crush,' he growled to the night. 'Get over it.'

But an adolescent crush wasn't what he was feeling. When his mouth had touched hers, a fire had reignited.

For her, too?

If it had, she wasn't letting on. Her armour might

be battered but it was still intact, and if he wanted any chance at all of persuading her to work with him, he needed to respect it.

'So leave her be.'

'Except to ask her to work?' He was arguing out loud with himself.

'Yes,' he told himself. 'She worked that first afternoon because she saw desperate need. She worked tonight for the same reason. At the moment she's giving you back-up when you most need it. Respect that, give her space, give her time.'

'But the way you feel?'

'Get over it,' he said harshly. 'You're not seventeen any more. Go find yourself a lady who wants you.'

'And isn't that the whole trouble?' he groaned, and punched a pillow. This island was small, and any affair he had, even asking someone on a date, led to expectations and complications.

Like tonight. One kiss…

Expectations and complications?

'Leave it alone,' he growled, and punched the pillow once more then gave up and got up and went across to the hospital to check on Henry—who was sleeping soundly and didn't need his attention at all.

He went back to bed and finally he slept, but when he slept he dreamed of Ginny.

She was an adolescent crush who'd turned into the woman of his dreams. The idea was romantic nonsense, he told himself, even in his sleep.

And down on the harbour… It was five in the morning and almost every islander was asleep, but Squid Davies was wide awake and pacing.

'It's coming,' he muttered. 'The big one's coming. I feel it in my bones.' He grabbed a piece of paper and started to write.

'Just in case,' he muttered. 'I'll be prepared even if they're not.'

CHAPTER FIVE

BEN DIDN'T SEE Ginny for days.

Henry spent four days in hospital in Auckland and then was transferred back to the island. Ben heard from his mum that Ginny had tried to persuade the old man to come back to the vineyard and stay with her, but Henry wanted to go back to his ancient cottage on the headland. It was too far from anywhere, he thought. He wouldn't mind talking to Ginny about it.

'But Ginny's doing all she can,' Ailsa told him. 'She's visiting him twice a day. There's nothing more she can do. There's nothing more anyone can do.'

So he didn't have an exc—a reason to talk to her. But finally Button's cardiac results came through.

There'd been a query on Button's medical records, tests taken but not recorded. Her family doctor had noted that slight heart murmur, he'd sent her to a specialist but then she'd been brought to the island and the notes she'd brought hadn't contained results.

It had taken a week's perseverance on Ben's part to get them. Laws protecting a patient's privacy were a concern, especially when the patient was four years old, one parent had disappeared to Europe and the other wanted nothing to do with her. Ben had run out of pro-

fessional ways of getting the results and had finally re-
verted to the personal. He'd rung Veronica's husband,
a man who blustered about not wanting anything to do
with a child who wasn't his but at least didn't hang up
on him.

'For now you're still legally Barbara's parent,' Ben
had snapped at him. 'I'm now her doctor, Ginny's her
acting guardian until the legalities are completed and
we need full access to her medical records. Do you
want her to die of heart failure because of your pride?'

The man had finally complied, and when Ben eventually received the results he swore.

There were problems. They'd have to be sorted. He
and Ginny had to talk.

It was Monday, a gorgeous autumn day. Ben did a
long morning's clinic then he needed to make some
house calls, and Ginny's house was first.

He'd just reached the vineyard gate when the earth
moved.

One moment Ginny was supervising Button eating her
boiled egg and toast. The next moment she was on the
floor and the world was crazy.

It was as if the whole house had been picked up and
was being violently shaken. Walls became floor, floor
became walls. Furniture was crashing everywhere.

She grabbed a chair but the chair slid sideways,
crashed, rolled, tumbled.

Button!

She was screaming. Was Button screaming? The
noise was unbelievable.

Somehow she grabbed the little girl as the chair
she'd been sitting on crashed almost on top of her. She

scooped her into her arms, and then the floor seemed to roll again.

The table. The table!

Drop and hold. Where had she heard that? In some long-ago safety lecture, maybe here in New Zealand when she'd been a child? New Zealand was known as the shaky isles for good reason.

There was another mantra. Get out of the house. Into the open.

But it was no use thinking that now, or trying to attempt it. This was like a wild, bucking, funfair ride, only there was nothing fun about this. Everything that wasn't nailed down was crashing around them.

She had Button cradled hard against her but she was struggling to hold her. She was fighting to stay on her knees.

The table... If she could get past these crazy chairs...

The table was big, solid, farmhouse wood. If she could get under...

Getting anywhere was impossible. Something sharp hit her head, and she thought, Drop further.

She dropped onto her side, ignoring the crunch of things breaking under her. Button was clinging to her, limpet-like, whimpering in terror, and Ginny could move where she wanted and she knew Button wouldn't let go.

Move where she wanted? That was a joke.

The table. She was three feet away. Roll. Roll!

The floor lurched again, tipping the other way, and under she went. She crashed into chair legs as she rolled but Button was with her, clinging so hard that Ginny had a hand free.

Grab.

She grabbed a table leg and clung.

She was under the table. The world was still rolling in great, fearsome waves, but the table and the floor beneath it were rolling with it and Ginny could hold and ride.

Thank God the house was single-storey, Ginny thought as she clung. And had an iron roof. No vast bank of heavy tiles.

Visions of knife-sharp iron flooded her mind but she shoved them away. Just hold on. Use her body to protect Button and hold on.

Wait until the earth found a new level.

Ben was just about to turn into the gate when the road buckled.

As buckles went it was truly impressive. The coast road was long and flat, and he saw the buckle start half a mile ahead of him, rising with a massive, unbelievable heave of solid earth. It hurled towards him, a great, burrowing mound, trees swaying, bitumen cracking and falling away, coming, coming…

It must have been seconds only before the great buckling mound hit him but he had enough time to think about getting out of the car and then to change his mind and decide to stay in the car but veer away fast from trees, head for the grassy verge away from the sea, pull to a halt. Or almost pull to a halt for then it hit and the car rose in the air as if it had been thrown.

It wasn't just the one wave. It was a series of massive jolting, shaking heaves, as if the world was shifting and not knowing where to settle.

He gripped the steering-wheel and hung on. It was all he had to hold onto—the car was like a bucking bronco.

Oh, God, his island.

And stunningly, even while he was holding on for dear life, he felt himself switch into doctor mode. Earthquake. Casualties. This was major.

Squid had been right. Never doubt the sages, he thought, and then he stopped thinking because he had to hold tight and nothing else could matter.

The car rolled—it almost rolled right over—and then, unbelievably, it rolled back again, righting itself with a massive thump.

What sort of power...? What sort of damage...?

Tsunami.

The vision crashed into his mind with sickening dread. Earthquake, tsunami. Get to high land.

Not yet. He could do nothing yet but hold on.

His seat belt was holding him safe—sort of. He was fine, short of the cliff caving in and his car sliding into the sea...

Not a lot of use thinking that.

Hold on. There was nothing he could do until the rolling stopped.

But he was still thinking medicine.

Casualties. He hardly dared think but already he knew the islanders were in real trouble.

One doctor.

No, two. First things first. He'd grab Ginny.

Please, God, she was okay.

Don't go there. He glanced towards the house and saw it heave and shift on its foundations. Please, hold.

He'd get Ginny, take her back to the hospital, leave Button with his mother...

His parents. The kids.

Do not go there.

Plan instead. The earth was settling. Panic was turning to focus.

He'd call the mainland, get help organised. Maybe he could do it now.

He flicked his phone. He had a signal.

And then he didn't.

The telecommunications tower at the airport must have toppled.

No phone.

The authorities on the mainland would figure it out anyway, he thought grimly. A quake this size would show on every seismograph in the world.

He had two nurses on duty at the hospital, with six more on call. How many could get there?

Roads would be cut.

Roads… How…?

The car jerked and bucked and his grip on the wheel tightened.

Ginny, he thought. Please.

He stopped planning. He held on like grim death and he said the word over and over and over.

Please.

It went on and on and on. Just when she thought it had ended it started up again. She couldn't move—she daren't. Yes, the safest place was outside but to get there she'd have to negotiate her way through the house. There were massive exposed beams in the historic homestead. She was terrified of those beams and the table was midway between two of them so she was staying right where she was.

Button was amazingly calm. She clung and clung,

and didn't say a word as they lay huddled under the massive table.

Weirdly, Ginny found herself singing, odd little nursery rhymes she'd heard from nannies as a child, and sometimes she heard Button add a word or two as well.

There was nothing and no one but the two of them and this table. The vineyard was miles from the nearest neighbour. The shaking went on.

She held Button, she clung to her table leg and she'd never felt so alone in her life.

One part of Ben was totally focussed on what was happening, seeing the cracks open in the road, watching parts of the cliff fall into the sea, watching Ginny's house buckle and sway.

One part of him was moving on, thinking tsunami warnings, casualty centres, evacuation plans, emergency resources.

The hospital was on high ground. It was weatherboard, and watching Ginny's house he thought weatherboard was the way to go.

But one of Ginny's chimneys had crashed.

Please…

Don't go there.

The ground was settling now, the massive undulations passing. Any minute now he'd dare to get out of the car.

And go see if Ginny was safe.

The thought of her inside, near that crashed chimney, made him feel ill.

But… It wasn't that he was especially worried about Ginny, he told himself. It was just because she was here, now. He'd watched her house heave—of course he was worried.

Plus she'd been part of his childhood. A friend.

But he knew there was more.

What were the levels of love?

It was hardly the time to think about that now. Finally the world was ceasing to shake.

Maybe it was worst on this side of the island, he prayed. Here the roads were buckled beyond using. Here huge trees had crashed. Here Ginny's house…

Was still standing. He could see broken windows and tumbled masonry. He thought suddenly of those massive beams above the kitchen and the thought had him out of the car and running before the earth had completely settled.

Ginny.

She should take Button out from under the table.

She was afraid to move.

The quake seemed to have passed. There were still tremors, but minor ones. She could venture out from under her table and make a run for outside.

She didn't want to. Here seemed the only safe place.

She stayed under her table and she held the silent Button and she hugged and hugged.

'It's okay, it's over,' she whispered, but she barely believed it.

'Ginny?'

The voice came from nowhere. No, it didn't, it came from the back veranda.

'Ben?' She could scarcely believe it. Ben! Here!

'Where are you?' he yelled.

'I-in the kitchen. Under the table. But the beams…'

She didn't finish. There was a series of crashes, like a bull moving through her living room, but maybe it was one desperate doctor hauling away the litter of damaged furniture blocking his path.

And then, unbelievably, he was under the table with her. He was gathering her—and Button—into his arms and he was holding them.

He held and held and her world changed yet again.

She'd thought it was over, but just as she pulled away a little, just as she relaxed and thought the world was settling, that Ben was here, that they were safe, another tremor hit.

It wasn't nearly as big as that first, vast wave, but it was big enough for Button to cling, for Ben to haul them both close again, for her to cling back.

And think again.

What she'd just thought.

Which was nonsense. Which was everything she'd vowed never to think again.

Safe in the arms of someone who loved her?

Life was a travesty, she thought as she clung, because she still needed to cling, for Button's sake as well as her own. Button was cocooned between them, safe, protected by their bodies, a Button sandwich between her two protective adults.

Button needed Ben.

For now Ginny needed Ben—but just for now. Only for now, she told herself fiercely.

This was crazy. This was an earthquake, for heaven's sake, so why was she suddenly thinking of James, of a marriage that had made her glow, had made her think this was happy-ever-after, had made her believe in the fairy-tale?

Why was she thinking of the travesty that marriage had turned out to be? Of infidelity, of shattered trust. Of anger, more, of hatred, that she was the one to live. Of the knowledge that her judgement was appalling, that trust was stupid, that love was for the pages of fairy-tales.

'Ginny...'

'Mmm.' It seemed almost wrong to speak, as if somehow voices might stir the demons to shake some more.

'We need to get outside.'

'I think I like my table.'

'I like your table, too,' he said. 'But there's the little matter of beams above us. We can't depend on them falling straight if this gets any worse. We need to risk it. Button, we're going to run. We're going to wriggle out from under here, I'm going to carry you, because I'm stronger and faster than Ginny...'

'Ginny,' Button said, and clung tighter.

'I can see Shuffles,' Ben said, lightly now, making it seem almost conversational. 'He's right by the door on the floor. If you let me carry you, we'll rescue Shuffles and take him outside.

Button considered. There was silence while they let her make up her mind and then she gave a decisive nod.

She turned within their sandwich squeeze and transferred her hold to Ben.

'Get Shuffles,' she ordered. 'Go.'

'Yes, ma'am,' Ben said, and touched Ginny's face— just fleetingly, but she felt herself flinch.

He gave her a sharp, questioning glance but the time for questions wasn't now.

'Let's go,' he said, and hauled himself backwards from under the table, holding Button and Button holding him, and there was nothing left for Ginny to do but follow.

Outside was weird.

It was as if a giant hand had picked up and shaken the house, leaving its contents a vast, jumbled mess. Outside it almost looked normal.

The veranda steps had cracked and fallen sideways. The downpipes were hanging at crazy angles, windows were broken and a chimney had crumpled. Otherwise you might almost look at it and think nothing had happened.

'Old and weatherboard,' Ben said. They'd scrambled out of the house, moving fast in case another tremor hit, but now they were in the yard between house and stables, with no trees close, nothing but open ground. There was a deep crack running across the width of the yard, a foot wide, heaven knew how deep, but they were well clear of it.

'Wooden houses seem to stand up to quakes much better than brick,' Ben said. 'Thank God most of the island houses are wooden.'

He turned and stared towards the town and Ginny could see his mind turning to imperatives. Medical imperatives? Plus the fact that his parents and siblings were in the valley.

'Tsunami,' he said, and just as he said it a siren started, loud and screeching, blaring a warning. Even as a child here Ginny had learned what it meant.

What Ben had just said.

'It's too close,' she whispered.

'What?'

'I did a project at school. Tsunamis come when quakes happen out to sea. This one was so big…surely the fault's right under us.'

'Let's not bet our lives on it,' Ben said grimly. 'Get in the Jeep, now.'

'I can—'

'Get in the Jeep or I'll throw you in,' he said grimly, and he grabbed her hand with his free one—he was still cradling Button with the other—and ran across the yard.

Seconds later they were bucketing across the paddocks, heading up the steep valley incline. Fences were ignored—Ben simply steered his battered Jeep between the posts and crashed straight through.

Tsunami.

The word was enough to block out everything else. She held Button tightly—Ben had obviously decided he wasn't wasting precious seconds fastening her into her child seat—and stared down at the sea. Willing it to be okay.

Willing a wave not to come.

It didn't. They reached the ridge above the vineyard and stopped, then climbed from the Jeep and watched the sea while the siren still wailed across the island.

Ben produced field glasses from the Jeep and his expression grew more and more grim as he surveyed what he could of the island.

Ginny didn't ask to see. She didn't want to see. She held Button and she thought this was a hiatus. The last moment before reality.

She thought suddenly of the day she and James had gone to the hospital for him to get tests. They'd been practically sure but not…not prepared. Did anything prepare you for such a thing?

The tests were run. 'Come back at six and get the results,' the oncologist had said, so they'd gone to the beach, swum, had a picnic, talked of everything under the sun until it was time to go back.

'If I'm okay we'll even have a baby,' she remembered James saying.

And she remembered thinking, Please, let this time not end.

Knowing that it would.

She was still watching the sea. Waiting for the world to end?

Ben was jabbing at his cell phone then turning his field glasses toward the island's small airport.

'The tower must be down,' he said, staring at the screen. 'I hoped it was just a glitch during the shake but everything's dead. We should be able to see the tower from here. There's no reception.'

Ginny hauled her phone out of her back jeans pocket and stared. No bars. Nothing.

'Oh, God,' she whispered.

'It'll be okay,' Ben said, and she saw the way he hauled himself under control. What lay before them might well be appalling. For him to be the only doctor… 'The guys on the fishing boats have radios that'll reach the mainland. A quake this big will be sensed from there. I'm guessing we'll get help fast.' His eyes roved over the island, noting signs of damage that from up here seemed small but she knew that once they got close it could spell calamity. 'Choppers can get here fast. An hour to scramble, two hours for the flight...'

'They'll come?'

'If they can't contact the hospital they'll come anyway. Hell, Ginny, I need to be there.' He winced as the siren kept on wailing and Ginny wondered whether if he wasn't saddled with Button and with her, he would have gone now, tsunami threat or not.

'If the coast road's out...we'll go overland as soon as the siren stops,' Ben said grimly, his field glasses sweeping slowly across the valley again. 'The coast road won't be safe. It'll be rough but the Jeep should do it.

'What...what's a few fences?' she said unsteadily, and Ben managed a smile.

'I hear the local landowner shoots trespassers on sight. Risks are everywhere.'

The local landowner would be her. She managed a smile back. 'You might be granted dispensation.'

'Dispensation. Wow!' And then his smile died. 'Ginny, will you help?'

'Of course I will.'

'No, *really* help,' he said. 'No holds barred. We'll need to leave Button with Hannah, as long as Hannah...' He broke off and went back to staring through his glasses and Ginny followed his line of sight and thought he'd be staring at an old wooden house in the middle of town that held his mum and dad and siblings.

'I think the hospital's intact. It's on high ground overlooking the harbour. It looks solid. I hope to hell our equipment's safe,' Ben said.

Ginny nodded. Ben needed to think of medical imperatives, she thought, or any imperatives rather than thinking about family, friends, for a quake of this magnitude had to mean casualties on a massive scale.

'Your family will be okay,' she said stoutly. 'Your house is as old and sturdy as mine, and your kitchen table's bigger. And I'm thinking your mum's the one who taught me about diving under it.'

'And Mum was preparing lamb roast for dinner tonight,' Ben managed. 'I hope she's taken the spuds under there with her. She should be peeling them now.'

She grinned, and then hugged him because she knew how hard it had been to joke—and then she pulled away because there was no way she wanted him to think a hug meant anything but a hug.

'Ginny,' he said, and put a hand to her face, and for the life of her she couldn't stop herself flinching again.

Why did she flinch? Of all the stupid... Wasn't it about time she learned some control?

There was a moment's loaded pause, a silence broken only by the wail of the siren. For a long, long moment Ben gazed down at her, as if he was seeing right inside her.

'What did that *bastard* do to you?' he asked at last.

No. One minute they'd been talking earthquake, thinking earthquake, feeling earthquake, and the next... this?

She stared at him, stunned to stupefaction. She didn't want him to see. She didn't want anyone to see.

'I won't hurt you, Ginny,' Ben said gently, and he touched her face again. 'How can you think I will?'

She shook her head. This was crazy. There was no way she was answering that, here, now, or at any time.

She'd made a vow. Life on her terms, now and for ever.

As long as this shaking world permitted.

'Of course I'll help at the hospital,' she said, far too quickly.

'Good,' he said, and moved his field glasses on. But she knew he wouldn't be deflected. He knew her, this man, like no other person had ever known her—and the thought was terrifying.

She went back to hugging Button. Apart from the siren, it was incredibly peaceful. It was a gorgeous autumn afternoon. The sun was sinking low on the horizon and the grass underfoot was lush and green.

But there were cattle in the paddocks, and every beast had its head up. Because of the siren?

Um…no. Because the earth had just shifted and neither man nor beast knew what would happen next.

And then the siren stopped.

Ben's field glasses swung around until he found what he was looking for.

'We send the siren out from four points of the island,' he said slowly, thinking it through as he spoke. 'The sirens are set off from the seismology centre on the mainland. They're supposedly quake-proof and they get their signal via satellite. If they've stopped we can assume that boffins somewhere have decided there will be no tsunami. Thank God.'

'Thank God,' she repeated, and once again she got an odd look, the knowledge that he saw more than she wanted him to see. Earthquake or not, she knew now that there was a world of stuff between them, and she also knew it was stuff he'd hunt down until it was in the open.

'It's okay, Ginny,' he said gently. 'We can work side by side, I promise. This is professional only. We treat it as such. We go see what the damage is and how best we can start putting things back together again. And we put everything else aside until later.'

CHAPTER SIX

ON TOP OF everything else, she was fearful for her farm manager. Henry now lived on the headland beyond the vineyard, on his own.

'His place is so remote. Ben, we need to check...'

'We can't,' he said, as gently as he could manage. 'Henry's four miles that way overland, the coast road'll be cut and we'll have casualties coming into the hospital now. Ginny, I'm sorry, but triage says hospital first. We have to get to town.'

She knew he was right but it didn't make her feel better. Her car was a sedan, not capable of going cross-country. Ben's Jeep was their only mode of transport. They needed to travel together and there was only one direction they could head.

Henry was on his own and it made her feel ill. How many islanders were on their own?

They headed down the valley. It sounded simple. It wasn't.

Driving itself was straightforward enough. Ben had wire cutters in the Jeep, so if they came to a troublesome fence they simply cut the wires. The ground was scattered with newly torn furrows where the earth had been torn apart, but the Jeep was sturdy and Ben was competent.

Ginny thought they'd get back to the hospital fast, and then they crossed the next ridge and her nearest neighbours came into view. Caroline and Harold Barton. Caroline was sitting by a pile of rubble—a collapsed chimney—and she was sobbing.

'He went back in to try and get the cat,' she sobbed. 'I can't get the bricks off him. And the crazy thing is…' she motioned to a large ginger tom sunning himself obliviously on a pile of scattered firewood '…Hoover's fine. Oh, Harold…'

There was a moan from underneath the bricks and then an oath.

'Would you like to stop reporting on the bloody cat and get these bricks off me?' Harold's voice was healthily furious.

Ben lifted Button from the Jeep and handed her over to the sobbing lady.

'Button, this is Mrs Barton and she's crying because she's had a fright,' he said matter-of-factly. 'But now she's going to introduce you to her cat. Caroline, your job is to keep Button happy. Ginny, how are you at heaving bricks?'

'Fine,' Ginny said, knowing how desperate Ben was to get to the hospital but knowing they had no choice but to help the hapless Harold.

Ten minutes later they had him uncovered and, miraculously, his injuries were minor.

'Felt the bloody thing heave so I dived straight into the cavity itself,' he said. 'It could'a gone either way, on top of me or around me, so I was bloody lucky.'

He was, Ginny thought as Ben cleaned a gaping gash

on his arm and pulled it together with steri-strips. It'd
need stitching but stitching had to wait. The important
thing to do now was stop the bleeding and move on.

Triage. The hospital. What was happening down in
the town?

Bricks had fallen on Harold's leg as well. 'There's
possibly a break,' Ben said, but Harold waved him away.

'Yeah, and you might be needed for something a bit
more major than a possible ankle break. Caroline can
put me on the tractor and we'll make our way down
to town in our own good time. With the cat. With this
ankle I'm not even going to be able to kick him so
there's not a lot of choice. Get yourself down to those
who need you, Doc.' And then he turned to Ginny. 'But
thank God you came home when you did, girl. When
you were a kid we always reckoned you belonged here.
Seems we were right. You've come home just in time.'

They passed three more houses, with three more
groups of frightened islanders. They crammed two
women, three kids and two dogs into the back. There
was nothing wrong with them except scratches and
bruises, but they were all stranded and they wanted,
desperately, to be in town with community support.

'I'm hoping someone's set up a refuge,' Ben said
tightly to Ginny. 'I need to be there.'

He couldn't be there, though. At the next farmhouse
they came to, an entire stone barn had collapsed. Once
again they found a sobbing woman but there was no humour about this situation. One of the women distracted
the kids while the rest grimly heaved stone. The elderly
farmer must have been killed instantly.

They left old Donald Martin wrapped in a makeshift shroud, they tucked Flora into the front of the

Jeep, and Flora sobbed all the way to the village—and hugged Button.

Button was amazing, Ginny thought. She was medicine all by herself. She even put her arms around this woman she'd never met before and cuddled her and said, 'Don't cry, lady, don't cry,' whereupon Flora sobbed harder and held her tighter. A normal four-year-old would have backed away in fear but Button just cuddled and held her as Ben pushed the loaded Jeep closer to town.

He was desperate, Ginny thought. The hospital, the whole town was currently without a doctor. It was now almost five hours since the quake. They'd seen a couple of helicopters come in to land and Ben had relaxed a little bit—'Help must be coming from the mainland.'—but she could still see the tension lines on his face. Why wasn't he at the hospital?

If he hadn't been calling in on her... If he hadn't been bringing Button's test results...

'Ben, I'm so sorry,' she told him from the back seat, and Ben swivelled and gave her a hard stare before going back to concentrate on getting the Jeep across the next paddock.

'There's no fault,' he said grimly. 'Cut it out, Ginny, because I won't wear your guilt on top of everything else. I don't have time for it.'

And that put her in her place.

It was self-indulgent, she conceded, to think of guilt. She was crammed between two buxom women. She had kids draped over her knees.

Ben didn't have time to think about guilt, she thought, and then they entered the main street and neither did she.

* * *

The first things they saw were road cones. Orange witches' hats were stretched across the main street, forcing them to stop.

The light was fading but they could see the outlines of the buildings. They could see devastation.

Porches of old, heritage-style shopfronts had come crashing down. A car parked at the kerbside was half-buried under bricks and stones—and maybe it was more than one car, Ginny thought, gazing further along the road.

Right near where they'd been forced to stop, the front of Wilkinson's General Store had fallen away. So had the front of Miss Wilkinson's apartment upstairs. The elderly spinster's bedroom lay ripped open as if a can opener had zipped along the edge. Her bedroom, with chenille bedspread, her dressing gown hanging on the internal door, her teddy bears spread across the bed, was on view for all to see.

She'd be mortified, Ginny thought, appalled for the gentile old lady. And then she thought, Please, God, that she's safe enough to feel mortified.

There were no lights. At this time of day the streetlights should be flickering on, but instead the scene was descending into darkness.

A soldier was approaching them from the other side of the road block. A soldier?

Ben had the Jeep's window down, staring at this uniformed stranger in dismay. For heaven's sake, the man even had a gun!

'The main street's been declared a red zone,' the soldier stated. 'It's too dangerous to proceed. My orders are to keep everyone out.'

'I'm needed at the hospital on the other side of town,'
Ben said with icy calm, and Ginny felt like reaching out
from the back seat, touching him, reassuring him—but
there was no reassurance to be had. 'I'm a doctor,' he
said. 'I have people here who need treatment.'

'Sorry, sir, you still need to follow protocol,' the soldier said. 'You can pull the car to the side of the road—
as far away from the rubble as you can, sir, and report
to Incident Control Headquarters.'

'Incident Control Headquarters?' Ginny demanded,
because Ben seemed almost speechless. She could see
where his head was. Soldiers coming in and taking control of his island? 'Where exactly is Incident Control
Headquarters?'

'Um…it's the tourist information centre,' the soldier
said, unbending a little.

'Thank you,' Ben said tightly, and parked the Jeep,
and he and Ginny ushered his tight little group of frightened citizens round the back of the shattered buildings
towards the sounds and bustle and lights of…Incident
Control Headquarters?

Here there were people everywhere. Floodlights lit
the outside of what was normally tourist central. Serious
men and women Ginny didn't recognise, wearing hard
hats and bright orange overalls, were spilling in and out.

Ginny was clutching Button and holding Flora's hand
with the hand she had spare. She was feeling ill. Ben
was carrying two of the toddlers they'd brought down
from the ridge, and he looked as grim as she felt.

It was almost five hours since the quake had hit, and
what five hours ago had been a peaceful island setting
had now been transformed. These people represented

professional disaster management, she thought. They'd have been brought in by the choppers they'd seen.

Kaimotu Island must now be officially a disaster scene.

And then there was Abby, flying down the steps to meet them. Abby was also wearing orange overalls and a hard hat. A grim-faced man came behind her, obviously keeping her in sight, but Abby had eyes only for Ben.

'Ben—oh, thank God you're okay,' the nurse said. 'I've been so worried. Where have you been? We've been going out of our minds. Your mum—'

'She's okay?' Ben snapped, and Ginny had a further inkling of what he'd been going through. What he still was going through.

'She's fine,' Abby said hurriedly. 'As far as I know, all your family is okay. Doug's out with the searchers. Your house is intact and your mum and Hannah have set it up as a crèche.'

'Flora!' It was a cry from inside the hall. A group of ladies was dispensing sandwiches. One of these ladies darted forward and Ginny realised with relief that it was Daphne Hayward, Flora's sister.

And then she thought, irrelevantly, I know these people. I haven't been near this island for twelve years but I know them.

I'm one of them?

'Can you clear the entrance, please?' a soldier asked, and they all turned round and glared at him, Ginny, too, and Ginny thought incredulously, I'm an islander.

And then Ben lifted Button from her arms and she let her be lifted because it was the natural thing to do, to let Ben help her.

Ben. Her friend.

Her island, in trouble.

'Why aren't you at the hospital?' Ben was asking Abby as he hugged Button close. 'Who's in charge there?'

'Things are as under control as they can be,' Abby said, but her voice was tight and strained. Really tight and strained. 'We've had four choppers arrive containing emergency personnel, including two doctors. Margy's doing triage, and every nurse on the island's with her. One of the helicopters has already evacuated Percy Lockhart and Ivy Malone—both have serious crush injuries. One of the doctors is a surgeon. He's reducing a compound fracture now—Mary Richardson's arm. It's bad, Ben, it's really bad.'

Her voice faltered and she motioned to the grim-faced man behind her. 'This is Tom Kendrick. I… We know each other. He's with Search and Rescue from the mainland. We've been out. They wanted a nurse who knew people. I… I…'

The stranger behind Abby moved in closer, and Ginny saw his arm go round her waist. That was odd, she thought, but Ben was standing really close to Ginny, and she was sort of leaning against him. In fact, her own arm was suddenly round Ben. It was because she needed contact with Button, she told herself, but she knew it was more.

She wanted contact with Ben, and if Abby needed contact with this stranger…it sort of gave her permission to ask for contact herself.

But even as she thought it, she looked at Abby's face, she saw the lines of strain and fear—and suddenly she got it.

'Abby, where's Jack? Where's your son?'

'On…on the bus,' Abby whispered. 'We've just come back to get the chopper. Tom's organising a drop of blankets and food.'

'What the…?' Ben started.

'It's okay,' Tom reassured him, solid, professional, assured. 'We had a tense time for a while when we couldn't locate the school bus but we have it now. One of the fishing boats has seen it from the sea. It's trapped on the coast road round past the mines at the back of the island. There's been two landslips and the bus is trapped between them. As far as we know, they're all fine, but we're not going to be able to get them out until morning. Hence the airdrop. We'll drop a radio in as well.'

'So it'll be okay,' Abby said, still in that tight, strained voice, and Ginny wondered what else was wrong. But she had to move on. They all had to move on.

'They need you at the hospital,' Abby said, forcing her voice to sound almost normal. 'Here's Hannah— Ginny, is it okay if Button goes with her? You and Ginny are needed for medical stuff. Please, go fast. There are so many casualties. But Tom and I need to go now. We need this food drop done before it's completely dark. Tom, let's go.'

New Zealand was set up for earthquakes. Emergency services stood ready twenty-four hours a day. It had been years since there'd been a major quake but that didn't mean they'd relaxed.

The personnel who'd arrived were moving with clinical precision. As Ben and Ginny walked through the almost abandoned town, skirting damaged buildings, they saw teams moving silently from house to house, quickly checking, in some cases with dogs by their sides, making sure everyone was out and then doing lightning assessments of each building.

Using spray paint. Numbers. Colours or degrees of risk. Miss Wilkinson's general store came under the 'Do Not Approach Under Any Circumstances' heading and Ginny thought bleakly of those little pink teddies and a dignified old lady having to bunk down in the school hall tonight without her dressing gown and her pink friends.

Ben was holding her hand. Ginny hardly realised it, but when she did she didn't pull away.

This was too big to quibble. If Ben needed reassurance…

She even managed a slight smile at that. Who was she kidding? Her hold on his hand tightened and he gave her a reassuring smile in the dark.

'We'll get through this.'

'Oi!' It was a soldier, one of the many patrolling the streets. 'You guys need to get to the evacuation centre. That way. This street's not safe.'

'Doctors,' Ben said briefly. 'We need to be at the hospital.'

And all of a sudden they had a military escort and Ben held her hand tighter and it seemed even more… right that she held his. And held and held.

It was so silent, so dark—and then they rounded the bend and the hospital was in front of them and it wasn't dark at all.

Kaimotu Hospital was a small weatherboard hospital up on the headland, looking over the town. Once it had been a gracious old house overlooking the harbour. Over the years it had been extended, with a brand-new clinic at the rear, a doctor's apartment to the side, the rooms expanded to make a lovely ten-bed hospital with most rooms looking out over the veranda to the harbour beyond.

It had been expanded even more now. Some sort of camp hospital had been set up on the front lawns overlooking the sea. It was a vast canvas canopy, lit by floodlights on the outside and by vast battery-powered lanterns inside. A huge red generator was humming from the side of the tent, and the lights were on inside the hospital.

Ginny, who'd thought bleakly of dealing with casualties in third world conditions, felt herself relax. Just a little.

'Docs,' the soldier escorting them said briefly, as yet another soldier came forward to greet them. 'Two of 'em. You can use them?'

'Doctors?' A fresh-faced kid who looked about eighteen pushed aside the canvas door and looked at them. 'Real doctors?'

'Ben McMahon and Ginny Koestrel,' Ben said, and held his hand out in greeting. 'I'm a family doctor with surgical training and Ginny's an anaesthetist.'

'Whew.' The guy whistled. 'I'm Dave Marr, doc with New Zealand Search and Rescue. We have Lou Blewit here as well but I want to send her back with the next chopper. I have a guy with a crush injury to his chest—breathing compromised. He needs a thoracic surgeon. If you guys can help…'

He was dressed in green theatre garb. He might look young but he didn't sound young, Ginny thought. He sounded every inch a doctor, like he knew exactly what he was doing.

Thank God for emergency personnel. Thank God for helicopters. If she and Ben had been on their own…

'You guys swear you're doctors?' Dave said, his tired face breaking into a slight smile. 'You look like chimney sweeps to me. Was that what kept you?'

'Digging the odd person out,' Ben said. 'We got here as fast as we could.'

'Well, thank God for it,' Dave said bluntly. 'From now on…yeah, we need diggers but we need doctors more. I have a truckload of casualties coming in now. You ready to deal with them?'

'Yes,' they said in unison, and Dave grinned.

'Excellent. You guys use the theatre inside the hospital—that's what you're familiar with. I'll stay on triage out here—this is my territory. By the way, you might need to wash. We've set up a washroom over there—we've attached hoses to the garden tanks out back but use a bit more antiseptic than usual because Abby tells us the tank often holds the odd dead possum. We're working on a safe water supply now.'

He glanced up as a battered farm truck turned into the car park. 'Here's the next load,' he said. 'Let's go.'

For the next eight hours Ginny and Ben scarcely had time to breathe.

Luckily most of the injuries were minor, caused by flying debris and masonry. The most common presentation was lacerations. Most of the island homes were weatherboard with corrugated-iron roofs. If they'd been brick homes with slate or tile roofs, the injuries would have been more severe, but corrugated iron, crashing down in sheets, could slice to the bone. Added to that, people had crawled out of collapsed buildings, trying to get out as fast as they could, often unaware that they had been crawling over shattered glass and crockery.

The wounds were caked with dust, and they couldn't be stitched fast.

Some people needed to be transferred to the mainland. Some would need plastic surgery to stop scarring for a lifetime, but there was enough work to hold Ben and Ginny in Theatre, working as hard and fast as they could.

They worked side by side rather than together, seeing two patients at a time. They shared a nurse—Prue, the youngest of the island's nurses—and they helped each other.

It was hardly best medical practice to operate on two patients in the one small theatre but it meant help was always on hand. If one of them got into trouble, Ben helped Ginny or Ginny helped Ben. Ben's surgical skills assisted Ginny, Ginny's anaesthetic skills assisted Ben…

And besides…

It settled her, Ginny thought as she worked through the night. The day had been terrifying. Just the fact that she had Ben six feet away, a solid, reassuring presence, helped her to focus.

There was no question that she was a doctor now. She'd walked away from medicine six months ago but now she was in medicine up to her neck.

And for the first time in years she felt grateful to be a doctor.

She'd helped Ben save Henry but she'd been almost

resentful that she'd been hauled out of her reclusive shell. Here there was no resentment.

She liked being able to help. She loved having the necessary skills.

The knowledge was almost like a lightning bolt. She remembered the early days of training, working as an intern. She remembered the almost terrifying sensation of making a difference to people's lives. The dependence on colleagues. The gut-wrenching pain of loss and the mind-blowing feeling of success. She remembered heading to the pub after work with a group of colleagues to unwind, joking about the macabre, understanding each other, knowing she'd be working side by side with them the next day.

Like she was working side by side with Ben now.

It had all stopped when she'd met James. Her social life had centred on him from that point on. She'd started specialist anaesthetic training.

She'd still worked in a team in Theatre but the atmosphere had subtly changed. She had become the girlfriend of a senior consultant and James had often stopped by, to watch, to give a little advice, to make sure everyone in the theatre knew she was his woman.

Why was she thinking of that now? She was cleaning slivers of glass from Bea Higgins's knees. Bea was seven years old, she'd been having a day off school when the quake had hit because she'd needed to go to the dentist, and had ended up crawling out of the Higgins's lean-to bathroom.

'And Mum says I still have to go to the dentist,' she said mournfully.

'Cheer up,' Ben said from the other side of the room. He was stitching an elderly farmer's arm—Craig Robb

had been trying to get his pigs out of their sty when
sheets of corrugated iron had fallen and slashed. Farmer,
not pig. 'Doc Dunstan's front porch has collapsed,' he
told Bea. 'You might not get a dentist appointment for
months.'

'Cool.' Bea grinned happily as Ginny dressed her
cuts and grazes. She'd hurt when the anaesthetic wore
off, Ginny thought, but kids bounced back. For most
of these kids this earthquake would end up being an
adventure.

And for the rest of the island? The damage didn't
seem massive. There'd been no tsunami. There hadn't
been any reports of multiple deaths—three so far, and
all of them elderly. Could the island get off so lightly?

But there might well be more casualties. There were
still the islanders who lived in outlying areas, where
searchers hadn't been able to reach. There was still a
trapped school bus.

There was still Henry.

'Worry about what's in front of you right now,' Ben
said.

She flashed a glance at him and thought again, He
knows me as no one else does.

The thought was terrifying, yet she was suddenly
no longer terrified. She was working side by side with
him, and no matter what was happening in the outside
world, she wasn't terrified at all.

All his attention should be on his island. All his focus
should be on deaths, injuries, damage.

Instead, he was working alongside Ginny Koestrel
and it felt…okay.

As a seventeen-year-old he'd thought he loved her.

Love was a pretty big word—a word he reserved for his family. There'd been a few women since Ginny, but not one he'd applied the 'love' word to.

His mother had been suggesting he could get together with Abby. Abby was competent, a caring professional, pretty, smiley, a great mum to her little boy. 'Does the fact that she has a child stop you being interested?' his mother had asked him recently, and he'd laughed. It made not one whit of difference. He'd lived in a household of twelve kids. If he didn't like kids he'd have gone nuts long since.

So what had been stopping him? He and Abby had dated a couple of times—yeah, okay, just social functions like the hospital fundraiser where it was easier to have a partner—but they had still been dates.

There'd been friendship and laughter, but not a single spark.

And here was this woman, this stranger, really, as he hadn't seen her for twelve years, working alongside him. She was a different person from the one he'd thought he'd been in love with all those years ago, yet sparks were flying everywhere.

How could there be sparks when he was so tired?

How could he hear her talk softly to Bea and crane his neck to hear, just to listen to her voice?

How could he get close? How could he brush away all the wounds that had been inflicted on her—for he knew there were deep wounds. How could he help her move on?

Move on towards him?

They ushered Craig and Bea out at the same time. Their two patients were welcomed into the arms of their re-

lieved relatives, and there was a moment's peace while
they waited for Dave to direct them to the next need.
The young nurse, Prue, was almost dead on her feet.
'Go home,' Ben told her. 'You've done brilliantly.'

She left and Ben put his arms around Ginny and
held her.

'So have you,' he said.

They stood at the entrance to the makeshift emergency hospital, and for a moment all was silent.

He kissed her lightly on her hair. 'You're doing a
fantastic job, Dr Koestrel,' he told her. 'As a medical
team, we rock.'

She didn't pull back. She was exhausted, she told
herself as he tugged her closer. It was okay to lean on
him.

The queue outside had disappeared. Islanders were
settling into the refuge centre or in some cases stubbornly returning to their homes. There'd still be myriad minor injuries to treat, she thought, but Dave hadn't
been waiting for them when they'd emerged this time.

There was this moment to stand in this man's arms
and just...be.

It couldn't last. Of course it couldn't. A truck arrived
and a weary-looking Dave emerged from the back.

'I need you to see two more patients and then I'm
standing us all down,' he said. 'I'm dealing with a suspected early labour—I'll stay with her until the team
arrives to evacuate her. I think she'll settle but I'm taking no chances.'

'Who?' Ben asked.

'A tourist,' Dave told her. 'She was on a boat in the
harbour when it hit.' He grinned. 'Which is something
of a relief because the islanders want Ben first, Ginny

as second best and me a poor last. But, as I said, it's easing. We have paramedics who'll stay on call for the rest of the night and I have another doctor flying in to take over from me. It's four now. If anything dire happens we'll call you out but you need to catch some sleep. The searchers will find more at first light so medically things will speed up again. Is there anywhere here you both can sleep?'

'My apartment's at the back of the hospital,' Ben said. 'If it's anything like the rest of the hospital it'll be unscathed. Ginny can stay with me.'

'I can give you a bed in a tent if that's not okay,' Dave told her, but Ginny shook her head, even though the tent might be more sensible.

But she didn't feel sensible. She was still leaning against Ben. She still wanted to lean against him.

But there were problems. She needed to focus on something other than this man's arms.

'Button…' she started.

'Whoops, I have a message about someone called Button,' Dave told her, looking rueful. 'One of the guys passed it on. The message is that Ailsa and Hannah said to tell you that Button and Shuffles are fast asleep and happy. They also said to tell you someone's left a basket of kittens with Ailsa because their laundry's collapsed and apparently Ailsa is a sucker for animals, so the message continues that Ailsa says Button would like a black one with a white nose. Button says she wants to call it Button, too.'

He grinned, pleased with himself for remembering the full gist of the message, and Ginny found herself smiling, too. It was exactly the kind of message she needed to hear. She found herself sniffing and when

Ben's arm tightened around her she didn't resist. How could she pull away?

Weirdly, her world, which had been shaken to the core years before, the day James had got his diagnosis, or even earlier, she thought, maybe even the day her father and James had taken her to dinner and hammered into her that she was a fool not to specialise, a fool to keep working in the emergency medicine she loved, seemed, on this day of all days, to be settling.

'You said…' she managed. 'You said…we have two more patients to see?'

'Minor problems,' Dave said. 'The searchers have just swept the wharf. Brian Grubb was trapped in the co-op storeroom when the door shifted on its hinges. He's cut his leg and needs an X-ray to eliminate a fracture to his ankle.

'We also have a Mr Squid Davies—a venerable old gentleman. The search dogs found him under a pile of cray pots and they've brought him in, protesting. He's had a bang on his head. I can't see any sign of concussion but he didn't have the strength to heave the pots off himself. He tells us he forecast the earthquake. He's busy telling all and sundry, "I told you so." Are you sure you can handle it?'

Squid and his end-of-the-world forecasting. Could she handle it?

She grinned at Ben and he grinned back.

'It'll be a pleasure to treat him,' Ben said, and his smile warmed places inside her she hadn't even known had been cold. 'We might even concede we should have listened.'

CHAPTER SEVEN

BEN TOOK ON Brian; Ginny took on Squid. Squid was brought in on a stretcher, but he was sitting bolt upright, his skinny legs dangling down on either side.

'I can walk, you fellas,' he was protesting. 'One hit on the head and you think you can treat me like a namby-pamby weakling.'

'Indulge us,' Ginny said, as the hefty paramedics transferred him smoothly to her examination couch. 'Come on, Mr Davies, lie down and let me see that bump on your head.'

'Since when have I been Mr Davies?' Squid demanded. 'I'm Squid. And you're the Koestrel girl. Bloody uppity parents. Folks say you turned out all right, though.'

'I think she's all right,' Ben said from the other side of the theatre. 'What about you guys?' he asked the paramedics. 'Do you think she's all right?'

There were grunts of agreement from the two burly paramedics, from Brian and from Squid himself, and Ginny thought, wow, she'd been in an earthquake, she'd spent half a day digging people out from under rubble, she'd been working as an emergency doctor for hours... and they thought...

'She's cute,' Squid decreed.

'Nah,' one of the paramedics said, eying her red hair with appreciation. 'It's politically incorrect to say cute. How about handsome? Handsome and flaming?'

'You've got rocks in your head, all of you,' Ginny said, as Ben chuckled. It was four in the morning. She felt punch-drunk. They all must be punch-drunk. 'Speaking of heads, lie down, Squid, while I check yours.'

'Won't,' said Squid.

'Lie down or I take over,' Ben growled, 'and we'll do the examination the hard way.'

'You and whose army?'

'Do you know how many soldiers we have outside? Lie down or we'll find a fat one to sit on you. Now.'

And there was enough seriousness in his tone to make Squid lie down.

Someone—Margy? —had been organised enough to find the islanders' health files and set them at hand. Ginny could see at a glance if there were any pre-conditions that could cause problems. She flicked through Squid's file fast while Ben started work on Brian. Ben knew each patient inside out; he didn't need their histories, but Ginny was wise enough to take care.

She flipped through Squid's history and did a dou-ble-take at his age. Ninety-seven.

Prostate cancer. Treatment refused. Check-ups every six months or so, mostly *or so*, because *regular* didn't seem to be in Squid's dictionary.

A major coronary event ten years ago.

Stents and bypass refused.

'There's nothing wrong with me but a bump on the head,' Squid said sourly. 'There I was, minding me own business, when, *whump*, every cray pot in the shed was on top of me. I warned 'em. Don't you stack 'em up there, I said, 'cos the big one's coming. Didn't I say the big one was coming, Doc?'

'You did,' Ben said wryly. 'I would have thought, though, with your premonition, you would have cleared out of the way of the cray pots.'

'I'm good but I'm not that good,' Squid retorted. He'd submitted as Ginny had injected local anaesthetic around the oozing gash across his forehead but he obviously wasn't worrying about his head. 'I was right, though. Wasn't I right, Doc? That German doc was right, too, heading for home. But you stayed here. And you, too, miss,' he said to Ginny. 'Did you listen? No.'

'Yeah, but I didn't get hit on the head with cray pots,' Ginny retorted. 'So I must have done something sensible. Squid, you have fish scales in this wound!'

'I was wearing me hat. There's always fish scales in that hat. Dunno where it is now; expect I'll have to go digging for it. Get 'em out for me, there's a lass, and make it neat. I don't want to lose me handsome exterior. Not but what I'm getting past it for the need for handsome,' he added, swivelling on the table to look thoughtfully at Ben. 'Not like you two. Not past it at all, not you two. At it like rabbits you were when you were kids. Going to take it up again now?'

'We were not,' Ginny retorted, 'at it like rabbits.' This night was spinning out of control. She was close to exhaustion, but also close to laughter. *At it like rabbits?*

'You woulda been if that gimlet-eyed mother of yours would have let you,' Squid retorted. 'But now you can. Got a littlie, now, though. Does that make a difference, Doc?' he demanded of Ben.

'That is not,' Ben said levelly, 'any of your business.'

'Island business is my business,' Squid said happily. The local anaesthetic was taking hold and any pain that might have interfered with his glorious I-told-you-so attitude was fading fast. 'That's why I warned you. The big 'un's coming. Did you listen? Not you. People are dead, Doc, 'cos they didn't listen.' He lay back, crossed his arms and his smile spread beatifically across his ancient face. 'Told you so. Told you so, told you so, told you so.'

'Ginny, could you give me a hand with Brian's X-ray?' Ben said, grinning across at Squid's obvious bliss. 'It'll take a couple of moments for that anaesthetic to work, and I'd rather not call any of the nurses back. Squid, I want you to lie still and keep quiet. We have patients resting just through the canvas.' Then, as Squid opened his mouth to protest, he put up a hand in a peremptory signal for him to stop.

'Squid,' he said sternly. 'Rest on your laurels. You said the big one was coming and it did. The whole island's in awe. Enough. Lie there and think about it, but while you're thinking, stay still. We're taking Brian next door for an X-ray and when we get back I don't want you to have moved an inch. Right?'

'R-right,' Squid said in a voice that told Ginny he wasn't quite as brave as he was pretending to be. He really was a very old man. He would have been scared.

She put a hand on his shoulder and gave it a gentle squeeze. 'This'll take no more than five minutes,' she told him. She'd checked his vital signs. She'd checked his pupils, his reactions. His bump on the head seemed to be just that, a bump on the head. 'You won't move, will you?'

'Not if you promise to keep looking after me,' Squid said, recovering, and Ginny smiled.

'I promise.'

'Then off you go, Brian, and let the lady photograph you,' Squid decreed. 'She's some lady, isn't she, Doc?

'I… Yes,' Ben said.

'Good call,' Squid said. 'I think I'm about to make another prediction. You want to hear it?'

'No,' Ginny and Ben said together, too fast, and they wheeled Brian out of the door towards X-Ray before Squid could say another word.

The X-ray took effort on both their parts. They were both needed to do the roll transfer that was part of their training. From there the X-ray went smoothly, confirming a greenstick fracture.

'I'll put a simple splint on it tonight,' Ben told Brian. 'We'll check it again tomorrow—it'll need a full cast but we'll wait until the swelling goes down.'

'Good luck,' Ginny said. Because she was feeling more and more like an islander, she gave the burly farmer a hug, then headed back to attend to Squid.

He was curled on his side, his back to the door.

'Sorry I've been so long,' she said cheerfully, and crossed the six steps to the examination couch.

But by the third step she knew something was amiss. Dreadfully amiss.

The stillness was wrong. She'd seen this.

Breathing was sometimes imperceptible but when it wasn't present, you knew.

She knew.

'Ben,' she called, in the tone she'd been taught long ago as a medical student. It was a tone that said, I don't intend to frighten any other patient but I want you here fast. Now.

She put a hand on Squid's leathery neck as she called, her fingers desperately searching for a pulse.

There wasn't one.

Ben was with her almost instantaneously, the door closed firmly between them and Brian.

They were alone in the room. Ben and Ginny and Squid.

Or Ben and Ginny.

'Oh, God, I shouldn't have left him.' Ginny was hauling the equipment trolley from the side of the room, fumbling for patches. No pulse... She didn't even have monitors set up. No IV lines. She hauled Squid's shirt open, ripping buttons.

She was barely aware that Ben was with her. Where was the laryngosope? She needed an endotracheal tube.

Panic was receding as technical need took over, and the knowledge that everything she needed was in reach. She put the patches on with lightning speed...

And Ben grabbed her hands.

'No,' he said.

What the...? She hauled back, confused. They had so little time before brain damage was irreversible. Did he want monitors? Proof? 'Ben, there's nothing—'

'Exactly,' he said, and his hands held hers in a grip that brooked no opposition. 'And that's the way he'd want it.'

'What do you mean? He's healthy. He was sitting up. It's only a bump on the head. Let me go!'

'No,' he said. 'Leave it.' And he held her for longer, while Squid's body settled more firmly into that awful stillness, while the time for recovery, for miracles, passed them by.

'Let me go.' She could hardly make herself coherent. 'Are you mad?'

'I'm not mad. Squid's ninety-seven, Ginny,' Ben said, and his voice was implacable. 'He's left clear instructions. You think he'd thank us for trying to resuscitate him?'

'He's well. It's just the shock.' She was still struggling but it was already too late. There'd been such a tiny window of opportunity. That Ben could stand there and stop her... That Ben could do nothing...

'He's your friend,' she hurled at him, and it was an accusation.

It was also true.

True for her as well?

When they'd been kids Squid had taught them to fish for flounder, to jag for the squid he'd taken his name from. He'd also shared the eternal supply of aniseed balls he'd always carried in his back pocket.

He was almost a part of the island itself. For Ginny... The thought that this was the end...

She gave one last despairing wrench and finally Ben set her free. But even as he did so, she knew it was too late. She knew it. She felt cold fury wash through her that she hadn't been allowed to fight. She wanted to hit out, hit something. Hit Ben?

'You know about medical DNRs,' Ben said, watching her, calmly questioning. Do Not Resuscitate. 'Squid signed one years ago.'

'But they're for people who have no chance,' she managed, thinking of a counsellor handing a form to

James, 'Do Not Resuscitate', and James screwing it into a ball and hurling it back.

'That's for people whose life is worthless. I don't need it, dammit.'

Her father had acted the same way. He'd had three coronary occlusions, a cardiac arrest, pacemaker fitted, defibrillator, there was nothing more to be done, yet he'd never have dreamed of signing a form that said 'Do Not Resuscitate'.

Do not go gently into that good night. Dylan Thomas's words had been her father and James's mantra, drilled into her with fury.

That anger was with her now. Not to be permitted to fight…

This was why she'd walked away from medicine, because she couldn't win. Because she wasn't good enough to win. To make a conscious decision not to win seemed appalling.

'Ginny, Squid is ninety-seven years old,' Ben said again, placing strong hands on her rigid shoulders. He must feel her anger but he was overriding it. 'He might look as if he's weathered to age for ever, but he's been failing for a long time. He has arthritis in almost every joint. He can't do the fishing he loves, and he's been getting closer and closer to needing nursing-home care. Add to that, from the moment the earth shook his face has been one vast smile. He was right, we were wrong. You don't think that's a good note to go out on?'

But how could death be a good note? 'We could have…'

'We could have for what, Ginny?' Ben said, still in that gentle yet forceful voice that said he saw things behind her distress and her anger. Things she didn't necessarily want him to see.

'You have to fight.' She could hardly speak. So many emotions were crowding in. James's words, flooding back…

You stupid cow, get the medication right, you know I need more. Damn what the oncologist says, give me more now!

'No,' Ben was saying. 'If we pulled Squid back now, what then? You know cardiac arrest knocks blood flow to the brain. You know the really old struggle to re-establish neural pathways. Ginny, he's left us at the moment of his greatest triumph and I for one wouldn't ask for anything better for such a grand old man.'

Anger was through and through her, but behind it was a fatigue that was almost overwhelming. It was like all the emotions that had built within her from the moment of James's death were here in this room, the armour she'd tried to place around herself shattering into a thousand pieces.

'I fight the battles I want to win,' Ben said. 'I wouldn't want to win this one.'

'You didn't want him to live?'

'I want everyone to live,' he said evenly, refusing to rise to the emotion she was hurling at him. 'But at ninety-seven I know where to stop. Ginny…'

'Don't Ginny me,' she whispered, and he touched her face, to give pause to the hysteria she was so close to. She flinched and he stopped dead.

'Is that what happened?' he said. 'Did James hit you because you couldn't save his life?'

There was a moment's deathly silence. Okay, more than a moment, Ginny conceded. There was a whole string of moments, packed together, one after the other, leading to a place where she was terrified to go.

'No,' she said finally in a dead, cold voice, a voice she scarcely recognised as her own. She glanced at Squid, at the peace on the old man's face, and she knew Ben was right. She knew it. She had no reason to be angry with him.

There was a time to die and that Squid had died at his moment of greatest triumph... *A consummation devoutly to be wished?*

Maybe, but that was the problem, she thought. James and her father had seen death as defeat. It was why, afterwards, she'd walked away from medicine. To see death, time and time again...

'No,' she said, and then decided it was time to be honest. 'Okay, once. Towards the end. Don't think of me as a battered wife, though, Ben. I was no doormat. Yes, I put up with abuse when he was dying, but he was dying. The one time he slapped me I walked away for a week. Then I had a call from the hospital saying he'd had a bleed. I had no choice but to go back. James lashed out because I was living and he wasn't. There was nothing I could do but put up with it until it was done.'

He did touch her then, a feather touch on her cheek. 'You should never have put up with it. Dying gives no one the right to abuse another. That someone could hit you...'

'It's okay.'

'It's never okay.'

'Yet you say Squid's death is okay.'

'You equate death with violence? It's not the same thing, Ginny, and you know it. Not a peaceful, timely death at the end of a life well lived.'

There was another of those silences. The searchers had ceased for the night, ready to start again at day-break. The stream of incoming patients had ended.

'Is this why you took Button?' Ben asked finally, heavily. 'Because you felt obligated? Like you felt obligated to return to James?'

'No.' She shook her head fiercely at that. 'No way. Do you really think of me as a wimp?'

'No, but—'

'I did go back to James because he was dying and there was no one else to care,' she said. 'But Button's no obligation. The way I see it, Button's the one true thing that's come out of this. Veronica and James can betray all they like, but to hurt Button… I'll love her and we'll make a new life for ourselves, without their shadows.'

'Good for you,' Ben said, a trifle unsteadily, and then he touched her face again. 'And this time you didn't even flinch. You're some woman, Ginny Koestrel.' He hesitated, glancing down at Squid.

'I'll organise this,' he told her. There'd be paperwork, formalities for Squid that had to be done and they had to be done now. Medical imperatives had to take over. 'You fix Brian's splint and then we need bed. We're both exhausted. Too much emotion. Too much work. Too much…everything.' His hands were on her shoulders again, but there was no force, only warmth and reassurance and friendship.

And something more?

'I…I do need to find Button,' she managed.

'Mum and Hanna have Button safe. They won't thank you for waking them, and you know they'll contact you in a heartbeat if Button needs you. My apartment's here. Stop fighting the world, Ginny. Squid's stopped fighting. It's time you stopped, too.'

It was four-thirty when Ben finally led Ginny into his apartment at the rear of the hospital. She was so tired she could barely stand. She should sleep in the search and rescue tents, she thought, or in the refuge centre or…or…

Or stop fighting. Stop thinking she had to fight.

'Bed,' Ben said. 'The bathroom's through that door. You want pyjamas, there're spares in the bureau, bottom drawer. They'll be big on you but they'll be comfy. There's a spare toothbrush in the bathroom cabinet.'

'You're ready for anything,' she murmured.

'I'm ready for any of my eleven siblings to land on my doorstep any time,' he said dryly. 'You try having brothers and sisters on an island as small as Kaimotu. *Ben, Mum'll have a fit if she sees me like this. Ben, I just need a bit of quiet. Ben, no one at home understands me.* This place doubles as the McMahon refuge centre.'

'You have lucky brothers and sisters,' she said wearily, and looked at the nice, big sofa in the sitting room. 'This'll do me nicely, as I suspect it does your siblings. Thank you, Ben. Goodnight.'

'You're using the bed.'

'I'm not taking your bed. There's no need. The way I feel, I'd sleep on stones.'

'Me, too,' he said, and then there was silence. A long silence.

Exhausted or not, things were changing. Twisting. It was like a void was opening, a siren was calling them in.

'I don't suppose,' Ben said, oh, so casually, 'that you'd like to share.'

'Ben…'

'No, okay, not an option,' he said hastily. 'I'd never sleep with a woman who expects a raised hand to be followed by a slap.'

'I know it wouldn't,' she said, astounded. 'I know it never would be.'

'And I'd never sleep with a woman who thought I might blame her for things that go wrong.'

That was a bigger statement. It was a statement to take her breath away.

Not all men were like James or like her father, the statement said.

Ben was her friend.

But Ben was standing in front of her now and she knew he was asking to be much more.

Sharing a bed…

More even than that.

'We do need to sleep,' she said uncertainly, but *more* was right in front of her, a huge, overwhelming impossibility that suddenly seemed possible.

To take a moment that had happened all those years ago—and take it forward?

Ben's hands were on her shoulders again—she was starting to get used to it. She was starting to get used to the feel of him. To the comfort of him. To security and to caring.

To love?

How could she possibly think that? How could she possibly fall in love again?

But right now fatigue was taking the edges off fear and caution and the knowledge that love could haul your life out of control and spin it into a crazy vortex of darkness. Right now there was only Ben, gently propelling her into his bedroom.

He proposed to sleep out here. Alone. Well, why not? He'd asked to share and she'd reacted with fear. The moment she had, he'd backed away.

He'd never push. He respected her.

Did she want respect?

The feel of his hands…

The knowledge that his body was right here, right now…

The fact that this was Ben…

Things were twisting, changing. She was feeling like a caterpillar cocooned in her impenetrable skin, only suddenly the skin was bursting.

She wasn't sure what was inside.

She wasn't sure, but Ben was here, now. Her lovely Ben.

No matter what this night had held, no matter about her armour, no matter about all her vows, this man was a huge imperative overriding all else.

Instead of allowing him to twist her away, to propel her away, she twisted back, so she stood within his hold, so close she could feel his breath, so close she could feel his heartbeat.

'Ben,' she said, and she looked up at him and he looked down at her and she knew she didn't have to say a word. Everything that had to be said had been said.

'You know I love you,' he said, and the world held its breath.

Love?

'I always have,' he said conversationally. 'I may not always have been faithful…'

'Not? When I'd imagined you pining for years and

years?' Somehow she managed to sound shocked, and somehow, amazingly, there was laughter in the room.

'No, but when you smacked Robbie Cartwright over the head with a wet chaff bag because he'd spilled my tadpoles and then went down on your hands and knees and scoured the mud until every last tadpole was saved…I fell in love with you then. Yes, Ginny Koestrel, there have been other women, as there have been other men for you, but our love was forged when we were eight years old and it seems it's there for life.'

'Ben…'

'And I'm not teasing,' he said softly, laughter fading. 'I have no idea why this emotion has surfaced again after all these years but it has, and if you'd care to share my bed…'

'But in the morning…'

'Can we worry about the morning in the morning?' he asked. 'Ginny, this is just for here, for now. It's been one hell of a day. Say no now and we'll sleep apart, but…'

'Yes,' she said. 'I'm saying yes.'

There was a moment's loaded pause. Maybe more than a moment. She looked up at him and he was so… solid. Here.

This man had been her friend for life. She'd walked away from him for all sorts of reasons, some of them right, some of them wrong, but now, for this night, he was offering her love and warmth and desire.

Love…

This wasn't a going-down-on-bended-knee love, she thought. This was a love born of friendship. She knew, she just knew, that taking what Ben was offering would never be used to hurt her, to hold her, to commit.

He wanted her in his bed now, in his arms, and there was no place she'd rather be.

'It's nearly five,' she whispered. 'We need to sleep.'

'So we do,' he said.

'So you'd best make love to me now,' she said, 'because there's no way I can sleep without it—except with drugs, and I don't hold with drugs when there's a very sensible alternative.'

'Is that what I am?' Amazingly laughter was suddenly all around them. 'A sensible alternative?'

'Yes,' she said, and she lifted her arms and wound them around his neck and then she raised her face to be kissed. 'My Ben,' she said. 'My prescription tranquilliser.'

'If you think I'm your tranquilliser,' Ben said, sweeping her into his arms and carrying her toward the bed, without so much as a hint of asking permission, 'then you have another think coming. Tranquilliser indeed. Is that what you really need, Dr Koestrel? Something to make you sleep?'

'N-no,' she managed.

'Excellent.' He lowered her onto the soft covers of his big, masculine bed and hauled his shirt over his head.

She'd seen this man's body—in swimming trunks, when he'd been seventeen.

She hadn't seen this. His body…his big, lovely body. It took her breath away.

'Ben…'

He stopped, the laughter disappearing again.

'Ginny?' His voice was tender and she knew if she said stop now, no would mean no.

Where did friendship end and love take over?

Right here, she thought. Right now.

'Come here,' she whispered, and she tugged him down to join her. 'You've done enough. The least I can do is help you get that belt unbuckled.'

He laughed and submitted. He was undoing the buttons of her blouse. It was already ripped. She should tell him to rip it straight off but he was over her, half straddling her, concentrating on each button, and her mind was doing some sort of weird shutting-down thing.

Only it wasn't shutting down. It was sort of…focussing. Every single distraction was disappearing to nothing. Earthquakes. Button. Patients. The past and the future. Nothing mattered. There was only this man carefully, painstakingly undoing buttons on a ruined blouse.

She put her fingers up and ran her palms down the length of his chest to where his belt was unfastened. She could go lower but Ben was taking his time and so was she.

The buttons were no longer an issue. He spread her shirt wide. 'You want me to tug it free?' he asked, and she grabbed both sides of the skimpy fabric and ripped.

'Wow,' Ben said. 'You want to do that to your bra as well?'

'You have to work for it,' she said, smiling and smiling, and he did, and then a few very satisfactory moments followed while he explored what was underneath.

She was on fire. It didn't actually matter if this night wasn't consummated, she thought hazily, but then his fingers drifted further, and she forgot any thoughts of lack of consummation. Consummation did matter. She wanted him. This was here, this was now. This was Ben.

And as a faint aftershock rippled across the island, waking weary rescue workers and causing islanders to hold each other tighter, Dr Ben McMahon and Dr Guinevere Koestrel didn't notice.

In a few short hours they'd be back in the wards, back to being emergency doctors.

For now there was only this night, this heat, this need.

For now there was only each other.

CHAPTER EIGHT

SHE DIDN'T WANT dawn to come. She lay encircled in Ben's arms and she thought if she didn't move maybe time would stand still. She was spooned against Ben's body, skin to skin, warm, protected…loved?

Somewhere out there was the outside world, responsibilities, cares, life, but for Ginny right now life was solely within this man's arms, and she wanted nothing more.

He was awake. She felt him shift slightly and the tingle of naked skin was enough to make her tremble. He kissed her hair and then tugged her around so she was facing him and he could kiss her properly. Deeply, achingly wonderful.

And then, as she knew he must, he set her back, holding her at arm's length, and they both knew the world needed to intrude.

'We've had four hours' sleep,' he said ruefully.

'Three and a half,' she said, and smiled, and he kissed her again.

'I know,' he said, half-mournfully. 'A man had the promise of four hours' precious sleep and suddenly there was a seductress in my bed.'

'You didn't appear,' she said smugly, 'to take very much seducing.'

'We need to go, Ginny.'

'We do.' She needed to find Hannah and check on Button, before heading back to the hospital. With the dawn the searchers would be out again and there'd be another influx of injured islanders.

Please, let the worst of it be past, she pleaded silently, and Ben kissed her again, but lightly this time, on the lips, and it was a kiss of reassurance.

'We can cope,' he said. 'Whatever the day brings, we'll face it. Ginny, will you share my bed again tonight?'

That was one to take her breath away.

'Ben...'

'I know it's too soon,' he told her. 'We're too stressed. This is hardly the time to be making a lifelong commitment and I'm not asking that. Okay, I'm not even asking for tonight, but if you're hanging around, wondering how to fill in time, and if the pillows up at the vineyard have dust on them, think of this as an alternative.' He touched her cheek, very gently, and his smile was a caress all by itself.

'Any time, my Ginny,' he said softly. 'This thing between us... I haven't figured it out and I know you're even further behind than I am, but I do know that I want you on my pillow, for tonight and for whenever you need me. I'll take my needs out of it for now because I know that they scare you. For now. I'm here, Ginny. I'll never hurt you and I'm just...here.'

For a while after that things got crazy. The two doctors with the rescue service plus every available nurse were fully involved caring for those who made their way to the extended hospital for treatment.

The main injury was lacerations, but there were broken bones, bruises that swelled into haematomas, twists, sprains and also fear. In some cases the fear was as much an injury as a bone break—a young mum who lived alone while her husband was away on a fishing trip was almost paralysed with terror and her terror was infecting her kids.

Medics turned into social workers, calling for help as they needed it. The young mum was matched with an elderly couple who had a lovely stable old weatherboard house that had remained unscathed. Their age meant they'd seen it all and they weren't the least bit bothered about what nature could throw at them, and they were warmly welcoming.

'Come and stay, as long as you like,' they told her when Ben contacted them and asked for their help, and Ginny watched Ben reassure everyone and she thought...

How could she ever have let herself believe family medicine was beneath her?

How could she ever have let James and her father persuade her?

Things still were changing inside her. They were twisting, jumbling, like the world had yesterday.

Last night had been world-changing for her. Today, working side by side with Ben, it changed even more.

She was so aware of him. She was so...

Discombobulated. It was the only word she could think of to describe how she felt. Weird, out of her body, where the only thing that kept her feet on the ground was seeing the next patient.

But finally they ran out of patients. By late morning the number of casualties was slowing to a trickle and she was able to surface and think of other imperatives.

She glanced around and thought, *I'm not needed here. Not for a while at least.*

'Ben, is it okay if I go and find Button?'

'Of course.' Hannah had popped in early to reassure Ginny that Button was fine but Ginny had been in mid-suture and hadn't been able to stop. 'I reckon she could do with a cuddle,' Ben told her.

'She's pretty good at giving them,' Ginny said, and Ben grinned.

'She is, that. So now you have two cuddlers. Off you go, Dr Koestrel, and find your alternative.'

And he kissed her, lightly, a feather kiss, but every eye in the big makeshift casualty ward was on them and she left with her face burning. She was feeling… feeling…

Even more discombobulated.

Practicalities. She needed to focus on what was necessary rather than what she was feeling, she told herself fiercely as she headed down from the hospital towards the town.

There were people everywhere. Even now, the chaos of last night was turning into organised chaos. Debris was being removed from the road, teams were going from house to house, inspecting damage, using paint to scrawl codes on each—'Safe', 'Safe With Care', 'Do Not Enter'.

And everywhere she went, people greeted her.

'Hey, Ginny, good to see you safe. You guys are doing a great job. So glad you're back. Great to have you here, lass, so glad you're home.'

This was….home. She knew it.

This morning she felt an islander. It was a strange sensation.

She'd never felt like she belonged, she thought. Had it taken an earthquake to make her put down roots?

And then she saw Hannah, heading up the road from Ailsa's house, carrying Button, and her stride quickened. Button. How fast had this little girl wrapped her way around her heart? She'd wanted so much to be with her last night. But then… But then…

To her dismay, she was blushing again, and she reached Hannah and took Button into her arms and buried her face in the softness of her new little daughter until the colour subsided.

As she knew she would, Button's arms wrapped around her in a bear hug.

'Ginny,' she said in satisfaction. 'Cuddle.'

It was the best thing. What was Veronica about, abandoning this little one? she thought. She'd lived with her for all of two weeks and already she was starting to think that if Veronica wanted her back she'd face a fight.

She needed to get those documents sorted. She needed to get the formal adoption through so that Veronica couldn't just swan in and take her away if the whim took her.

Ben would help.

All this she thought in the moments she took out to let her colour subside, to let the warmth of Button settle her, to feel even more that this was her home.

'How frantic are you?' Hannah asked when she finally emerged from her bear hug, and Ginny smiled ruefully.

'Sorry.' On impulse she hugged Hannah as well, with

Button sandwiched between. 'I haven't even said thank you yet. Taking her in last night...'

'It was the least I could do, and I always do the least I can do,' Hannah said cheerfully. 'Mum and I had six toddlers between us. But no tragedies. They're all kids of those caught up in rescue efforts, like you and Ben.' Then her face clouded. 'But I heard Squid died.'

'Yes.' There was nothing else to say.

'Ben will be upset,' Hannah said quietly. 'He loved that old man.'

He didn't try to save him, Ginny thought, but she didn't say it. Ben's reasons were sound; she knew they were, but they took some getting her head around. She should have her head around it. Her reaction was illogical but it was still there.

You fought to the end, and if you failed...

Failure. It slammed back, right there and then, standing on the rubble-strewn main street with Hannah watching her curiously and Button still clinging, nonjudgmental, her one true thing.

Was that why she loved her? Because Button would never judge her?

Would Ben ever judge her?

This was crazy. She gave herself a fierce mental shake and turned her attention back to the question Hannah had asked first.

How frantic are you?

'The worst of the rush is over,' she told her. 'We have four doctors, five nurses and for the time being not enough patients. Please, God, it stays that way.' She hesitated. 'I thought...if I could find a car... Henry's on his own out at his cottage behind the vineyard. I just met Ella—she's his closest neighbour but they were in town when the quake hit and haven't been back. Ella has a sprained wrist and is staying put. That means Henry's on his own. Ben and I drove down from the vineyard yesterday so I know a route we can take and we've already chopped the fences. I might just go and check.'

'Send a team,' Hannah said, and Ginny gazed along the street at the organised troops of orange-clad workers moving methodically from house to house.

'It's just one old man in a tiny weatherboard cottage,' she said. 'It's hardly worth a team and if I know Henry he'd be furious if I sent strangers.'

'So let him be furious.'

'No.' Ginny shrugged. She'd had enough blame in her life, she didn't need to wear this. 'It's easy enough to check and it's safe enough. I'll take one of the hospital vehicles.'

'You can take Mum's,' Hannah offered. 'It's four-wheel drive and it has a child seat.'

'Why—?'

'Um…that's why I was coming to find you,' Hannah said diffidently. 'There's been a bit of a drama with the school bus. Nothing dreadful,' she added as Ginny flinched. 'It was stuck between two landslips. They had a kid missing but they all seem to be accounted for now and as far as I know there's no casualties. But they're bringing them into town by boat now and lots of their mums and dads are still stranded in outlying parts of the island. So Mum and I have been asked to help. If you're sure where you're going is safe…could you take Button with you?'

She thought about it. The route she and Ben had taken yesterday had been bumpy but sound. They'd checked the farmhouses along the way so there'd be no huge dramas to find.

She could stop in at the vineyard, check the house was okay, maybe pick up a few things she would need if they were to stay in town. She'd take no risks.

And at Henry's cottage…

The worst she'd find would be an injured old man, but she was more likely to find him distressed than injured. And angry that she'd come?

Button could defuse that, she thought. She might even help.

'Take a radio with you,' Hannah urged. 'The rescue co-ordinator is giving them out. You'll need to tell him where you're going. Oh, and I'm off to let Ben know about the bus. He's been worried about Abby. I'll let him know where you've gone as well. Is that okay?'

She shouldn't take Button. She held her and thought there were risks. But the risks were small, and with no one to mind her… The alternative was to leave Henry without assistance he might need.

She could do this. It'd be safe.

'You do that,' she said, and gave Hannah another swift hug. 'And tell Ben I'll be fine. We'll all be fine. Let's hope we've heard the worst of the news about this earthquake. It's time to come out the other side.'

'She's gone where?'

'Up to Henry's.' Hannah suddenly sounded scared and Ben caught himself. He'd reacted with shock, and given a moment's thought he had himself together. The route they'd taken yesterday was safe enough. She had his mother's car, which was as tough as old boots. She was sensible.

'She took Button,' Hannah said, and he had to fight shock again.

But it was still reasonable. Woman heading off to check on an elderly neighbour, taking her daughter with her. Via a safe route. Taking a radio.

She was sensible and she'd be even more sensible with Button with her.

'Mum and I are heading down to the harbour to be there when the kids come in,' Hannah said. 'You want to come? Abby will be there.'

She was still matchmaking, Ben thought, humour surfacing. Ailsa and Hannah—plus half the island— had been trying to get Ben and Abby together for years.

It wasn't going to happen. They were friends but there'd never been that spark.

Like the spark of last night?

Last night hadn't been a spark, he conceded. It had been wildfire. A meeting of two bodies that ignited each other.

Ginny had ghosts.

He could lay ghosts to rest, though, he thought as Hannah waited for his reply. He could work with whatever demons she had; she lived here now and he had all the time in the world.

Except he wanted her in his bed again, tonight.

'It's Ginny, isn't it?' Hannah said cheekily.

And he wished he was busy. He needed a whole busload of casualties to come in the door this minute to stop the prying, laughing eyes of his little sister seeing far more than he wanted her to see.

'You're sure she's taken a radio?'

'Cross my heart and hope to break a leg. We walked to the co-ordination centre together. She's got more safeguards in place than you can shake a stick at. You know, Abby's been out all night with the most gorgeous rescue paramedic. You're not worried about Abby?'

'Not if she has the most gorgeous rescue paramedic with her.'

'But if it were Ginny?' Her eyes danced and she held up her hands. 'Okay, big brother, no more questions. I don't think I need to ask them anyway. I'm off to do some serious childminding.' She glanced around the makeshift casualty ward where medics were working efficiently and well. 'You know, if this place stays quiet you could even follow Ginny.'

'She doesn't need me.'

'She might,' Hannah said airily. 'You never know.'

It was kind of eerie retracing the route she and Ben had followed yesterday. Then their minds had been set to crisis mode. They'd faced fear and tragedy, and they'd known they had to get down to the hospital fast.

Now the crisis seemed to be over. It was a gorgeous autumn day. The rolling hills were bathed in warm sunshine, the cattle had gone back to grazing and only the occasional fallen tree or weird gash across a paddock indicated anything had happened.

The gashes were easy to avoid. They seemed to happen in fault lines, where the earth underneath had simply pulled apart. They didn't look deep but Ginny didn't need to find out how deep they were.

She could still see the tracks they'd made yesterday, driving the truck cross-country over the lush pastures. She kept to the tracks. She didn't deviate to the houses she passed—she knew they'd been checked. The fences were all slashed thanks to yesterday's efforts so she didn't need to stop until she reached the vineyard.

Her house was still intact.

She climbed from the car, lifted Button out and stood looking at it. The long, low homestead showed superficial damage—a couple of broken windows, downpipes skewed, the front steps to the veranda twisted away and one crumpled chimney—but nothing major.

The house had been shaken and then put down again on the same foundations and she stood and hugged Button and looked at it and felt her eyes well with tears.

Why? This had been her parents' holiday retreat. This place had only been home for her for six months.

But that's what it was. Home.

This island was home.

Ben was home?

She had a tiny flash of longing. She and Ben. Kids, dogs, family. Here?

Whoa, that was like a teenager sitting in class signing her name Ginny McMahon, over and over again. She'd actually done that when she was seventeen. Dumb. Emotional. Not based on facts.

But it might be, she thought. Last night had been real. Last night Ben had said he loved her.

So many emotions. She stood in the sun in the stableyard and for a moment she simply gave in to them. Yesterday the world had shaken, but for her, now, the world had settled, and her foundations seemed surer.

'This is home,' she whispered to Button. 'We'll fix this up. It's big and solid and safe. We can live here for ever and ever.'

And Ben? Big and solid and safe?

So sexy he made her toes curl?

That was way too much to think about right now. Ben and what had happened last night was an image, a presence, a sensation that had her retreating fast to the practical.

She and Button ventured round the back of the house to the kitchen. She turned on the hose—miraculously the water tanks were still standing and she still had pressure. Button's favourite occupation was still to stand and point the hose, and the late-producing tomatoes were wilting.

'Give them a big drink,' she told her, and knew she had a few minutes to enter the house. If she avoided standing under the beams she'd be safe enough. She needed to collect urgent belongings, things they'd needed to stay in the town for a few nights.

With Ben?

Don't go there. She was starting to feel…just a little bit foolish. More than a little bit afraid.

Get on with it. Move on, she told herself, and get back to the hospital. She might be needed. Coming up here was a bit irresponsible.

Unless Henry did need her.

She headed back out to the garage and grabbed bolt cutters for hacking through fences if needed, and then popped a happy, soggy Button back in the four-wheel drive. Henry's cottage was further out on the headland. The track seemed to be okay. There weren't any significant ruts or crevices, though at one place there was a small landslip partly blocking the way.

'Nothing to this, Button,' she told the little girl as they edged past. 'We'll reach Henry's cottage in no time. It'll be fine.'

And then they topped the next rise and saw the cottage and it wasn't fine at all.

Ben was starting to worry. It seemed simple, logical even, for Ginny to drive to Henry's. It didn't even seem risky to take Button with her. Childminders were at a premium, the way seemed safe and Ginny wasn't one to take risks.

So why was he worrying?

It wasn't as if he didn't have enough to do. The boatload of school kids had arrived, with myriad cuts and bruises to be checked. There was nothing serious but most of these kids had parents who'd spent a sleepless night imagining the worst, and every cut needed to be checked.

Besides, to a traumatised five-year-old a bandage was a badge of honour, a signal to the world that he'd been doing something dangerous. It was therapy all by itself, Ben thought as he applied a much-too-big plaster to Rowan March's grazed arm. He'd applied antiseptic with liberal abandon as well, so Rowan headed off with his parents, plus a bright orange arm and a plaster to brag about. He was all better. And suddenly there were no more kids.

'We have a bit of medical overkill.' Margy was clearing trays, keeping a weather eye on the door. 'So many helpers... The guys have been wonderful, though. Four deaths, five major injuries, minor injuries arriving slowly enough to be dealt with promptly, and teams are reporting most properties have been checked.'

'I should have sent a team out to Henry's,' Ben growled, and Margy frowned.

'Didn't Max and Ella check on him?'

'Apparently not. Their daughter's here in town. They came down in a rush and stayed.'

'I'll ask one of the rescue guys—'

'There's no need. Ginny's gone up there.'

'Has she now.' Margy eyed him thoughtfully. 'And that's why you seem distracted?'

'I'm not distracted.' Then he shrugged and grinned. 'Or not very.'

'You want to follow her up there?' Margy raised a quizzical eyebrow and smiled. What was it with the people around him? Was he that transparent? 'Surely she shouldn't be out there by herself.'

But one of the searchers was coming in now, cradling his arm. He needed to be seen to and the two fly-in doctors were taking a break. Margy and Ben were it.

'I don't have time.'

'But when the others come back on duty?'

'She'll be back by then.'

'So she will,' Margy said, pinning on a smile. 'So you can stop worrying.'

'I've got you worrying now,' he said.

'She's a sensible woman.' But Margy was starting to look worried.

'Will you cut it out? There's no reason to worry.'

'Except that if it was my Charlie I'd be worried,' Margy said. 'And the way you feel about Ginny…'

'What the…? I do not feel—'

'Sure you do,' she said, cheering up. 'You think you can sleep together on this island and not have every islander know in five minutes?'

'Margy! We were exhausted. She needed to stay in my apartment.'

'Of course,' Margy said equitably. 'But if you slept

on the sofa I'm a monkey's uncle and if you're not feeling like I feel about Charlie, when you're looking the way you're looking…'

'Will you cut it out?'

'Yes, Doctor,' she said meekly. 'Anything you say, Doctor. But let's get this arm seen to and get you up the valley to rescue your lady.'

Henry's cottage was ramshackle. He'd run a small farm up here before her parents had employed him, but he'd let this place go. He'd only left the vineyard six months back, when arthritis had overtaken him, and he'd refused Ginny's offer to stay in the caretaker's residence permanently.

The old cottage, therefore, was hanging together with rotting timbers and rusty nails. Ginny had been out here a couple of times to see him. She'd been horrified but he wouldn't move.

And now…maybe the time for him to move was gone. The entire building had folded in on itself. The chimney looked as if it had crashed down, bringing the rest of the house with it.

It looked like a huge bonfire, set and ready to go.

And where was Henry?

'Stay in the car, Button,' Ginny said, handing Shuffles over. 'I need to see…'

'Henry,' Button said, and Ginny wondered how much this little girl understood. Henry had been down in the vineyard teaching Ginny to prune. He'd shown Button how to build Shuffles a little house with the clippings and then, the last time Ginny had come up here, the day after Henry came home from hospital, Henry had made Button red cordial, which she liked very much.

'I don't know where Henry is,' Ginny conceded. 'But you stay in the car while I look.'

'Okay,' Button said happily, and Ginny left the doors open so the sun wouldn't heat it up too much and turned her mind to Henry.

Somewhere in this mess, an old man...

The house was on the headland overlooking the sea. From here you could almost see to the mainland. A sea eagle was soaring in the thermals, seemingly having given up on fishing for the day just to soak up the sun. There seemed no urgency at all. How could anything dreadful happen on such a day?

Where was Henry?

'Henry?' It was a cautious call, and produced nothing. She tried again and put a bit of power behind it.

'Henry!'

And from the ruins...

'Well, about time. I've bin thinking I was going to have to chop me leg off with a penknife, only I can't reach a penknife. You want to get me out of here, Ginny, girl?'

Ginny, girl. He'd called her that all her life, she thought as she tried to get closer, tried to figure where exactly he was.

Feeling ill.

She should have insisted he stay with her. She thought suddenly that this man was more of a parent to her than her own parents were. Henry at the vineyard, Ailsa in town, her friend Ben—those were her people.

'Are you hurt?' she called, shifting to the far side of the house, calling loudly because he was far in, she could hear it from his voice.

'I'm stuck. Bloody piano came down on me ankle.

I can still wiggle me toes. It got me sideways, like. I never even played the thing either. My May only got it 'cos she liked the look of it.'

He was sounding brave but she heard the pain and weakness behind the bravado. But how to get him out? She was looking at vast sheets of roofing iron topping a crumbling mess.

'I need to call for help,' she told him. 'Can you hold on for a bit?'

'Can you get me one of them intravenous line things you docs have? You could feed it down through the cracks with a bit of beer in it. A man 'd feel better with a beer in his belly.'

'You're still recovering from a stomach ulcer,' Ginny retorted. She had him pinpointed now, she thought. From the sound of his voice he was near the remains of the main chimney but completely under the roofing iron. 'No alcohol for you!'

'No, ma'am. But you're calling for help?'

'You'd better believe it.'

'Ben!'

Ben had just finished splinting the fractured arm. It was a vicious break; it'd need setting by a decent orthopaedic surgeon, but he'd done enough to make the guy comfortable. He was starting to clear up when Don Johnson, the island's fire chief, stuck his head around the door. 'Can I have a word?'

'Sure. You settle down on the pillows, Mac,' he told the guy he was treating. 'You'll be on the next chopper out of here.'

'Chopper'll be half an hour,' Don said across him, glancing at Mac with concern. 'Do you have decent painkillers on board, Mac? Can you wait until next trip?'

'Sure,' Mac said. 'Broken wing is all. I can still handle a shovel if you let me.'

'I don't need a shoveller,' Don said, but he sounded worried. 'What we need is more vehicles. Ben, Ginny's just contacted base. She's up on the headland past her place and Henry's trapped under his collapsed house. I'm hauling a team together now. Are you free as soon as we are?'

'I'm free now,' Ben said.

It was the longest wait. There was nothing she could do but sit in the sun by the ruin that was Henry's house, and cuddle Button and talk to him. If she tried to climb onto the ruin to rip up the sheets of iron that hid him from view, she could bring more down on the man beneath. She had to sit and wait, sit and wait, and Henry knew it.

'So tell me why you never came back?' Henry asked, and she shook herself and thought it was she who should be asking questions, she who should be focussing on keeping him distracted.

'I did come back.'

'From the time you were seventeen… Your parents came back every summer and played the landed gentry. Why not you?'

'I guess I didn't…like playing the landed gentry.'

'Or were you scared you'd fall harder for our Ben?' Henry said. 'That's what my May said. "She's fallen for that lad in a big way," she said. "If she comes back next summer they'll be together for life, mark my words," and then you never came back. So what was it about our Ben that scared you?'

'Nothing.' She was holding Button on her knee, making daisy chains to keep the little girl occupied. She was as close to Henry as she dared to go.

'Something did,' Henry said, and she heard the pain in his voice and knew he was trying hard to find anything—anything to distract him. 'You don't need to tell me, but May said you were as besotted with him as he was with you, and then you disappeared. It seemed dumb to us.'

'It was too hard,' she said, and she didn't say it loud enough. In truth it was barely a whisper.

'You still there?' Henry's voice rose sharply and she caught herself. This wasn't about her. This was about Henry and distraction and nothing else.

And maybe…maybe it was time to say it like it was.

'I wasn't brave enough to love him,' she said. 'I was seventeen and my parents treated this place as an escape. That summer…I told my mother I was in love with Ben, and she laughed. And then she told me exactly what would happen if…if I was stupid.'

'What would happen?'

His voice was so thin she was starting to panic. He sounded so weak there was no way she could do anything but tell him the truth.

'My dad was a powerful man,' she said. 'He was at the top of his field and he was wealthy to boot. Very, very wealthy.'

'You know, I figured that,' Henry said dryly and Ginny managed a smile.

'So he had friends all over the world. Friends in most of the major teaching hospitals. Friends in Auckland. The head of medical training for Auckland Central was a house guest here that summer. Dad said he only had to drop a word. He said nursing was a much more suitable profession for someone of Ben's background—his words, not mine. He said it was fine for a kid like Ben to have aspirations and he could have any aspiration he wanted except his daughter. And if he was to keep wanting me then his plans to be a doctor would be pulled from under his feet, just like that. So be a good girl, Ginny, he said. Let him down kindly and move on.'

'So that's what you did.'

'That's what I did,' she said drearily. 'And, of course, he was right. We were only seventeen, and it even seemed sensible. Medical school seemed exciting. The way I was feeling seemed dumb. I managed to dump Ben like it was my idea. But if I'd had the courage to maybe keep writing, keep in touch, who knows? But I couldn't write without crying and then I met James and it was the easy way out. Now I'm so, so sorry.'

There was a long silence, a silence that stretched until she got scared.

'Henry?'

'I'm still here,' he said, almost amicably. 'And Ben could have written, too. Is he sorry?'

'I don't know,' she said, confused.

'Bet he's not,' Henry said. 'He's a guy. I'm seeing a pattern here. I know it's sexist, but *women*. You know, my May once dropped her best meat platter—a plate she inherited from her mum who inherited it from her mum. So she's standing there staring down at five or six bits of broken crockery and she's welling up with tears and saying, oh, Henry, I'm so sorry, I'm so sorry. Like she's apologising to me, or to the shades of her mum and her grandma, but who's hurting? Daft woman. Hell, this piano hurts. You think they're coming?'

'They're coming,' Ginny said, and they were, at least she thought they were. In the distance she could see a Jeep, coming fast. 'At least…I hope…I think Ben's here.'

'Thank God for that,' Henry said morosely. 'A nice shot of morphine'd be useful and I hope he has tin cutters.'

'Or a crane,' Ginny said, hugging Button and climbing to her feet to wave to the approaching Jeep. 'I'm sorry I haven't been more useful.'

'Oh, for heaven's sake, you know where you can put your sorry,' Henry snapped. 'Let's put the past behind us and acknowledge all we both want is Ben.'

CHAPTER NINE

BEN WAS ALONE. Ginny had called for the cavalry and the only one who had come was Ben. That was fine, as far as it went—the hard hug he gave her when he arrived was reassuring, as far as it went—but she wanted more.

Did Wellington have these sorts of problems? Ginny wondered. Did 'Get the fourth infantry division to the front now' mean get them here after the fourth infantry division had finished dinner and put their boots on? Or after the fourth infantry had coped with a wee crisis like fighting five French divisions down the line?

Something must have happened. There must be another catastrophe somewhere, because there was no back-up in sight.

Meanwhile, she and Ben walked carefully around the ruined house, with Ginny carrying Button, while Ben tried to assess how he could get in there.

There seemed no safe way, but Henry's voice, which had risen in hope when Ben had arrived, was now a thready whisper.

And then, appallingly, Henry started to sob.

It wasn't loud sobbing, the kind of wail you'd expect to hear from loss, but the slow rasp of someone in unbearable pain, someone who'd held up as long as he could but had now reached the edge.

'I'm sorry,' he gasped. 'No, don't tell Ginny I said that. I'm not sorry, it's just this damned piano is heavy.'

Ben headed for the radio. 'Where the hell are you guys?'

'The church has come down,' Don barked at him. 'We have three old ladies trapped in the rubble. They were trying to rescue the altar cloths, for heaven's sake, in a building categorised as unsafe. It's okay, we'll get 'em out, but what's worse, the land behind has slipped and our vehicles are trapped. No, it wasn't another tremor, it was just damage we couldn't see—the rise behind the church must have been waiting to fall since the quake. We're organising vehicles on the other side but I reckon it'll be another half-hour before we get up to you.'

'I don't think he can last half an hour,' Ginny whispered. They'd gone back behind Ben's Jeep to radio where Henry couldn't hear. 'Ben, there's a sliver— a small cavity round the back. If you hold Button I could...'

He'd already seen the cavity she was talking about. It was a tiny hump in the caved-in iron. He'd shone his torch in and seen nothing but rubble, but at that point they were only maybe ten feet from where Henry was lying. If they could reach Henry... Even an arm or a leg might be enough to inject painkillers. As well as that, if someone could just be here with him it could make all the difference.

An elderly nurse, an old-school martinet, had instilled *Just being there* into Ben in his first year as an intern.

'Don't be scared of getting personal, Doctor. All these new-fangled drugs and treatments, they don't matter half as much as human contact, and don't you forget it.'

He hadn't. He wasn't forgetting it now.

They'd been talking to Henry—of course they had. Ginny had persuaded Button to sing her favourite song, *'Happy Birthday to Button'*, to Henry, and he knew it helped, but touch…

The way Henry sounded…

'You can't,' he said harshly to Ginny. 'I'll go.'

She drew back, appalled. 'No!'

'Hang on. It's okay if you go in but not me?'

'No,' she said, more urgently. 'I'm smaller.'

'And I'm stronger.'

'What if the roof comes down?'

'So what if the roof comes down?' he said. 'Ginny, you know as well as I do that if we don't get drugs on board soon we'll lose him—we can both hear it. I'm only going under iron. You suggested it. I'm the one to do it.'

'No!' It was a cry of terror.

'Yes,' he said. 'Ginny, I'll concede there's a risk. I think it's small but it's still there. With that in mind, I'm a bachelor with no dependants, and you, my love, like it or not, are a mother with a dependent four-year-old. Your job, I believe, is to keep the home fires burning, take care of the children and prepare slippers and pipe for when your man comes home.'

'Ben!' Despite the gravity of the situation she choked on laughter.

'That's right, my love, I'd like a nice Irish stew when I come out, please, with golden syrup dumplings on the side.' He was shoving gear from his backpack into his pockets as he spoke; syringes and vials, wrapping the vials in dressings to keep them unbroken. Then he gave her a swift, hard kiss, the sort of kiss a man should give his woman as he went off to battle—and he was gone.

She could help him for the first part. At the edge she helped him clear loose rubble, and then as he worked his way under the iron, he shoved stuff sideways and she reached in and helped him haul it clear.

There'd been some sort of sideboard at the side of the room. It formed a kind of base so the roofing iron hadn't been able to reach floor level.

Once the rubble had been exposed they saw clearly what was happening. The sideboard was too low for Ben to go under it; there was no way they could shift it and neither would they want to—it could bring the whole roof down even further—so Ben had to manoeuvre his way round the sides.

It was filthy, dangerous, even foolhardy, but Henry had grown silent. Ginny had stopped protesting, but she felt sick.

She felt worse when Ben managed to get around the massive sideboard, gave a grunt of satisfaction and hauled himself further under and she could no longer see him. There was now nothing else she could do.

She went back to Button. They started making daisy chains again but Ginny was doing it by feel.

She was watching the crumpled roof and she was watching the track down the valley.

Please, let it not collapse.

Please, let help arrive.

'Talk to me,' she pleaded, and Ben grunted back.

'It's pretty hard to talk with a mouth full of grit.

Henry, I know now why we haven't heard from you for a while. You couldn't, I don't know, whistle or something, just to let me know where you are?'

There was a faint attempt at a whistle and Ginny managed a smile and went back to daisy-chain-making as if her life depended on it.

'We need a conversationalist,' Ben grunted, his voice muffled almost to incomprehension. 'Go on, Ginny, tell us a story.'

'Story,' Button said in satisfaction.

Ginny thought, Story? What sort of story?

Ben was inching his way through rubble. Henry was lying trapped in pain. Button was looking up at her expectantly.

She'd been in pressured situations before, but none like this.

Tell us a story.

'Once upon a time,' she said, feeling helpless, and Button beamed and bounced on her knee.

'I like stories.'

'You need to stay quiet,' Ben growled. 'Shush, Button, we all need to hear.'

A story.

Stories don't have to be made up, though, Ginny thought, floundering for inspiration. Stories could be real.

'Once upon a time there was a little girl called Ginny,' she said, and Button squeaked in surprise, but then put her hands firmly across her small mouth as she remembered the rules.

'Ginny's mum and dad brought her to the island but she was very lonely,' Ginny continued. 'She didn't have any friends but she had beautiful clothes.'

'I remember those clothes,' Ben said, muffled, and there was a thump and grating of metal on metal and Ginny's heart almost hit her ankles. But her job wasn't to quiver with fear. She was the storyteller.

'Ginny's mum and dad were busy,' she said. 'They were always busy. So they asked someone else to take care of Ginny. The lady's name was Ailsa and she had a little boy called Ben. The first time Ben met Ginny he pointed to her pretty white pleated skirt and he snickered.'

'I did not,' the voice from under the tin said.

'What's snickered?' Button asked.

'Laughed. He laughed at my white pleated skirt.'

'That wasn't nice,' Button said.

'I didn't think he was a very nice boy,' Ginny agreed. 'But then he offered to take me tadpoling. You've seen tadpoles, Button. We caught some last week, remember?'

'Yes,' Button said, wiggling more firmly onto Ginny's lap. 'I like this story.'

'As long as I stay the good guy,' Ben said. 'Henry, mate, could you grunt or something? I should be able to see you soon.'

'Grunt,' Henry managed. 'Will that do? Keep going, girl.'

'So he took me tadpoling,' Ginny said. 'Out the back of town there's a farmer's field with a lovely, wide pond. It's a great place for catching taddies.'

'I know it,' Henry said, sounding strained to breaking point. 'You nearly here, lad?'

'Reckon I'm three feet from your feet,' Ben said, sounding just as strained. 'Oi, storyteller, get on with it.'

She couldn't bear it. If the iron came down…if anything happened…

Get on with it.

'So Ben took Ginny to the pond,' she managed. 'And he said the best taddies were on the far side. Now, the farmer had left an old bath lying near the pond. I don't know why, but Ben said it was a good old bath and he used it as a boat. The only problem was there was a hole where the plug should be.'

'Didn't you have a plug?' Ginny asked, and astonishingly Ginny heard Ben chuckle.

'Shush, Button,' he said, mock-sternly. 'This is a very good fairy-tale and I like the ending.'

'Shush yourself,' Ginny said tartly, and it was almost as if he was standing beside her, grinning. Her Ben…

'There was clay by the pond,' she made herself continue. 'So Ben showed Ginny how to make a ball of clay mixed with grass, and shove it into the hole in the bath. Then Ben climbed into the bath and used a pole and pushed himself all the way across the pond and back. He'd obviously done it lots of times because he was very fast.'

'Old trick,' Henry muttered. 'I did that when I was a lad. Got into all sorts of trouble. Hey…'

'Yeah, that's me touching your arm,' Ben said. 'Can you see the flashlight?'

'Can I…? Answer to me prayers,' Henry said, his voice breaking. 'Lad…'

'Hold still. I can reach enough of your arm to give you a shot of something to take the edge off the pain.'

'I'm scared of needles,' Henry retorted, and the old Henry was back. Human contact…the best medicine in the world. Ben was in there with him, and Ginny heard the easing of the old man's terror.

'Be a man and put up with it,' Ben retorted. 'Quick, Ginny, get to the exciting part.'

'So then Ben brought the bathtub back to Ginny's side of the pond,' Ginny said, and for the life of her she couldn't keep her voice steady. 'And Ben made her make her own plug out of clay and grass and fill the hole. And then he pushed her out into the pond and told her how to use the pole to push herself across the pond. The pond wasn't deep but it was very, very muddy. And Ginny wasn't good at rowing. So she was slow, and because she was slow the plug in the bath slowly melted.'

'What does that mean?' Button asked, trying hard to keep up.

'It means,' Ginny said direfully, 'that Ben had tricked Ginny. The hole in the bath was open again and the water was pouring in and Ginny stood in the bath and yelled to Ben to help her but he stood on the bank and laughed while she sank into the mud. And her lovely white pleated skirt got covered with mud, and her pale pink cardigan was ruined and her nice curly hair got soaking wet and there was even a tadpole in my…in her hair. And then Ben strode into the pond and rescued…'

'Rescued Ginny,' Button crowed.

'Rescued the tadpole,' Ben said, and even Henry chuckled.

There was a long silence. This was surreal, Ginny thought, sitting in the bright sunlight on this gorgeous autumn morning, where everything seemed perfect, where underneath the ruin one man was fighting for his life and another was putting his life on the line to save him.

'And then did she cry?' Button asked in a small voice, and she had to go back to the story. To how she'd felt as an eight-year-old, standing shoulder deep in mud while this strange boy carefully disengaged a tadpole from her curls. Knowing she'd go home to her parent's disgust. Knowing she'd been tricked. Knowing she looked appalling.

'No,' she said softly, and added, because suddenly it seemed important, 'No, she didn't cry because he saved the tadpole. Just like he's saving Henry now.'

'Oi,' Henry said, and his voice was now sleepy instead of pain-filled. 'Are you comparing me to a tadpole?'

'No,' she said. 'But you're being saved by a hero and all the best stories have heroes.'

'And heroines,' Henry muttered. 'And then they all live happily ever after. Is that you, girl? You're ready for your happy-ever-after?'

'We'll get this roof off you guys first,' she said. 'And then we'll see.'

'That sounds promising,' Ben said, and there was strain in his voice now. What sort of situation was he in? He sounded as if he, too, was in pain. 'So, in your story…the heroine falls in love with her hero?'

'Maybe she did,' she said. 'Maybe he was the first person she'd met who cared more for tadpoles than for pleated skirts.'

'That,' said Henry, 'is just plain weird.'

'Maybe it is,' Ben said. 'But it's important. So the heroine might have fallen in love?'

'The best heroines do,' she whispered.

'Pardon?'

'The best heroines do,' she yelled, and she yelled

too loud but it didn't matter. Her Ben was underneath
a ruined house, risking his life, and nothing was more
important than that.

'A truck's coming,' Button said.

Ginny swivelled and stared down the valley and a
truck *was* coming—no, two trucks.

'The cavalry's here,' she told the guys under the
house, as she recognised Don Johnson and his fire
crew. 'Let's get you guys out and concentrate on fairy-
tales later.'

'Let's not forget to,' Ben said. 'I have a feeling the
end of this one's pretty import—'

And he got no further.

The aftershock was the biggest yet. It rolled across
the island as a great, rolling swell. The iron of the house
heaved and shifted.

Ginny heard Ben yell once, just once, and then she
had to grab Button and hold her and crouch down until
the land settled.

Until the world settled in its next new place.

The fire crew had to stop while the world shook but no
more cracks appeared in the earth and as soon as things
settled Don ordered his crew forward.

They topped the rise and saw the ruins of Henry's
home. A great sheet of roofing iron was ripped almost
all the way along and on top of it a woman was tearing
at it with her bare hands.

Ginny.

'They're in there,' she screamed at them as Don and
his crew reached her. 'Henry and Ben. Ben… The iron's
come down. Get it off them. Please, get it off them. I
can't bear it. Oh, Ben… Oh, Ben, my love, no…'

* * *

If it hadn't been for the dust they would have been fine.
Or sort of fine. The world gave a giant heave, the mass
of iron and debris above them rolled and shook and
shuddered, there was momentary pressure on Ben's
chest that took his breath away but then the iron shifted
again and the pressure eased—and the heaving stopped.

He was fine except the torch had rolled somewhere
out of reach, beaming a useless stream of light into un-
reachable darkness. The air was clogged with a dust so
thick he couldn't breathe and Henry was rasping with
ever-decreasing strength.

What was it they said in planes? Fit your own mask
first and then help others around you?

First make a mask.

He was trying to haul his shirt off but there wasn't
enough room to manoeuvre. He needed to rip the thing
and who would have guessed how strong shirts were?
Note: remember to buy cheaper ones. He couldn't get
his hands apart wide enough to wrench it.

He had a sudden flash of memory of Ginny's shirt
ripping…how many hours ago?

Ginny.

Above him he could hear her sobbing, ripping away
at the tin, her voice filled with terror. He wanted to reassure her, to tell her he'd be fine, but he wasn't yet. It
was so hard to breathe.

Finally the shirt gave way, and he wrenched again,
hauling the arms off so he had two long strips and large
panels front and back.

What followed was more ripping and then wriggling
in the darkness, trying to get cloth on his face and the
sleeves around to tie his makeshift mask on. But when

he did, the relief was almost instant. The appalling, clogging muck was kept out by the barrier.

Now for Henry.

'Ben? Henry?' Ginny was screaming from above but there was no way he could use precious air to call back. He had to get closer to Henry. He had to.

He heaved himself forward, risked bringing the entire sheet of rubble down on them, but he had no choice. Before it had simply been enough to reach Henry, to get the drugs to his arm, but now he had to get to his face; he had to fit a mask. The drugs he'd given him would depress his breathing still more.

He was hauling at the rubble, pushing forward—and miraculously something moved, gave and he could pull himself the last foot forward and feel Henry's head.

'Mate…Henry?'

He got no answer—Henry's entire focus was on his weak, rasping breaths.

'Help me, Henry,' Ben managed, and swept a handful of dust from the old man's face and somehow managed to get the back of his shirt across it. He was clearing Henry's mouth, shifting muck the old man was clearly unable to shift himself. 'Breathe through the cloth. Breathe…'

'They're coming, Ben, they're coming,' Ginny called from above, and he gave up trying to tie Henry's mask in place. It was too hard. He didn't have enough breath left himself. He simply lay full length in the filth and held Henry's makeshift mask in position and willed Henry to keep on living.

Ginny'd tell them where he was. Ginny'd bring in the troops.

Ginny…

The thought of her up there in the sunlight was his one true thing. He thought of her again as she'd been at eight years old, standing in tadpole territory, and he thought how he'd decided he had been stupid asking her to marry him when he'd been seventeen.

He should have asked when he was eight.

'Just keep breathing, mate,' he told Henry. 'Just keep on breathing, one breath after another. Over and over. Breathe, breathe, breathe, because Ginny's up there waiting for us, and I, for one, have unfinished business with the lady. I suspect she loves us both and, dammit, I suspect if we die she'll blame herself. She's dumb like that, but there it is. For Ginny's sake, we keep on breathing.'

Don's crew consisted of eight emergency workers, tough, work-ready men and women who were trained to cope with stuff just like this, a few who'd been in earthquakes before, who understood about risk and urgency. This was no massive collapse of stone. It simply needed strength, skill and the right equipment, all of which they had.

Ginny had been trying to haul sheets of iron back from where she'd last heard voices. Don put her aside, snapped a few incisive questions and then set his crew to work.

In less than five minutes the vast sheets of tin were rolling back, exposing what was beneath.

What was there was a massive pile of rubble, dust, grit—and two prone bodies, one almost completely covering the other.

For one appalling moment Ginny thought they were both dead. She'd backed to the edge of the ruin to give the guys space to move but she hadn't been able to take her eyes from what was being exposed.

Two bodies...

And then one raised his head, revealing a makeshift mask and a face so caked in dust it was unrecognisable. But, of course, she recognised it.

Ben.

'I'm fine,' he said in a voice that wasn't the least bit fine; it was the merest croak through the mask. 'And I reckon Henry'll be okay, too, once we get this piano off his leg.'

And miraculously there was a grunt of agreement from Henry.

Ben was hauled to safety first. They tugged him to his feet, he staggered but then stood, unhurt, whole.

Ginny started breathing again. She hadn't been aware she'd stopped but her body sucked in air like she'd been drowning.

Ben. Safe.

He didn't come to her. Instead, he watched as four strong men, one at each corner of the piano, acting in unison, lifting the thing clear. And Henry was out, free.

There was stuff to do. Somehow she shifted into doctor mode, adding to Ben's in-the-dark care, setting up IV lines while Ben snapped orders to keep Henry's spine steady, watch for his hips and beware of a possible broken pelvis as they transferred him to a rigid stretcher to carry him back across the ruins.

But Henry was giving sleepy directions himself. 'When are you going to get a tarp here to cover this? There's stuff here worth saving. Be careful of that piano.'

And Ginny knew, she just knew, that he'd be fine.

Finally, finally there was time for Ben to turn to her, for Ben to take her in his arms, to hug her close.

'About time,' Henry said weakly from his stretcher. 'We've only been waiting twelve years for this to happen.'

There was laughter, filled with relief, but Ginny hardly heard it. Ben had her in his arms, against his heart. Her world folded into his; into him. Heart against heart.

He kissed her hair and then he tilted her chin and he kissed her on the mouth, a full, public proclamation that this was his woman, his love.

She melted into him. This proclamation was okay by her. What were her qualms anyway? Last night had been the beginning of the rest of her life. Why had she ever thought she wasn't brave enough to start again?

How could she not when that start was Ben?

There was slow clapping. Somehow they broke apart and found everyone was looking at them, cheering, and Henry was even leading the clapping from his stretcher.

Ben smiled and smiled at her. Her love. Her Ben.

And then he looked around, still smiling, and said, 'Where's Button?'

She'd forgotten Button. In the midst of her terror her thoughts hadn't swerved from the two men fighting for their lives in the ruins. When the second tremor had hit she'd almost thrown Button into the Jeep. She'd said stay, and she'd run.

But now…

She was standing in the arms of Ben, who was safe, safe, safe, and a little girl who depended solely on her was no longer where she'd left her.

Ginny was no longer in Ben's arms. She was staring wildly around her.

'Button!' Her yell sounded out over the valley, echoing back and back and back.

The Jeep was empty. She stared back at the ruins. Surely she would have seen… If Button had come anywhere near the ruins, she would have noticed.

She should have noticed. What sort of a mother…?

The cliff…

But Ben was before her.

'Button's missing,' he snapped to the team around him. 'Four years old. Priority one.'

Triage… When faced with an emergency, take time to assess then look at worst-case scenarios first. That meant no matter who was yelling, who was bleeding, you took the time to assess, see the guy with the grey face clutching his chest, know that even though it might simply be shock and bruising you checked that out first.

So head for worst-case scenarios first. The worst scenario was that Button was buried under the debris…but maybe it wasn't. Because Ben was turning away from the ruin and striding—no, running—towards the cliff.

The cliff. Dear God.

Below was the sea, fascinating, awesome for a little girl who had no sense of danger.

Ginny gave a sob of terror and followed, but Ben was before her.

He reached the edge.

'Here,' he snapped back at them. 'She's slipped down a bit but there's a ledge. Button, don't move. Sweetheart, I want you to play statues, don't move at all. I'm coming down.'

And just as he said it a tiny tremor, the vaguest hint

of an aftershock, rocked the world. It may have been tiny but it was too much for what must have already been a weakened stretch of headland.

A crack opened between Ginny and Ben. A tiny crack, but it was widening.

Ben gave a yell of warning. 'Ginny, stay where you are.'

And then he slid over the edge of the cliff, helpless, as the crack widened still further and the land seemed to slide toward the sea.

What did you do when your life crumpled before your eyes?

Nothing?

There was nothing she could do. She stood numb with shock and terror while around her men and women leapt into action.

They'd been in earthquakes before? Disasters? They must have been for instead of standing like useless idiots they had ropes out of the truck, they were gearing up with harnesses and shackles, and Don was edging out to where the edge of the cliff was a crumpling mess of loose dirt.

Someone was holding onto her, a woman who seemed just as competent as the men but whose job, obviously, was to keep her out of harm's way.

'We're belaying down,' she told Ginny. 'Hold on, love, Don's good. If anyone can reach them, he can.'

The world held its breath. There was no way anyone else could go near the edge—the headland was still crumbling, and another tremor could hit at any moment.

Don edged out, slowly, slowly. Dirt was breaking away as he moved, but he was testing the footing each

time before putting his weight on it. He was safe; they'd
fastened the rope onto the Jeep and the crew was guid-
ing it to keep it steady but the last thing they wanted
was to cause further collapse.

And then Don was over the edge and lower, lower.

'They're here.' His voice crackled through the radio.
'Send down two harnesses, a big 'un and a little 'un.
The kid looks okay and Ben's holding her. Ben's shoved
Button against the cliff face. He looks in pain—he's hit
something but he's conscious. He's kept her safe from
the landfall. Harnesses fast would be good. It'd be a bit
of a waste to lose them now.'

A bit of bruising and confusion—that was Button.

One fractured pelvis—that was Henry.

Pain, dropping blood pressure, possible internal injuries, that was Ben. Ginny set up IV lines, gave him
pain relief, tried desperately to be a doctor rather than
a woman whose man was in mortal danger.

They called in the chopper, and Dave, the doctor
Ginny had met the night before, came with it. Dave took
over from Ginny, examining Ben fast, concurring with
what she thought—or hoped. Was it foolish to hope for
the best? 'Query ruptured spleen,' Dave barked into the
radio—there were directives to take them straight to
Auckland—and then there was nothing Ginny could
do but hold Button and try to stop shaking.

'Take Ginny down to the med centre,' Dave told the
team as the chopper prepared to take off. 'She'll need
something for shock.'

'I don't,' Ginny said as she watched the chopper lift.
She'd said goodbye to Henry—and to Ben—but it had
all been done in such a rush there'd been no time to

talk. Ben had taken her hand and gripped hard, but she wasn't sure if it had been need or pain making him hold on so tight.

She wanted, so much, to go with him, but her priority had to be Button.

She'd forgotten Button once. Not again.

She felt sick to the depths of her soul.

'You idiot.' She heard James's voice echo back to her, words that had been said over and over in their marriage. 'You don't have the brains you were born with.'

She stood in the morning sun and let the words play and replay.

It was her fault that Ben could be so hurt.

Even Henry... She should have insisted he stay with her at the vineyard. She should have...

'Come on, Ginny, let's get you down to the hospital,' Don said, and she shook her head.

'I'm fine,' she said dully. 'No thanks to me, but Button and I are okay. I can still drive. Thank you all for your care, but I need to manage by myself.'

'On a scale of one to ten, how bad's the pain?' Dave asked Ben as the chopper headed out over the sea.

'Eleven,' Ben said morosely, and then at Dave's look of alarm he shook his head. 'Sorry. Seven, I guess, so, yes, I would like a top-up. There's just a few more things going on.'

'Like leaving his lady,' Henry said from beside him. They'd set both patients up with headphones so they could speak to each other. 'He'll be feeling bad because of Ginny.'

'Ginny seems okay,' Dave said, startled. 'She's a competent woman.'

'Yeah, she's a competent woman and a fine doctor,' Ben managed through his pain. 'But the lady has demons. I thought I'd slayed enough of them to break through, but something tells me Henry and I have conjured up a whole lot more.'

She drove carefully back into town, filling her mind with plans, figuring how she needed to get the house inspected and repaired, get the manager's residence liveable for Henry, persuade Henry to stay, get her and Button back to the vineyard.

Her list was vast, and she concentrated on it fiercely, because if she didn't concentrate, fears broke in. As well as that, the voices flooded back, accusing, and it was too hard to cope with.

She'd had a whole lifetime of not being good enough, and she was weary to the bone.

'I am good enough,' she said out loud, finally cracking and letting the voices hold sway. Trying to defend herself by facing them down. 'I will look after Button. I will.'

'And that's all,' she added in a less fierce voice, a voice that was an acknowledgment that she couldn't fight failure on more than one front. 'That's all I'm focussing on. I might love Ben. I might even love medicine, but I stuff things up and I won't risk it any further. I'll help Ben with emergency medicine until he finds someone else but that's all. It's Button and the vineyard and nothing else.'

CHAPTER TEN

A WEEK LATER Ben went out to the vineyard to find her. When he arrived Ginny was hammering boards onto the veranda of the vineyard manager's residence. Button had a hammer as well and was banging everything in sight. Ginny paused in her hammering as the car approached, but Button kept right on going.

His mother had driven him up from the town. She paused at the gate—there seemed to be unstable ground along the driveway and she wasn't risking driving further—and looked at the woman and child in front of them.

'You sure you want to do this? Do you want me to wait?' she asked.

'Nope,' he said. 'Ginny will drive me back.'

'You might have trouble getting her out of here,' Ailsa said worriedly. 'Okay, it's not the shaky ground I'm worried about. I know you can go cross-country. But she's wounded and retreating, Ben. More wounded even than you are.'

'What, worse than a ruptured spleen?'

'You don't have a spleen any more and Ginny still has her wounds,' Ailsa said sternly. 'Her father was a bully and a thug, and her mother was appalling. I know you love her but even when she was a kid I could see her shadows. From what I hear, her marriage has just meant longer ones.'

'I can cope with shadows,' Ben said, but uneasily because he wasn't sure that he could.

'Good luck,' his mother said, and leaned across and kissed him before he climbed out of the truck, carrying his grandfather's old walking cane for support. His ruptured spleen had been removed by laparoscopic surgery, he was recovering nicely but he'd been bruised just about everywhere it was possible for a man to be bruised. His mother had been fussing, and maybe she had cause.

'Give me a ring if you don't get anywhere,' she said now, and glanced ahead at Ginny. 'You might need more than a walking stick to get through this pain.'

'If I travelled by helicopter to Auckland with a ruptured spleen, I can get through anything,' Ben said, but Ailsa still looked doubtful as she drove away.

Ginny had seen him arrive. She'd started walking towards them, pausing to fetch Button. It seemed Button wasn't to be allowed out of her sight.

She stopped coming towards him when Ailsa drove away.

'H-hi,' she managed, and then the doctor part of her took over. 'Surely you shouldn't be out here, walking. I... Can I get you a chair?'

'I'm fine,' Ben said, and then they both looked at the walking stick. 'And I'm tough,' he said, like he was convincing himself. He managed a grin. 'Chairs are for wusses. Thanks for the flowers.'

'They were...the least I could do.'

'And you always do the least you can do? That's Hannah's line, not yours.'

They were twenty yards apart. It was slow going with his walking stick—he had a corked thigh that was still giving him hell a week after the event—and Ginny had stopped and wasn't coming any closer. 'I thought you might visit,' he said. 'I sort of hoped.'

'I phoned.'

'To enquire. And then didn't ask to be put through. Coward.'

'On the card I said I was sorry,' Ginny managed. 'There didn't seem anything else to say. I *am* sorry, Ben. I can't say more than that. So why would you want to see me?'

'To ask you to marry me.'

Marry...

The word was huge. The word was impossible, Ben thought as he watched all the colour drain from her face. Maybe his plan to put it all out there hadn't been such a good idea after all.

'Ben...'

'What happened wasn't your fault,' he said. 'Nothing's your fault. You're my Ginny and I'm your Ben. Bad things happen but whenever they do, we face them together.'

'You wouldn't want to share...my bad things.'

'Ginny...'

'I always get it wrong,' she blurted out. 'I try and try but it never turns out right. Even Button...I'm so scared of caring for Button. I know she has no choice. I know she needs me, but she'd be so much better with someone who can love without messing things up.'

'That sounds...' He sorted his words carefully, fighting for the right ones. 'As if you're seriously thinking of stepping away.'

'I can't,' she said. 'Not from Button.'

'And from me?'

'Yes,' she said. 'From you.' It was a bald, harsh statement, and he thought suddenly of the harsh things Ginny had said to him when she'd been seventeen, and how he'd believed her and had let her go.

It'd be easier to be a caveman, he thought suddenly. It'd be over the shoulder, a bit of manly exercise lugging her back to his lair and he'd have her for the rest of her life. But now...he had to make her see sense.

'Do you love me?' He asked it like it was the most natural question in the world, like it was totally reasonable for a guy who ought to be in bed to lean on his walking stick in the midday sun and wait for an answer to a question of such import that it took his breath away.

But there'd never be a better time to say it, he thought.

Maybe there'd never be a good time to say it.

He watched the doubts flash across her face, the fear, and he drove his advantage.

'Yes, my first question was marriage,' he conceded. 'That didn't get me anywhere, so let's try this from a different angle. No lies, Ginny. Do you love me?'

'Too...too much,' she whispered.

He nodded. 'As a matter of interest, did you love me when I was seventeen?'

'Yes, but—'

'So what Henry told me was true. We shared a ward in Auckland and he told me. You tossed me over because your old man made threatening noises about my career.'

'He shouldn't have told—'

'Henry shouldn't have told me?'

'No.'

It was too much, he thought. He was aching all over. She was standing there in her faded jeans, dirty from pruning grapes, holding Button's hand, and she was just as unattainable as she'd been at seventeen. Dammit, did she really expect him to walk away?

'Henry shouldn't have told?' Suddenly he was practically shouting—okay, he was shouting, and he might frighten Button but Button looked interested rather than scared. 'Henry shouldn't have told? What about you? Why didn't you say it like it was and we could have faced it down together? You don't need to fight shadows yourself. Think about the immorality of your father's threats. Think about the sheer cowardly bullying of your husband, the guy who's making you shrink now and look like a scared rabbit because somehow you think it's all your fault that I'm angry. Do you love me, Ginny?'

'Yes, but—'

'Then that's all I need right now,' he said grimly. 'Go take a shower. We're going to a funeral.'

'Ben…'

'If you think I'm letting you lock yourself away all over again, you have another think coming,' he snapped. 'I shouldn't be here. I'm incapable of driving. I'm walking wounded standing in your driveway and I promised Squid that I'd speak at his funeral.' He glanced at his watch. 'In forty minutes from now. So Hannah's meeting us at the church to take care of Button and you're going to get yourself into something a wee bit cleaner and then you're driving me to the funeral. And then you're coming in with me, Ginny, like it or not. You're part of this island. I need you, Ginny.'

And then he softened as he saw her face. She looked like a deer trapped in headlights, but he wouldn't—he couldn't—let her walk away.

'I can't do this alone, Ginny,' he said, and he held out his hand. 'One step at a time. I won't talk marriage. I won't even push the love bit, but I will push belonging. Squid knew you as an islander, as do I. You were with us when we needed you most. This is to say farewell to one of us. Ginny, come with me, just for now.'

'You mean you come with me,' she said with an attempt at humour. 'I appear to have the only set of wheels here.'

'That's why I need you, Ginny, love,' he said. 'That and about fifty other reasons and a lot more besides. Come on, love, it's a date you can't refuse. Let's go and say goodbye to Squid.'

She sat in a pew at the back of the crowded church. Ailsa squashed in with her and gave her a swift hug.

'Ben's been asked to do the eulogy,' she said. 'He and Squid were friends. He's feeling it.'

And she fell silent as if she was feeling it, too, and Ginny was left with her own thoughts.

Love? Marriage?

She'd just hurt him, as she'd hurt him already.

That had been her cowardice talking. That had been the shades of her parents and James.

But to hurt someone else…to expose Ben to mistakes she'd inevitably make? How could she do that?

Ailsa's hand gripped hers.

'He loves you with all his heart,' she whispered. 'Go on, Ginny, love, jump.'

Was she so obvious? She dredged up a half-hearted smile as they rose for the first hymn.

Jump? And that was all she had to do. Jump, dragging Ben with her. And what was at the base of that leap?

The hymn ended. Ben was in front of the congregation, in front of the plain, wooden coffin, holding a sheet of paper before him. 'Squid asked me to speak today,' he said, and her heart turned over. 'And everyone here knows Squid. He liked to predict what would happen so he made sure. He wrote this just before the earthquake, just in case, telling me exactly what to say.'

There was a ripple of laughter, and then the room fell silent. Squid had been an ancient fisherman, a constant presence on the waterfront since childhood, and the island would be the poorer for his going. Besides, who would predict disaster now?

'It wasn't my fault.'

Ben's first words—Squid's first words—hauled Ginny from nostalgia and regret. They were her words, she thought in confusion—or maybe they weren't.

She'd spent a childhood trying to desperately defend herself with those words—*it wasn't my fault*—only to learn it was easier to appease and accept.

It was my fault.

'"Me heart's been giving me trouble for a couple of years now",' Ben read, following faithfully the script on the page. Unconsciously, his voice even sounded a little like Squid's. '"Doc's been telling me I ought to go to mainland to get one of those valve replacement thingies but, sheesh, I'm ninety-seven—I might be even older when you hear this—and who wants stuff inside you that don't belong.

"'So I'm sitting on the wharf enjoying me last days in the sun and I'm starting to tell all you fellas there's a big 'un coming. An earthquake. Be good if it did, I'm thinking, only to prove me right, but I sort of hope I'm wrong. Only then I'm reading in the papers there's two scientist fellas somewhere who are in jail because they didn't predict an earthquake and I reckon the world's gone mad. If I'm wrong then it's my fault? If I'm right is it my fault 'cos I didn't yell at you louder? Fault. Like Doc telling me I need a new valve. Is it his fault I'm lying in this damned coffin?'"

There was a ripple of uneasy laughter through the church. Ginny had heard the island whispers, and sometimes the voices had risen higher than whispers. 'Someone should have warned us. Who can we sue?'

She thought of James, apoplectic with fury because she'd tried to inject a drug he'd needed and had had trouble finding a vein. Lashing out at her. 'It's your fault I'm in this mess.'

It was totally irrational, but blame was a powerful tool. When all else failed, find someone to blame.

"'You want me to cop it so you'll all feel better?'" Squid—Ben—said from the pulpit. "'No way. That's what I want to say here. That's the reason I didn't ask to get wrapped in a tarp and tipped over the side of me fishing boat out at sea before I'd had this nice little ceremony. I reckon if I'm right about the quake and it sets me ticker off—and I know it might—you might be sitting here shaking your fist at me coffin, saying the mad old coot caused this mess.

"'So I just wanted to say stuff it, no one causes earthquakes so don't dare stop drinking beer at me wake if it's happened. I want a decent wake and I want you to pour a bit of beer over me coffin and then toss me out to sea with no regrets and say I'm done. Great life. Great times. Great island. Merv Larkin, notes on me snapper spot are written on the back of the calendar of me dunny. That's it, then. There's me legacy. See you."'

Ben paused then. There were more ripples of laughter but Ginny still heard the odd murmur. There had been blame. Ben was watching calmly as islanders elbowed each other.

She knew the mutterings. 'If Squid knew, why didn't he say just how bad it'd be? Why didn't he talk to the mainland scientists, shove it down their throats, get official warnings out?'

'He really didn't know.' It was Ben now, Ben speaking his own words, and suddenly he was looking at Ginny. Straight at Ginny. He was smiling faintly, and suddenly she knew that his smile was meant only for her.

'A hundred years of living, and you know what Squid knew for sure?' Ben said. 'That no one knows a sausage. We can make guesses and we make them all the time. I'll cross this road because chances are a meteor's not going to drop on my head. That's a guess. It's a pretty good guess, and Squid's earthquake prediction was a pretty good guess, too, backed up by a hundred years of Squid's grandpa telling him the signs. But, still, unless Squid got underground and heaved, it wasn't his fault.

'Meteors are sitting over everyone's head and one day they'll drop, nothing surer, and we just need to accept it. Anyway that's all I need to say except we were blessed to have Squid. We should have no regrets except that even though he's left his snapper spots, his best crayfish spots die with him. We loved him, he drove us nuts and we'll miss him. That's pretty much all we need to say, except he left enough money for everyone to have a beer or a whisky on him. Bless him.'

There was laughter, but this time it wasn't uncomfortable. There was the odd sniff and the organist belted out a mighty rendition of what must surely be the island's favourite hymn by the strength of the island voices raised in farewell.

And then six weathered fishermen led by a limping Ben carried the coffin from the church, the hearse carried the coffin down to the wharf because after all this he would be buried at sea—and then the island proceeded to the pub.

'Shall we join them?' Ailsa asked, and Ginny realised Ailsa had been holding her hand all the time. Even while singing.

As if Ginny was her daughter?

She wasn't this woman's daughter.

She could be.

Courage.

'I'm a wimp,' she said softly, and Ailsa followed her gaze to where Ben was talking to the pallbearers while they watched the hearse drive slowly through the still rubble-strewn streets down to the harbour.

'You trusted,' Ailsa said. 'You trusted your father and you trusted your husband. It's no fault to trust, child. But you know Ben would never hurt you.'

'It's not that. I just…mess things up.'

'Like Squid messed the island up,' Ailsa said briskly. 'Nonsense. You want to take that attitude, then you are a wimp. Get a grip, girl, go for what you want and stand up for yourself. Now, you want to head for the pub for a bit of Dutch courage? Squid's prepaid for the very best beer—and whisky all round.'

'I need to think,' Ginny said, and Ailsa shook her head and tugged her forward.

'Nonsense, girl. You need to belong.'

CHAPTER ELEVEN

BEN AND THE pallbearers accompanied the coffin out to sea. Ginny headed to the pub and ordered a glass of Squid's excellent whisky but only one, she told herself, because she really did have some thinking to do.

Serious thinking.

She was an accepted part of the island, she thought. No one looked askance at her; in fact, she was being treated with affection.

'Word is you've had a rough time of it,' one of the farmers who lived beyond her vineyard said. 'Doc says we're to leave you be, no pressure, but don't you bury yourself too long, girl. We need you.'

'I know the island needs a doctor...'

'Not just that,' the man said. 'I know this sounds dumb but you're an islander. You always seemed one, not like your mum and dad, but even when you were a little tacker it was like you were coming home every time you came here. And we don't like losing islanders.'

He stared into his beer and gave a rueful smile. 'We don't even like losing ninety-seven-year-olds who smell like smoked mackerel and prophesy doom. We'll miss him, like we're missing you, girl. Doctor or not, this is your home.'

There wasn't a lot she could say after a speech like that. She hadn't brought enough tissues. Dratted funerals. Dratted islanders.

Dratted Ben.

She took her whisky and escaped out through the beer garden, through the back gate she and Ben had sneaked through when they had been under age, then out along the path that led to the island's best swimming beach.

It had barely been damaged by the quake. A few rocks had rolled down the gentle slope but the path was fine. She headed down, slipped off her shoes and went and sat on a rock and stared out to sea. Towards the mainland.

You're an islander.

She was crying good and proper now. There weren't enough tissues in the world for how she was crying, and she didn't care.

She didn't cry. Until she'd come back to the island she'd never cried. Not once, not at her father's funeral, not once when James had been diagnosed and died. So why was crying now?

Who knew? She didn't. She was so out of control she felt like she was falling, and when Ben sat down beside her and put his arm around her and pulled her into him, she had no strength to pull away.

She was falling and he was the only thing stopping her.

He took the whisky glass carefully out of her hand—the thing was half-full and one part of her still acknowledged it was excellent whisky and Squid would probably haunt her if she spilled it. Ben set it on the rock beside them, and then he carefully turned her towards him and tugged her into his arms.

'I...I'm soggy,' she managed, and it was almost impossible to get that much out.

'You're allowed to cry at funerals.'

'I don't.'

'Because you're not allowed to?'

'I don't cry. I won't cry,' she said, and cried some more, and the front of his shirt was soaked and she was being ridiculous and she couldn't stop.

'I'm...I'm sorry...'

'Ginny...' He hauled back from her then, held her at arm's length, and his face was suddenly as grim as death. 'Don't.'

'Don't...'

'Don't you dare apologise,' he snapped. 'Not once. You know what you did when I sank your bathtub?'

'I threw...I threw mud at you.' How did people speak through tears? It looked so elegant in the movies—here it felt like she was talking through a snorkel.

'And very appropriate it was, too,' Ben said, the sternness replaced by the glimmer of a smile. 'And then?'

'And then you said if I didn't tell your mum what you'd done, you'd give me your best taddy—the one that looked like it'd be a bullfrog to beat all bullfrogs.'

'A supreme sacrifice,' he said nobly. 'And I watched you care for him and skite about him to the other kids...'

'I did not skite!'

'You skited. And then I watched you let him go—my bullfrog—and I swear he or his descendants are around here still, thinking they owe their whole family lineage to you. That pond was full of ducks. He'd have been a goner but you were his lifesaver and not me. You know what? I should have just said sorry and kept the bullfrog for myself. But I didn't feel sorry. I felt...' He smiled at her then, a killer smile that had wobbled her heart when at eight years old and was wobbling her heart still.

'I felt like it was the way things were,' he said. 'I covered you with mud so you got to raise my bullfrog. But you know what? I loved watching you raise my bullfrog. There wasn't a single bit of sorry left in there.'

'Ben...'

'If we married,' he said, and the smile had gone again. 'That's what I'd want. Not one single bit of sorry.'

'You can't want to marry me,' she whispered. 'To take me on with all my baggage. To help raise another man's child...'

'It's like the bullfrog,' he said softly. 'You'd give your baggage to me and I'd take it on and you'd watch me care for it and it'd be like caring for it yourself. That's the way I see it. That's the way it's always been for us, Ginny. Not a single sorry between us, now and for ever.'

'But I hurt you.'

'And I pressured you. Pushing a seventeen-year-old to marry me... We both needed a life before we settled down. It seems like I've had a happier one—I've had some very nice girlfriends, thank you very much, all of whom sound nicer than your creepier James, but I'd prefer if you don't ask me about them, and you can tell me as much or as little about James as you want. All I'll tell you about my girlfriends is that not a single one of them would have raised my tadpole into the fine specimen of a bullfrog he turned out to be. So no sorry, Ginny. Get every tear you need to shed, shed them now and then move forward.'

She couldn't talk. What was it with tears? If she was Audrey Hepburn she'd have whisked away the last tear-drop from her beautiful eyelashes and would now be fluttering said eyelashes up at her love.

Where were tissues?

'Here,' Ben said, and handed over a man-sized hand-kerchief.

'A handkerchief,' she said, sidetracked. 'A handker-chief?'

'I never go to a funeral without one,' he said. 'You'll note the left-hand corner is already a little doggy.'

She choked and he tugged her close again and then he simply held her; he held her and held her until fi-nally she sort of dried up and she sort of pulled herself together and she sort of thought...that this was okay.

That this was where she belonged.

That this was home.

But to let go of the baggage of years? To let go of sorry?

'If you're still harping on sorry, then I see your duty is to catch me a very big tadpole for a wedding gift,' Ben said, putting her away from him again.

And she choked again. 'How did you know what I was thinking?'

'I just do. I always did. Like you know me, my love. You know we fit. Maybe it's time we acknowledged it.'

'Button...Button might like to be a flower girl,' she said, and his face stilled.

'I didn't know you were thinking that.'

'I'm thinking all sorts of things,' she admitted. 'So many things you can't possibly keep up.'

'So one of them might be that you'd marry me?'

'Only if I can get braver.'

'You're brave already,' he said steadily. 'You took Button on without a backward look. You didn't walk away from James, no matter how he treated you. It's not bravery that's missing, my love. It's the ability to stand over a smashed vase or a broken leg or a patient we lost no matter how we worked to save him and say, "This is life." That's all it is, life. It'll throw bad things at us, you and I both know that, but it'll also throw joy. Joy, joy and more joy if you'll marry me.'

'Ben—'

'You weren't responsible for James' death. You know that,' he said. 'Say it.'

'I wasn't responsible.'

'Or for your father's death or for his disappointment that you didn't win the Nobel Prize before he died.'

'I guess…'

'And your mother's appalling disappointment that you turned out not to be blonde.'

'Hey, I wouldn't go that far,' she said, suddenly realising her tears had gone. She wasn't sure what was taking their place—some emotion she'd never felt before. Liberation?

Freedom?

'It was a heinous crime not to be blonde,' she managed, and Ben grinned.

'Yes, it was. So can you stand in the dock, look your accusers in the face and say it wasn't your fault?'

'I guess.'

'You want to have fun?'

'Fun,' she said, and the word was weird. Foreign.

'I'm not marrying you unless you turn back into the Ginny I knew,' he said. He motioned to the gently sloping rise behind the beach. The earthquake had shaken free a great swathe of loose, soft sand. It looked…sort of poised.

Poised to slide straight down the slope into the shallows beneath it.

'The Ginny I know would ride that slope,' Ben said.

'I'd get wet.'

'You're already soggy.'

'So I am.' She looked at him, her gorgeous, kind, clever Ben, her love who'd magically waited for her for all this time, who'd made her see what she should have been yelling at the top of her lungs for years.

'I believe I'm about to burst a few chains,' she said, and Ben looked startled.

'Pardon?'

'You don't know what you're getting into. If it's not my fault I'll break cups all over the place. And…' she eyed the sandy slope thoughtfully '…I'll get sand in my knickers. But I won't do it alone.'

'I don't want you to do anything alone any more,' he said, and then added a hasty rider. 'Within reason. It seems to me you've been on your own all your life. You hook up with me, you have a whole island. We're part of a community but we're a team. You and me, Dr Koestrel. Together for ever.'

'Prove it,' she said, and he blinked.

'What?'

'Remember all those years ago when I wanted to be your friend. Prove it, you said, by rowing this bathtub all the way across the pond.'

'Haven't we moved on from that?'

'Maybe you have,' she said. 'But I'm still wary. See this slope? It's gentle sand—a gentle slope. It shouldn't hurt someone who had his surgery laprascopically and I'll kiss the bruises. Together or nothing, Dr McMahon.'

'I'll get sand in *my* knickers.'

'Yes, you will,' she said serenely, because suddenly she was serene. She was happy, she thought incredulously. She was totally, awesomely happy. She was in love, in love, in love, and miraculously the man she loved was smiling at her, loving her right back, and all she was asking was that he slide on a little sand for her.

She thought of the impossibility of asking either of her parents to do such a thing, or James, and she wondered why she hadn't seen it? The fault had never been in her. It had been in them. They'd chosen the wrong daughter, the wrong wife. Their perfect daughter, perfect wife was maybe out there somewhere but it wasn't her, and whoever it was who wanted to be blonde and perfect and servile, well, good luck to them. It wasn't her.

'Slide or nothing,' she said.

'You will kiss the bruises? Slide and everything?' Ben asked, and that gorgeous twinkle was back, the twinkle she'd first met twenty years ago, the Ben twinkle, of mischief, life and laughter.

'Everything,' she said, and turned and headed up the sand bank, and she knew he'd follow.

And he did.

Two minutes later two very wet, very sandy doctors emerged from a shallow wave, laughing and spluttering, and Ben was holding Ginny and Ginny was holding Ben, and she knew that here was her home.

Here was her love. Her life. Her whole.

And then—after all the bruises had been very satisfactorily kissed and a few other places besides—because it seemed like the right time, the right place, the right everything, Ben took Ginny's hand and led her back to the pub. Squid's wake was just starting to wind up but most of the islanders were still there.

They turned to stare in amazement at the picture of the two sodden island doctors, Ben's suit dripping, Ginny even wearing a bit of seaweed.

They stood in the doorway and Ben held Ginny's hand tightly while the voices faded and every eye was on them.

'We have an announcement to make,' Ben said to the whole pub, the whole island, the whole world. 'I'd like to tell everyone who's listening that Ginny has just agreed to marry me. And, Squid, if you're listening up there, no, it's not your fault but you lent a hand. The lady loves me, ladies and gentleman, and the next ceremony on this island's going to be a wedding.'

And so it was.

Ginny's wedding to James had taken place in Sydney's biggest cathedral, with a luxury reception in a lush ballroom overlooking Sydney Harbour.

Ginny's wedding to Ben took place in the small island chapel where they'd said goodbye to Squid, and the reception took place on the beach.

Simple, Ginny had decreed, but she didn't quite have her way. The islanders prepared a party to end all parties. Ailsa made her a dress that was breathtakingly lovely, with a sweetheart neckline, a cinched waist and a skirt that flowed out in a full circle if she spun.

And she did spin, as Ben took her into his arms and proceeded to jive instead of doing a bridal waltz.

'You can't waltz on sand,' he decreed, and she didn't think she could jive on sand either, but it seemed she could.

And did.

So did Button, dressed in a gorgeous pink dress the same style as Ginny's, jiving along with Henry, who was enjoying himself very much indeed. He was back living in the manager's residence at the vineyard now, pottering in the vineyard, falling in love with Button, deeply content with the way life was turning out. Looking forward to Ben and Ginny and Button sharing the big house.

He'd decreed Button was now his family, as was the tiny black and white kitten that followed Button everywhere. As for Button, she was pretty much in heaven. The heart specialist had decided surgery would be necessary to repair a slight abnormality but it could wait, he said. No rush. No drama. For now they could settle into what they were.

Family.

The islanders had lit the campfire to beat all campfires. Dusk was settling into night. The local band was playing its collective heart out, there was enough food for a small army, people were dancing, singing, gossiping, rolling tired children in rugs and settling them to sleep on the sun-warmed sand...

'This'll go on for hours,' Ben said into her ear, and she felt so happy she could melt.

'Let it.'

'But you're my wife,' he said. 'Is it my fault that I want you now?'

'Yes, it is,' she said serenely. 'All your own fault. I take no responsibility.'

He grinned and held her tighter. They danced on, drowsy with love and desire, knowing they had all the time in the world for each other, but there was still this desire to have that time now.

No one looked like going home. No one wanted this party to end.

'Tell you what,' Ben said. 'Why don't we have a medical emergency?'

'An emergency?'

'A serious one,' he said. 'Did you know you can make your own phone ring?' And he twirled her over to a place where the fire torches were less bright, he whirled her round so his bride was between him and any on-lookers—and, lo, his phone rang.

'Uh-huh?' he said in a voice that carried. 'Goodness, that sounds serious. Really? Well, if you say so, we'll be on our way right now.'

He replaced his phone in his jacket pocket and turned to face the bemused islanders—and his bemused and brand-new wife.

'We have an emergency on the other side of the is-land,' Ben said. 'It needs two doctors. Sorry, guys, keep up the party, but you need to excuse…my wife and me.'

There was a ripple of laughter and more than one mutter of disbelief.

'What sort of emergency?' someone yelled.

'Heart,' Ben said promptly. 'You can't mess with hearts.'

'Whose?' someone else yelled.

'Patient confidentiality,' Ben said. 'How can I tell you? All I can say is that it's a multiple problem. Two hearts that need attention. Ginny…Dr Koestrel can care for one, and I'll take the other.'

There was a whoop of delighted laughter. 'You're making that up,' someone else yelled. 'You just want to get away all by yourselves!'

'So what if we do?' Ben said, taking his bride by the hand and then changing his mind and sweeping her into his arms to carry her up the beach, to his waiting Jeep, to the night beyond, to the future together.

'So what if we do?' he said again. 'This is my love and my life. Have you seen my bride? If we did want to get away, all on our own, it's not our fault. It's life, guys. It's life and laughter and love and it's our future, just beyond the campfire. And, fault or not, we're stepping into it, right now.'

* * * * *

ALWAYS THE HERO

BY
ALISON ROBERTS

First published in Great Britain 2013
by Mills & Boon, an imprint of Harlequin (UK) Limited.
Harlequin (UK) Limited, Eton House, 18-24 Paradise Road,
Richmond, Surrey TW9 1SR

© Alison Roberts 2013

ISBN: 978 0 263 89907 8

Harlequin (UK) policy is to use papers that are natural, renewable and recyclable products and made from wood grown in sustainable forests. The logging and manufacturing process conform to the legal environmental regulations of the country of origin.

Printed and bound in Spain
by Blackprint CPI, Barcelona

Dear Reader

I live in Christchurch, New Zealand, and on the 22nd February 2011 our city suffered a catastrophic earthquake. As a paramedic, I was privileged to be within the Red Zone in the early hours and days, but people the world over soon became aware of the heroism of our emergency services like firemen, police officers, paramedics and USAR teams. And not only the professionals. Many of our heroes were ordinary people who just happened to be thrown into extraordinary circumstances.

Disasters bring out the best in the vast majority of people, and I've learned that they can have some other interesting effects. The rate of deaths from heart attacks increases, for instance, but it's balanced by an uncannily similar increase in births. People make big decisions, too, especially about relationships, as the reminder of how precious life is makes us realise what's really important. I heard of many people who made a lifelong commitment to each other in the wake of the Christchurch earthquake.

Marion Lennox and I didn't set our *Earthquake!* duet in Christchurch, for obvious reasons, but we were drawn to explore the emotional repercussions of a natural disaster.

My people, Abby and Tom, certainly needed something earth-shattering to get them back together and make sure it works this time.

I have every confidence that they will have a very happy future.

I hope you'll agree :-)

Happy Reading!

With love

Alison xxx

Alison Roberts lives in Christchurch, New Zealand, and has written over 60 Mills & Boon® Medical Romances™. As a qualified paramedic, she has personal experience of the drama and emotion to be found in the world of medical professionals, and loves to weave stories with this rich background—especially when they can have a happy ending. When Alison is not writing, you'll find her indulging her passion for dancing or spending time with her friends (including Molly the dog) and her daughter, Becky, who has grown up to become a brilliant artist. She also loves to travel, hates housework, and considers it a triumph when the flowers outnumber the weeds in her garden.

Recent titles by Alison Roberts:

NYC ANGELS: AN EXPLOSIVE REUNION~
ST PIRAN'S: THE WEDDING!†
MAYBE THIS CHRISTMAS…?
THE LEGENDARY PLAYBOY SURGEON**
FALLING FOR HER IMPOSSIBLE BOSS**
SYDNEY HARBOUR HOSPITAL: ZOE'S BABY*
ST PIRAN'S: THE BROODING HEART SURGEON†

~*NYC Angels*
***Heartbreakers of St Patrick's Hospital*
**Sydney Harbour Hospital*
†*St Piran's Hospital*

These books are also available in eBook format from www.millsandboon.co.uk

CHAPTER ONE

'WHAT'S SO INTERESTING out there, Abby?'

'Nothing.' Abigail Miller jerked her gaze away from the window, sending an apologetic smile to the young woman who'd asked the question.

It wasn't a completely truthful response. There was a lot to be seen out of the window of this consulting room in Kaimotu Island's medical centre. The modern building that housed the consulting rooms and surgical facilities was attached to the old wooden cottage hospital that had been built many years ago on a prime piece of land.

Being on top of a hill, they had one of the best views—encompassing the township where most of the permanent community lived and the small, sheltered harbour against a backdrop that had ragged bush-covered slopes created by an ancient volcano on one side and a seemingly endless ocean on the other.

She could see a gorgeous, fresh-out-of-the-box April autumn day for one thing, with the intense blue of the sky only surpassed by the deeper blue of the sea. A stunning stretch of golden sand on a beach bordered by huge pohutukawa trees. She could even see the red stars of their flowers, which were unusually long-lasting this

year. She could see people on the main street of the village, stopping to talk to each other as they went about
their tasks for the day, the pace of life here encouraging them to take their time and stop to smell the roses.

It was a view Abby adored but she'd seen it many
times a day for more than five years, now. There was
no excuse to be caught staring out the window during
working hours. Especially right now, when she was in
the middle of a heavy outpatient clinic and the island's
only doctor at the moment, Ben McMahon, was out on
a house call.

She'd been actively trying to persuade mothers to
bring their children to this clinic for weeks, determined
to make sure that every baby and preschool child on the
island was up to date with their vaccinations. She had
a responsibility to keep things moving as efficiently
as possible because she'd hate Ben to come back and
find chaos.

Ruth had her six-week-old baby, Daisy, in her arms
and a very active toddler, Blake, who was trying to
climb up onto the examination couch.

'You want to sit up there?' Abby scooped up the little
boy and sat him on the bed. 'Don't move, okay? We'll
both get into trouble if you fall off.'

Coming up to two years old, Blake was overdue
for his protection against some of the more dangerous
childhood viruses like measles, mumps and chicken-
pox. Baby Daisy was due for her polio drops as well
as an injection. Right now, Blake was grinning up at
Abby but he'd be crying very soon, unfortunately. It was
never enjoyable having to inflict pain on small children,
even if it was for the greater good. Ignoring the ping of
a heartstring, Abby reminded herself that she could at

least cheer the older children up pretty fast with a bright 'I've been brave' sticker and a sugar-free jelly snake.

Maybe that reluctance to inflict pain could explain the procrastination of getting caught by the view.

Except it was more than that. Abby had been the clinic's senior nurse for years now. She was experienced and professional, and personal feelings were not allowed to interfere with her job. What was bothering her so much? She couldn't help another frowning glance outside as she went to the fridge to collect the vaccines she needed.

Ruth removed her breast from Daisy's mouth and got up from her chair to have a look out the window herself, rocking baby Daisy when she started grizzling about having her feed interrupted. A moment later, she was also frowning.

'You're right,' she told Abby. 'Something doesn't feel quite right, does it?'

'You feel it, too?' Abby was holding the small glass vials in her hand, warming them up so the injections might be less painful. 'It's weird, isn't it?'

'There's nothing out there that I can see.'

'No. It's kind of like that feeling you get when you've gone on holiday and you're on the plane and then you suddenly wonder if you've left the iron on, or a tap running or something.'

Ruth laughed. 'Can't say I've ever worried about an iron. We're lucky to get enough hot water from solar power. Clothes stay wrinkly in my house.'

The laughter broke the shared unease.

'My mother used to tell me off for worrying too much,' Abby confessed. 'She said I was a born worry-wart and I was never happy unless I had something to worry about and if there wasn't anything real, I'd just make something up.'

And that was definitely a truthful statement.

Of course she was an expert in the mental game of finding potential causes for a premonition that something bad was going to happen. She'd been doing this kind of thinking since she was three years old. Imagine a disaster, think of every possible reason for it to have happened and then take steps to make sure it *didn't* actually happen.

It was why she'd come to Kaimotu Island in the first place, wasn't it?

Why she hadn't even tried fighting to keep the man she absolutely knew would prove to be the love of her life.

'Maybe it was that earthquake a few weeks ago,' Ruth suggested. 'It was enough to get everybody a bit on edge and old Squid hasn't helped with his forecasting doom and gloom about the "big one" being so imminent. There's a few people upset at the way he chased off the last of the summer tourists.'

Abby laughed. 'And then all we get is that tiny tremor the other day that most people barely noticed. I hear that poor Squid's been getting a hard time about that being the "big one".'

Ruth grinned. 'Squid says they'll all be laughing on the other side of their faces soon enough.'

Abby shook her head. Even the larger of the two tremors had been pretty minor. Certainly not enough to make anyone take any more notice of what the island's oldest fisherman, Squid Davies, had to say about it being a warning of the kind of quake his grandfather had experienced here. It had just been a bit of a rattle.

The kind anyone who'd grown up in New Zealand was familiar with.

'Jack said it was really fun at school the next day. They got to practise their "Drop, Cover and Hold" emergency drill. I think the kids all thought it was just as good as a game of sardines, squeezing in under their desks.'

She snapped off the top of an ampoule and put the needle of a tiny one-mil syringe in to suck up the contents.

'Ahh....' Ruth was nodding. '*That's* what it is.'

'What what is?'

'Why you're on edge and staring out the window so often.'

Abby raised her eyebrows. She was all set to give Daisy her shot now but she stood there for a moment, holding the kidney dish, waiting for Ruth to elaborate.

'Jack's only just started school and he's your only child. I remember what that was like, wondering if anyone else could take care of your baby as well as you could.'

'I've been working since Jack was three. He's been in day care and play groups for half his life, just about.'

'Yeah, but he's off on the big junior school trip today, isn't he? My Brooke and Amber have gone, too. The hike to the shipwreck this morning and then the visit to the old copper mines after the picnic?'

'Mmm.' Abby bit her lip. 'I would have gone as parent help but I'd already organised this clinic and I couldn't postpone it when I was out there trying to persuade everyone to come.'

Ruth was right. Anxiety about her precious little boy

was undoubtedly the cause for her underlying sense of unease.

Abby's sigh was part relief, part exasperation. Enough of this.

She could hear a child crying in the waiting room outside and had to hope people weren't getting too impatient. It would be disappointing if some of them changed their minds about being here after all her hard work of talking to parents at the local schools and playgroups recently. Ben's younger sister Hannah was in charge of keeping them all organised and entertained but there was only so much a seventeen-year-old could do to manage a room full of youngsters.

Ruth was exactly the kind of result Abby had wanted when she'd embarked on this project. Kaimotu Island, being so isolated from the mainland, attracted people who wanted to live an alternative lifestyle and Ruth and her husband Damien lived with their six children in a converted train carriage out on the edge of the bush. They supplemented their self-sufficient lifestyle by making pottery that they sold to the influx of visitors in the summer months.

Totally against the idea of vaccination, Ruth and Damien had had a huge fright last year when one of their older children had needed urgent evacuation to a large hospital after developing complications from measles.

Thank goodness they weren't so isolated that evacuation wasn't a viable option in emergencies. Abby had been in the early stages of pregnancy when she'd first arrived here and potential complications for herself or her baby had been a real worry, to put it mildly. Mix some medical knowledge in with the fervent imagination of a born worrier and obsession was well within grasp.

Reassurance had come from both the impressive skills of the doctor here, Ben McMahon, and how well the clinic was set up to either cope with a serious emergency or stabilise a patient for evacuation. And it wasn't so far by small plane or helicopter. Only a couple of hours. There was usually an abundance of private aircraft available, too, in case the mainland rescue chopper was otherwise engaged.

Thanks to the stunning scenery and the facilities that some of the vineyards had developed, Kaimotu Island was becoming an increasingly sought-after venue for weddings and honeymoons.

Predictably, Daisy's eyes widened in outrage at the prick of the needle and then she erupted into ear-splitting wails. Seeing Blake's bottom lip wobbling, Abby sighed. Why hadn't she done Blake's vaccination first? Daisy wasn't old enough to put two and two together and realise that the nurse was torturing small people in here.

Ruth was offering Daisy her breast in the hope of consoling her by finishing her interrupted feed. Abby took the jar of jelly snakes and put it on the edge of her desk.

'Me?' Blake asked hopefully.

'Very soon,' Abby promised.

'No,' Blake shouted. *'Now.'*

Abby managed a smile but the tension was skyrocketing. Heading for her desk to collect Blake's file, her gaze snagged on the photo taking pride of place beside the phone.

Taken on the first day of school just a couple of

months ago, Jack's proud grin lit up his little face. A cheeky grin beneath mischievous dark brown eyes and a mop of soft, black curls. Something huge and warm welled up inside Abby and she felt some of the tension evaporate. It was always so grounding to be reminded of her love for her son. The reason she'd come here had been to keep him safe and give him the best possible start in life.

It was great that he was out having a real boy's adventure today. The teachers and other parents would be looking after him. He wasn't going to wander off and drown or topple into an abandoned mine shaft. It was ridiculous to even allow the fear of such scenarios to enter her head but they'd been there ever since Jack had started to get mobile and had crawled into his first spot of bother and revealed what a handful he was going to become.

She didn't need the photograph to remind her of what hovered in the back of her mind every single day. It was more than looks. It was a whole personality.

Jack was the spitting image of his father.

The man she had loved so much.

The man she had chosen to lose.

'Did you get put on the naughty step?'

'Reckon it was worth it.' Thomas Kendrick threw a lazy grin in his colleague's direction as he headed for the comfortable armchair in the staff quarters of the mainland rescue base.

The most recent addition to the elite team of paramedics, Felicity, shook her head. 'I'd heard you were a bit of a cowboy even before I applied for the job here, you know. Yesterday was the first time I'd actually seen you do something so reckless, though.'

Tom shrugged. Okay, the job had been a bit wild. And, yes, he'd taken a fair risk climbing under the un-secured car wreck at the bottom of a cliff as it had tee-tered on rocks, far too close to the boiling surf, but it had been the only way to get the unconscious driver out.

'You were just as keen as I was, Fizz. You would have been the one to crawl inside if I'd let you.'

'Yeah...' Her grin was unrepentant. 'It was awesome, wasn't it? And we got her out. Alive.'

They had. But Tom had known there would be re-percussions. Felicity had sustained a fairly major lac-eration to her arm in the process and was now stitched up and in a dressing that had to be kept dry. She was off active duty for a few days. And Tom had received a warning from an exasperated base manager.

'Look, we both know you live for the adrenaline rush, Tank. And we both know you're the best in the business. But there are limits, okay? Start taking notice of the boundaries or I'll have to take this further than a verbal warning. You nearly broke one of the crew. That's not on.'

Fair enough. It hadn't been his fault that Fizz had got injured, though. She had simply refused to do what he'd told her and stay put, off the slippery rocks, until he'd retrieved their patient. She was too young. Too eager. And not just when it came to the job. The look she was giving him now was unambiguous.

'I'm off active duty, Tank. I'm...frustrated.'

Tom ignored the invitation in her eyes. It would be all too easy to start an affair with Felicity. The other guys on the base were probably taking bets on how long it would take this time. And they were probably getting a bit puzzled by the fact that Tom couldn't seem to summon the interest.

Maybe the game of starting something he would only want to finish not so far down the track was finally getting old. Been there, done that. Too many times.

'You could come and help me with a…a stocktake, maybe…'

Counting supplies in the storeroom was not what Felicity had in mind. Good grief…at *work*? Maybe he did push the boundaries when it came to saving lives out in the field but, dammit, he had some personal boundaries. Funny that the prospect of an illicit thrill wasn't even enough to spark real desire, though.

He shook his head. 'I'm going to hit the gym. Doubt if we'll get another job before the shift's over.'

He knew she was watching him as he left the room. He knew he could pretty much click his fingers and get her into his bed if he wanted. Was that the problem? That there was no challenge involved?

The rescue base pilot on duty, Moz, was running on the treadmill. He raised a water bottle in salute as Tom entered the small fitness centre. The paramedic standing in for Fizz was Frank and he was currently using the rowing machine.

That wasn't the name his parents had given him, of course. It was short for Frankenstein and had been bestowed after an accident had given him an impressive facial laceration. The scar from the injury was virtually invisible, now, but the nickname had well and truly stuck.

Stripping off his overalls, Tom moved to the weight machine, wearing only a pair of shorts and a singlet.

He flexed his muscles and started to warm up slowly. Keeping in shape was taking more effort these days but it was worth it. He'd earned his own nickname years ago due to his physique, along with his impressive height.

Thomas the Tank Engine. Unstoppable.

The weights on the machine rattled loudly and Tom narrowed his eyes as he watched them. The whole machine was rocking now and he wasn't touching anything.

'What the hell is that? An *earthquake*?'

'Didn't feel a thing.' Moz was still pounding the treadmill at a good pace.

'I felt it.' Frank was looking interested rather than alarmed in any way.

An earthquake you were aware of was pretty unusual for Auckland, but not unheard of. They had minor tremors all over the country on a regular basis. If that was it, it was nothing to write home about.

Frank was already moving to his next activity. 'Just a seismic burp,' he said. 'No biggie.'

'Might be the tail end of something that was pretty big for someone else,' Tom suggested.

Frank grinned. 'That would make up for a quiet day, wouldn't it?'

Moz mopped the sweat from his brown with a hand towel but didn't slow down. 'Dream on,' he called.

Tom laughed. They would probably all do exactly that for the next few minutes. Good distraction from the pain of pushing yourself physically, anyway, imagining an event that could provide the kind of job they all dreamed of.

Tom took a deep breath and released it. He was feeling good now. Life was full of exciting possibilities. You just needed to be in the right place at the right time.

And keep yourself fit.

Tom added more weights and settled into his routine.

The tremor on Kaimotu Island started exactly the way the others had in the last few weeks. A sharp, unpleasant, jolting sensation.

But instead of fading away, this time the intensity built up with a speed too fast to process. It wasn't until she was virtually thrown off balance and only stopped herself falling by catching the edge of her desk that Abby realised that something huge was happening. She watched the jar of jelly snakes float through the air and then smash into shards on the floor. The fridge door had opened and its contents were starting to spill out. The revolving filing system, filled with thousands of patient files, was rocking violently and spewing paper in all directions.

Even then, it was all happening too fast to feel any fear. Blake had been thrown off balance but was still on top of the examination couch. Any second now, though, he would be on the floor amongst the broken glass and whatever else was about to come loose. It felt like Abby was trying to move against the deck of a violently rolling ship as she lunged towards the toddler.

'Under my desk,' she shouted at Ruth. 'Quick.'

She had to shout. It wasn't just the crashing and banging of things falling around them, there was a peculiar roaring sound. As if a huge jet was trying to land on the narrow, unsealed road that led to this hill-top hospital.

Catching Blake in her arms, Abby made a dive for

her desk. She felt something crunch under her knees but was oblivious to any pain. The shock of being narrowly missed by the computer monitor crashing off the desk beside her was more than enough distraction. The fridge had not only emptied its contents on the floor but now it was trying to walk through the debris, tilting ominously as it rocked from side to side.

Was the solid wood of the desktop going to be enough to protect them if the fridge fell over? Was the building going to stay upright? Vicious sounds of windows exploding and a scream from the waiting room gave Abby another surge of adrenaline, and it was then that the first shaft of pure fear sliced through her.

'Hang on,' she told Ruth. 'It's got to stop. It'll be okay.'

Who was she trying to reassure? The terrified mother who was clutching her infant with one arm and hanging on to a leg of the desk with the other? The small boy in her own arms, who was rigid with terror?

Herself?

All of them. It felt like this was never going to stop. The floor was tilting beneath them and still things were coming off the walls and shelves above, like the framed certificates that showed the qualifications Abby had worked so hard for. Heavy medical textbooks and the plastic models of joints that she used for educational purposes. Her whole world seemed to be literally crashing down around her.

And then, finally, it began to fade. The shaking stopped. The roaring noise and the sound of things breaking stopped.

Even the sound of her own breathing stopped.

Abby had never heard a silence quite like this.

Heavy.

Dead.

The moment when the world changed irrevocably.

And that was the moment that real fear took hold. When it had all stopped but you couldn't know if it was about to start again.

Or what had happened to everybody else.

Oh, God… *Jack*…

CHAPTER TWO

THE PILOT TOOK the rescue helicopter in a long, slow sweep over the length of Kaimotu as they made their final approach.

Most of the island appeared to be covered in native bush with little in the way of buildings. Housing was concentrated along the longest stretch of beach and the hills at one end. This was where the wharf was located and the community's centre, which contained the public buildings, including schools and business premises.

It was also where the major damage from the earthquake had been focused according to the patchy reports that had been coming in for nearly two hours now. The tremor that Tom and his colleagues had felt had indeed been the tail end of something much bigger. A seven point four earthquake with its epicentre right beneath Kaimotu Island. Probably right beneath its most densely populated area at this time of day, unfortunately. Reports contained the information that there were a lot of people injured. Possibly trapped in collapsed buildings.

The landing coordinates were for the field close to the medical centre, which was often used for evacuations from the island. This was the first time Tom had ever been here but it was hard to appreciate the natural beauty of the isolated island with the amount of adrenaline he had coursing through his body. Exchanging a glance with Frank as they hovered over the centre of the tiny township, where the buildings had taken the brunt of the damage, he could see that his mate was as wired as he was.

Here they were, the first responders, quite possibly the only responders for some time, and they were facing what was probably going to be the biggest job of their careers.

'There it is.' The voice of Moz, the pilot, sounded deceptively calm. 'The medical centre. Hang on to your hats, boys. Let's get this baby on the ground.'

In their bright red overalls, still wearing their white helmets with the rescue service insignia on the front, hefting only their backpacks full of emergency gear, Tom and Frank ducked beneath the slowing rotors and ran for the steps leading up to the modern buildings attached to the old, wooden hospital. A sign indicated that this was the island's medical centre—the place they'd been instructed to report to first.

Even before they got through the door they could see the place was crowded. There were people milling around inside and out and the veranda of the old hospital was packed.

It had been two hours since the quake had struck. The initial tsunami warning had been cancelled when it had become clear that the quake hadn't been centred out at sea. Were people staying on higher ground anyway, just in case?

How many of the walking wounded had made it this far? How many had been carried here? Tom had no idea what was available in terms of medical staff and resources. He had to hope that somebody competent had taken charge and would be able to fill him in. Where would they be needed most? How on earth would they even begin to triage this situation?

The waiting room was packed to the gills. The sound of children crying and the sight of so many pale, frightened people galvanised Tom into action.

'Who's in charge here?' he asked the person closest to the door, a middle-aged woman who was holding a bloodstained dressing against long grey hair that was matted with blood.

'The nurse. A— *Ahhh*…' The word turned into a shriek of fear as the building shook. Children screamed. Somebody tried to push past Tom to get to the door. Everybody else was moving now, too. Gathering children into their arms and either crouching over them or turning to flee.

Tom turned to say something to Frank but all he could manage was a quiet but fervent oath. The aftershock was over almost as soon as it had begun but his heart was still picking up speed as he surveyed the room, wondering if the building was about to come down on them all.

'It's just an aftershock.' The clear notes of a woman's voice cut through the sounds of panic. 'We have to expect them. You're all safe in here. Mike and Don have checked the building. It's solid.'

'Who are Mike and Don?' Frank's query came as Tom tried to see past all the people and find the woman who'd spoken. There was something about that voice that had made his gut tighten instantly. Sent a tingle down the length of his spine. 'And where are they now?'

'Let's find out.' Taking a step forward, Tom found a

space magically clearing, the way it usually did when they arrived on scene. They had come to help. They knew what they were doing. Their arrival was always welcome.

He could see the back of the woman now. A long blond braid hung down over a navy blue uniform. Tom felt that kick in his guts again but the sight of long blond hair always did that to him, didn't it? Ever since…ever since…

Abby…

'It's definitely broken,' he heard her tell a teenage boy as she finished winding a crepe bandage to hold a cardboard splint in place on his arm.

Now that her name was filling his head, it was easy to recognise that voice. Clear, soft notes that got a husky little edge to them when she was stressed. Or when she was…

No. Tom had to force that particular association out of his mind as fast as it had entered but it was by no means easy because there *was* a husky edge to her voice right now.

'It won't hurt so much now it's immobilised but I'm sorry, Sean—there's nothing more I can do right now. We'll all have to wait until help arrives.'

'It's here,' the boy told her, staring up at Tom, his eyes wide. 'Right behind you.'

The woman rose to her feet in a graceful movement, turning at the same time. Tom could clearly see the relief in her eyes as she registered the bright uniforms of the helicopter crew. And then he saw the shock as she caught his gaze.

As she recognised him.

'Oh, my God… *Tom…?*'

The shock was mutual. Tom had thought that being on an island in the aftermath of a massive earthquake was the only thing he'd be expected to have to deal with.

But he'd been so wrong.

Seeing Abby again was…was such a shock he couldn't even begin to process it.

That hair, with its gorgeous golden-honey colour and the length that made it so damn sexy when it brushed on naked skin.

Her voice…

Those huge blue eyes that darkened in colour if her mood was extreme. They were as dark as he'd ever seen them right now. She was shocked. Afraid.

Of *him*?

It was another reaction that Tom had to squash. This wasn't about them right now. It couldn't be allowed to be. And this was most certainly not the time or place to try to process anything so personal.

So Tom simply nodded. And acknowledged her.

'Abby.'

It was just a name but the weight that single word could carry was overpowering. It wasn't just a person he was acknowledging. Behind that name swirled deep, personal things. Huge, *painful* things that Tom had thought were long since dead and buried. He could feel them hovering over him in this instant, waiting to punch him in the gut with far more force than seeing her hair or hearing her voice had done. Stab him in the heart, even.

They couldn't be allowed to get even remotely closer. Not here, not now. They were in an emergency situation that was far bigger than a reunion between two people whose relationship had turned to custard.

'Fill us in,' he ordered Abby. 'Communication's been very patchy and we need to know what we're dealing with, here.'

She nodded. 'The cell phone tower is out of action. They've been using the coastguard radio to communicate with the mainland but nobody's been back to update us. We had no idea when help would start arriving. Come with me.'

Abby led them to what had been her office.

Tom Kendrick was here.

Here. Right behind her. As huge as he'd ever been in both his physical size and the sheer presence his personality emanated. Just as breathtakingly gorgeous as he'd ever been, too, with those strong features and dark eyes and that deep, commanding voice. A crisp, professional voice right now but Abby knew how it could soften. How both that voice and those eyes could make her think of melted chocolate.

Oh…dear Lord… The past was crashing all around her, just like all that stuff that had come off the shelves of her office during the big quake.

Small, paper-sized things, like finding out they had the same favourite foods. Sweet, jelly-snake kinds of things, like how good the sex had been. Huge, fridge-sized things, like the way she couldn't have imagined her future without him as a part of it.

She couldn't handle this new bombardment. Her world had been turned upside down and shaken far too hard already. Abby walked ahead of Tom, frantically trying to find the emotional equivalent of a solid desk to crawl underneath, but every instinct was urging her to run. To get out of there—away from Tom—

to find Jack and then just keep running. The way she had when Jack had been no more than a positive line on a pregnancy test?

No. Her first instinct then had been to run back to Tom, hadn't it? Despite the fact that their relationship had already hit the rocks. She'd chosen to run later, when she'd had time to think about the implications of a future that included him.

Something like a sob was building inside her chest, making it impossible to take a breath. She couldn't run because she was desperately needed here.

And she didn't even know where Jack was right now, so she could find herself running totally in the wrong direction.

The hovering terror had just been magnified.

She didn't know whether Jack really was safe.

And…what if Tom found out about Jack?

She had to hold it together. She would be no use to anyone if she fell apart. She had to hang on to the mantra that Ruth had given her within minutes of the quake. Jack was safe. All the children on the school trip, including her Brooke and Amber, would be safe. They were miles away from the township and village and the falling debris that was hurting people.

They were probably the safest people on the island and the teachers would be looking after them. The only reason that they weren't already in the school hall that was being used as an evacuation centre was because something had happened to close the cliff road. They might have to walk instead of riding in the old school bus.

Time had passed in a blur since that initial terror.

That first stunned silence, when the wail of the tsunami-warning siren could be clearly heard, hadn't lasted long.

Panicked people were heading away from the harbour's edge and uphill towards the hospital. Others began rushing away from the medical centre when it was discovered that the cell phone tower was obviously not functioning and there was no way for anybody to find out whether loved ones were okay. The first injured people began to arrive and Abby had to check on the mostly elderly inpatients in the old hospital wing.

She needed Ben to be here. And Ginny, the doctor who'd helped out recently, although she was refusing to fill the gap that had been left when the last doctor had resigned. She wouldn't refuse now. They needed all the help they could get.

Thank heavens for Ruth. She'd started by reassuring Abby about the children and had then carried on to be a tower of strength in assisting her to create some order amongst the chaos. With Daisy strapped to her chest in a sling, and Blake being looked after by Hannah, they'd checked on everybody they could find and dispensed both first aid and as much reassurance as they could muster. They'd been ready for contact from the local policeman and volunteer fire brigade when it came and had begun to coordinate a response.

More people who needed medical attention had begun to arrive at the centre and the men had driven off to assess the damage in the township. Now Ruth was sitting at the desk in Abby's office, trying to record and coordinate information about who was missing, injured or might need evacuation to the mainland.

Ruth looked up as Abby entered the office and she had tears of relief in her eyes as she registered the men with her. 'Oh, thank God you're here.' She tilted her head to see past the two men.

'It's just us, so far.' It was the man with Tom who spoke. 'We got dispatched as soon as it was known that the epicentre of the quake was in a populated area. When contact was made and we heard about injuries and trapped people, a full response was put into action but it takes time to scramble the right people. There's another chopper and a light plane coming that are carrying two doctors, a mobile triage unit and a USAR team with a search dog, but it'll be at least an hour until they're due to land.'

Tom was looking at Abby.

'Who's in charge of the overall incident control?'

Abby heard her breath come out in an incredulous huff.

He didn't seem to be having any trouble dealing with the fact that they were seeing each other for the first time in nearly six years. Maybe it was so far in the past he didn't have things hurtling around in his head, like the image Abby suddenly got, of being cradled in his arms. That magic time when desire had been temporarily sated and the world had never seemed so perfect.

Maybe he didn't have things crashing around in his head or his heart, because it had never meant that much to him in the first place. She had to hold on, here. To stop allowing the past to intrude and assume an importance it had no right to have. She had to focus. To respond to Tom as the person he was at this moment. A rescuer. A skilled professional who was doing exactly what he should be doing and focusing on his job.

But...this was an *incident*?

No. This was far more than a mere incident. Her

whole community was in danger. People she loved. A place she loved. The sanctuary she had sought years ago that had embraced her and kept her safe. More importantly, had kept Jack safe.

Until now.

But this was Tom all over, wasn't it? This wasn't about the people and their broken lives. This was about the adrenaline rush of a big job. Of the opportunity to put himself in danger to save others.

Not her problem. Abby could hear the almost desperate whisper in the back of her mind. Not anymore.

Tom was staring at her. Holding her gaze but keeping anything personal well shuttered. If he knew what she was thinking—and, given what she knew about him, he probably did—he wasn't about to let it interfere with his work.

Oh…help. For a heartbeat, Abby was caught by that intense stare. Or rather by what she could see around it. The gorgeous olive skin and strong features that spoke of Maori heritage. Those dark, dark eyes. The soft, dark waves of hair.

An adult version of her precious Jack.

She couldn't go there. Couldn't waste another second thinking about what Tom looked like. Or how it made her feel, seeing him again like this.

'Mike Henley is our senior police officer. He's working with Don Johnson, who's the chief fire officer. They have about twenty people who work in the volunteer fire brigade and have had some training in rescue. We also have our island coastguard guys. They've set up headquarters in the information centre, which is on the main street at the ferry terminal end. A boat radio is being used to contact the mainland. The cell phone tower is down.'

'What medical staff are available? Where are your doctors?'

'We only have one full-time doctor on the island at the moment—Ben McMahon. He was out on a house call when the quake happened and we haven't heard any news since. There is another doctor but she's not working officially and I have no idea where she is at the moment. Apart from that, we have four nurses. Two of them are on duty in the hospital. The others are on their way and they're going to help look after injured people after we've assessed and stabilised them.'

'We?'

Abby felt a flush of colour stain her cheeks. 'So far it's only been me. Fortunately there hasn't been anything major arriving.'

'We need to get to the information centre. And we need a medical team to work with. What's the most serious case you've got in here?'

'There's nothing life-threatening. Bruises, lacerations and a few broken bones. One of our other nurses who's coming in is trained in first aid. It's under control.'

'Good. You can come with us, then.'

It was a gasp rather than a huff that escaped Abby now. 'I don't think so…. This is where people are coming for treatment.'

'If they can get themselves here, they're not the victims we need to worry about first. We've got doctors arriving very soon and they can base themselves here. You're an experienced emergency nurse, Abby. We're going to need more than one team to check the township and triage for injuries. Frank can lead one. You can come with me. I take it you know the layout of the town?'

'Of course. I've been living here for five years.'

A flicker crossed Tom's face as he registered that this was where she'd come after they'd split up. A frown that suggested he couldn't understand why. It was gone as fast as it had appeared but Abby was aware of a flash of…what, satisfaction? *Relief?* He wasn't as unaffected as he was managing to appear. He hadn't forgotten everything because he hadn't cared enough.

Yes. It was a kind of relief. She wasn't the only one who was finding this painful.

'Good.' Tom's gaze had shifted away from her. 'You'll know the people as well, then. Could be a valuable asset.'

Torn, Abby twisted her head to look at Ruth. She could see her own reaction reflected back. She was a valuable asset here, too, wasn't she? This felt like the right place to be. Where she had access to medical equipment and drugs and where Ben and Ginny would come to help.

This was where someone would come to reunite Jack with his mother.

And…and it was a much safer place to be than out there in the unknown, where things were wrecked and dangerous and where she could be at serious risk if there were any more of those horrible aftershocks.

But these new arrivals were the experts. They also had medical qualifications that exceeded her own. Ethically, she had no choice. She had to follow orders.

'Let's go.' Frank was staring out the window. 'We're wasting time here, mate.'

Tom's glare was holding Abby. Pulling her in.

'I can't go out like this.' Abby held out her bare arms and looked down at the flimsy material of her uniform.

'There's the overalls in the back of the Jeep,' Ruth reminded her. 'And the helmets.'

'You've got a four-wheel-drive vehicle?' Tom was moving towards the door. 'Excellent. Let's move.'

The Jeep was one of the clinic's vehicles, modified to have a stretcher clipped in the back and equipped with emergency gear. The island's equivalent of an ambulance. Ben had the other one.

'Go, Abby,' Ruth urged. 'We can cope here. People need you.'

Abby nodded. She had no choice. Tom was already halfway out the door. Frank was holding back, waiting for Abby to go ahead of him.

'Send someone to find me,' she told Ruth, 'if you hear anything at all about Jack.'

'Of course I will. He'll be fine, Abby. They all will.'

But Ruth's lips trembled. She had two daughters on that school trip, didn't she? Did she have to try and make Abby believe they were all safe in order to keep herself focused?

'Who's Jack?' Frank asked as he followed Abby out of the door. 'Your husband?'

'No.' Abby took a deep breath as she tried to push her own fear back into its box in the corner. 'He's my... my son.'

Tom heard.

Abby had a child? A *son*?

Of course she'd moved on. It had been nearly six years since they'd been together. How old was this Jack?

A baby? A toddler, maybe. Couldn't be any older unless she'd moved on and replaced him pretty damn fast.

'So you've got a son?' The words escaped as Tom climbed into the front passenger seat of the Jeep.

Abby reached to switch on the ignition. 'Mmm.'

'And he's in day care or something, because you're working?'

She might have nodded. It was hard to tell because she was turning her head to see whether Frank was on board and the door was closed. It was also quite possible she was avoiding answering him by simply pretending she hadn't heard his question.

'How old is Jack?' Tom knew it was none of his business. He had no right to ask personal questions and it was entirely inappropriate given the circumstances but the idea that Abby had moved on so conclusively...had had a *child* with her new man was sitting in his gut like a hot rock right now. Burning, even.

The vehicle lurched forward with enough force to make him think about fastening his seat belt instead.

'Sorry,' Abby said. 'Haven't driven this beast for a while. It's a bit rugged.'

'No worries,' Frank said dryly. 'We just won't hand you the controls for the helicopter any time soon.'

Even when Abby was used to the clunky transmission again, the ride was no smoother. The road was badly damaged with parts that had risen into hillocks and other parts sunken and cracked. There were pools of...

'What is that?' Abby asked.

'Liquefaction,' Tom responded. 'Silt gets driven up through the earth. Don't drive into it. It may be filling a sinkhole and could be deep. We'd get stuck.'

Abby was now manoeuvring the vehicle very competently, driving onto the grass verge at times to avoid obstacles. For a moment, Tom stopped looking through the windscreen to spot hazards and looked at her face instead.

He saw a grimly determined profile. She must be scared stiff, he thought. She'd never been into the adrenaline rush of facing danger. She was the total opposite of someone like Fizz. Unlike any of the women he'd ever been attracted to or involved with—before or after Abby, in fact—and maybe *that* had been the attraction in the first place. It had also been the reason it could never have worked long-term. He needed to remind himself of that. Had to fight an undercurrent happening here that he didn't even want to try and identify.

And Abby was not only facing potential personal danger here. This was her home now and people she knew well could be amongst the dead and injured. And her child was missing? Yet here she was, totally focused on what had to be done. Heading further into danger?

Tom felt a strong impulse to send her back up the hill when he and Frank had been delivered to where they needed to go. To keep her safe.

Except they needed all the medical assistance they could get. The whereabouts of the only other medics on the island were unknown. Sure, the volunteer fire brigade or civil defence guys here would be trained in first aid but he'd seen Abby in action in an emergency department. He knew she would be as capable as he was of getting an IV line in under difficult circumstances. Assessing someone's injuries. Intubating them if necessary. She was more than capable. Abby was gifted.

Working as a GP's nurse on a remote island must be sadly underutilising her skills.

If hitting another bump wasn't enough to bring his train of thought instantly back to his present surroundings, entering the main street of the village certainly was.

'Oh...my God,' Abby breathed. She slowed the vehicle, looking stunned as she took in the scene.

It must have been a very picturesque shopping centre with its old, heritage brick and stone buildings preserved and restored to enhance it as a tourist destination but they were always the type of buildings that came off worst in an earthquake. Shop facades and chimneys had toppled. Walls had crumbled, leaving skeletons of wooden framing and rooms exposed like an open doll's house.

A car was buried under a crushing mound of bricks, with only the front wheels and bumper clearly visible.

'Hope there wasn't anybody inside,' Frank said quietly.

A few metres on there was another mound of bricks and timber. There were several men here, frantically pulling at chunks of rubble. They flagged down the Jeep.

'We need help. There's someone under here.'

'Are they calling?' Tom asked.

The man shook his head, his face twisted with distress. 'We can see her foot.'

Tom took a deep breath. 'I'm sorry, mate, but there's no chance she'll be alive under there.'

'I know...' The man dragged in a ragged gulp of air. 'But we've got to try...'

'You need to keep yourselves safe.' Tom pointed upwards. 'Another aftershock could bring that lot down. Who directed you to dig here?'

He shook his head. 'We just arrived.'

'Follow us to the information centre. We're going to get a plan in place for a systematic search and rescue effort. We'll need all the help we can get.'

He turned to Abby, who was staring in horror at the gap the men were opening up in the pile of rubble. Could she see the part of the woman's body being exposed? Was it someone she knew?

He wanted to reach out. To touch her arm and offer encouragement. Strength. Or comfort, maybe. But he would be crossing a boundary to do that. The same boundary that made it inappropriate to want to send her back to the hospital to protect her. They were no longer in any kind of relationship. Quite the opposite, and Abby would not want to reach out in any way. The boundary was an almost palpable thing. Like a glass bubble encasing Abby.

'Drive on, Abby,' Tom said quietly. 'We can't stop.'

This was far, far worse than Abby had anticipated, but it felt so unreal she knew she wasn't going to fall apart. It was like being transported onto the set of a disaster movie and she was merely a character waiting to play her part depending on the instructions of the director.

Feeling as though she was on autopilot, she kept the vehicle going until they reached the other end of the main street. The wharf end, where the ferries berthed. She could see a police car among all the vehicles parked outside the information centre, a modern hexagonal structure that was central enough to make it an excellent choice as an operational hub.

The men who were currently the directors looked as though they were up against it.

The island had three police officers and Mike Henley was the most senior. The biggest 'incident', as Tom would call it, that Mike had had to deal with in recent years had been a private yacht that had gone aground in rough weather on Elephant Rocks, which were far enough offshore to have made the rescue fairly dramatic.

Mike's best mate was Don Johnson, who was the chief fire officer for Kaimotu Island. He was also in charge of civil defence and the coastguard and, in fact, he'd been the one who'd dealt with the Elephant Rocks incident very competently.

Both men had come past the hospital on the way into the town's centre as soon as this emergency had struck and they'd taken the time to check, as best they could, that the building that would be required for providing medical aid was safe to be inside. When the two men saw Abby come into the information centre with Tom and Frank, their relief was obvious. Expert help had started to arrive, at last.

And Abby was proud to introduce him to Tom. If anyone had asked her who she would want to turn up if she was ever in a dangerous situation and needed her life saved, Tom Kendrick would be at the very top of her list.

Even after they'd broken up.

Maybe even more so, because she knew that Tom still wouldn't hesitate to do whatever it took to save her, even if it meant he was putting his own life at risk. And it wasn't because he was stupid and a cowboy, as some had accused him of being. Or that he had some kind of death wish. He could calculate those risks perfectly well. He was just prepared to push the boundaries further than most.

Abby was a born worrier. She could conjure up imaginary disasters with no effort whatsoever. The habit was as ingrained as the way she tied shoelaces or slept with her head cradled in the crook of her elbow.

What would Tom think if he knew about some of the fantasy situations she'd come up with over the years? The ones that always ended with his appearance to make everything okay? The ones where he saved her and held her in his arms afterwards as if she was the most precious thing on earth? Or the ones where he saved Jack and recognised his own son?

Oh…help…

This was no fantasy. Abby stood quietly to one side as the group of men taking control of this rescue operation made swift plans. The wall behind them was covered with the kind of brochures the tourists were looking for the moment they arrived on Kaimotu Island. Invitations to charter a fishing vessel or go scuba diving. Pictures of people happily abseiling, mountain biking or taking a vineyard tour. The kind of activities Kaimotu was famous for and which now seemed no more than fantasies themselves.

A map of the township was on a table and grids had been drawn on it. There were cans of spray paint in a box on the floor. They were going to be assigned areas and would spray information on the walls about what they found. Whether there were people trapped. Or needing urgent attention for their injuries. Or dead. If they came across serious injuries, they could only take the time for an initial stabilisation and then summon backup for transportation to the hospital. They had to keep moving as fast as possible.

There was no way Tom's presence was going to be enough to make everything okay here, either. It was going to take a lot of people and a lot of time. They were facing a gruelling night of probably grim and possibly dangerous work.

There was also absolutely no chance of Tom taking her in his arms and holding her, and that was a good thing. She was over him. She'd spent years getting over him and she couldn't afford to let those protective walls around that place in her heart fall apart.

And surely there was no chance that Tom would instantly see himself in Jack, was there? She'd managed to avoid letting Tom know exactly how old Jack was, which would be a dead giveaway, and there shouldn't be any need for the two of them to be in the same place at the same time.

When Jack and the other children turned up, they would be cared for in the community centre. She would be able to get there and reassure herself that he was fine and then she could have him go to Ben's parents, Doug and Ailsa. Or Hannah, up at the hospital.

Somehow she had to keep Jack hidden from Tom.

At least until she had some time to try and think this through.

Abby barely heard the last instructions being issued by Tom and Mike and Don. She tightened the straps on her backpack full of medical supplies.

'So you'll be Tom's partner,' Mike said, as though summarising everything she hadn't heard clearly enough. 'You're going to triage the northern half of the village but if we need you for major medical stuff, you'll be contacted by radio.'

Abby could only nod.

Tom's *partner*.

How ironic was that?

At least they had an urgent mission to focus on. No time for anything personal to interfere with the job that needed to be done.

No time to herself to try and think things through.

To try and deal with the awful dread that she had, in fact, done a terrible thing by not making more of an effort to tell Tom about Jack a long time ago.

CHAPTER THREE

THE CHOPPING BEAT of a hovering helicopter was loud enough to preclude the need for any conversation as Tom and Abby stepped out of the information centre, which had now morphed into the island's incident control headquarters.

Abby was shading her eyes against the lowering sun to peer upwards.

Tom raised his voice, although the chopper was moving again, now. 'That'll be the extra doctors arriving. And maybe the first USAR team members. Hopefully with a search dog.'

He saw Abby close her eyes for a moment and take a deep breath, as though summoning a fresh burst of courage. He had to fight the urge to touch her. To offer her some of *his* strength.

'Who else will come, do you think?'

Tom didn't have to raise his voice any longer. 'I imagine the army will be involved by now. If they've got an Iroquois helicopter available they can dispatch a few troops, which will be useful. It would be good to have more space available for evacuating any serious trauma, too.' He glanced down at the map in his hand. 'Let's get going. Where's Hickory Lane? That's the southern border for our search area.'

'A few blocks up this way.' Abby set off. 'It's got a bakery on one side called The Breadbin and the Fat Duck café on the other side. There's a big metal duck sculpture that hangs off the side of the café. You can't miss it.'

Except the quirky café icon was no longer hanging off the brick wall. It was buried somewhere beneath the rubble. There were several local men standing in the middle of Hickory Lane, where it branched off the main street.

'Hey, Abby,' one of them called. 'You okay?'

'That's Jim,' Abby told Tom. 'He's our butcher. His shop's a bit further down.'

She stepped closer to the men. 'I'm fine, Jim. What about you? Oh, help…look at your hands.'

The middle-aged butcher was still wearing his blue-and-white-striped apron but it was filthy. His arms were just as grimy but they were also scratched and bruised-looking. His hands were a mess, his knuckles ripped and bleeding.

Tom saw them cupped in Abby's much smaller hands. He saw the expression on Abby's face. This man wasn't just the local butcher. He was someone Abby cared about. Part of a community she cared about. A place and a way of life that made *him* an outsider.

He didn't like that feeling.

'It's nothing.' Jim dismissed Abby's concern but his smile was grateful. 'I've just been shifting a few bricks.'

'A few!' One of the other men gave Jim a friendly thump on his shoulder. 'This man's been a right hero. Single-handedly dug at least three people out from

under where they got buried here.' He pointed at the
Fat Duck.

'Everybody inside got out in time,' Jim told them.
'But poor Miriam got hit in the head by a brick or something. And some others got under the picnic table. They
got buried good and proper.'

'Where's this Miriam?' Tom asked.

'We just sent her up to the hospital. Used the back of
Johnno's ute. She should be there by now.'

'And the others?'

'Not too bad. We sent them all off to get checked,
though.'

'So the café's clear of people?' Tom had his can of
spray paint ready. 'Are you sure about that?'

Jim nodded. 'Business was pretty quiet. Miriam was
last out. She was making sure all her customers were
safe first, bless her.'

'Right.' Tom sprayed the word 'Clear' and the time
on a window that was still intact. He could see inside
the café. There were tables with plates of uneaten food
on them. Toppled chairs and an abandoned handbag
that was spilling its contents into the puddle created by
an overturned water cooler. They needed to move on.

'Let's go, Abby. Next building. We'll do the rest of
Hickory Lane and then come back to the main street.'

'What can we do to help?' Jim asked.

'Best thing you can do is head for the information
centre. They'll be organising teams and giving out some
safety gear and radios and things. We don't want you
just off on your own. It's too dangerous.'

'I don't think there's anybody up Hickory Lane,' another of the men said. 'My wife and kids were along
there and they got out fast. Everyone panicked and ran

when they heard the siren go off. Someone said they should all go to the community centre in the new school hall.'

'We'll check anyway,' Tom said. 'But thanks.'

They moved swiftly along the narrow lane, climbing over rubble to peer into buildings. Yelling as loudly as they could.

'Is anyone here? Can you hear me?'

There could be people buried or too injured to respond but they would be found later by the urban search and rescue teams and the dogs in a second sweep. Right now, the priority was to try and get an idea of the big picture and find anything urgent that could be dealt with fast.

Back on the main street they came across another knot of people, these ones in front of the hardware store. They spotted the overalls and helmets Tom and Abby were wearing and backed out to make room amongst the rubble.

'We can hear someone,' a man said, clearly distressed. 'Groaning.'

Sheets of corrugated iron from the veranda roof along with timber beams were making it impossible to get any further. As they stood there, something rolled from higher up, bounced and narrowly missed Abby as it fell with a crash.

Tom gripped Abby's elbow and hauled her back. 'Everybody move back,' he ordered. 'We're going to have specialist teams here very soon.' He marked a sheet of iron beside where the men had been working. 'Trapped 1', he painted. '1725 hours'. He added an arrow pointing to the interior of the shop.

As if to back up his words to the locals, a group

wearing the bright orange overalls of a USAR team appeared on the main street, walking down from where the last helicopter had landed beside the hospital. One of them had a dog, which was straining at its leash.

'Where's the info centre?' one of them called.

'Keep going that way,' Tom directed, pointing. 'And take these guys with you. We need to clear this zone of civilians.'

He and Abby moved on. The next building they checked was a book-and-toy shop. Nobody answered their calls and he was about to declare it clear when he heard a cry from Abby. She climbed over a shelf teetering on a pile of dislodged books and headed deeper into the shop.

'Abby, stop! We don't know if it's safe.'

'It's Millie,' Abby shouted. 'Tom...come here, *quick*...'

The shop had been created inside an old cottage. A brick chimney had collapsed and brought down part of a heavy slate roof. Trapped beneath a beam of wood and a shower of bricks was a woman who looked to be in her eighties.

The heavy beam was directly over the woman's chest, weighted down at one end by most of the chimney bricks.

Abby was bent over the woman's head, desperately searching for signs of life. Breathing. A pulse. Tom could see that she wasn't going to find any. He crouched beside her.

'It's too late,' he said firmly. 'I'm sorry, Abby, but we have to keep moving.'

'But it's *Millie*...' Abby was crying. 'She's known every child on the island for generations, now. She has a story circle every Saturday morning when she reads to them. Everybody loves Millie. She...she just helped Jack choose his backpack and pencils for school...'

Tom froze. 'What did you just say, Abby?'

'That everybody loves Millie. We can't just leave her here like this.'

'About Jack.' Yes, it was a tragedy that an old lady every child on this island loved had been killed, but Tom couldn't give it any head space whatsoever. Something huge was exploding inside him. 'He's at *school*?'

Abby scrubbed tears from her face, making huge streaks amid the dust and grime already covering her skin. She gulped in air, trying to get herself under control, but she was nodding. 'He started a few weeks ago. He's on his first school outing today and I still don't know if...'

As if a switch had been thrown, Abby suddenly stopped crying. She went very, very still.

It was happening for her as well, Tom realised.

The world had stopped spinning because it needed to adjust the tilt of its axis. That 'something huge' still splintering inside Tom meant that his world would never turn in quite the same way again.

Slowly, Abby raised her gaze from Millie to Tom. Her eyes looked enormous and her face, beneath the grime, was as white as a sheet.

'Oh...*God*...' she whispered.

She had no one to blame for this but herself.

Abby had just walked off the edge of the precipice without even looking. She'd told Tom *exactly* how old Jack was. Five years and a few weeks. Given this man's intelligence, it would probably only take him two sec-

onds to do the maths. To work out that nine months before Jack was born had been when they had been utterly
in love. Unable to keep their hands off each other. Not
always as careful as they could have been about protection because they had been blinded by how strongly
they had felt about each other.

As blind as she had just been, stepping—no, *throw-
ing*—herself off anything remotely resembling safe
ground. But finding Millie dead had been the last straw,
hadn't it, on top of the terror of the earthquake and the
dreadful anxiety about Jack's whereabouts and safety.

The shock of seeing Tom again and the relentless
punches of seeing the worst of the damage as their
search progressed. Knowing with more and more clar-
ity just how big a disaster her community and home
had suffered.

She'd snapped. Somehow it had all coalesced into
grief for a pillar of her small community and her own
connection with this sweet old lady. Her son's connection.

Tom was rising from where he'd been crouched beside her. In slow motion, as if he was trying to counter
the effects of being shot with a stun gun. And when
he was on his feet, he stood as still as a stone. His lips
barely moved as he spoke.

'Who's Jack's father, Abby?'

She couldn't say anything. Couldn't move. Couldn't
even breathe.

He knew. Of course he knew. He just needed to hear
her say the words. The way people did when someone
they loved had just died. It wasn't real until you heard
the words.

'It's me, isn't it?'

She still couldn't make her lips move. Or take enough of a breath to push it out and make words.

A glance up showed a muscle twitching on Tom's jaw. He was processing this. He was shocked, of course, but he was also…furious?

Yes. When he spoke, his voice was dangerously controlled. Almost too quiet to hear.

'And you didn't think to tell me?'

Now Abby could move. She pushed herself to her feet.

'I tried to.'

A snort escaped Tom. 'Funny…I don't remember that.'

'You weren't there. You…were off on a mission.'

It had been the final straw on that occasion. Confirmation of why their relationship could never have worked. Why it could have ruined more than one life if Abby had gone through with her intention to tell Tom he was going to be a father.

'Oh…so you couldn't have waited an hour or so?'

'I… You… It was after we'd broken up, Tom.'

He turned a glare on Abby that made her flinch. 'And that makes it okay? To *pretend* that you were going to tell me? Or maybe you did turn up at the base. After you saw the chopper take off, perhaps? When you knew I wouldn't be there?'

That wasn't fair. Abby opened her mouth to snap that he could go back and check the visitors' sign-in log if he thought she was lying but she didn't get a chance to speak. There was an ominous rumble and the ground began to shake with the biggest aftershock yet.

Abby started to turn her head to look for something to shelter under but felt herself being grabbed before she had time to think, let alone spot something. Her feet left the floor and, even as things rattled and more bricks came in through the damaged roof, Tom was moving at speed.

The aftershock had stopped by the time he reached the street but he didn't let go of Abby. He let her put her feet on the ground but kept her pinned with one arm, looking around and up as he assessed their safety, pulling her out of range of anything that could come loose and fall from roof level.

A four-wheel-drive vehicle was coming up the street. Mike Henley was driving.

'You guys all right?'

A burst of something like hysterical laughter almost escaped Abby. All right? Millie was lying dead in the shop they'd just escaped from. She could have just been killed herself. She was terrified. She didn't know where her son was or if he was all right. Tom had just learned that he was a father. Jack was *their* son.

No. It was inconceivable that either of them were 'all right' at this moment.

'I'm on my way to check the airstrip after that aftershock. There's an Iroquois on the way in. They've got army troops on board and a couple of structural engineers who can assess buildings properly. Oh, and, Abby?'

'Yes?'

'The crew of a fishing boat spotted the school bus. It's trapped on the cliff road between a couple of big slips. They've seen a bunch of kids and adults waving at them so we can assume everyone's okay. Including your Jack.'

'Oh...oh...' Abby's legs were threatening to give

way. She was shaking all over and suddenly Tom's arm
holding her up was very, very welcome. 'Oh, thank
God…'

'Doesn't look like there's any way to clear the slips
and get them out tonight but they're talking about using
a chopper to drop some food and blankets to get them
through the night. Right… Gotta go.' Mike gunned the
engine. 'You two should stop for a break soon. There's
a lot of teams ready to take over.'

One of those teams was just down the street, in fact.
In front of the hardware store where Tom had left the
painted message about someone being trapped. They
weren't trapped any longer. A man's body, strapped to
a back board, was being carefully lifted over the man-
gled iron and other debris.

Tom and Abby hadn't even scratched the surface of
the conversation they needed to have but they weren't
going to get a chance to continue it right now, either.
Tom's radio crackled into life.

'Medic needed. Outside the hardware store on main
street. Man having trouble breathing.'

Another voice came on that sounded like Frank. 'I'm
five minutes away.'

Tom keyed the button on the radio. 'We're on to it.'
He'd let Abby go to reach for his radio but it wasn't a
problem. Her legs were steady now.

Jack was safe. He wouldn't even see anything terrible because, by the time the slips were cleared and the
children rescued, any bodies or badly injured people
would be out of public view. There was nothing Abby
could do to speed up his rescue so she could direct all
her energy to helping Tom. And with the fear about
Jack vanquished, she was aware of a new burst of en-

ergy, which was just as well seeing as she had to trot
to keep up with him.

He wasn't looking at her and seemed to be occupied
in getting his backpack off without slowing down the
pace. Was he still furious with her? Of course he was,
but having a medical emergency to deal with meant
that they wouldn't be having any personal conversa-
tions any time soon.

The longer it took the better, as far as Abby was concerned. It was a conversation to be dreaded, that was for
sure. Except, curiously, she was aware of a trickle of relief that the truth was out. The burden of guilt had been
there from the moment she'd left the rescue base that
day without having spoken to Tom, and it had grown,
bit by bit, over the years. Grown faster in the last few
weeks since Jack had started school because most of
the other children had dads and he was starting to ask
some pointed questions about why he didn't.

Awareness of any personal sense of relief evaporated
as they reached the USAR crew, who had rescued the
trapped victim from the hardware store.

'You know him?' Tom asked Abby.

'Of course. It's Harley. Owner of the shop.' Abby
crouched beside the man and touched his shoulder.
'Harley? Can you hear me?'

Harley's eyes opened. So did his mouth and he tried
to speak but he was struggling to breathe. Beside her,
Tom was fitting the earpieces of his stethoscope but
still looking up.

'What the story?' he asked.

'Chest and leg injuries, from what we could see.
He was under the counter but a steel beam had come
down on top of that. Took a bit of digging out and

his breathing seemed to get worse pretty fast after we pulled him out.'

Tom used the shears he carried clipped to his belt to cut clear what remained of Harley's thick shirt. He listened to his chest for only moments. 'Find the chest drain kit, would you, Abby? He's got a tension pneumothorax.'

The chest injuries were allowing air to get into the wrong places, compressing Harley's lungs. It could stop his heart functioning if they couldn't relieve the pressure. Abby opened what she recognised as the airway roll in Tom's pack and found the wide-bore needle she knew he would need. By the time he had a pair of gloves on, she had an alcohol wipe opened and ready for him to grab, as well as the three-way stopcock and tape that would be needed to complete the procedure.

'Thanks.' Counting down the rib spaces, Tom cleaned the area the needle would penetrate. 'Can you check his leg injury and get a blood pressure while I do this?'

Abby used the shears to cut Harley's trousers. 'Femoral fracture,' she reported.

'I don't carry a traction splint.'

'It's not mid-shaft.'

'Okay. How 'bout starting an IV so we can get some pain relief on board?'

'Sure.'

They were working in far from ideal circumstances with their patient on a plastic board in the rubble of his collapsed shop. Their resources were also limited and people around them were in a hurry to move on, so there was unspoken pressure, yet to Abby it felt as if she and Tom were working together as a smooth team.

She reached around him to get what she needed from the pack and paused in what she was doing to comfort Harley when he groaned loudly.

Tom had punctured the space between Harley's ribs and advanced the cannula far enough to release the pressure of the air filling his chest cavity. Almost immediately his breathing improved. Abby had the tourniquet on his arm and slid a cannula into place as Tom attached the three-way stopcock to the chest cannula and taped it into position. He might be busy with his own task but he wasn't missing anything Abby was doing.

'Nice work,' he murmured, as Abby flushed the IV access now established in Harley's arm. 'Could you draw up some morphine?'

Of course she could. The praise was remarkably sweet and with Harley now in no immediate danger thanks to their intervention, she could feel proud of what she and Tom had just achieved by working together. She'd only ever done this kind of work in the safe environment of an emergency department. Was this what his job was like every day? Stressful procedures under trying conditions to save lives?

As soon as Harley was stable, arrangements were made to move him up to the hospital.

'He should probably get a proper chest drain inserted before they fly him out,' Tom said. 'Either that or keep to a low altitude.'

The light was starting to fade noticeably by the time Harley was being taken away.

'Take a break,' one of the USAR team advised. 'You're not needed urgently right now and none of us know how long the night's going to be.'

'When did you last eat?' Tom asked Abby.

'I skipped lunch,' she admitted. 'I was a bit nervous about the big clinic I had on for this afternoon. And I didn't eat much breakfast because I was a bit on edge about...about...'

'Jack's first school outing?'

'Mmm.'

Tom said nothing more. Instead, he steered Abby away from the hardware shop. Away from the street, even, towards a small grassed area near the Fat Duck that had a child's play area and a bench seat for supervising adults. He sat down and Abby had no choice other than to sit down beside him and eat the muesli bar he produced from a pocket.

'Hardly ideal,' Tom said wryly. 'And I probably shouldn't be taking the time for personal issues but if we're on a break, I can't see the harm. And I really do want to know. I think you owe me that much, Abby.'

Abby's heart thumped. Was he going to suggest she was lying again? About Jack's paternity, perhaps? That would hurt. Badly.

'Know what, exactly?'

'Why you didn't tell me.'

They were sitting side by side. Close enough to touch but there was a gap between them. Abby stared straight ahead of her, her gaze fixed, unseeing, on the child's slide. Where they were, and the emergency situation they were in the middle of, seemed to fade into the background. Abby mentally stepped back in time. To another situation that had been just as tense in its own way.

'I did intend to,' she said quietly. 'I went to the hospital but they said you'd discharged yourself. Against doctor's orders. They said you'd be at home, that it would be a couple of weeks before you were signed off as fit to fly, so I went to your apartment. When I found nobody was home, I decided you'd be hanging out at the base. Not the ideal place to break news like that but you hadn't returned any of my calls.'

She heard Tom's breath escape in an angry kind of hiss. 'You never left any messages.'

'Well…now you know why.'

'No.' The word was clipped. 'I can't say I do.'

Abby had to turn and look at him, then, because she didn't understand. She encountered a dark and determined gaze. Tom was still angry. He wanted answers. And he deserved the truth, didn't he? He was right. She owed him that much. A lot more, probably, because… he'd given her Jack, hadn't he?

'I don't know why you didn't wait. Why you didn't make any more of an effort to tell me.'

'It was because you were off on a mission,' Abby said. 'When your doctors must have told you it wasn't a good idea after you'd had a punctured lung. It was then I knew I…I just *couldn't* tell you.'

Abby had to bite her bottom lip hard to stop tears coming. Good grief, she seemed to be crying at the drop of a hat today. Emotional overload. How unfair was it to have so many huge things in her life crashing around her at the same time? She had no idea whether her little house was still standing or when she would get to cuddle Jack again. Seeing Tom after all these years would have been quite enough of a shock all by itself.

Cuddling Jack… Oh, Lord… The relief of hearing that he was safe was wearing off now. Abby was desperate to take her son into her arms and hold him tightly. So tightly he could never wriggle free and get into danger ever again.

Yet again she had to fight back tears. The physical activity on top of the totally shocking emotional roller-coaster she was on was taking its toll. Abby felt too exhausted to take any notice of the alarms ringing in her head as she crossed barriers that had been there for a very, very long time.

'I never told you much about my childhood, did I?'

'I know you lost your parents early and that you were brought up by your grandparents in a little country town.' Tom turned his head to survey what had been Kaimotu village. Was he thinking that she'd come to a place like this because it had reminded her of where she'd been raised?

He was closer to the truth than he realised.

'My parents were both mountaineers,' she told him. 'Famous for their achievements. They once did seven of the world's hardest climbs in a seven-month period. They wrote a book about it.... *Lucky Number Seven*.'

'And that's how they died? In a mountaineering accident?'

'Yep. They both got swept away by an avalanche. Their bodies were never recovered.'

'God, that's awful. How old were you?'

'Nine.'

Tom was looking at her. She could see the sympathy but she could also see a question mark. What did this have to do with her not telling him he was going to be a father?

'I was really proud of Mum and Dad,' Abby went on. 'I absolutely adored them but as I got older I began to understand how dangerous their passion was. I'd beg them not to go. And when they did, which was at least once a year, I'd stay with Gran and worry myself sick that something bad was going to happen.' Her voice wobbled and began to fade. 'That they'd never come back...'

It seemed perfectly natural that Tom take hold of her hand and hold it. Squeeze it, even.

'But...' He stopped himself after the single word, but it was enough for Abby to realise he still didn't get it.

'You were off on a mission, Tom. You lived for the danger of your job—just like my parents lived for the danger of the mountains. You obviously still do. When I found out you'd gone out on a job that day, I suddenly realised what it would be like if I told you that I was pregnant. If you decided that you wanted to try and make things work, maybe. That you might want to be a father.'

She could feel the shock wave through her hand just before Tom released it abruptly.

'*Might* want to be a father? What the hell is that supposed to mean? That I wouldn't be prepared to take the responsibility? That I wasn't capable of stepping up to the mark?'

'No. It wasn't like that. It was—'

'What made you so damn sure I would have been a bad father?'

'*No.*' The word was even more vehement this time. Torn out of Abby. 'The opposite of that. You would have been a great father. The best. Just like you were in everything you did.'

The best paramedic.

The best lover...

She had to make him understand somehow, because Abby knew this would be very, very important for trying to move forward from this. For all of them. She sucked in a deep breath as she felt Tom's stunned silence as he processed her words. And suddenly—surprisingly—she felt calm.

'Jack would have had a hero for a dad,' she continued quietly. 'Someone a little boy would grow up worshipping. And at some point he'd start to understand how dangerous that job was. He'd start getting scared.'

Tom was absolutely silent beside her. Abby was looking straight ahead again and she had the impression that Tom was doing exactly the same thing. That it was too hard for him to look at her as she spoke. She wasn't finished yet, either. She had to keep going. Make him *really* understand.

'He'd start to realise that all those unknown people who were sick or hurt were somehow more important than *he* was. That every time his dad answered the call to go to one of them, there was a chance that he'd never come back.'

Abby had to scrub at her face and sniff loudly. Where were these tears coming from?

'I know what it's like to live with that fear,' she added brokenly. 'I didn't want it for my child. It was right then, when I found you'd gone off on a new mission when you hadn't even recovered from getting hurt in the last one, that I knew I had to find somewhere my baby would be safe. And keep him safe for as long as I possibly could because…'

Because that baby had been a part of herself.

A part of Tom.

The man she loved with all her heart and soul.

It was on the tip of her tongue to let that spill out, too, but Abby stopped herself just in time. Tom didn't need to know that. The consequences of him finding out he was a father were enough of a worry. She didn't need to make it worse by making herself vulnerable as a woman as well as a mother.

'Just because…' she finished lamely.

Tom was still sitting there silently. Maybe he would have said something but the air around them was filled with the distinctive heavy sound of an approaching Iroquois helicopter.

The hard-core rescue personnel were going to arrive in droves now and the operation to save and protect the community of Kaimotu Island would move into a new, intense phase. They couldn't stay sitting here in a quiet corner, ignoring what was really important right now.

And the four-wheel-drive vehicle that Mike had taken away to check the condition of the runway was coming back down the hill. At some speed, given the appalling condition the road was now in.

He slammed on the brakes when he spotted Abby and Tom sitting on the bench.

'Thought you'd be back at HQ,' he said. 'You won't have heard.'

Abby's heart skipped a beat. Was this going to be news about Jack?

'They're getting a food parcel together. It's your pilot who's going to do the drop, Tom. Moz? He's asking where you are.'

'What?' Tom reached for the radio clipped to his overalls and then swore softly. 'How the hell did I miss dropping that?'

'It's probably back at the hardware shop where we were working on Harley,' Abby said. 'Do we need to go and look for it?'

'No.' Mike shook his head. 'Jump in and come with

me. We're running out of time because they don't want to do it after dark. You could go, too, if you like, Abby. You might get to wave at Jack, at least.'

If she liked?

Was he *kidding*? Abby jumped to her feet. Tom already had the door of the vehicle open for her to climb in.

He had an odd expression on his face.

Because he might get to wave at Jack, too? See his *son* for the first time?

Abby's hand was shaking as she reached to slam the door shut. As unbelievable as this day already was, the tension had just increased by several huge notches.

CHAPTER FOUR

THE INFORMATION CENTRE was a hive of activity as Abby and Tom arrived back in the gathering dusk.

Outside, portable generators were powering spotlights that illuminated vehicles being stocked with various supplies and people moving both towards and away from the operational hub.

Inside, the space was far more crowded and noisy than the last time Abby had been in there.

When she'd been delegated as Tom's partner. Before he'd had any idea of the real partnership they still had. One that would change the shape of the future for both of them.

The partnership of being parents…

Not that Abby could give any head space to a future that wasn't immediate. Even the excitement of possibly seeing Jack very soon was being pushed aside in the face of this controlled chaos.

How many choppers had landed on the island in the last couple of hours when she'd been working in what remained of the island's village? Or had a ferry arrived? The centre was crowded with strangers wearing the overalls and hard hats that were the uniform of people who knew how to handle an urban disaster.

One of them was wearing a fluorescent vest that had the insignia 'Incident Commander' on its back. Tom headed straight for the man but Abby had stopped in her tracks, overwhelmed by the noise and activity.

There were locals in here, too. Mike Henley was looking exhausted as he was being interviewed by a television crew and reporters.

'Yes. In hindsight, I suppose we could say that the minor tremors recently were foreshocks, but nobody can predict a major earthquake. I'm sorry, but you'll have to ask an expert those kinds of questions. We have more important things to deal with at the moment.'

'How many confirmed deaths have been reported so far, sir?'

'Three.' The grim lines on the senior police officer's face deepened.

'Can you release any names?'

'Not yet. Not until the victims have been identified and their next of kin notified.'

Other people were bustling past the obstruction the knot of media personnel were making. Someone had an armload of blankets.

'Put them in the ute outside, Kev,' someone else called. 'Who's got the food parcels?'

'Report of person trapped.' A young man waved a radio above his head. 'Building down and the dog handler reckons they've got someone alive in there.'

The reporters' attention swerved instantly away from Mike. The incident commander turned away from his conversation with Tom.

'Blue team? Over here.'

There was a surge of movement as a group of rescuers responded to the summons.

Abby still hadn't moved. Her body was aching, she realised. Especially her knee. She'd banged it on something, way back, but had no idea when. There were too many things happening around her and her head was spinning.

The relief of knowing Jack was safe was disappearing beneath fear again. She wouldn't really believe it until she could hold her son in her own arms. And what about all the other people she cared about so much on the island? Like Ben McMahon, who'd been her colleague and friend for so many years now. Where was he? He should have turned up hours ago, as soon as the disaster had happened. Or maybe he had. He could be up at the hospital right now, operating on a badly injured islander, perhaps.

Somebody here must know about Ben. And his parents, Doug and Ailsa, who, ever since she'd arrived here pregnant and vulnerable, had been like the parents Abby had never really had. Catching her breath, Abby looked around. She didn't even know how people had fared in their houses. If houses were still standing.

The smell of hot food caught her nose. In the corner of the information centre a table had been set up to dispense food and hot drinks to the rescue workers. Abby recognised the older woman who was clearly in charge. Daphne Hayward—the kind of pillar of a small community who was always in exactly the place she was most needed, usually with her sister, Flora, by her side. The 'Hayward girls', as they were known locally, always knew what was happening.

Finally, Abby could move.

'Daphne…do you know anything about Ben? He

went out on a house call and didn't get back before the quake hit. I haven't heard anything...'

'Sorry, love. I haven't heard about Ben, either. Ailsa said she's sure he'll be fine. He'll be busy helping someone or other.... The phones aren't working.' Daphne's face creased in sympathy. 'You must be so worried about your little Jack but isn't it good news about the bus being spotted?'

'Mmm.' Abby choked back a sob. 'We're going out there...with food parcels...' She turned her head, trying to see where Tom was.

He was coming towards her through the crowd and his gaze caught hers. It felt like a solid connection. A path he was travelling to get to her side.

And it felt wonderful. The confusion—even the exhaustion—Abby had been aware of since coming into the centre was suddenly gone. Tom would be by her side any second now and then they would go and do whatever had to be done. Together. And she could cope, because she'd have Tom beside her.

Daphne was prattling on, telling her as much news as she could in a short space of time. Trying to offer her a cup of tea, as well, but Abby was moving again now. With Tom.

Heading for the door and the vehicle that would take them to the helicopter.

But she came to another sudden stop right outside the door of the information centre because there was a new crowd of people blocking the entrance. People she knew.

Ben...and Ginny...and Daphne's sister, Flora, and a whole bunch of children. But it was Ben that Abby couldn't take her eyes off.

'Ben—oh, thank God you're okay. I've been so wor-

ried. Where have you been? We've been going out of
our minds. Your mum—'

'She's okay?'

Oh, help… She could see the fear in his eyes. Ben
didn't know that his family were safe. Wherever he'd
been, he obviously had no idea what was happening
in the township. Or up at the hospital. She had to reassure him.

'She's fine. As far as I know, all your family is okay.
Doug's out with the searchers. Your house is intact and
your mum and Hannah have set it up as a crèche. Oh…'

Another look at the children Ben had collected and
the mention of the McMahon house being used as a
crèche had reminded her of how much this family had
done for her when she'd first arrived. When Jack had
been a baby.

Jack…

'Can you clear the entrance, please?' A soldier was
waving at them. Abby glared at him and didn't move.

'Why aren't you at the hospital?' Ben asked. He had
Ginny's little girl, Button, in his arms now.

Abby hurriedly tried to reassure Ben that things were
under control. That there were people who knew what
they were doing in charge at the hospital. That she'd
been out on the front line where things were really bad.
She could feel her fear rising again as she spoke.

She could feel Tom moving closer behind her and
she had to introduce him to Ben.

'This is Tom Kendrick…. I…we know each other.'

Abby had to bite her lip. Would it be obvious to Ben
that Tom was a grown-up version of Jack? Or maybe
Ginny would see it because she hadn't watched Jack

growing up and she was seeing everything on the island with fresh eyes because she'd only returned recently.

No. Surely it wouldn't occur to either of them. They all had far too much to deal with and it had nothing to do with Jack's possible paternity.

'He's search and rescue from the mainland. We've been out. They wanted a nurse who knew people. I...I...'

Tom was even closer to her now. Abby could feel his arm go around her waist. Good grief...if it hadn't occurred to Ben to wonder about just how well they'd known each other in the past, this would be a dead give-away. And how hard would it be to put two and two together after that? She wasn't ready for other people to know about Tom being Jack's father so, despite longing for that contact and the reassurance it could convey, Abby moved swiftly away from the touch.

'I'm...I'm fine,' she said.

Ginny was staring at her. 'Abby, where's Jack?'

'On...on the bus.' And it was getting darker by the minute. They really had to get moving but Ben and Ginny needed to get brought up to speed, didn't they? Her mind a swirl of anxiety now, her voice faded to almost a whisper. 'We've just come back to get the chopper. They've organised a drop of blankets and food.'

What if they couldn't take off in time? Or if the teachers decided to walk everybody out along the cliff road? To climb over the obstacle of the slip? In the dark, with those rocks and the crashing surf so far below...?

'What the...?' Ben stopped speaking. He was staring at Abby now, too. Or had his gaze caught the fact that Tom's arm had come around her waist again and that, this time, she hadn't moved out of range.

'It's okay,' Tom was saying calmly, over her head. 'We had a tense time for a while when we couldn't locate the school bus but we have it now. One of the fishing boats has seen it from the sea. It's trapped on the cliff road round past the mines at the back of the island. There's been two landslips and the bus is trapped between them. As far as we know, they're all fine, but we're not going to be able to get them out until morning. Hence the airdrop. We'll drop a radio in, as well.'

'So it'll be okay.' Abby forced the words out. She had to believe them. It was about more than getting Jack back to a safe place. Much more.

Ginny was frowning at her now. Trust another woman to pick up on an undercurrent and wonder what was going on. Abby took a deep breath.

'They need you at the hospital.' Persuading Ben and Ginny to move on to where they were needed and allow herself and Tom to do the same was suddenly paramount. 'Here's Hannah. Ginny, is it okay if Button goes with her? You and Ginny are needed for medical stuff. Please, go fast. There are so many casualties. But Tom and I need to go now.' Abby moved away from his touch, leading the way. 'Let's go.'

Finally, they were airborne.

'We'll be there in no time, don't you worry.' Moz was happy to be doing something useful. He threw a grin sideways at Abby, who was sitting in the front of the helicopter but, from where he was sitting in the back, Tom could see that the reassurance hadn't softened the lines of tension in her face. She didn't say anything in response to Moz. She just nodded tersely and stared straight ahead into a dusk that was almost complete darkness.

Just as well the helicopter had a night sun. They could shine the powerful beam of light down onto the drop area and make it safe for Tom to winch down the supplies they were carrying. Or maybe even find a safe place to touch down. How happy would Abby be if she could bring her son on the return trip? No reason not to. They had plenty of room to include a small boy.

Her son.

His son.

Oh…God… For however long this short flight took, there was nothing else Tom needed to be doing. There was nothing to be talked about between the three people confined in this flying bubble. For the first time since this bombshell of news had landed on him, Tom was alone with his own thoughts.

Abby hadn't followed through with telling him she was pregnant. There was anger there. Lots of it. He'd had the right to know. He could have stepped up to the mark if he'd had the opportunity, but he'd simply been dismissed. Not even consulted.

What would have happened if he *had* known? How would he have reacted? If he was going to be honest with himself, Tom knew he probably wouldn't have reacted well. He'd never even considered taking on the responsibility of having kids. No way. Good grief, he'd broken up with Abby because she'd become an anchor. Trying to hold him back from doing the job that was his life because it was dangerous. She'd only been his girlfriend. Having a family—a *child*—would have chained him to an even bigger anchor. There was no way it wouldn't have slowed him down. Clipped his wings.

No. He wouldn't have reacted well to the news. He would have been horrified. But he would have stepped up to the mark. He would have tried to make things work with Abby again and a part of him—maybe a huge part—would have been relieved to have her back in his life.

He'd missed her far more than he'd ever admitted, even to himself.

Moz was following the ribbon of the cliff road at a fairly low altitude. Tom could see the dark spikes of rocky coastline now that they were away from the beaches on the more inhabited side of Kaimotu Island. He could see the white foam of big waves breaking and the inky darkness of dense bush on the hills. This was wild country.

Beautiful but very isolated.

And this was where Abby had chosen to come to have her child. To raise him.

Not because she thought he'd make a terrible father, though.

Because she thought his son would have grown up thinking he was amazing. A hero.

A sensation Tom couldn't identify squeezed in his chest. Pride? Lots of people thought he was a hero. How many times had he had his photo in the paper or letters written to the rescue base praising his efforts to save the life of somebody's loved one? No, it was more than pride. It was something huge.

The idea of being loved by a child? That that child would learn to live with fear? A fear of losing *him*?

That was why Abby had been like she'd been about his job. Not initially, but after he'd been injured. She'd wanted him to be more careful. He'd seen it as her trying to clip his wings and hold him back because she didn't understand his passion and was trying to control him.

But she'd been scared.

The way she'd been scared about losing her adored parents.

Because…she'd loved him? *That* much?

Nobody had ever loved Tom that much. He hadn't wanted them to, had he?

It made life easier because you never had to get close enough to return a love that big, and that way you were never in any danger of being hurt by rejection.

Had he learned that lesson before he'd even been old enough to know what any of it was about? His teenage mother had never been in a position to raise him herself. As part of a huge, extended family, he'd been passed from household to household over the years. Always cared about. Loved, even, but somehow always on the periphery of the inner circle of family.

Maybe he'd coped with any sense of missing out by the adrenaline rush of danger that had always garnered attention. Being made a fuss of was a kind of love, wasn't it? That mechanism had started too early to remember, as well, but there was a photograph around of the cast he'd had on his broken arm when he'd fallen out of a tree, aged only two.

His mischief as a youngster had been the stuff of family legend. His exploits as an adult, after he'd discovered that taking risks was deemed far more acceptable if they were taken on behalf of others, attracted just as much attention. And all the women in his life had applauded his career, the same way that Abby had at the beginning of their relationship. Most of them, of the same ilk as Fizz, had urged him on to greater accomplishments. Bigger risks.

Because it wouldn't have mattered that much if he didn't come back?

Now Tom had another weird squeezing thing going on in his gut. Pretty much like the first one. He could see it wasn't pride, now. It was more a self-esteem thing. Feeling important. Not for the heroic or dangerous things you did for a job but simply because of who you were.

It was definitely a weird sensation and it was new but it wasn't entirely unpleasant.

'Almost there, Tank.' Moz was slowing the chopper. 'This looks like the first landslide coming up.'

Another glance down and Tom was again struck by the wildness of the landscape below.

He heard Abby's gasp as the bus came into view.

'Target sighted,' Moz said. 'We'll go around and get lower. Turning downwind.'

Abby's tension was palpable now, over and above the vibration of the helicopter. Every fibre of her being was focused on seeing her child. Making sure he was safe. Holding him in her arms, maybe.

Tom closed his eyes in a long blink. Imagine someone caring so much about you that they took you to the most isolated place they could find to try and keep you safe?

Was Jack a lucky kid?

Or was he being suffocated?

He wouldn't want his son to grow up to be a sissy. Was he a frail kid? Was that why Abby was so worried? Maybe he wore glasses and kept his nose buried in a book all day or too close to a computer screen for hours at a time.

Well…if that was the case, maybe Jack *did* need a father figure in his life. Maybe he wasn't too late to step up to that mark after all.

The chopper was much lower now. Hovering. It was time for Tom to do his job. To open the door and set up the winch to lower the parcel.

'Checking winch power,' he announced.

Moz turned on the night sun. They could see the bus and the crowd of children waving up at them. And the adults, who were keeping them well within a safe range. Abby was straining against her safety harness, focusing intently on the brightly lit scene below.

'Where is he?' she cried. 'I can't see Jack anywhere.'

'There's a lot of kids down there.' Moz sounded as calm as he always did. 'He'll be there somewhere. Speed back, Tank. Clear door.'

Abby was shaking her head. 'I'd see him, I know I would.'

'He might be inside the bus.' Tom was turning on the radio clipped to the outside of the blanket bundle. There was no way it could be missed, so they would be able to communicate clearly with the people on the ground within the next few minutes. 'We'll know pretty soon. Hang in there, Abby.'

He slid the side door open. 'Door back and locked,' he told Moz. 'Bringing hook inside.'

He attached the hook to the big parcel. 'Moving box to the door,' he informed Moz. Now he had to get permission to stand on the skids and control the winching process. 'Clear skids.'

'Clear skids,' Moz confirmed.

He had to make sure the parcel landed safely away from any people, which wasn't a simple process. Too far one way and the vital supplies, especially the radio, would go over the cliff and into the sea below. Dense bush on the other side of the cliff road could make it impossible for the people to find it in the dark.

There was enough clear road between the landslides, though. Enough to land on, except that it was a risk that wouldn't be deemed worth taking given the dangers on either side of the narrow road.

Tom watched the distance between the parcel hanging on the end of the winch line and the road below.

'Minus fifteen,' he told Moz. 'Ten...nine...eight...'

And then it was almost on the ground and the attachment was disengaged. Someone was running towards the parcel while others were keeping the children in a close knot beside the bus.

Tom picked up his radio.

'Hello?' he called. 'Hello, hello? Do you read?'

There was silence but he could see a man hunching over the big parcel. Reaching for the radio.

'Hello?' Tom tried again. 'Push the button on the top when you speak.'

A crackling noise came through, along with the end of an unintelligible sentence.

'Try again,' Tom directed. 'Hold the button and keep it down. Can you hear me?'

'Yes...' The word was a shout.

'You have food and blankets. We're looking at ways of getting you out but it won't be till daylight, now. Is there anything else you require urgently?'

'Yes.'

Tom was aware of Abby twisting in her seat. Of her eyes widening. An urgent message was coming silently.

Ask about Jack.... Please, Tom.

'What's the problem?' Tom had to stay professional here. He couldn't single out a particular child to ask about, even if was his own son.

'We have a child missing.' The man had figured out the radio now. 'He was still in the old copper mine when the quake struck and the walls collapsed at the entrance.'

'Only one child?'

'Yes. A teacher has stayed behind. We could hear him calling.'

'Is he injured?'

'Don't think so. Don't know. We came on the bus to get help and that's when we got stuck. It's not far to the mine from here but we decided it was too dangerous to send anyone back. It's been hours…'

Tom didn't need to hear how hard it was for Abby to control her breathing right now. He knew the answer to his question before he even asked.

'Who's the child?'

'Jack Miller. He's only five, poor little guy. Just started school a few weeks ago.'

Tom heard a low oath from Moz underscoring a stifled sob from Abby. He took another look at the stretch of road between the landslips.

The risk might not have been justifiable a few minutes ago but there was no question about it now.

'Take us down, Moz,' Tom said quietly. 'We're needed here.'

CHAPTER FIVE

ABBY HELD HER BREATH as the helicopter came down to land on the narrow road in the dark. She wished she had a hand to hold.

Tom's hand?

She could see how intently Moz was concentrating on controlling the aircraft so she knew this was not an easy task. It could be that it was actually far more dangerous than she knew. She didn't want to know. She just wanted to be on the ground.

Moving.

She had to get to Jack. Her own safety was almost irrelevant at this moment.

'Good job, mate.' There was a note in Tom's voice as they touched down and the rotors began to slow that suggested to Abby that she had been right in thinking that this landing had been dangerous. They'd taken a risk here.

Because Tom had suggested it?

Abby's flash of gratitude was swiftly displaced by the desperate need to get out of the helicopter. To find a way to reach that mine and start searching for Jack. She fumbled with the clasp on her safety harness. It was Tom who reached through from the back and re-leased the catches.

'Follow me,' he directed. 'And keep your head down. The rotors haven't stopped.'

'Why not?' Abby's head turned sharply back in the pilot's direction. 'You're coming, too, aren't you, Moz? We need all the help we can get.'

Moz and Tom exchanged a long glance. And then Moz reached to flick some switches and Abby heard the engine noise change. It was shutting down.

'I'm in.' Moz nodded. 'I'll grab what we've got in the way of ropes and stuff. You guys go and get briefed.'

The man who'd retrieved the air-drop parcel and the radio was waiting for them. Dennis Smythe, born and bred on Kaimotu Island, was the senior teacher of the junior school. Usually laid back and well in control of any trouble a bunch of kids could manufacture, he looked anguished right now.

'Abby, I'm *so* sorry. I can't believe this has happened to Jack, of all people...'

Words were torn from Abby. '*How* did it happen?'

'We were getting on the bus to come back to school. He was right at the end of the line. Apparently he re-alised he'd dropped something when we were exploring and he was off like a little rocket back into the mine to try and find it. His teacher, Shelley, tried to stop him but couldn't so I took off after him, but that was when the quake hit. I...I was thrown off my feet. The kids were all panicking... It was complete chaos for a bit.'

Abby could only nod. She would never forget those interminable seconds of the initial quake. The terror of feeling like the world was in the process of ending.

'We could hear Jack calling,' Dennis continued. 'Just

faintly. We couldn't get inside the entrance because the beams had come down with a ton of rocks and other stuff. We knew we needed help but the phones weren't working.'

'The tower came down.' Abby was trying hard to listen but the information was coming too slowly and there wasn't enough of it. But she could see how hard this was hitting Dennis and, whatever had happened, it hadn't been his fault. He'd had the responsibility for a lot of people, most of them children, and she knew he would have done his absolute best.

'We decided the quickest way to get help would be to take the bus and we needed to get the others to safety, as well. Shelley volunteered to stay at the mine so she could try and talk to Jack and keep him reassured that help was on its way.'

'What…what was he calling? Is…is he hurt?'

'Shelley didn't think so. He was scared, of course. He…he was calling for you, Abby. Calling "Mummy"…'

'Oh…oh, *God*…' Abby had to press a hand to her eyes. She felt Tom step closer and felt his arm go around her. The touch was starting to feel familiar again and it was an offer of strength she couldn't refuse. Abby leaned into him and tried so hard not to give in to the tears that wanted to come that she could feel her whole body trembling.

'Tell us everything you can,' Tom instructed. 'How well do you know this area?'

'Like the back of my hand,' Dennis told him. 'I grew up here, mate. Right below here is the beach that was the best place on the island for some serious surfing. There's a track that leads down the cliff somewhere close. And a jetty. I reckon we could get these kids out by boat but I wouldn't try it in the dark. No way.'

'How do we get to the mine? Along the shore?'

'No, that wouldn't work. There's only one track and you can't get back up past the bay. I reckon you'll need to get into the bush and head up. You could clear the slip where it started and then get back down to the road. Couple of kilometres on and you'll find the road to the mines. It's signposted. Or it was, anyway...' Dennis started to rub his forehead. 'I don't know if anything's like it's supposed to be anymore. What's happened in town? Has anybody been hurt? I've been worried sick about Suzie. She's pregnant, you know. About three months along.'

Abby took a deep breath. A very deep breath. Dennis and Suzie had married only last year.

'It's bad, Dennis, but a lot of help's arrived from the mainland. Experts, like Tom here. I haven't seen or heard anything about Suzie but that's a good thing. It probably means she's okay. Tom, will the radio work to contact someone like Mike Henley?'

'Yes. I just need to change the channel being used.'

'Can you do that now? There must be so many parents who're desperate to know their children are okay and then...and then can we get going? To the mine?'

It was dark now and Tom's eyes were dark anyway so Abby shouldn't have been able to see his expression of complete understanding so easily.

Other parents were desperate, yes, but they were about to find out their children were safe. To be able to talk to them even, maybe.

She was the only one who couldn't get that reassurance.

Yet.

But there was more than sympathy in that gaze. There was the reassurance that only Tom could give her right now.

We'll find him, Abby, the look told her. *We can do this. Everything's going to be okay.*

There had been a point in Abby's life when she had trusted Tom absolutely. But he had broken that trust when he'd ended their relationship. Broken her heart. Could she believe in him again? Trust what that look was telling her?

Yes, she could. She *had* to.

Moz had coils of rope over his shoulders and a backpack stuffed with everything else he could find that might be useful.

Tom tightened the straps on his backpack, which contained all the medical supplies they might need.

Abby was given a pack with a couple of blankets and some of the food and water they'd brought there.

They all had hard hats on with lamps that were now glowing. Heavy boots that would help them cope with the terrain. Overalls that would help protect them from superficial injury. And determination that they were going to succeed on this unexpected mission.

They were all grateful for the overalls as they pushed their way uphill through native bush that had a dense undergrowth of scratchy punga ferns. They kept as close as they could to the side of the slip and eventually came to where the land had been shaken loose and had started the slide. The trees above still seemed soundly rooted and gave them a secure passage to the other side and then they had to get down the steep hillside again, slipping frequently and catching themselves on nearby tree trunks. Once, Abby missed a catch and fell, sliding a long way before coming up against a larger fern.

Tom's heart skipped a beat. He was by her side in seconds, helping her as she struggled back to her feet.

'Are you okay?'

'I'm fine. Keep going, Tom. I'm *fine*.'

She wasn't. She may not have been injured by the fall but she wasn't fine. How could she be?

Abby knew her son was in danger. Possibly trapped and hurt. She'd just fought her way up a slope that had been enough to drain Tom's energy but she'd refused a water stop at the top. She was hurtling downhill now and it would have been that speed and determination that had made her slip in the first place.

But she wasn't about to stop. Or even slow down, thank you very much.

She was fearless right now. A woman who was going to do whatever it took to save someone she loved. She was staring at him, still radiating that fierce resolve to carry on.

The direct beam of Tom's headlamp pointed above her head but Abby was bathed in the surrounding circle of light.

She was filthy. Her overalls were splattered with the same mud that streaked her face. The long plait of her blonde hair was coming unravelled and was festooned with twigs and pieces of fern frond. A deep scratch on her cheek was adding blood to the grime. Any vestige of make-up she'd been wearing had long since vanished.

But her eyes shone with determination and an inner strength that Tom had never recognised in Abby. And her lips trembled with a vulnerability that he'd also never known about because she'd kept it so well buried.

At this moment, in possibly the most isolated place in which he'd ever been, Abby Miller was *the* most beautiful woman Tom had ever laid eyes on.

And there was that odd squeezy sensation in his chest again. The same as he'd got in the wake of imagining someone loving him so much they couldn't bear anything bad happening to him. The same, only different, because it was like he was transmitting that sensation now instead of simply receiving it.

He didn't want anything bad to happen to Abby. He wanted to protect her.

But he also wanted to cheer her on.

Maybe *this* was pride. He was proud of Abby.

His breath felt ragged as he dragged it in. Was his hand actually shaking as he reached out to check whether that cut on Abby's cheek needed attention before they carried on?

'What's up, Tank?' Moz's voice carried easily from a fair way further down the slope. 'I think I can see the road again.'

Abby pulled her face away from the touch of Tom's fingers. With even more of an effort she pulled her gaze away from what she could see in his eyes.

Admiration?

Tenderness, even?

She could have drowned in that look. Just as well, the sound of Moz's voice carried so clearly.

'It can wait,' she told Tom. 'It's just a scratch.'

Her knee could wait, too, even though it was hurting badly now. By the time they reached the road it was getting hard to disguise the fact that she couldn't put her whole weight on that leg. What would Tom do if he saw her limping?

Carry her to where her son was?

Probably.

She couldn't let that happen. She couldn't let herself be dependent on Tom in any way.

Not physically. And definitely not emotionally. Dear Lord…even under these circumstances, that touch of his fingers on her face had woken memories that had pushed insistently into her mind as she'd walked on.

The way he'd once played with her toes, for example, when they'd been curled up on a couch together, watching television. Idle touching that would morph into a truly excellent foot massage until they both lost interest in the movie and her feet would be neglected in favour of more exciting parts of her body for him to touch.

The way he'd held her head when they'd kissed, with his fingers woven through her hair and pressing onto her scalp.

The way he would lie beside her, when they were both completely naked, usually in the aftermath of making love, and he would use his fingertips so gently. He would trace the entire outline of her body as if he was drawing her shape in sand. Or committing it to memory.

How could a single touch unleash so many memories? Abby had had no idea they were still lurking so close to the surface. She had to bury them and make sure they were deep enough this time. She had to protect herself.

She could do this. Shut the memories away and not react to any touch, accidental or otherwise. And she'd make sure she didn't start depending on Tom. Not emotionally and not physically.

Not even as a co-parent.

He might think he wanted to get involved in Jack's life now but how long would that last? How available would he be if some exciting mission came up? What if Jack was holding his breath, waiting for his dad to make an appearance at a school play or a prizegiving and Tom didn't show up because he'd been called back to work or his helicopter happened to have crashed on that particular day?

Oh…good grief…

Abby allowed enough of her weight to go onto her bad knee to send a sharp twinge right through her body as a kind of wake-up call.

As if she didn't have enough to worry about right now. Yet here she was, imagining a worst-case scenario for something in a future that wasn't even on the horizon. Tom hadn't even met his son. He certainly hadn't said anything about wanting to be a part of their lives.

They had turned off the main cliff road now, where the signpost to the tourist attraction of the old copper mine was still standing, albeit at a drunken angle.

Maybe it was some kind of a defence mechanism, Abby excused herself. By looking into the future, perhaps she was giving herself the reassurance that they would get through the tension and fear of their present situation.

That Jack would be okay and he'd go on to do a school play or excel at something enough to be deemed worthy of a special prize. Not that she needed him to win any prizes. All she wished for was that her little boy would be safe. And grow up happy.

So why did she invent disasters for the future? Was she incapable of imagining something wonderful?

Like…like Jack getting his first puppy, for instance. His face shining with joy. His dad on the floor beside him, playing with the pup and offering silly suggestions for names. His mum there, too. Taking pictures to add to the family album. Laughing at the puppy's antics. Knowing that this happy moment would become a treasured memory.

Abby's breath escaped in something far too close to a sob.

This was why she conjured up disasters and not joyful moments. Because the pain of knowing those moments would never happen was too much.

The longing *hurt*, dammit. And, right now, it was worse than ever because he was here. And he'd touched her face as if he cared and it had made her remember too much.

Tom had slowed his pace. He'd heard that sound of distress she'd been unable to stifle.

'You're limping.' The words were an accusation.

'I'm fine.'

'Dammit, Abby. Be honest for once. What's hurting?'

Abby almost laughed aloud. He wanted her to be honest? If he knew what had really hurt her, he'd run a mile.

That joyous glimpse into an imaginary future for her would no doubt represent a disaster for Tom Kendrick. A family hanging around his neck like a millstone. Holding him back from the adrenaline rush of hurling himself into danger at every opportunity. Of being a real-life hero. Admired by all and loved by many.

That sweet-little-puppy scenario she'd lost herself

in for a few moments wasn't going to happen. Not in this lifetime.

'It's my knee,' was what she did say. 'I gave it a bump, way back, when the earthquake first happened. It's just getting a bit stiff now, that's all.'

Moz had come back to where Tom was walking more slowly beside Abby.

'How far have we still got to go?' he asked.

'I'm not sure,' Abby said. 'Not too far, I think.'

For a minute or two the three of them walked in silence.

'Hey...' The call was female. And faint. 'Is someone there? I can see a light. Help...we're up here. *Help*...'

Tom's voice rang out clearly in the night air. 'We're coming,' he shouted. 'Hold on...'

The teacher who had stayed behind at the mine, Shelley Carter, was young, in her early twenties. By now she'd been alone out here for many hours. She was exhausted and scared and when she saw Moz, Tom and Abby arriving, she burst into tears.

It took a while for Tom to be sure she wasn't injured in any way and to get the information he needed to start assessing the situation.

'It wasn't so bad while it was still light.' Wrapped in a blanket now and drinking a bottle of water from the supplies they had brought with them, Shelley was finally calm enough to talk, although her voice was very hoarse. 'The aftershocks were really scary but I could keep busy, you know? And I could talk to Jack. Well, yell at him, anyway...' She drank some more water. 'I've almost lost my voice.'

The first thing Abby had done when they'd arrived

at the scene had been to get as close as she could to the entrance and start calling.

'Jack? Jack, can you hear me, darling? Mummy's here. We're all here to rescue you. Jack? *Jack?*'

There'd been no response to her calls and Abby had stopped for now. She was standing nearby, her arms wrapped around her body, her bottom lip caught between her teeth, staring at Shelley as she talked.

From where he was crouched beside Shelley, Tom glanced up at Abby and then back to the young teacher.

'How long ago did you last hear Jack?' he asked quietly.

Shelley shook her head. 'I'm not sure. I've kind of lost track of time, you know? I guess it was after it got dark. I had to stop trying to shift rocks and stuff. And I couldn't yell as loudly because I was already starting to lose my voice.'

Abby's head flicked back and the light from her helmet raked over the blocked entrance to the mine. Another light was moving further away as Moz explored the site.

'Maybe...maybe he fell asleep,' Shelley whispered. But fresh tears rolled down her face. She was thinking exactly what had gone through Tom's mind and what he knew would be filling Abby's.

That Jack might be unconscious rather than asleep. Lying inside that mine somewhere, badly hurt. Dying, even...

Tom heard Abby suck in a breath.

'What made him go back inside like that?'

'Action...Man,' Shelley gulped.

Abby groaned. 'I *told* him he couldn't take him to

school. He must have hidden him inside his school bag when I wasn't looking.'

'What are we talking about here?' Tom was frowning. Why had Jack disobeyed his mother? Was he a naughty kid?

Because he didn't have a father around?

'Action Man.' Abby shook her head. 'It was his birthday present when he turned five. He'd been desperate for one.'

'It's a toy? A...a *doll*?' Oh, man, this was getting worse.

'Kind of.' But Abby had a poignant smile tugging at the corner of her mouth. 'It's an action figure. Special operations kind of hero doll and you can bend the joints to do almost anything. Action Man can climb table legs and abseil off the top of doors and parachute out of trees. He can do pretty much everything a little boy can dream of being able to do himself, I guess.'

Ohh...

Tom found himself smiling. If he'd had a doll like that when he'd been a kid, maybe he wouldn't have collected so many bumps and bruises and broken bones trying stuff out for himself.

'Tank?' Moz was still a short distance away. 'Come and have a look over here.'

'Tank?' Shelley looked at Abby as Tom pushed himself upright. 'I thought his name was Tom?'

'It is,' Abby responded. 'Tank's a nickname. You know, like Thomas the Tank Engine?'

Tom heard Shelley giggle behind him. 'That's what we need,' she said to Abby. 'A real-life Action Man.'

Tom strode towards where Moz was. That odd little

smile was still curling one side of his mouth. Because Abby had remembered his nickname?

No. It was more like he could imagine a little boy making his toy climb a table leg. Maybe making him talk at the same time. Being so attached to that toy that he'd rebelled against his mother's orders and sneaked him into a hiding place in his school bag. Clearly, his worry that Jack was a sissy was unfounded. He was starting to get a picture of what Jack was like.

His son was becoming a real person....

'Look.' Moz directed the beam of his headlamp. 'There's a gap here where the beams have crossed. If we shift a few rocks, we might be able to get access.'

How dangerous would that be? How precarious was any space left inside this mine entrance? How many aftershocks were still to come and how strong would they be? Enough to bring another load of rocks and earth down to bury any gaps?

One of those gaps contained his son.

'Let's do it.' Tom had already positioned himself beside one of the larger boulders. He put his shoulder against it and waited until Moz joined him. 'Ready? On the count of three. One...two...*three*...'

Abby was beside them by the time the boulder had rolled clear.

'Oh, my God...' she gasped. 'There's a *gap*.'

'Stay clear,' Tom ordered. 'We don't know which way these rocks are going to roll. You can come and have a look when there's something to see, okay?'

It took a remarkably short time for the two men to shift the boulders and the gap was easily big enough for them to get inside. Tom would have preferred to keep

Abby well out until they'd assessed how safe it was but she was having none of it.

Shelley was more than happy to stay where she was, wrapped up in her blanket, but Abby was right behind them as they entered the pitch blackness of the old mine entrance.

Only the beams around the end of the tunnel seemed to have collapsed. Inside, the roof and walls still had their tunnel shape. A few rocks had fallen further in but there was enough space to climb over them. They still couldn't see what lay ahead.

'Jack?' His voice bounced off the wall and echoed in the tunnel as Tom shouted. 'Jack? Can you hear me?'

'*Jack...*' Abby yelled as soon as Tom stopped. 'Jack, where are you?'

She hauled in a breath to call again but Tom gripped her arm. 'Shh...'

Abby's jaw dropped in shock but then he saw that she understood. If they kept yelling themselves, they wouldn't be able to hear a response, especially if it was faint.

And there it was. Very faint. Sounding sleepy.

'*Mummy...?*'

Abby's head swivelled so that she could catch Tom's gaze.

Had she really heard what she thought she'd heard?

Tom gave an imperceptible nod and Abby pressed a fist to her mouth. Trying to control herself so that she wouldn't burst into tears of relief? She was still holding his gaze and Tom could feel his own throat closing over a rather large lump. What he couldn't decide was whether that was due to the sound of that small voice or the relief he was feeling because Abby was so relieved.

She was still scared, though. And he was still holding her arm. He gave it a squeeze to encourage her. She would want to sound strong for Jack. She wouldn't want him to know how scared she was.

'*Yes...*' The word came out as a whisper so Abby had to try again. 'Mummy's here, Jack. We're coming to get you. Are you...? Does anything hurt?'

'I'm cold, Mummy. I want to go *home*.'

'I know, darling.' Tom could see that Abby had her eyes shut now. He could see the way her lips trembled when she wasn't talking but, amazingly, she was sounding incredibly strong. Confident. 'It won't be long now. We're coming to get you, okay?'

A faint sobbing could be heard now. '*Mum—mee...*'

The sound of Jack's voice was faint enough to be coming from a long way into the mine. Just how far had they taken the children exploring? Or had Jack missed where he'd dropped his toy and kept running in panic during or after the earthquake?

Abby was moving forward now, eager to find Jack. It was Moz who yelled a warning.

'Abby, *stop...*'

She turned her head towards Moz so she wasn't looking where she was going. Thank God her steps had faltered at the warning because Tom's light now zeroed in on what lay ahead. Where the floor of the tunnel simply disappeared.

His heart in his throat, he launched himself towards Abby, catching her in his arms and hauling her backwards.

'What the—?' Abby struggled in his hold. 'Tom, let me *go*.'

Tom had to struggle to take a normal breath, waiting for his heart to get back to a normal rhythm.

'Abby.' He kept his tone as calm as he could. 'Look…'

Abby looked. She sagged in his arms, and knowing that she could now see the danger, Tom let her go. Let her sink to her knees and stare over the edge of where the floor of the tunnel simply stopped.

'There must have been another tunnel running beneath this one.' It was Moz who spoke first. 'Something's given way to create this sinkhole.'

'How far does it go?' Abby's voice was shaking. 'And how do we get down?'

Tom's heart sank. How could he tell her that they had no idea how deep the hole was? Or how stable the sides of it were? That any movement could send a pile of earth and rocks cascading down to bury both Jack and anyone who was crazy enough to climb down?

He couldn't, that's all there was to it.

'I'll go down with a rope,' he said quietly. 'And see how far I can get.'

'Uh…Tank…' Moz's tone was a clear warning. He knew how far out of any acceptable protocol Tom was stepping.

'Can you anchor the rope?' Tom didn't give Moz the chance to voice any doubts. He used his headlamp to survey the surroundings. 'We'll use that beam, there. That'll hold most of my weight. You'll just need to feed me the length.'

Silently Moz took a long coil of rope from his shoulder and the two men moved to set up. Abby stayed by the edge of the hole.

'We're coming, Jack. Did…did you find Action Man?'

'No-o-o…'

'Doesn't matter, darling. We'll get you a new one, I promise.'

'But I want *my* Action Man.'

Tom had one end of the rope secured around his waist. Moz had another section of it around his own waist. Between them, the rope snaked around the solid beam that was part of the tunnel support.

'You sure about this, mate?'

Tom simply turned away and walked to the edge of the hole. Of course he was sure. It was his son who was at the bottom of that hole.

The walls were sloping to start with and it wasn't difficult to climb down. The rope was only needed as insurance so far but the danger was an unknown quantity and Tom moved very carefully. When his foot sent a shower of dirt and a small rock plunging down, he stopped and held his breath.

'Jack?' Abby shouted from above. 'Are you okay? Did anything hit you?'

'No…' came the small voice. 'It's okay, Mummy. I've got a roof.'

A *roof*?

Tom inched his way down until he could go no further. He was at a point where the huge beams from the tunnel above had wedged themselves in a criss-cross pattern across the hole, leaving only a small gap in the middle.

They seemed solid enough. Tom knelt on one of them to peer through. His lamp lit up a kind of rough cavern beneath. At least twenty feet further down he could see a jumble of rocks and piles of earth. But nothing else.

'Jack?' His voice felt weird and the name of his son

came out too faint to be useful. He cleared his throat. 'Jack? Can you hear me, buddy?'

Silence. And then something pale appeared in the dark shape of a huddled child amongst the boulders as a small face turned up towards the light.

'Who're you?' A frightened little voice.

'I'm...'

I'm your dad, Jack.

'I'm Tom...a friend of your mum's. I've come to get you out of here.'

Except there was no way he could get down to Jack. No way in the world he could push his huge frame through the only available gap. They needed help from engineers, here. Some heavy-duty equipment, which might have to be brought over to the island from the mainland. Diggers. Cranes. Oh, God. How long would that take?

Abby's headlamp was shining on the same place his was.

'What's the problem, Tom?'

'I can't get through the gap. It's too small.'

'Jack's small. Can't he climb up to it?'

Tom had to swallow hard. 'No. He's a good twenty feet further down and he wouldn't manage the climb.'

'I could get through that gap.'

'No way, Abby. It's far too dangerous. Stay where you are.' The beam he was cautiously kneeling on was solid enough but Tom wasn't about to push his luck any further. He could feel a sponginess that instinct told him was a very clear warning. One good aftershock and this whole lot could shake loose and tumble further.

No way on earth was he going to let Abby risk her life here.

Tom turned his attention back to what lay between him and rescuing Jack. Could he find another gap? Somehow move one of these beams?

He reached out to test the earth around where one end of a beam was wedged. The dirt crumbled in his fingers and, weirdly, some of it seemed to fly up and ping off his helmet.

Tom stopped what he was doing.

Another shower of earth rained down. A small stone sounded like the graze of a bullet on his helmet.

Realisation hit far too late.

Appalled, Tom looked up again but he knew he wouldn't see the beam of Abby's headlamp where it had been.

She was already halfway down the slope of the sink-hole, without even the protection of a rope. He saw the moment the small boulder she was using as a hand grip came loose from the surrounding earth.

The moment that Abby began to slip.

CHAPTER SIX

IT HAPPENED TOO FAST to feel any fear.

That reaction came seconds later, kicking in the moment Abby felt the grip of Tom's arms as he caught her and stopped her fall. When she realised she was safe, in that powerful hold, hearing the fervent relief in the oath that escaped Tom's lips, along with her name.

'*Abby...*'

As if *her* safety was the most important thing here. The way he said her name touched something very deep but Abby could ignore it far more easily than that touch on her face a while back. It wasn't *her* safety that mattered. And, anyway, she was relatively safe again now. More importantly, her impulsive action of climbing into the sinkhole hadn't made things worse. What if she'd dislodged enough debris to send the whole lot crashing down to bury Jack?

Jack.

Abby pushed the fear aside. Wrenched herself out of Tom's arms so that she could drop to her knees and put her face into that gap between the beams.

She could *see* him.

And he looked so small and vulnerable. Dirty and

scared and all hunched up in a little ball. Somehow Abby choked back a sob and even managed to sound calm.

'Hey, sweetheart…'

'Mummy.' Jack started to cry. 'Can we go home now? I d-don't like it down here.'

'I know, darling. You just hold on tight. We're going to get you out of there.'

'Abby…' The way Tom said her name this time was very different. A warning rather than a prayer of thanks. A warning that she was promising something they couldn't deliver?

'I can get through that gap,' she told Tom. 'I'm sure I can.'

'And then what?' Tom kept his voice low so that Jack couldn't overhear. 'Drop twenty feet and break your leg? So that we've got two people to try and dig out?'

'You're not using your rope. You can tie that around me.'

'No. I won't let you do this, Abby. It's far too dangerous. We have no idea how stable any of this stuff is. We'll radio for backup. Get some engineers and USAR guys here.'

'And how long will that take?'

They both knew the answer to that. *Too long.*

'You can't stop me, Tom.'

'Oh, I can, Abby.' It was more than a warning now. More like a threat.

'That's my *son* down there,' Abby hissed.

Tom just stared at her silently. He didn't have to say it. It was *his* son down there, too.

As if nature was impatient with the stand-off, a rumble of sound echoed in the mine shaft and the ground shook. It wasn't a big aftershock but it was enough to

remind them all of how they came to be here in the
first place. Of just how dangerous it was. That they all
needed to get out of there as fast as possible and the
clock was ticking loudly.

Abby had to bite her lip hard to stop herself crying
out in fear. Jack screamed. Tom's face was grimmer
than she'd ever seen it. Even when he'd been lying in
his hospital bed, telling her that their relationship was
over. That it could never work so the best thing for both
of them would be to walk away now before anybody
got really hurt.

It had been way too late for her by then. It wasn't too
late now but it soon could be. For Jack. And for them.
Was Tom going to learn that he was a father and then
lose his child on the very same day?

No. It wasn't going to happen. Abby wasn't going
to let it happen. She'd rather die trying to prevent it.

'You can't do this, Abby.' Tom's tone was curiously
hollow.

'I can't *not* do it,' was her response.

'You guys okay down there?' Moz was at the rim of
the sinkhole, the rope he'd been monitoring wrapped
around his waist instead of the beam, now.

'So far,' Tom said grimly. 'Chuck that rope down
here, will you, Moz? Abby's going to try and get down
to get Jack.'

'*What?* Oh, man…' Moz sounded shocked.

'Just do it,' Tom ordered. 'Chuck the rope.'

Moz did it silently. Maybe nobody argued with Tom
when he used that commanding tone. Abby wasn't about
to, either. Not when he was knotting the rope into a kind
of harness and giving her instructions about how she
could use the underside of the criss-crossing beams to

get to where she could find a foothold to help her get down to the bottom of the sinkhole.

There was no going back as she squeezed herself through the tight gap between the beams. Having achieved that, she found herself suspended in midair, groping for a handhold to start trying to move sideways. The rope bit painfully under her arms and between her legs. The dank smell of damp earth filled her nostrils and she had no way of knowing whether anything she held on to would be strong enough to take her weight. Or whether the earth would start moving again, and that would simply be the end of it all.

Abby had never done anything this dangerous in her whole life. It would have been impossibly terrifying if it wasn't for the fact that she was doing this to get to Jack. Having been compelled to start and now on her way, however, she couldn't deny the underlying thrill that was interlaced with the terror. The adrenaline rush was unexpectedly powerful. Exhilarating, even.

And it certainly helped that she had Tom watching her back. Keeping his headlamp where it was needed and talking her quietly through the ordeal.

'There's a rock...to your left...down about a foot.'

'Stay where you are. Catch your breath.'

'You can do this, Abby. You'll have to jump the last bit. I can take some of your weight so you'll land softly.'

Then she was down.

Checking Jack out all over. 'Are you sure nothing hurts? Nothing at all?'

'No. I just want to go home.'

Abby's voice wobbled. 'Not before I get a squeezy hug.'

Tears came then, but only a few. The clock was ticking even more loudly in this potential tomb. They had to get out in case another, larger aftershock happened.

'How will we do this, Tom?' Abby called. 'Do I take my harness off and put it on Jack?'

'No-o-o...' Jack might consider himself to be getting too big for squeezy hugs but he clung to Abby fiercely now. 'Don't put me down, Mummy. *Don't.*'

'I'll send down another rope,' Tom called back. 'You can put it round Jack but we won't use it unless we have to. Do you think you can climb back up while you're holding him?'

'Yes.' Abby made sure she sounded confident but she had no idea whether she was capable of doing this. She swallowed hard and put her mouth close to Jack's ear. She could feel his warmth. The tickle of his soft hair against her face.

She was halfway towards succeeding in what had seemed like an impossible mission such a short time ago. There was more than the thrill of the danger, now. Abby could sense how overwhelming it would be when they got through this and were safe again.

'You'll have to help me, Jack. You'll have to hang on like a little monkey so I can use my hands to help us climb. Like…like Action Man would. Can you do that, do you think?'

Jack nodded but his bottom lip wobbled. 'I couldn't find Action Man,' he said sadly.

The end of the new rope was dangling above her now. Abby wound it around Jack and tied the best knots she knew how. If, God forbid, she fell or dropped him on the way up, Tom would be able to save him. 'It doesn't matter,' she told Jack as she worked. 'We'll get you another Action Man.'

'But he won't be *mine*.'

Abby was already moving. She hitched her son more securely against her body. 'Hold on really, really tight,' she instructed. 'This is the biggest squeezy hug you're ever going to have to give me, okay?'

'Okay.'

It was much harder getting back up, with the extra weight of Jack. Painful, too, with the rope continuing to bite into her body from the moment Tom had used his weight to help her up that first bit, which she'd jumped on the way down. Was he trying to make it easier by taking some of the weight?

By the time Abby got up to the level of the wedged beams, she could hear that Moz had joined Tom in the hole. Why? Surely they needed someone up on solid ground in the tunnel in case something went wrong?

And then she realised why both men had put themselves in more danger. This was the point where she had to let go of Jack because there was no way she could fit back through that gap while she was holding him. Tom was lying above the gap and he had his head and arms through it.

'Moz has got Jack's rope, Abby. You need to hold him out. Jack? You need to grab my hands, buddy, so I can pull you up.'

'*No-o-o...*' Jack clung more tightly. 'Don't let me go, Mummy.'

'I have to, baby. Just for a few seconds. And then it'll be my turn to come through the hole and I'll never let you go again if you don't want me to. Okay?'

'*N-o-o-o.*' Jack was sobbing. Terrified.

'Tom's my special friend,' Abby said desperately. 'He's your...' *Dad*. The word so very nearly slipped out.

'That makes him *your* special friend, too. He won't let anything bad happen to you, I promise.' She was prising Jack's arms and legs from around her body, unaware of the tears coursing down her face. 'Tom's like...he's a real-life Action Man, Jack. This is what he does. He saves people.'

Jack's sob ended on a hiccup. He'd turned his head to see if he could see this real-life Action Man. All either of them could see was the blinding glare of the headlamp, of course, and the two big hands waiting to catch hold of Jack, but having his attention diverted even for a moment was enough for Abby to break the hold.

She lifted her son away from her body and turned him to face outwards. She stretched her arms out to the limit of their capacity. Holding her baby over what now seemed like a huge, huge drop.

Jack shrieked in terror but his arms had gone out instinctively to find something to hold on to. Instead, Tom's hands had circled the small wrists.

'Pull us back, Moz.'

Abby saw Jack's little legs disappear through the gap. She was shaking like a leaf now. No way could she manage to get over there and back through that gap by herself.

She didn't need to. A moment later she felt the rope around her body tighten.

'Your turn, Abby. I've got you. I won't let you fall.'

It only seemed a blink of time since Abby had been trying so hard to hide the fact that she was limping so that Tom wouldn't notice. So that he wouldn't scoop her up and make life easier for her. Since she had resolved so firmly not to allow herself to depend on this man again. Somewhere in the back of her mind, now, there was an echo of something that could have been an ironic chuckle. Who had she been trying to kid?

She was dependent on him for her very life at this moment and she knew without a shadow of doubt that she could trust him. There was nobody else alive that she could give this kind of trust to.

So, when he had taken her whole weight and pulled her to the relative safety of the other side of that gap, it seemed only natural that he would keep pulling until he had her so tightly clasped in his arms it seemed like he never intended to let her go.

And it was just as natural that breaking such awful tension would release a flood of emotion from Abby. That she was laughing and crying at the same time. Holding Tom just as tightly as he was holding her. That his head was bent over hers and they were pressed so close together that when she moved her head, her lips brushed Tom's cheek. That when his head moved in response, it was their lips that brushed.

The intensity of the emotions spiked to become utterly confusing. Overwhelming. Not that there was any time to process any of it. Moz was right there beside them. And Jack, who sounded more scared now than he had at the bottom of the hole.

'Why are you crying, Mummy? What's the matter?'

Did Tom's hold soften or had Abby wrenched herself free? She couldn't tell. The need to touch her son was overwhelming.

'Nothing's the matter, darling. I'm just happy that we're out of the big hole. That we're safe.'

'We'll be a lot safer when we get right out of this damn tunnel.' Tom's voice was a growl. 'Let's move.'

* * *

The anger should have evaporated long ago.

The relief of getting Abby back through that gap should have been almost enough. Getting all three of them out of the sinkhole with assistance from Moz certainly should have done it.

But it hadn't.

Tom was at the rear of the small procession finally making its way out of the mine shaft. He knew he had been far too curt in ordering everybody to get moving but this wasn't the place for celebrating success. They could do that when they were safely clear of a space that could close in on them with a decent aftershock.

Why was he still so damned *angry*?

Maybe it was just a kind of chemical reaction. There were too many, powerful emotions roiling around inside him and, because they were all mixed together, they were producing an explosive heat. Did it just *feel* like anger because he had no other yardstick to measure it by?

He'd certainly *been* angry. With Abby, for refusing to listen to reason and putting herself into such a dangerous situation. With himself, because he'd had no choice but to allow her to in the end. She'd been right. Trying to save Jack had been a no-brainer. It couldn't *not* be done. And she'd been the only person physically capable of fitting through that gap.

And she'd done it. She was amazing. He should be full of admiration for her courage. Pride, because she wasn't a stranger and he had the right to be proud of her. Relief, because she hadn't been killed and he didn't have to face the prospect of never seeing her again for as long as he lived.

Was that why he was so angry?

Because he still *loved* Abby?

He'd never felt anything like when he'd pulled her through that gap and had kept pulling until he'd had her as close as it was possible to have anybody who was fully clothed in rescue gear. He had felt Abby's heart pounding against his chest. Against his own heart. He'd felt the huff of her breath as she'd sobbed with relief and the tight grip of her arms around his neck. He'd felt the sweet brush of her lips against his cheek and then the explosion of sensation when they'd touched *his* lips.

An accidental kiss?

Of course it had been. But if he'd needed a slap in the face to wake him up, it had certainly done the trick. Of course he still loved Abby.

The knowledge had been waiting to punch him from the first moment he'd seen her in that waiting room, hadn't it?

Had he really thought it was simply ancient history? That he'd buried his feelings for Abby so well, along with everything else about that break-up, that it had become impenetrable?

And now there was Jack.

It had been Tom who'd carried the small boy out of the sinkhole. In his arms. He could still feel the clutch of those skinny arms around his neck. The sturdy little legs around his waist. He was such a small person. So incredibly vulnerable.

He hadn't been crying, though. He was just as brave as his mother.

Maybe just as brave as his father?

Oh…man… Yes. These feelings were overwhelming. The build-up of pressure was unbearable.

Moz and Abby, who was now carrying Jack, were ahead of him. Without thinking, Tom lashed out with his heavily booted foot, kicking at a pile of rock and earth. The debris scattered but it wasn't enough. He kicked it again for good measure and felt a shaft of pain in his ankle as a larger rock moved.

Good.

Tom sucked in a breath. It was a tiny vent for the pressure inside but it helped. He paused for a moment to wriggle his foot and check that he hadn't been stupid enough to injure his ankle, and it was in that moment that his headlight caught the shine of something pale in the rubble.

Frowning, he stooped and brushed some more earth away. The pale thing was plastic. The head of a doll. A male doll, who was wearing camouflage clothing.

Action Man? It had to be.

Tom had a grin on his face as he eased himself through the gap that had allowed them access to the mine shaft in the first place.

Mission accomplished.

He brushed some more dirt off the toy and waited a minute or two until Shelley and Moz had moved away from where Abby was sitting with Jack in her arms, a blanket now draped over her shoulders. Shelley was helping Moz go through the backpacks, looking for something for Jack to eat and drink.

Tom walked towards them, holding Action Man behind his back, a little unsure how to present his find.

Good grief…he was feeling *shy*?

He was certainly feeling something that wasn't anger anymore.

Seeing Abby sitting there, holding her son, *their* son,

was doing something very odd to that mix of emotion in his gut. Tom could feel his throat closing up. A weird prickle at the back of his eyes.

Tears?

The thought was shocking enough to stop him in his tracks for a moment.

They were safe. His son. The woman he still loved.

There was peace to be found in that realisation. The kind of satisfaction that came with the success of any tough job and then some. Then a whole heap more because he had a real connection to these people.

Tom swallowed hard. He moved again. Got close to Abby and Jack and then crouched down into a squat.

'Guess what I found?'

He'd never forget the way Jack stared at him with those wide, startled eyes. The way his grubby little face lit up with the biggest grin in the world when he saw his beloved toy.

The ordeal was forgotten.

'You okay, buddy?' Tom had to check. 'Nothing hurts?'

Jack shook his head.

'Not scared anymore?'

He shook his head again. He clutched Action Man a bit tighter and then his grin reappeared. A cheeky flash that Tom recognised.

God knew, he'd seen it in photographs often enough. In the mirror, even.

'I *was* scared,' Jack whispered. 'But now I liked it.'

A huff of sound came from Abby and Tom's gaze shifted to capture hers. They both knew exactly what Jack meant. That he might have been terrified at the time but now that it was all over, he wouldn't mind

doing it again because the way he felt now made it all
worthwhile.

How was it possible to feel such an instant bond with
another human being? That simple, childish logic had
gone straight to a place in Tom's heart that nobody else
had ever touched.

Even Abby. This small child, who'd probably never
experienced anything really dangerous because he had
such a protective mother, understood exactly why Tom
did what he did.

Could he feel that same exhilaration without knowing what it was? Tom could recognise the fizzing sensation running through his veins. He'd experienced it
often enough. It was the thrill of still being alive after
the adrenaline rush of facing danger had receded.

When you knew you were safe and you could breathe
again. When everything about life seemed to have more
colour. More meaning. The time when it was so obvious that life was worth living.

Shelley came back with water and muesli bars for
Abby and Jack. They all needed to eat and drink something and then they could get moving. It would be a long
haul getting back through the bush to where they'd left
the helicopter, especially with a small child to carry
now. And with Abby's sore knee.

Except maybe they wouldn't have to after all. As the
light brightened a notch, Tom could hear something
that swiftly became the recognisable chop of an Iroquois helicopter.

They had sent in the troops.

Moz let out a whoop and pumped a fist in Tom's
direction. He grinned back. Things were looking up.

And then he looked back to where Abby was now

standing with Jack. His son was bouncing up and down, pointing at the approaching helicopter. He held his mum's hand on one side. The pointing hand was still firmly clutching Action Man.

Tom could feel his grin fading.

How come he'd never realised this before?

That it wasn't the absence of danger that gave you that feeling that life was worth living.

It was *this* feeling. The connection with other people. *Love.*

The realisation was shocking. It pretty much contradicted the premise his life had always been built around.

What the hell was he supposed to do about that?

CHAPTER SEVEN

IT WAS SO QUIET.

Everything and everyone on Kaimotu Island seemed to be caught in a stunned silence.

It seemed that the worst was over. They could expect a lot more aftershocks, of course, but none of them would be anywhere near the intensity of that first dreadful quake.

Abby was back at the information centre where the focus was now on looking to the immediate future rather than urgent rescue missions.

Everyone was accounted for. Those unfortunate enough to have been trapped in buildings had been rescued. Anyone who had suffered serious injuries had been airlifted to the mainland. Engineers were swarming over the township, assessing whether it was safe for people to go back to their houses and start cleaning up.

For the first time, Abby spared a thought for her own cottage. Until now, whether her home had survived the quake had been inconsequential compared to Jack's safety. Now all she wanted to do was to take her son and…and go home.

She had never been this exhausted in her life. Too tired to eat, even, despite the fact that the Hayward sisters were providing delicious bacon butties straight off a barbecue for anyone who wanted breakfast. They were fussing over Jack, who sat at one end of the long table, eating bacon with one hand and still clutching his Action Man toy with the other.

Tom was beside him, clearly enjoying his own generously stuffed sandwich, talking with other rescue personnel between bites. There were a lot of people here. Stood down from active duty now because they were all well overdue for a rest and, as far as anybody could tell, nobody was in imminent danger any longer.

The rest of the school children were being taken off the beach below where the bus was stuck. Moz had gone out on the boat so that he could get back to the helicopter and retrieve it. In just a few hours, he and Tom would be expected to take that helicopter back to their Auckland base and step back into their own lives.

What would happen then?

Tom hadn't said anything about where they would go from here.

He hadn't said much of anything at all, really, since they'd all come out of the mine shaft.

And Abby hadn't said anything much to Tom, either, because what she needed to say was so big she had no idea where to start.

He had saved her son. *His* son. Nobody else would have even attempted that dangerous rescue. Apart from herself, of course, but she could never have done it without Tom.

The debt of gratitude was too deep to measure but it came with a mix of fear, as well. What might Tom expect in return? How much was this going to change their lives?

'You okay, Abby?' Mike Henley looked pale with fatigue. 'I heard about what happened up at the mine. He's quite something, isn't he?'

Had Mike noticed that she was standing here by herself, staring at Tom Kendrick? Oh, help... How many other people had noticed?

And he was standing right beside Jack. How long would it take for somebody to notice the physical similarities between Tom and Jack? It was amazing that one of the Hayward sisters hadn't spotted the exciting discovery and said something already, but maybe everybody was just too tired right now.

'I'm okay, thanks, Mike.' Abby tried to sound convincing. 'I just want to get home and see what state the cottage is in. Get some sleep, maybe. Do you know where Ben is? I'd better find out if I'm needed up at the hospital first.'

'What's needed is for you to get some rest,' Mike told her. 'You and Jack. We've got plenty of people holding the fort for the moment. Ben and Ginny are coping up at the hospital. Did you hear that Squid Davies died?'

'Oh...no. What happened?'

'The search dogs found him under a pile of cray pots but he seemed to be okay. Had a bump on the head but he wasn't keen on being dragged up to the hospital. Apparently Ben and Ginny fixed him up and left him to have a rest while they went to treat someone else and when they went back, there he was. Dead.'

Abby swallowed back the prickle of tears. 'Ben must be devastated. He and Squid were such good friends.'

'I think Ginny was more upset about it, actually. Ben's saying that we have to remember that Squid *was* ninety-seven years old and he'd had a great life. And he had been having a few problems with his ticker. Ben reckons he died peacefully. People are already saying that he died with a smile on his face and a bubble over his head that read, "I told you so."'

Abby had to smile. It was true. Squid had been forecasting the 'big one' for a while now and nobody had taken any notice. Being proved right was a pretty good note to go out on. Especially when you'd reached the grand old age of ninety-seven.

Would she live that long? Get to see her grandchildren having children, maybe?

Maybe she'd still be living alone in her little cottage. Wandering down to sit on a pile of cray pots and enjoy the sunshine. Remembering Squid and his prophecy of doom.

The prospect was a long way from being appealing.

'I'll get hold of the engineers,' Mike was saying now, 'and see if they've had a look at your place yet. Then I'll organise some transport.'

'We can walk,' Abby protested. 'It's not that far.'

'You're dead on your feet, Abby. You look like you've been run over by a steamroller.'

Abby had to smile. It felt like that, too. Physically and emotionally. Her feet felt like lead as she started moving again.

'You had enough bacon, Jack? It's time we went home.'

'Can Tom come, too?'

'I…uh…' Abby managed to avoid catching Tom's gaze. He had crashed back into her life and already seemed to have penetrated too far, too fast past its safe boundaries. The home she'd created in the last six years was the only part of her life he hadn't entered. Could she cope with having to share that, as well?

'Tom's got things he has to do,' she told Jack. 'With… with the helicopter and stuff.'

'It'll be a while before Moz gets back.' Tom's voice sounded deceptively calm. 'I'd like to see that you both get home safely.'

'Cool…' Jack grinned up at Tom. 'I can show you my tree hut. I built it all by myself.'

'Did you, now? Didn't Action Man help?'

'Nah… I built it when I was *four*.'

Tom looked suitably impressed. 'I'd like to see that.'

Abby closed her eyes as she took a slow breath. It hadn't taken much building. It wasn't even a tree hut, really. Jack had discovered the hollow centre of the old macrocarpa hedge that ran along the back of their garden and he'd claimed it for his 'hut'. It was his favourite place to play. A place that only special people were invited to visit.

She'd never been allowed to crawl inside. Jack had sawn off some tiny branches to make a hole big enough for her to deliver snacks and drinks but it was *his* space and she respected that.

Now he was inviting Tom to see it. He didn't even know that this man, who'd been a complete stranger until a few hours ago, was his father, but already there was a bond there that she felt excluded from.

And it wasn't a nice feeling. On top of everything else, it was simply too much to cope with and Abby had the horrible feeling she might burst into tears.

'Abby? We've got a Jeep going your way. Engineers tell me your chimney's come down but the rest of the house is sound. Bit of a mess with broken crockery and stuff, that's all. Will you be okay to start sorting that yourself?'

'She won't be by herself.' It was Tom who spoke. 'I'm going with them. Moz can contact me by radio when he's back. Or you can get hold of me if I'm needed elsewhere.'

'You're on stand-down for now, mate. You've done more than enough.' Mike gripped Tom's shoulder. 'We can't thank you enough. I'm sure Abby feels the same way.' He was smiling at Jack now.

Abby hurriedly scooped her small son into her arms. It would look pretty churlish if she refused Tom's intention to accompany them to see what needed to be sorted out at the cottage. And she was too tired to argue. This was clearly going to happen and somehow, she had to deal with it.

The driver of the Jeep was Ruth's husband, Damien.

'Ruth's at home with the kids now,' he told Abby. 'We got off lightly. Something to be said for living in a train carriage, I guess. Lost some of the pottery in the shed but that's all. I wanted to do something to help the others.'

He had plenty more to tell her about in the short drive.

'There's offers of help pouring in from all over New Zealand. Tradesmen are offering to donate their time to help rebuild things and others are already donating money to buy the materials. Kind of restores your faith in human nature, eh?'

'I'm often amazed by the good things that can fall out of what seems like a horrible package no one would want to accept.'

Tom's words were quiet. They were in response to

Damien's comment. But his eyes were fixed on the rear-view mirror and it felt like he was talking only to her. Funny how reflected eye contact could feel just as intense as the real thing.

Did he mean meeting her again?

No. She ignored the skip her heart took. He meant finding out about Jack. Learning that he was a father.

It didn't take long to get to Abby's house, a stone's throw from the beach. Small and old, the weather-board dwelling had a corrugated iron roof now heavily dented by where the brick chimney had toppled and come crashing down to leave only a few jagged bricks at roof level.

'That'll need covering before it rains,' Tom observed. 'Lucky you had an iron roof. Something like tiles and you would have found that pile of bricks right inside your house.'

'Mmm.' The agreement was somewhat strangled. That pile of bricks was a tiny patch of destruction compared to what had happened elsewhere but it was a very personal patch and Abby had to blink back tears as she looked at it.

It felt like she had a similar pile of rubble somewhere deep inside her. The barrier between her life before and after Jack had come into it?

The safety walls?

Tom gave himself a mental kick.

What a stupid observation to have made about the chimney. No wonder Abby had made that dismissive sound. Or that she was now walking away from him.

It was more than reluctance to engage in conversation, though, wasn't it?

Abby hadn't wanted him to come here at all. She was reluctant to invite him any further into her life, and fair enough…he got that.

But this was also where Jack lived and surely he had the right to see where his son had been living for the last five years?

Where he'd been cradled and fed as a newborn?

Where he'd taken his first wobbly steps?

Spoken his first word?

Made his first tree hut?

An entire lifetime for Jack so far, and Tom hadn't been remotely aware of any of it. He'd missed out on so much. But if he gave that any more head space, that anger that he'd been so aware of when he'd been stomping his way out of the mine tunnel could resurface. If he didn't want to miss out on a whole lot more of Jack's life, it would be advisable to make sure it didn't.

So Tom allowed himself only a frown. A scowl that was directed squarely at Abby's back as she opened the front door of her cottage. He couldn't maintain the scowl, then, because his eyebrows shot up.

'Your door's unlocked?' Super-safety-conscious Abby didn't even bother making sure her home was secure these days?

'No reason to lock it,' she said. 'Not in the off-season, anyway. The only time stuff is likely to get stolen is when there are thousands of tourists around.'

'Mmm…' It wasn't lost on Tom that the sound he made was a perfect echo of Abby's reaction to his comment about the chimney but he didn't like the idea of Abby taking safety for granted. For herself or Jack.

Abby ignored his response. Holding Jack's hand, she walked down the short hallway into the space at the back of the cottage—a room that ran the width of the house and contained both a kitchen and living area.

The chimney stack might have fallen outside the house, but bricks and mortar and a lot of dust had also tumbled down what remained of the structure and had billowed out into the room. What looked like dirty icing sugar coated ornaments and pictures that had fallen from the mantelpiece and a heap of books dislodged from shelves.

Chairs had toppled beside an old, scrubbed pine dining table and a light fitting dangled from a wire, well below where it had been attached to the ceiling. It was the kitchen that had suffered the most damage, however. Cupboard doors were open and their contents of crockery and glassware lay in broken piles on the dusty wooden floorboards.

'Careful, Jack,' Abby said. 'Don't walk there.'

'Why not?'

'The broken bits have got sharp edges. I don't want you getting cut.'

Tom found himself nodding agreement. Not just because he didn't want Jack getting injured, either, but because this sounded more like the Abby he knew. The safety-conscious one.

He had learned so many things about this woman in less than a day. He'd learned that she was a fiercely protective mother and that she had more courage than you could shake a stick at and that she was terrified of losing the people she loved because of the way her parents had been ripped out of her life. It was a relief to recognise something he could remember. Like the way she'd always checked that the door was locked.

And double-wrapping a broken glass in newspaper so that the person collecting their rubbish wouldn't get cut.

Jack's eyes were wide. 'It's messy,' he announced.

Abby actually smiled. 'It's okay, hon. Mess is something we can fix.'

'Will my tree house be messy, too?'

'I wouldn't think so.'

'Can I go and see?'

'Sure.' Abby lifted Jack over the broken crockery, her own boots crunching through the shards as she carried him to the French doors beyond the dining table.

Tom noticed the garden now. A small area bordered by a thick green hedge. The clothesline was a rope tied to a tree at one end and a branch of the hedge at the other, propped up in the middle by a tall, forked branch of driftwood. There were Jack-sized clothes pegged on the line, along with towels and some very feminine underwear.

Deliberately averting his gaze as soon as he realised it had been snagged, Tom looked at the vegetable patch on the other side of the garden, which was clearly carefully tended. Jack was heading towards the hedge behind the vegetable patch, to one side of the gap cut into the tall hedge to leave an archway effect. The gap was filled by a wooden gate and a view of the beach and sea on the other side.

The sun was climbing higher into the sky now and the sea looked astonishingly blue. The garden had a shady area under the tree the clothesline was attached to and Tom noticed the old tractor tyre that had been filled with sand from the beach. A rather rusty toy digger and some plastic dinosaurs were arranged around the edge. Had Jack played in that when he'd been younger? Maybe while Abby had been tending the vegetable garden?

His voice felt curiously raw when he spoke. 'This is an amazing spot,' he said. 'What a great place for a kid to grow up in.'

Abby turned slowly to meet his gaze but she didn't respond immediately. There was a question in her eyes, as if she was waiting for him to say something more. Something about the disadvantages of growing up without a father, perhaps?

But Tom didn't say anything like that. He held Abby's gaze and then he smiled. 'He's a great kid, Abby. You must be very proud of him.'

She nodded slowly. She smiled but her lips wobbled. She opened her mouth as if she was about to speak but no words came out.

And Tom got that, too. Where could they start? With how he'd recognised himself in Jack so instantly when he'd said, 'I was scared but now I liked it'? With whether they told Jack that he was his father before or after they talked about where they went from here?

'There's an awful lot we need to talk about,' he said into the silence. 'But right now we're both beyond exhausted and we need time, and I think you've got enough on your plate.' He let his gaze sweep the domestic devastation around their feet.

Abby's breath came out in a big whoosh as though she'd been holding it.

'Thanks,' she whispered.

'What can I do to help?'

Abby shook her head. 'I think I need to get some sleep. I'm sure Jack does, too. Then I'll do a bit of tidying up and find out what's happening at work. Whether I'm needed there.'

'Have you got food in the house? Is your water working?'

'I'll check.' Abby's feet crunched again as she moved to the kitchen bench. She turned on the tap and nodded. 'It looks fine.'

'Power?'

'I've got a generator in the shed.'

'Let's check that.'

The generator appeared to be undamaged. Abby started to walk back to the house in front of Tom but then stopped and turned to face him.

'Tom…I haven't said thank you. Not properly. I…I don't know how…'

Her eyes looked huge. And were such a dark blue that Tom knew these words were coming straight from her heart. He had to swallow around the lump in his throat.

'There's no need,' he said gruffly.

'There is.' He could see the muscles move in Abby's throat as she swallowed hard. 'I know how dangerous it was to rescue Jack and I know that if it hadn't been you there, it probably wouldn't have happened, and… and I just want you to know how much that means to me. Jack's…he's my whole life…'

'It was you that rescued him, Abby.'

'I couldn't have done it by myself.' Abby gave a huge sniff and offered him a wry smile. 'And you know something else?'

'What?'

'I think I kind of get why you do what you do, now. It's pretty amazing, doing something that dangerous and saving a life.'

'Mmm…' Tom couldn't identify the emotion welling up inside him. Pride that Abby respected what he did for a living? Or was it relief that they were connecting on this level?

Hope for something he couldn't define yet? Some kind of future?

'It's kind of like a drug, isn't it? That feeling when you know you've succeeded?'

'Yeah…it is.'

'I wonder if that's how my parents felt when they'd conquered a mountain. If they got addicted to that adrenaline rush and the euphoria that would have come after it when they knew they'd survived.'

Tom opened his mouth. He wanted to tell Abby that she might have learned what drove him, but this experience had taught him something much bigger. That what was important in life wasn't the adrenaline rush or the euphoria but the connection between people. The kind of connection he'd felt when he'd seen Abby holding Jack outside the mine.

He'd just experienced an echo of that extraordinarily powerful feeling when Abby had been telling him she understood why his job was so important to him.

But he couldn't tell her any of that. Because she might push him away? Yes. The risk was too big to take because he'd not only lose her this time, he'd lose Jack as well.

But he had to say something.

'They got it wrong,' he said softly. 'You didn't just lose your parents. They lost you. And they'll never meet their grandchild.'

Abby blinked, her eyes going misty as she absorbed his words. For just a moment they were caught and Tom knew she understood that he was trying to tell her how much *he* cared.

And it felt…like the pieces of something broken were fitting themselves back together. As if a magic spell had been cast and Abby would open her mouth and say something that would provide the glue to hold those pieces in place.

She did open her mouth.

'Tom…I…'

'Tom…' Jack's face appeared through the branches of the hedge. 'Come and see. It's not messy in here.'

'I'm coming, buddy.' But Tom couldn't move just yet. He searched Abby's face and held his breath, waiting for her to finish whatever it was she'd been about to say.

But the spell had been broken. A second ticked past, feeling like much, much longer. And then another one.

And then Jack was right beside them, impatient to show Tom his tree house. Tugging on his hand.

'Come and see,' he implored. 'You *promised.*'

Tom was too big to crawl right inside the small space but he could fit in far enough to admire the dim cavern created by the twisted trunks and branches overhead and the carpet of long-dead needle leaves on the ground. There were more plastic dinosaurs in here. A tiny, wooden child's chair. And a shoebox.

'That's Action Man's bed,' Jack told him. 'For when he's tired.'

'I'll bet he's tired now after the big adventure you guys have just had.'

'Mmm.' Jack's face twisted into a gigantic yawn at the mere mention of being tired.

'Might be time that you and Action Man and Mum

all had a bit of a nap in the house. Shall we go and see what Mum's doing?'

'Okay.' Jack wriggled back out of his cubby hole. He still had Action Man clutched in his hand. 'He wasn't scared, you know. When he got buried in the mine.'

'Not even a little bit?'

Jack thought about this. 'Maybe a little bit,' he admitted. His big brown eyes were worried, though. Was he admitting some kind of failure?

Tom bent down so he could talk very quietly. Man to man.

'It's okay to be scared, Jack. Everybody gets scared sometimes.'

'Even if you're brave?'

'Especially when you're brave. You can only *be* brave if you get scared.'

Jack was frowning hard. Trying to understand.

'If you're not scared then there's nothing you need to be brave about, is there?'

'No-o-o…' Jack bit his lip but then his face lit up. He understood. He took a deep breath. 'I was really, really scared,' he whispered. 'When I was all by myself in the big hole.'

Tom nodded solemnly. 'That's how I know that you're really, really brave.'

Jack's little chest puffed out with pride but his face was very serious. 'Were *you* scared, too?'

'Oh, yeah…'

Jack nodded, satisfied. And then he nodded again as if coming to a decision. 'We won't tell Mummy we were scared, eh?'

'Nah…I reckon it can be our secret.'

This time they shared a smile. And then they started walking back to the house.

'I could tell you another secret,' Jack offered.

'What's that?'

'Well, Nathan at school's got a tree house, too, only his is really in a tree. You have to climb a ladder to get into it. He says he built it all by himself but it's not true. His dad built it.'

'Dads like doing that kind of stuff. And Nathan might have helped a lot.'

'I guess.' Jack was silent for a moment. They had reached the French doors of the cottage by the time he spoke again. 'I haven't got a dad,' he said.

Abby was picking up pieces of broken glass and putting them into a cardboard box. The piece she was holding dropped with a clatter as she heard Jack's words and then she froze, crouched on the floor in front of them.

'I'd really *like* to have one,' Jack continued. His tone was light. Conversational almost. He was looking up at Tom. 'D'ya think *you* could maybe be my dad?'

Oh, man… Here it was, being offered to him as if it would be the easiest thing in the world to step into his son's life. Except, of course, it wouldn't be.

Abby shot to her feet. There was a look of utter panic in her face as she turned.

'Tom lives in Auckland, Jack. It's a long way away from here.'

Something huge welled up inside Tom at the prospect of being dismissed like this, but he kept his tone as light as Jack's had been.

'It's not that far.'

'Far enough.' Abby's words sounded choked. She

was staring at him. Warning him not to go any further down this track. Not yet.

Maybe not ever?

They *were* too far apart for this but it had nothing to do with the physical distance between their homes. That factor paled into insignificance compared to what Abby was really talking about—the emotional distance between them.

For now, Tom knew he had no choice. He had to respect that. Even if it was killing him.

Abby was still staring at him in horror.

Jack was staring at him, too, looking hopeful.

Tom was spared having to find an answer for either of them by his radio crackling into life.

'Tank? You there, mate? Do you read?'

He unclipped the radio and pressed the button. 'Loud and clear, Moz. What's up?'

'We're good to go. Someone's on the way to collect you and bring you up to the helipad. Should be a vehicle just about there.'

Sure enough, a car's horn could be heard tooting outside.

'Roger that,' Tom said. 'On my way.'

He reattached his radio. Jack was looking impressed. He'd totally forgotten the question he'd asked and Tom wasn't about to remind him.

'I've got to go, buddy.' He ruffled Jack's hair. 'But I'll see you soon, okay?'

Abby followed him out of the front door and down the path. 'Why did you say that? He'll be asking me every day now, waiting for you to come back.'

Tom stopped walking just before he reached the waiting vehicle and turned to face Abby. It was important that she heard every word.

'I said it because it's true. I *will* be back. As soon as I can arrange something.'

Abby sucked in a breath but he didn't give her time to say anything.

'I intend to be part of Jack's life from now on,' he told her. 'I'm not sure how it's going to work but there's no way I'm walking away from my son.'

Or you, he wanted to add. *Not this time.*

He managed to hold those words back. Abby had enough to process in coming to terms with the fact that her son now had a father in his life.

'Bye, Abby.' The urge to reach out and pull Abby close was overwhelming. Almost as great as it had been when he'd pulled her through the gap in the sinkhole. But it wasn't the same. She and Jack were both safe, now. In their own home. There was no reason to pull her close and hold her tight. To wish for even an accidental kiss.

He couldn't even hug her like a good friend saying goodbye. The depth of emotion she was clearly coping with herself, judging by the darkness of her eyes and the tight way her lips were pressed together, was screaming a warning that it would not be a good idea.

He had to touch her, though. It was just his hand that he reached out. Just his thumb that he used to brush her cheek with a feather-like stroke.

'I'll be in touch,' he promised.

And then he had to get into the vehicle and be driven away from the beach-side cottage. In a very short space of time he would be in a helicopter, being flown away from Kaimotu Island.

He'd never been here before. He'd been here for less than a full day.

How on earth could it feel like this?

Like he was ripping out his heart and leaving it behind?

CHAPTER EIGHT

THE FUNERAL FOR Squid Davies was held three days after the big quake, and the small chapel was stuffed to the gills and overflowing outside with almost every adult islander. Everybody had loved Squid—the indomitable old fisherman who had been an island icon for as long as anybody could remember.

Abby was sitting in a back pew beside Ben's father, Doug McMahon. Ailsa sat on his other side and she had Ginny beside her. Ginny had her eyes fixed on Ben as he moved to the front of the chapel to give the eulogy. Ben was still using a cane to help him walk, thanks to the injuries he'd suffered only a week ago after rescuing Henry from under a piano. He was only just out of hospital and he looked very pale.

The look on Ginny's face advertised something more than concern for his physical wellbeing, however. There was something on the young doctor's face that struck a very poignant chord with Abby.

She loves him, she thought. So much that she can't imagine her life without Ben in it.

Abby knew what that kind of love was like. How it could make your life unbelievably wonderful. How it

could come so close to destroying it when things went
wrong.

Like they'd gone wrong for her and Tom.

'Squid asked me to speak today, and everyone here
knows Squid,' Ben began. 'He liked to predict what
happens so he made sure he wrote this before the earthquake, just in case, telling me what to say.'

A ripple of laughter echoed in the space but Abby
didn't join in.

She wished someone was around to predict what was
going to happen for her.

Tom was coming back.

And the prospect was deeply disturbing.

For the last few days Abby had been doing what everybody on the island was doing right now: trying to get
her life back to some semblance of normality. Thinking about Tom coming back made it seem impossible.
Nothing was ever going to be 'normal' again.

Ben's quiet words from Squid about his health issues
and how nobody had listened to his predictions flowed
over her head. He absolved everyone from blame in
the end, saying that nobody really knew anything, you
could only guess about what the future held.

Despite Abby's penchant for guessing the worst possible scenarios, somewhere between Squid's funeral
and school reopening a few days later, she realised that
thinking about Tom coming back was giving her a small
thrill every time it happened. A curl of sensation that
flickered somewhere deep in her belly.

She recognised that sensation. From way back, when
she'd first noticed Tom in his rescue overalls, delivering a critically ill patient to the emergency department

in which she'd been working. It had begun to happen whenever she'd heard the swishing sound of the automatic doors to the ambulance bay opening. Or caught a flash of red clothing amongst the emergency services personnel. It had been the thrill of anticipation laced with attraction.

Desire, laced with hope.

In some form, Tom intended to come back into her life. Did it matter that he was only coming back because of Jack?

Well…yes and no.

No, because otherwise he might not have chosen to come back at all.

But yes, because Abby would never know if he might have wanted to see her again if Jack didn't exist.

Abby knew perfectly well she could be setting herself up for renewed heartbreak if she allowed hope to bloom. And what if they *did* rekindle something? Just because she had new insight into the extraordinary satisfaction that could come from putting your own life on the line to save another, it didn't mean that she was prepared to let her son risk the devastation that could come from loving a father who had that kind of addiction.

But any choice in the matter had been taken out of her hands the moment she'd confirmed Jack's paternity, hadn't it? She couldn't protect Jack now. He had the right to know who his father was and to have a relationship with him. Tom had had those rights for even longer and Abby knew she'd been wrong in keeping her secret. Tom had every right to be furious with her.

Maybe that was why she hadn't heard from him yet. Was he consulting a solicitor, maybe? Asking about his entitlements as a father? About potential custody of his son, even?

Oh…God… She was doing it again. Dreaming up the worst possible scenario. Messing with her own head by dredging up the past or worrying about the future so much she lost sight of the good things that were happening in the present.

And, despite the huge trauma of the earthquake, the grief over people who had lost their lives and the enormous inconvenience of trying to work around services and supplies that were broken or missing, there *were* good things happening.

Ben and Ginny, for one.

The confusion and longing she'd seen in Ginny's face at Squid's funeral had been replaced by a glow of pure joy. She and Ben were engaged now, planning a wedding, as soon as things got a little closer to being normal around here, and a future that would see them living and working together as an integral part of a community of which they were both an important part.

Abby might have come here as a stranger but she felt part of it now, too. She was as happy as everybody else about the news. And she was a part of something much bigger, too. Something that was making her feel like a 'real' islander.

The community of Kaimotu Island had always been tight knit but there was a new and powerful bond forming in the wake of the disaster. People whose houses had been damaged more than others were taken into the houses of neighbours or friends while repairs were done. The cabins in the camping grounds were all occupied.

People whose businesses had been closed because of

damage to the town centre were offered new premises, some of them in caravans, and the local men who were part of civil defence used their status to go into places deemed off limits to the general population to retrieve stock and whatever else was needed to make a start in getting businesses and trades operating again.

Heavy machinery had arrived by vehicle ferries and there were diggers and cranes all over the place. Supplies of timber and roofing materials were stacked in huge piles near the jetty. Owners of bed-and-breakfast establishments and motels had opened their doors to volunteers willing to come from the mainland and share their expertise and labouring skills. There were builders and engineers, electricians and plumbers. Counsellors, even, who wanted to help people deal with the trauma. And there were others, who just wanted to offer their time and muscles.

One of them was Tom.

He just turned up at the hospital one day, about ten days after he'd left. Abby was in the clinic's reception area, chatting to Ben's sister Hannah. The afternoon clinic wasn't due to start for an hour and there were no emergencies on the way in that they knew about so they both turned to see who was coming unexpectedly through the door.

They both instantly forgot whatever it was they were talking about and simply stared as Tom walked towards them. He was grinning at Hannah.

'Hi, there.'

'Hi.'

Hannah sounded a bit breathless. Impressed, even though Tom obviously hadn't come by helicopter and he wasn't wearing his rescue service overalls or anything else that advertised his profession as an elite paramedic. This was just Tom, in faded blue jeans and a black T-shirt, with a bag slung over his shoulder, but to Abby, he'd never looked better. Or more important. Abby was more than a bit breathless herself. Maybe she'd forgotten *how* to breathe.

He'd come back.

Whatever this new chapter in her life held, it was about to begin. Abby's mouth felt dry and she noticed that Tom's grin faded as he turned his gaze from Hannah to meet her gaze.

'Hey, Abby…I'm back.'

Stupidly, all she could do was nod. This was huge. Scary but…exciting, too.

'I've taken a couple of weeks' leave,' he told her. 'I offered my services to come and help with the clean-up. There's a briefing for the group I came with this afternoon but I wanted to come and say hi first.'

Abby nodded again. A smile wanted to emerge but her lips wouldn't cooperate. 'Hi,' she managed.

Hannah was still staring. 'You're one of the air-rescue guys, aren't you? You came here when the earthquake first happened. You took Abby away with you.'

'I sure did. I needed her.' Tom was smiling at Hannah again. He flicked a glance back at Abby but she couldn't read it. Had he ever *really* needed her?

'And you rescued Jack out of the mine. Everybody was talking about that.'

'Were they?' Another glance came Abby's way but this time the raised eyebrow made it easy to read. What else had everybody been talking about? The physical similarity between him and Abby's fatherless son, perhaps?

Abby took a deep breath. 'Hannah, this is Tom Kendrick. He's…he's an old friend from when I used to live in Auckland.'

'Ohhh…' Hannah was a teenager. She was primed to read between the lines and pick up on any potentially romantic nuances. Her smile revealed the conclusion she had come to. The glance she gave Abby was impressed. Then she smiled at Tom.

'Where are you staying? In the camping ground?'

'Not sure yet.' The glance Abby got this time was lightning fast. Almost embarrassed?

Hannah hadn't missed it. Her smile widened. 'Nothing wrong with a couch,' she offered.

'*Hannah!*' Abby's jaw dropped. Having Tom here on the island again was one thing. Having him staying in her small cottage would be something else entirely. She tried to shake off the intense shaft of *that* sensation in her belly and found she was actually shaking her head. 'How 'bout you go and check if there's a clean sheet on the bed in the consult room?'

Left alone with Tom, Abby didn't know quite what to say. She fiddled with the papers on the reception desk, putting the list of the outpatient appointments on the top. There were a lot of them, as many islanders continued to recover from minor to moderate injuries sustained in the quake. She could feel the steady impact of Tom's gaze, however, and had to raise her eyes.

'I want to get to know Jack,' Tom said quietly. 'And I want him to know that I'm his father.'

Abby nodded. Swallowed hard. 'I want that, too.'

'I'll probably be quite busy during the days with the working party.'

Abby nodded again. It wouldn't leave that much time to spend with Jack, would it? She took a very deep breath.

'The couch isn't that big,' she said, 'but…if you want to stay…'

The silence seemed to tick on. And on…. Abby couldn't look away from Tom. Did she want this? To have him in her house when she woke up in the mornings? To have time with him in the evenings after Jack was sound asleep?

Oh, yes…

This was for Jack, she reminded herself desperately. This wasn't about Tom wanting time alone with her.

But the look in Tom's eyes suggested that could be part of it.

His nod was decisive. 'I'd better get to the briefing,' he said. He hefted his bag and turned to leave but then looked back. And smiled. 'Thanks, Abby.'

The agonising over what Abby might be thinking about how and when to tell Jack he had a father turned out to be one of those bridges that hadn't needed crossing.

It just happened. On the very first evening when Tom turned up with his bag and Abby casually told Jack that Tom was going to be staying for a bit to help people fix up their houses.

Jack's nod was solemn.

'Are you going to be my dad while you're here?' He made it sound like it was no big deal.

Tom had trouble making more than a vaguely non-committal sound as he met Abby's gaze over the top of their son's head. He knew his face would be asking a very big question but he wanted to convey reassurance as well.

He fully expected to see a flash of fear in Abby's eyes and he wasn't going to rush this if she wasn't ready.

But, amazingly, what he could see was something soft. And warm.

'Um…' Abby had to clear her throat. 'Not just for while he's here, Jack. Tom's going to be your dad…well, for ever. He…he always has been.'

Jack's eyes seemed to fill half his face and his mouth was an O of amazement. Tom dropped to his haunches so that he was on the same level as this small, astonished person.

'I didn't know about you before,' he said carefully. 'But I'm here now.'

'Why didn't you know about me? *I've* always been here.'

Something poignant twisted inside Tom at the childish logic. He had no idea how to answer the question and he didn't have to look up to sense Abby's tension. Or know that she was feeling guilty. She was responsible for Jack spending his first five years without a father. For him not knowing he had a son.

Tom expected to feel the heat of the anger that had been swirling within touching distance ever since he'd found out. Oddly, though, it didn't seem to be there right now. He'd come here knowing he was taking a big step into a new future. A whole new path, even. And it was the future that mattered, not the past. No…it was right now that really mattered.

If this was going to work—this 'being parents' stuff—he and Abby needed to support each other.

Besides, it was easy to step away from something that would hurt Abby. You didn't do things that you knew would hurt someone you loved.

Maybe Abby didn't have any reason to think that he had anything worthwhile to offer her after the way he'd pushed her out of his life years ago, but right now he had the opportunity to make a new beginning.

'It happens,' he told Jack quietly. 'Sometimes people are friends. Even really, really good friends and things happen that makes them think they don't want to be friends anymore.'

Jack was nodding. 'Like me and Nathan. When he wouldn't let me climb up the ladder and go in his tree house. I *cried*.'

It was Tom's turn to nod his understanding. But that twisting thing was happening inside again and he had to swallow to get rid of the tight sensation in his throat. Had Abby cried after he'd pushed her away? When he'd told her it wasn't going to work? That his career was what he lived for and he couldn't be with someone who was going to clip his wings and hold him back?

'But you and Nathan are friends again now?'

'Yes. I'm going to his birthday party next week. We're going to *sleep* in the tree house.'

'I'm not sure about that, hon.' Abby touched Jack's head. 'You'll have the party in the tree house but you might have to sleep in the real house.'

'Why?'

'Well, what if you needed to go to the toilet in the middle of the night? You might forget where you are and fall down the ladder.'

'I wouldn't forget, Mummy. That's silly. I'd remember cos I'd be there and I'd *see* the ladder.'

'You might be really sleepy and think you were dreaming.'

Tom could easily think *he* was dreaming right now. He could feel Jack's small hand on his knee as the little boy edged closer. With Abby's fingers still resting on that silky, dark head, they were all connected.

A...family?

'Can I call you "Dad"?'

The need to know the reason why Tom had been absent in his life up till now seemed to have been forgotten. Or maybe it had simply been deemed unimportant.

Tom tried to smile but his lips wouldn't quite cooperate. 'If that's okay with Mummy, it's fine with me.'

He had to close his eyes for a heartbeat because that stupid word made him wince. Fine? Tom had no idea what it was going to be like having someone call him 'Dad', but he did know it was far too huge to be encompassed by that little word.

He could still feel the touch of Jack's hand on his knee as he crouched here on the floor of Abby's living room. He could feel the connection right through to Abby and he knew that she still had her hand on his head. The feeling of connection strengthened as he heard her soft words.

'It's who you are, Tom. Of course it's okay with me.'

Tom opened his eyes to find Jack staring at him. Then the small boy twisted his neck to look up at his mother.

'Are you and Dad friends again now? Like me and Nathan?'

The tiny silence seemed huge. Filled with how easily the title of fatherhood had fallen from Jack's lips. His acceptance had been instant. Unquestioned. But

how was Abby feeling? Tom could feel the thump of
his heart as he waited for Abby to answer.

'Yes.' Abby's gaze shifted from Jack to Tom. 'I think
so.'

Her eyes were dark enough to show strong feelings.
As strong as what was stealing *his* breath away? Did she
think that there was a possibility of more than friendship?

Did she *want* that?

'I think so, too,' Tom said, amazed at how calm he
sounded. At the smile he managed, while still holding
Abby's gaze. She was the one to break the connection,
first looking away from Tom and then ruffling Jack's
hair before lifting her hand.

And then she turned away.

She had to find something to do with her hands. Something that didn't require any brain power because whatever she had between her ears had turned into some
kind of mush. Just as well, the dinner dishes were still
piled up on the kitchen bench and it was only a step or
two away. Behind her, she could sense Tom getting to
his feet. She could hear Jack bouncing.

'Come and see *my* room. I've got books and trucks
and…and a helicopter just like yours…'

The voices faded and Abby was left trying to find
something solid in the mush of her thoughts.

Hearing her son call Tom 'Dad' like that. As though
a missing piece of his life had simply been slotted into
where it belonged.

As if they were a real family.

The way Tom had looked at her when she'd said that

she thought they were friends again. As if there was something much, much bigger than friendship on offer.

Just the sheer, overwhelming presence of him in her home hunched down like that, with those faded jeans emphasising the muscles in his thighs and that soft, old T-shirt clinging to the equally impressive outline of his shoulders and chest. He could have remained standing and commanded a physical control of this space with no effort at all. He could have taken emotional control, too, and simply told Jack what he needed to be told.

But he hadn't. He'd handed that control to her and his eyes had told her that whatever *she* wanted was okay. He would back her up if she wasn't ready for this. It had been *her* call.

And it had been easy to know what to say. Even when her approval had been sought about whether it was all right for Jack to call him 'Dad'.

Dad. Daddy. The word held such power because it took Abby straight back to her own childhood. To when she'd had a 'real' family and life had seemed perfect. And even after so many years, the pain of missing her parents could sneak up and hit her like a sledgehammer and bring tears to her eyes. A painful lump to her throat.

On top of feeling like, somehow, a real family had been born again just now. When she'd been looking down at Tom, keeping her hand on Jack's head as if that would somehow steady her and remind her that he was hers and always would be. When she'd probably seen too much in that dark gaze of Tom's.

He was here for his son, not to be with his son's mother. Somehow, she had to remember that.

With the last of the pots on the draining-board, Abby

wiped her hands on a tea towel and straightened her back, then walked out of the kitchen.

'Jack? It's time to get your pyjamas on and clean your teeth, ready for bed.' She poked her head through the doorway. 'It's a school day tomorrow.'

Oh, help. Tom was sitting on the end of Jack's bed. Half lying, in fact, propped up on one elbow. Jack was lying on his stomach and their heads were almost touching, bent over the glossy pictures of a book about dinosaurs. They both looked up at the same time and if her heart had been wrenched any more, it would have torn into little pieces.

They were *so* alike.

And she loved them. *Both* of them.

If she didn't get some protective barriers up there was no way she was going to cope with having Tom here, getting to know his son.

Keep busy, she ordered herself. Focus on Jack. On work. On the house. Whatever it takes. In a couple of weeks, Tom would be going back to his own life. To the career that meant more to him than anything or anyone else. She had to keep her distance because there was no way she could stand the heartbreak of losing him for a second time.

'I'll find some bedding,' she added, turning away, 'and make up the couch for you, Tom. You've probably got an early start tomorrow.'

How could time be passing so fast?

The days were full-on, with early starts and late finishes. The bonus of volunteer labour was being well used and Tom was happy to be in the thick of it. There were roofs to be patched and made weatherproof after chimneys had fallen, and mounds of bricks and rubble to get shifted. Damaged septic tanks were being replaced and there was a lot of digging that had to be done by hand in awkward places.

Hefty framing was going up around heritage buildings that could be saved but which needed to be protected from further aftershocks in the meantime.

Many of the people Tom was working with were also volunteers from the mainland. He even knew a few of them, including a trio of firemen from Auckland that he'd met at more than one major accident scene. He didn't join them for a few beers after the manual labour was finished for the day, though. While he was enjoying being part of the recovery process, it hadn't been the primary reason for this visit to Kaimotu Island.

The other volunteers had no idea of the real reason he'd come back so soon but there were a lot of locals in and around the working parties and it only took a day or two before Tom realised he was getting some significant looks along with friendly slaps on the back here and there that other volunteers didn't seem to be given.

How could he have forgotten how small communities worked? He might have stayed in blissful ignorance a little longer, too, except that a Jeep slowed and then stopped just in front of him on a morning when he was headed into a site on the main street. A route that Ben McMahon was taking to get up the hill to the hospital.

Ben got out of the Jeep and leaned on the door as he waited for Tom to catch up. 'Hey, Tom… Haven't seen you for a few days and I've been wanting to say hi. How's it going?'

'Great. I think we're beginning to see a bit of progress. Still a lot to be done, of course.'

'It's people like you that are going to make it happen faster. We're all very grateful.'

Tom shrugged off the praise. 'How's it going up at the hospital? I heard you've had to evacuate a ward after they found some cracks.'

'Safety precaution. It's probably only cosmetic but there's a team of engineers coming to give it a thorough inspection today.'

'Abby says you're pretty stretched for manpower still. It's great news that Ginny's going to come on board.'

Ben's grin lit up his face. 'Sure is. I'm the luckiest man alive.'

Tom grinned back. Everybody knew that there was a wedding in the near future for Ben and Ginny. That Button was going to have a real family. An amazing family, from what Tom had been hearing. The kind that cemented communities like this together in the best possible way. Ben's parents were astonishing in their capacity to care for so many people. It was always a highlight of Jack's day when he got to go to the McMahon homestead after school to be looked after by Hannah.

He was wearing Abby down at the moment, begging for one of the kittens that Ailsa was caring for. Button had a black one with a white nose, apparently. Jack wanted the one that had odd black and white splotches all over it. He had already named it Checkers.

'And I'm not the only one with great news,' Ben added. 'I think Jack's the happiest little boy alive right now.'

'He's got the kitten?'

'What? No, I don't know anything about a kitten. I'm talking about him not only having a dad but having one that everybody knows is a real hero.'

'Ohh…' Tom was embarrassed. 'He told you?'

'Actually, it was Button who told us, but I think he's told everybody else. It was news at school the day after you got here.'

Tom's embarrassment deepened. This was pretty personal stuff to have broadcast. And what would people think? That he hadn't wanted to have anything to do with his son until now?

'I didn't know,' he said quietly. 'I probably never would have known if the earthquake hadn't brought me here.'

Ben nodded. 'Abby made that very clear. That she hadn't told you she was pregnant. That it wasn't your fault.'

Tom winced. 'I wouldn't go quite that far. It was my fault that the relationship didn't work out.'

There was a genuine sympathy in Ben's gaze and his eyebrows had an encouraging lift but he didn't say anything. Maybe his own current state of bliss made him want things to work out for everybody. And he knew Abby, didn't he? He had to know what an amazing person she was. But he didn't know *him* that well and they were blokes, for heaven's sake. Neither of them would be remotely comfortable getting onto emotional territory. Besides, they both had important jobs to get on with.

'I'm working on that.' Tom managed a grin.

Ben's face lit up again and Tom got another one of those friendly back slaps. 'Good luck. And consider yourself invited to the wedding, if you can make it.'

'The reception's going to be a beach party,' Abby told Tom later that night, when he mentioned meeting Ben

and getting an invitation to the wedding. 'And I've had
a sneak preview of what the wedding dress is going to
be like. Ginny will look stunning.'

'I'm sure she will.' Tom's smile looked a bit strained
and Abby wasn't surprised. Men like Tom weren't into
the whole marriage thing, were they? It was the kind of
anchor that heroes functioned better without.

Hmm. Awkward. And Jack wasn't even around to
defuse this sudden atmosphere by launching yet another campaign that would result in him getting his
own kitten. That morning's attempt had been a portrait
of Checkers that was now held in place by magnets on
the front of the fridge. He wouldn't be bursting into the
room any time soon, either, because this was the sleepover night for Nathan's birthday party.

It was, in fact, the first night that Abby and Tom had
been alone together in the cottage.

Oh…help. Awkwardness had just gained an edge
of real tension.

As if she wasn't totally aware of Tom all the time,
anyway. Having him sitting to eat with them at the table
or crowding the small kitchen to wash up afterwards.
Seeing him come out of the bathroom after a shower
with his hair in spikes and his chest still bare, or, worse,
when he passed close enough for her to smell the clean
dampness of his skin. To feel its heat.

Having Jack always there had made it easy to fight
the awareness. And the desire that licked at its heels.
Until it was safe to go there when she was in her own
bed, wrapped in the privacy of darkness.

How was she going to distract herself now? Keep
herself safe?

The meal was over. The dishes were done. The little

house was very quiet without Jack. Abby could hear the wash of the nearby waves and the forlorn cry of a seagull.

She could wash her coffee mug, at least. Pushing her chair back, Abby got to her feet. 'It'll be a real island do,' she said a little too brightly. 'Something happy everybody can look forward to. You should come...' Oh, Lord, why had she said that? 'I guess you won't still be here, though...'

Tom had got to his feet, as well. He was following her with his own empty mug. 'Would you like me to still be here, Abby?'

'I...' Abby shook off a wave of longing. Her next words came out more harshly than she'd intended. 'What's the point in even asking, Tom? There's nothing here for *you*.'

Tom's mug went down onto the bench with a loud thud. 'What's that supposed to mean? Do you think the fact that I've got a son means *nothing* to me? That *you* mean *nothing*?'

'N-no...' Abby gulped. She meant something to him? What, exactly? 'I was talking about your career. What's most important to you. You couldn't live here.'

Tom took a step closer. 'But you and Jack could come and live in Auckland.' He was speaking more quietly now. With an intensity that revealed this wasn't the first time he'd thought about this. 'We could be a family, Abby. We could...we could get married.'

It was that tiny hesitation that broke Abby's heart. That...*reluctance*. Or an acceptance of the inevitable? He would be marrying her only for Jack's sake. To make them a family.

The result might be something Abby had dreamed of

countless times but the means of getting there was not enough. Not nearly enough. She shook her head with a sharpness that spoke of despair.

'Kaimotu's our home,' she said. 'We're happy here.' Up until a few weeks ago she would have automatically added, *We're safe here*. They still were, emotionally.

Or were they? Jack already adored his father and she…well, any safety barriers she'd had around her heart had been showing cracks ever since Tom had shown up so unexpectedly in her life again. And those cracks were widening as she stood here in the silence. Tom seemed to be waiting for her to say something more.

'What makes you think it could possibly work?' she whispered. Okay, maybe the sexual tension had been there on both sides but he hadn't even tried to kiss her, even though they'd been living in the same house. Jack's house. 'It didn't before.'

'We were good together.'

Abby's breath huffed out in an incredulous snort. 'Good? You told me I was holding you back. Clipping your wings. How does that suddenly become *good*?'

'It's different now.'

'Because of Jack?'

'No.' Tom was still standing very close. His eyes were fixed on Abby's. 'I was wrong. I didn't understand.'

'Understand what?'

'What happened to you when you were just a kid. When you lost your mum and dad.'

Abby huffed again. It was almost a sob. 'And how exactly does that make a difference?'

'If you understand *why* someone feels the way they do, you can work around it. Find a way through.'

When had she wrapped her arms around herself like this? She hadn't even noticed but now she was holding herself tightly, as if she needed comfort.

What was going on here? Why was she feeling so devastated? This was what she wanted, wasn't it? For her and Tom to be together again? So why was she arguing? Trying to push him away?

Because nothing had really changed. If they were together, she would still have to live with that fear of losing him, even if Tom thought he could 'work around it'.

But...she understood, too, now, didn't she? What drove him? She'd felt it herself, when they'd rescued Jack. She'd told him she understood.

No wonder he was looking bewildered. As confused as she was feeling. She screwed her eyes shut tightly, trying to sort out the whirl of conflicting thoughts.

She could feel Tom moving closer.

She felt his breath on her skin. The touch of the pad of his thumb on her lips that made them part instantly in a response that had become hard wired years ago and simply couldn't be overridden. The soft touch continued to trace her bottom lip and Abby couldn't fight the wave of sensation that rocked her all the way to her toes.

She felt her head tipping back. This track was well worn into her cell memory, too. In a heartbeat it would be Tom's lips instead of his thumb touching hers and... *yes*...he would slide his fingers into her hair like that— the press of his fingertips as arousing as the magic he could make with his lips and tongue.

The desire Abby had been fighting ever since she'd first laid eyes on Tom again became incandescent. The heat was obviously contagious because Tom stripped off his T-shirt moments later and then helped Abby shed hers. The garments puddled on the floor beside them and then there was a moment's absolute stillness as they stood there, simply looking at each other.

Abby drank in the sight of him. He was the most beautiful man she had ever seen. All that glorious, olive skin covering sheer masculine power. The irresistibly vulnerable copper discs of his nipples and the invitation of that soft arrow of dark hair that dragged her gaze down to where the denim of his jeans cut low across the ridges of a totally ripped abdomen.

Her fingers itched to release the button on those jeans. To hear the delicious slide of the zip opening. She knew what she would find and…dear Lord…she'd never wanted anything this much.

But Abby dragged her gaze up because she could feel the touch of Tom's gaze warming the soft swell of her breasts as they pushed against the lacy cups of her bra. She could sense that his fingers were itching, too. To reach behind her and unfasten the clasp of that small undergarment.

But as she looked up, so did Tom. No wonder it's called 'eye contact', Abby realised. The touch wasn't physical and yet this was the most powerful grip in which she had ever felt herself held.

The touch of souls rather than bodies.

Abby felt as though some force was lifting her. As though her feet were no longer touching the floor, and she recognised this feeling as easily as her skin cells remembered Tom's touch.

This was love.

For both of them.

Could they make it work? *Really* work this time?

Impossible to think into the future right now. Abby's

ability to leap ahead and think of everything that could possibly make something *not* work failed her completely this time. She couldn't think a week ahead. Or even a day.

Ten seconds was about all she could manage. No, less than that. Just as long as it took her to stand on tip-toe and lean forward so that she would feel the press of Tom's bare skin against her breasts. To wind her arms around his neck and pull him in for the kiss that would take them straight to her bed.

The future could wait.

Thinking could wait.

All Abby wanted to do was to sink into this astonishing explosion of sensation. Pure bliss.

All she wanted was Tom.

CHAPTER NINE

BLISS HUNG AROUND.

Somewhere very close to the surface of your skin, Abby decided. The memory might not be as intense as the real thing but it was still magic. It sparked little curls of something delicious deep in her belly, and made her feel as if her bones had softened. And she knew it made her smile because Jack noticed sometimes.

'Why are you smiling, Mummy?' he'd ask.

'Because I'm happy,' she would tell him. 'Because I love you so much.'

And that would send little Jack on his way. Before his busy day could be interrupted by one of those annoying squeezy hugs.

It didn't take much to scratch the surface and release a little bit of that bliss, either. Just the sound of her phone indicating a text message could do it these days because it was usually Tom. He'd be asking about what Jack had been up to that day or how work was going for Abby and he'd sign himself 'T' with an 'x' for a kiss.

The sight of a particularly dark head of wavy hair or some other physical similarity that reminded her of Tom could lift that release catch, too. Of course, Jack reminded her of what Tom looked like on a daily basis and always had but that never triggered the bliss thing. No. That sparked a much softer sensation as she thought of a small boy worshipping his father as he grew up and the two of them getting closer and closer. Eventually being men together.

With a small sigh that acknowledged the complexity of what was happening in her life, Abby let something else trigger a release of that seemingly endless supply of bliss—the soft caress of a sea breeze on the bare skin of her arms, which made her think of a whisper of touch from Tom's lips.

'Are you happy, Mummy?' Jack asked. 'You're smiling again.'

'Mmm. I'm happy, hon.'

'Because we're going to Auckland?'

'I guess. It's a beautiful day for a ferry ride, isn't it?'

'I haven't seen a whale yet.'

'You might. We saw lots of dolphins, didn't we?'

Jack cupped his hands around his eyes to pretend they were binoculars but he couldn't keep his attention on the sea. 'Are we going to live in Auckland, Mummy?'

'No, hon. We're just going to visit for a day or two.'

'To see my *dad*.' Jack bounced up and down in excitement.

'Hold on to the rail,' Abby ordered, but she was still smiling. Despite repeated warnings to herself not to get her hopes up too high, she had to admit she was feeling more than a little bit of that excitement herself.

Or was it trepidation? Would Tom ask her to marry him again? And if he did, would he expect an answer this time? What could she tell him? That one night of bliss wasn't enough to turn her life upside down and hang her future on? Or, more importantly, Jack's life and future?

Not that she and Tom were likely to get any significant alone time. Just as they hadn't in the remainder of his visit after the night of Nathan's birthday party. It had been two weeks now since his volunteer stint had ended and he'd gone back to the mainland. The idea of marriage hadn't been raised again before he'd left, or since, in any text message or phone call. He was giving her space to think about what he'd said in the wake of their amazing night together, thanks to Jack's sleepover.

His words had hung in the darkness of her bedroom, almost shining with their intensity.

'I have to go back to Auckland soon, Abby. To my job. Like you said, there's nothing here for me on Kaimotu, career-wise.'

And there was everything for Abby and Jack. A home. A job. An amazing community.

'But I'm Jack's father and it's…it's incredible. *He's* incredible. I can't tell you how it makes me feel because I can't even describe it to myself but it's…it's huge, Abby.'

She had only been able to nod, her head brushing the side of Tom's chest, right beside his heart. She'd felt like that when she'd first held Jack as a baby, seconds after his birth. The world had changed for ever in that moment and her tears had been born from both amazement and joy.

'I want to be the best father I can be,' Tom had told her, and Abby had only been able to nod again.

Those tears at Jack's birth had held sadness, as well. That there had been no father for her baby boy by her side to share the miracle. Guilt that she had been keeping this all for herself.

'I know it would be a big move for you and Jack to come to Auckland and it's too much to ask for right away but...I need to see Jack. As often as I can.'

And Jack needed to see his father. Abby had known that. She'd accepted it without question.

'Just come,' Tom had whispered into her ear as he'd held her close. 'Please. Even if it's only for a day or two.'

When Abby had booked the ferry tickets within days of Tom's departure, it had been his final words she'd kept hearing.

'Come soon. I'm going to miss you. *Both* of you.'

Jack's excitement only grew as the ferry moved through the Hauraki Gulf towards the sprawling city of Auckland.

'Look, Mummy. There's so many *boats*.'

'They're yachts, hon. See the sails? They call Auckland the "City of Sails" because so many people have yachts.'

'Does my dad have a yacht?'

'I don't know.'

'I'll ask him,' Jack said happily.

For the next few minutes they watched the pleasure crafts crowding the harbour waters and then the lovely harbour bridge as it drew steadily closer, but Abby wasn't really taking much notice.

She didn't know if Tom was into sailing. She didn't know anything about what his life away from work was like now. He was probably addicted to adventure sports like abseiling or parachuting. How would a child fit in with any of that?

What if he *did* have a yacht? Auckland had one of those 'four seasons in one day' types of climate. Tom could sail off with Jack on a lovely sunny morning and then a storm could blow in and they could end up in big trouble in the open sea and Jack could fall overboard and…and *drown*…

Oh, for God's sake. Abby gave herself a mental slap. Give him a chance, she told herself, without immediately envisaging a disaster.

Tom was meeting them off the ferry today. They would drop their bags at the motel where Abby and Jack were to stay the night and then they would have the rest of the day together.

Abby swallowed her concerns and smiled at Jack as he turned his imaginary binoculars onto her.

She would give Tom a chance. It was going to be interesting to see what he'd come up with for them to do today. More than interesting. Nerve-racking, because it was possible that three people's futures could be influenced in a major way by what happened today.

'Where are we going, Dad?'

'To the motel. To drop off your bags.'

'Why can't we stay at your house?'

'Because you need a bed of your own and my house is too small.' Tom had to avoid a sidelong glance to where Abby was sitting in the front passenger seat of his car. Abby wouldn't need a bed of her own. Damned frustrating to think of her sleeping in a motel tonight but he was treading slowly here. Carefully. Because of Jack.

She wouldn't even be here today if it wasn't about Jack spending some time with him, would she?

But it was *so* good to see her again.

He'd had his doubts. Of course he had.

There'd been a definite 'Oh, my God what was I *thinking*' moment when he'd stepped back into the familiar comfort of the house he shared with Moz and had realised that if he and Abby and Jack became a family, it would mean losing almost everything that was familiar and comfortable. That wave of…fear, almost, at the thought of such a different future had been thankfully receding a little more every day.

Even his long-held fear that having a family would somehow hold him back in his work was fading, too. He wasn't being any more cautious in what he did. If anything, he might be pushing the boundaries a tad further just to prove a point. He certainly didn't feel like his wings were being clipped in any way and yet there hadn't been a single day—a single hour, in fact—that he hadn't thought about Abby.

And Jack, of course. The relationships were very different but they were equally intense. Was one more important than the other?

Maybe the difference was that his relationship with Jack was simply there and all he had to do was make it as good as it could be. He was Jack's father and always would be.

A relationship with Abby, however, would have to be earned. And it might be harder to do that the second time around, because he had to try to undo the damage that had been done. When he'd made her feel like she wasn't as important as his career. That he didn't want her in his life because she would hold him back from being the person he wanted to be.

Whatever. It was important that they both have a good day today and Tom had given the matter a great deal of thought ever since Abby had texted to let him know she was bringing Jack to visit.

'Where are we going now?' Jack asked, as Tom drove them away from the motel.

'To the zoo.'

'What's a zoo?'

'Jack!' Abby sounded astonished. 'You know what a zoo is. Don't you?'

There was silence from the back seat.

'Jack?'

'I wanted Dad to tell me,' said a small voice.

Tom caught Abby's gaze and they shared a flash of something. Amusement tinged with apology on Abby's part and amusement mixed with maybe pride on Tom's part. It was something warm and adult that understood what was going on in a small boy's head. Something very poignant about Jack having to confess his attempt to connect with his father.

Tom shifted his gaze to the rear-view mirror so he could see Jack. 'Auckland zoo is special,' he told his son. 'It's been there for nearly a hundred years and it has hundreds of different sorts of animals and birds.'

'Has it got lions?'

'Yep.'

'And tigers?'

'Yep.'

'And monkeys?'

'Loads of monkeys. And chimpanzees and orang-utans and I'm not sure but there might be gorillas, too.'

'What else?'

'Have you ever seen a giant weta?'

'Ew…' Abby made a face. 'We get those at home. I'm not so keen on big bugs.'

'There's meerkats. There are people tunnels and you can climb through them and pop up into these Perspex bubbles and there you are, in the middle of the meerkat enclosure.'

'Oh, I'd love to do that.' Abby grinned. 'What do you think, Jack? Wouldn't that be fun?'

'Mmm. What else is there, Dad?'

'Have you ever seen a hippopotamus?'

'No-o-o...' Jack's eyes were round. 'I've never seen a hit...a hittopopamus.'

'Hippo-pot-amus,' Tom said slowly.

'Hitto-pop-amus,' Jack said, even more slowly.

'Close enough,' Tom said. His gaze slid sideways and this time there was pure amusement in the shared glance with Abby. The odd nerves that had been plaguing him about whether the zoo was the best idea for a day together disappeared completely.

This was going to be great.

Abby knew she'd never be able to decide what her favourite moment of this day had been because they were all so different and they each had their own magic.

Just walking along the miles of pathways, being parents and each holding the hand of the small boy between them, had been special.

'Swing,' Jack had commanded. 'Make me a *monkey*.'

And Tom and Abby would share a glance and mouth a silent count of three and then both lift Jack's feet off the ground in a big, forward swoop that made him shriek with delighted laughter.

The meerkats made them all laugh and shared laughter was absolutely the best, Abby decided.

Then again, the private, telepathic kind of laughter

that passed between Tom and Abby with Jack's continued inability to pronounce 'hippopotamus' gave her heart an even more memorable squeeze.

And the bliss had been almost overwhelming when it had surfaced as she'd watched Tom eating an ice cream and catching a drip on the cone with his tongue. It had come supercharged with a hefty kick of desire, this time, thanks to the reality of his physical presence, and it had only got stronger as Abby had sensed the way he'd been watching *her* eat her ice cream.

Jack had been oblivious to the atmosphere above his head but Abby had barely noticed the alligators because she'd been concentrating so hard on trying to get her wayward thoughts under control.

In the end, however, there had really been only one moment that had stolen the limelight from them all, due to its significance.

They'd had afternoon tea at a café and had then wandered to a lovely grassy area near a band rotunda. Maybe they were all reluctant to head for an exit and finish their day at the zoo. The grass was long enough to be soft and tickly and there was a gentle slope under a tree that Jack spotted.

'Wanna see me do a roll, Dad? All the way down the hill?'

'Sure do.'

They both sat on the grass in the shade of the tree and watched Jack roll down the slope.

'I remember doing exactly the same thing when I was about his age,' Tom said with a note of wonder in his voice. 'It was a hell of a lot of fun.'

'Nothing to stop you doing it again,' Abby said with a grin.

Tom grinned right back. And then he simply turned sideways, lay down and started to roll, gathering speed fast.

'Look out, Jack, Dad's coming after you.' Abby had trouble shouting because she was laughing so hard.

But then Tom reached the bottom of the slope and rolled right into Jack and caught him in his arms, and her laughter died as she watched the rough and tumble between a father and his son as if it was an instinctual thing.

It was such a pure moment. A joyous moment.

Okay, there had to be a potential for Jack to get injured, but Abby wasn't thinking about any future catastrophe. She was absolutely in the moment and it felt utterly safe. Even if something *did* go wrong, Tom was here and he would look after them.

He would always look after them and keep them safe.

And Abby realised that she'd spent the whole day amongst wild animals. There'd even been a leopard or a cheetah or some big cat being walked around on a leash by a handler and not once today had she imagined something horrible happening.

Well, she'd thought about Tom's imaginary yacht and Jack falling off and drowning but that had been before she'd been in Tom's company.

Before she'd felt so…safe.

Before she'd felt like she'd come home.

Yes, Abby knew perfectly well that there would be heartbreak if she lost Tom but if she didn't accept that future risk—something that might never actually happen—then she could never have this *now*.

And this now was absolutely perfect.

It was in this ultimately memorable moment that Abby gave Tom her heart.

Completely and for ever.

Even if they didn't end up being married or together as a family, it was too late to lock her heart up and constrict her life by trying to keep it safe. Her heart was Tom's. For better or worse, for richer or poorer. In sickness or health or even death.

He was her man just as decisively as Jack was her son.

Their son.

Her smile was misty as she watched Tom and Jack coming back up the hill on all fours, being tigers, maybe. Tom got to her first and flopped onto his side, propping his chin on his hand.

She was still smiling and Tom smiled back.

'Have I ever told you how gorgeous you are?'

He looked pretty gorgeous himself, with his hair all rumpled and bits of grass stuck in it. With his dark eyes still alight from the fun of the rough and tumble.

Or were they alight with something else?

They were so close. Abby could just lean forward and snatch a kiss. The sudden gleam in Tom's eyes suggested both his understanding and agreement and a tiny quirk of his lips was an irresistible invitation, but just as Abby tossed her braid over her shoulder so it wouldn't flop into Tom's face, a small human missile landed on top of him from the other side.

'*Gotcha.*'

'*Oof...*' Tom wrapped his hands around Jack's midriff and lifted him as if he weighed nothing. 'You sure did get me, buddy.'

Jack waved his arms and wriggled his legs but Tom's

hand held him securely out of harm's way and then he tickled him and Jack shrieked with laughter and wriggled harder.

Abby could only laugh as well, tucking the disappointment over losing that kiss somewhere deep enough for it not to matter.

There was plenty of time.

Wasn't there?

Talk about bad timing.

Abby had been about to kiss him when that human missile had found its target.

Tom put Jack down and looked at his watch. 'If we head away now, we'd have time to drop into the rescue base. Would you like to see where I work, Jack?'

'*Yes.* Can I have a ride in a helicopter?'

'I'm not sure about that. Not today, anyway,' Tom added, as Jack's face fell. 'You could sit in one, though, and pretend you were driving.'

'Do I get a helmet?'

'I'm sure we can manage that.'

'Let's *go.*' Tom held out his hands to tug his parents from where they were still sitting on the grass.

So they went. Tom's crew was off duty but Moz was apparently there talking to a mechanic who had been called in to look at a helicopter. Frank was using the gym and Fizz was there, too, apparently watching Frank use the gym. Was there something going on that he didn't know about?

'Can't stay away from the place, can you? Fizz, this is Abby and this is Jack. My son. I told you about him.'

'Yeah…' Fizz grinned at Jack and then eyed Abby.

'Abby, this is my crew partner, Fizz.'

Abby eyed Fizz.

Frank caught Tom's eye and grinned. Both men could feel the wary vibe that had sparked instantly between the two young women.

'I'm working out,' Fizz said to Tom. 'See?' She opened her hand to show him a soft ball in her palm. 'Building up strength in my wrist.'

She was still wearing a protective bandage on her wrist, although the stitches were long gone and she'd been back on active duty for the last two weeks.

Jack's eyes were round. 'What happened to your hand?'

Fizz laughed, her gaze flicking towards Abby before moving to Tom. 'Your dad broke me.'

Tom cleared his throat—an annoyed sound. There were small ears here that might not detect a joke.

'Fizz hurt her arm when we were out on a job,' he told Jack.

'Yeah…' Fizz grinned at Jack again. 'We had to crawl into a crashed car at the bottom of a cliff with waves crashing around us. It was awesome. D'you want to be a helicopter paramedic when you grow up? Like Dad?'

'Yeah…' But Jack was biting his lip. He didn't sound confident, and why would he, when Fizz was making it sound so dangerous?

'Let's go and see a helicopter,' Tom said.

'The BK's out on a job,' Frank said. 'MVA up north. It'll be a while.'

'Backup's on site?'

'Yeah. The mechanic's going to have a look at that faulty fuel gauge. Moz is a bit worried it might be more than that.'

'They won't mind if Jack sits in the pilot's seat for a few minutes?'

'Might come and see how things are going myself.' Frank picked up a towel and mopped his face.

Fizz threw the soft ball into a bucket of hand weights. 'Me, too.'

The base manager was in the staffroom as they all trooped through.

'You must be young Jack,' he said. 'My word, you look like your dad, don't you?'

'Yep.' Jack stood on tiptoe to make himself taller. He stepped closer to Tom, who put his hand on his son's head.

He'd never felt so proud in his whole life.

'I'll bet you—' The base manager broke off his sentence as a signal announced an emergency radio message coming in. He moved swiftly towards his office and, with the door open, they could all hear as he picked up the microphone.

'Rescue Base One. Go ahead.'

'Rescue Base One, we have a priority one call from Kaimotu Island. I'll patch you through.'

Priority One meant a life-threatening emergency. They all knew that, apart from Jack, but the little boy went as still as everyone else as they listened. Could he feel the professional interest from Frank and Fizz? The alertness with which he himself was now listening? Or was it the flash of fear on his mother's face as she heard Ginny's familiar voice?

'Rescue One? We have a twenty-three-month-old boy, Blake Taggert, who's choking. Came in with a GCS of eight and deteriorating vital signs. Dr McMahon's tried to remove the obstacle with Magill forceps but without success. We're going to secure his airway with a cricothyroidectomy but we need urgent backup and evacuation.'

The base manager shook his head. 'Hold on.' He released the button so that Ginny couldn't hear him and turned towards Tom, looking rueful.

'It's a no-go for us. We'll have to see if the air force can help. It'll be an hour before the chopper's clear of that MVA and the backup's out of action.'

'They might not have started working on it yet. It's only a fuel gauge.'

'Kind of important when it's a distance that's pushing fuel capacity,' Frank reminded him.

'And it would be out of order,' the base manager snapped.

'I'd go with you.' Fizz had a sparkle in her eyes. An interesting mission with the added frisson of potential mechanical problems? She wanted in.

Was she crazy?

Was *he* crazy, even thinking about what he was thinking about?

Abby would think so. But when he caught her gaze, her eyes were shining, too. With tears.

'Poor Ruth,' she whispered. 'She must be frantic. Imagine if it was Jack and we were that far away from backup?'

That did it.

'I'll go,' Tom announced. 'If Moz is okay with the mission.' He was quite confident that the pilot would be prepared to take a small risk in a situation where a child's life was at stake. And the base manager might grumble and fuss but he'd find a way to bend the rules.

'Cool,' Fizz said.

'But no more crew,' Tom added. 'The less weight we have the less fuel we'll need so the gauge problem won't be such a major one.'

Tom left the base manager to update Ginny on what might be possible and moved swiftly towards the helipad. He knew Abby was following him. Any second now she would probably touch his arm and he'd stop and turn and have to see the plea in her eyes for him not to do something that must seem dodgy to someone who didn't know this business.

She wouldn't want him to risk his safety. For Jack's sake, now, as well as her own.

This was it. The crunch test of whether having Abby back in his life was going to mess with his career. A blinding flashback to the crux of why it hadn't worked the first time round.

Abby did touch his arm.

Tom did turn around.

But what he saw in her eyes wasn't fear. Not for him, anyway. It was fear for Ruth and Damien, parents of a small boy. An understanding of the agony they must be going through. An understanding of what only Tom could offer by way of help.

She hugged him goodbye swiftly, knowing she would have to get out of the way as preparations became fast and focused.

'Thank you,' was all she said. And then... 'I love you.'

That was when Tom kissed her.

Hard.

Right there on the helipad in front of everybody, including Jack. His words were far more private, however.

'See you soon, babe. I love you, too.'

CHAPTER TEN

IT WOULD BE HOURS before Tom returned.

There was the flight time to Kaimotu Island, the time needed to make sure little Blake was stable enough to travel, the trip back and then more time at the specialist paediatric hospital handing over his care before the chopper returned to base. There was probably a heap of paperwork that would need to be completed on top of that, especially given the protocols that must have been broken to send an aircraft out when it had been stood down for repairs.

Repairs that hadn't even been started.

Oh…help. It would be so easy to let her imagination conjure up a juicy disaster scene or three but Abby was determined not to go there. She wasn't going to let Jack see how worried she was.

They waved until the helicopter became no more than a speck in the distance and then Abby looked down to find Jack scowling up at her.

'Why are you *smiling*, Mummy?'

Was she? Abby touched the tip of a finger to the corner of her mouth and, yes, there was a faint tilt there.

Because, despite her worry, she was still singing

inside? Bathed in the glow that Tom's last words had given her?

I love you.

Were there any other little words in the universe that were that powerful?

Actually…maybe there were. Those four words *'I love you, too'* were more powerful because they confirmed something that was reciprocal. That brought people closer and cemented a relationship.

Her. And Tom. And Jack.

A real family.

So it was no wonder she was smiling a bit, was it? Not that Jack understood. Or approved.

'You shouldn't be happy,' he told his mother.

'Why not?'

'Because…' Jack sniffed. 'Because Dad's gone far away.'

'He'll be back soon.'

Jack's mouth turned down at the corners. 'He said we could have hamburgers and chips for dinner and that there was a big playground just for kids at the hamburger place. Will he be back in time to take us?'

'Hmm. Maybe not this time, hon.' Abby crouched down beside her son. 'But you might have to get used to things like this happening sometimes. It's what your daddy does. He's gone to rescue a very sick little boy. Brooke and Amber's little brother, Blake. Amber's in your class at school, isn't she? Imagine how sad she'd be if someone like your daddy *didn't* go and help make Blake better.'

Jack scowled harder but scuffed his foot thoughtfully, digesting Abby's words.

'Tell you what.' Abby straightened and took Jack's

hand. They both needed distraction for a while, didn't they? 'Let's say goodbye to everybody here and how 'bout we get a taxi and go into the city? We can look at all the boats and find that hamburger restaurant and have dinner. Then we can go back to our motel and that way Dad will know where to find us. He might even be back in time to tuck you up and say goodnight.'

And then she and Tom would have some time alone.

Time to talk. To touch. To simply *be*.

Together.

Abby closed her eyes and blew out a long, long breath. The next few hours could well seem interminable.

They were. They were over an hour checking out all the yachts down at the viaduct and another hour watching Jack tucking into a hamburger and playing with a crowd of other children in the extensive indoor playground. By the time they arrived back at the motel it had been well over three hours since the helicopter had taken off from the rescue base.

More than enough time for it to have reached Kaimotu and for Blake to be on the way back. Was he all right? Had they needed the surgical intervention? Somebody would be able to tell her. With Jack happily splashing in the bath and playing boats with a plastic scrubbing brush, Abby picked up her mobile phone and made a call to Kaimotu Hospital.

'*Ben.*' She hadn't been expecting him to answer. 'How's Blake?'

'Crisis over, thank goodness. We're still monitoring his breathing and he's obviously got a very sore throat but it's hardly surprising when you've tried to swallow a small, plastic aeroplane with sharp wings, is it?'

Ben's chuckle was wry but Abby was pushing away the cloud of relief to try and find what was ringing such a loud alarm bell in her mind. Was it because Ben knew what it was now that had caused the airway obstruction?

'You had to operate?'

'Not in the end. Once he was completely unconscious, there was no spasm to fight and I managed to get it out with the forceps. Not a moment too soon. Poor Ruth was beside herself.'

'I'll bet. Oh, I'm so glad to hear he's okay.' He must be more than okay if Tom had decided not to transfer him for follow-up.

The alarm bell rang louder.

'How long did it take for the chopper to get there?'

'We're still waiting,' came Ben's response. 'It hasn't shown up.'

It was Frank who answered Abby's call to the rescue base seconds later.

'I'm so sorry, Abby,' he said grimly. 'We don't know what's happened yet. All we know is that the chopper didn't make it to Kaimotu and it's not visible on radar. Last radio contact was two hours ago. A search plane's been dispatched.'

Abby felt curiously calm. It was probably the only benefit of a tendency to imagine the worst-case scenarios on an automatic basis. It meant that when they did happen, you didn't crumple up in shock because you'd been expecting them. You were ready.

'Can you call me, please?' Her voice only shook a little. 'Just as soon as you know anything?'

'Of course. Hang in there, Abby. Tom wouldn't give up without a bloody good fight. Especially now.'

Abby swallowed hard. 'Why especially now?'

Frank's voice was gentle. 'Because he's got so much to fight for, hasn't he?'

He meant Jack, Abby thought, as she ended the call. And…maybe me, too?

She did crumple then. Onto the couch, dropping the phone beside her so that she could bury her face in her hands.

She hadn't practised this scenario, had she? The one where she had to tell Jack that his daddy wasn't coming back.

Not tonight.

Not ever.

She'd thought about having to do it and the prospect had been horrific enough for her to keep Jack's existence a secret from his father.

Now her worst fear had been realised. No, it was worse than that. Jack had only just discovered his dad and fallen in love with him and now he was going to lose him. Thanks to her, he'd already lost all the years he could have had with his father in his life. How long would it be before her son could put those pieces of his life's jigsaw together and hate her for what she'd done?

She could see it now. He'd be maybe ten or eleven and he'd demand to know why he'd only had a few weeks of having a dad. He'd accuse Abby of—

Whoa. Why on earth was she doing this?

She didn't need to imagine a future disaster.

She had one happening right now.

Somehow she was going to have to tell Jack what had happened to Tom's helicopter.

To Tom.

Oh, God… The grief was pressing closer. She needed to get Jack into bed and sound asleep before that phone call came to confirm the worst. At least that way she'd have the rest of the night to try and find the best words to tell Jack.

And then they'd have to go home.

Only…Kaimotu Island would never really feel like home again, would it?

Home was where Tom was.

Didn't they say that you never really knew how precious something was until you lost it?

Well, they were right.

Tom had never given much thought to how precious his own life was until he was seriously contemplating the end of it.

As his helicopter spiralled down towards the ocean somewhere in the middle of nowhere, about halfway between New Zealand and Kaimotu Island.

Moz was swearing like a trooper. It wasn't just the fuel gauge that was faulty. Some major fault had wiped out so much they couldn't even send out a radio distress signal. They were just about to disappear off the radar and nobody would know why.

Except they would know why. This was happening because he'd put his hand up to take a risk. Pushed the boundaries like he always did, but this time he'd run out of luck.

And it wasn't just himself he was hurting. His best mate, Moz, was going down with him. And he was leaving the woman he loved behind.

Leaving the son he was only just getting to know.

Maybe he'd never stopped to think how precious his own life was because he'd never had that much to lose before. Maybe he'd avoided having that much to lose because then he'd be too aware of it and that was when you could start getting spooked. And then you couldn't do this kind of job as well as you might otherwise be able to.

Not that Tom had time to think about all that on the way down but there was plenty of time to think as they floated in their tiny emergency raft on that vast, icy ocean.

It was a miracle that they'd survived the crash. Even more of a miracle that a spotter plane had found them within hours and another rescue chopper could be scrambled to winch them out of the sea.

They had radio contact now. Had Abby been told they were safe and on their way home? That Blake had been airlifted from Kaimotu and was doing well in hospital on the mainland? Tom tried a patch from the helicopter to Abby's mobile phone but it rang and rang until he got voicemail.

He didn't want to leave a message.

He wanted to talk to Abby.

He *needed* to talk to her. So much that he couldn't go home to sleep when he and Moz had finally been checked out and then discharged, and had escaped from their base manager's relief disguised as anger over the foolhardiness he'd let them talk him into.

He had to go to Abby's motel and tap softly on the door, hoping that he would only wake her and not Jack, as well. That she wouldn't be too scared at having someone knocking on her door at some ungodly hour of the night.

* * *

The soft tapping on the door finally penetrated the numbness that Abby had wrapped around herself.

With her heart hammering, Abby got slowly to her feet. They'd sent someone to tell her in person, hadn't they? That was why she'd never received the phone call she'd been dreading so much.

She couldn't do this. Halfway to the door Abby stopped and had to stifle a sob with her fist. This was unbearable.

'Abby?' The voice was as soft as the knocking had been. 'Are you there?'

The voice was little more than a whisper but it was instantly recognisable. Abby could feel it slice through the numbness and bring every cell in her body back to life so intensely it was physically painful.

She threw herself at the door, fumbling with the lock in her haste to haul it open.

'Oh, my God…' she sobbed. 'You're still *alive.*'

And then Tom was through the door and filling the small space. Wrapping her in his arms and holding her so tightly her feet were off the floor and she couldn't take a breath but it didn't seem to matter because she'd never, *ever* been this happy.

Nothing was said for the longest time. They held each other very tightly and then Tom sank onto the couch with Abby still in his arms. She curled onto his lap with her arms still around his neck, gazing at his face as if she had to check that every pore of his skin was still intact. And then she had to touch and *feel* the reality of him. It was only then that their lips met in the gentlest kiss ever. The heartbreaking tenderness of that kiss sparked tears that rolled unheeded down Abby's face.

'I thought I'd lost you again,' she finally whispered. 'I…I've been sitting here for hours, wondering how on earth I was going to be able to tell Jack.'

'But they should have told you I was safe a long time ago. I tried to ring you myself from the chopper but all I got was voicemail.'

'What?' Abby blinked. 'But my phone was right beside me on this couch.'

They both looked for the phone but couldn't see it. Tom let go of her long enough to dig in the space between the cushions. He held up the phone and pressed a couple of buttons.

'It's been on silent,' he said. 'Looks like you've got a few voicemails here, babe.'

'Oh, no…' Abby groaned. 'And I've just been sitting here, imagining the worst when I didn't need to. That's the story of my life, isn't it? Imagining the worst and then avoiding it so it can't happen.'

'Like avoiding me, because I couldn't give you what you needed?'

'Not anymore.' Abby felt curiously shy as she met Tom's gaze. 'I realised today that it was too late.'

There was a flash of alarm in Tom's eyes now. 'Too late? You mean…for us?'

Abby wanted to smile but it didn't happen. Her lips wobbled instead. 'No…the opposite. Too late for me to try and keep my heart safe. It's yours, Tom. Whether or not you want it, it's yours. For ever.'

'Oh, I want it. You can't begin to know how much.' He pressed another of those exquisitely tender kisses on her lips and then tucked Abby's head against his shoulder, resting his cheek on her hair.

She was pressed against his heart. She could feel

its steady beat right through her body. Could feel her own heart rate slowing a little until the beats matched.

'I realised something, too,' he said softly. 'It made more sense today but I realised it a while back. When we all got out of that mine safely.'

Abby felt his chest swell as he took a deep breath. For a moment she couldn't feel his heartbeat so clearly and then his ribs sank again and she could feel that comforting thud and her own breath came out in a contented sigh.

'I've spent my whole life chasing danger,' Tom went on. 'Because I thought that was what made life worth living. Not the danger itself but that rush of feeling safe afterwards. I never knew how wrong I'd got it all. Until I met you and even then I didn't understand.'

Abby was puzzled. She tilted her head, trying to find the answer in Tom's face, but he just smiled at her.

'I always went for women who were just as crazy as me.'

Abby's heart skipped a beat. 'Women like Fizz?'

A tiny nod. 'And you were the absolute opposite. So safety conscious. I thought that you would stop me chasing danger and getting that feeling that life was so worth living afterwards.'

'I don't want to do that.' Abby pushed herself to sit upright so that she could make sure Tom understood properly. 'I never want to do that. I know I'm not as brave as someone like Fizz but—'

Tom stopped her rush of words with a gentle finger on her lips. 'Shh…' He was shaking his head. 'Let me finish.'

Abby shushed.

'The thing that I realised properly today is that it

isn't where the feeling comes from. An adrenaline rush
might make you *feel* more alive for a while but what
makes life worth living is *this*…'

He kissed her again. And again.

'I love you so much, Abby. You make every breath
worth taking. You *are* my life. You and Jack. You're
my people. My family.'

As if on cue, a small, sleepy figure in a pair of pyjamas patterned with bright green dinosaurs stumbled
through the door of the motel's tiny living area, his
Action Man doll dangling head down from one hand.

Jack blinked. And then he smiled.

'Hi, Dad,' he said. 'You came home.'

'Yeah…' Tom's voice sounded a bit choked. He held
one arm out to invite Jack closer for a cuddle but then
his gaze caught Abby's and held it as he tugged her
closer as well.

'I came home,' was all he said.

It was all he needed to say. They were finally together. A family. And Abby knew they would stay that
way and she would make the most of every single minute of it.

Home.

Maybe that was the most powerful word in the universe.

Jack's sleepy feet had brought him close enough to
be scooped up by Tom to join Abby on his lap. She put
an arm around her precious son, as well. It was a tangle of arms and she ignored the painful poke from the
foot of the plastic doll. This was a squeezy hug to end
all squeezy hugs.

Because it was their first family hug. Abby knew
with absolute certainty that it would be the first of a

countless number. That, maybe, in the not-too-distant future, there would be even more of a tangle of small limbs and plastic toys to contend with.

Somehow, over the top of Jack's tousled curls, Tom managed to find Abby's lips for a kiss just for her.

'Marry me?' he whispered.

Abby could only nod, her heart too full for her head to find words. It wasn't much of an answer to a proposal, was it?

She'd kiss him again, she decided. Properly. Just as soon as they'd tucked their son back into bed.

* * * * *

A sneaky peek at next month...

Medical Romance

CAPTIVATING MEDICAL DRAMA—WITH HEART

My wish list for next month's titles...

In stores from 6th September 2013:

- ❏ The Wife He Never Forgot – Anne Fraser
- & The Lone Wolf's Craving – Tina Beckett
- ❏ Sheltered by Her Top-Notch Boss – Joanna Neil
- & Re-awakening His Shy Nurse – Annie Claydon
- ❏ A Child to Heal Their Hearts – Dianne Drake
- & Safe in His Hands – Amy Ruttan

Available at WHSmith, Tesco, Asda, Eason, Amazon and Apple

Just can't wait?

countless number. That, maybe, in the not-too-distant future, there would be even more of a tangle of small limbs and plastic toys to contend with.

Somehow, over the top of Jack's tousled curls, Tom managed to find Abby's lips for a kiss just for her.

'Marry me?' he whispered.

Abby could only nod, her heart too full for her head to find words. It wasn't much of an answer to a proposal, was it?

She'd kiss him again, she decided. Properly. Just as soon as they'd tucked their son back into bed.

* * * * *

A sneaky peek at next month...

Medical Romance

CAPTIVATING MEDICAL DRAMA—WITH HEART

My wish list for next month's titles...

In stores from 6th September 2013:

☐ The Wife He Never Forgot – Anne Fraser

& The Lone Wolf's Craving – Tina Beckett

☐ Sheltered by Her Top-Notch Boss – Joanna Neil

& Re-awakening His Shy Nurse – Annie Claydon

☐ A Child to Heal Their Hearts – Dianne Drake

& Safe in His Hands – Amy Ruttan

Available at WHSmith, Tesco, Asda, Eason, Amazon and Apple

Just can't wait?

Visit us Online

You can buy our books online a month before they hit the shops! **www.millsandboon.co.uk**

Special Offers

very month we put together collections and
nger reads written by your favourite authors.

ere are some of next month's highlights—
d don't miss our fabulous discount online!

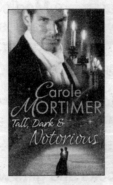

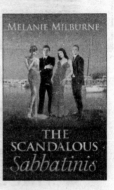

sale 6th September   On sale 6th September   On sale 16th August

Save 20%
on all Special Releases

Find out more at
www.millsandboon.co.uk/specialreleases

*Visit us
Online*

Join the Mills & Boon Book Clu.

Want to read more **Medical** books?
We're offering you **2 more** absolutely **FREE**

We'll also treat you to these fabulous extras:

- Exclusive offers and much more!
- FREE home delivery
- FREE books and gifts with our special rewards scheme

Get your free books now!

visit www.millsandboon.co.uk/bookclub
or call Customer Relations on 020 8288 288

SUBS/ONLINE/M1